Pride, Prejudice and Paintings

Jessica DiPalma

Copyright © 2022 Jessica DiPalma

Printed in the United States of America

Pride, Prejudice and Paintings/ DiPalma- 1st Edition

ISBN: 978-1-953610-21-8

1.Title.
2. Fiction>Romance.
3. Fiction>Arts. Painting.
4. Fiction>Female authors.
5. DiPalma.

NFB
<<<>>>
NFB Publishing/Amelia Press
119 Dorchester Road
Buffalo, New York 14213

For more information visit Nfbpublishing.com

There are many artists mentioned in this novel. All are real except for Sébastian Reno. While Reno is a figment of the author's imagination, he represents all artists who have inspired and helped to shape the lives of others through their art.

Chapter One

Exhaling a deeply held breath, Bennet Reynolds slowly opened her eyes. It hadn't worked. She was still standing in what was possibly the slowest moving line in history. With two people waiting to be served in front of her and a row of customers at the register to her left, she was beginning to ignore the logical side of her brain and succumb to the irrational fear that she would never make it out of this coffee shop.

It all ends here, she silently tortured herself. *You are never leaving this line, so your career will be over. Worse than that, your mother's greatest fear will be realized and you will die a lonely spinster with the entire world seeing you for the colossal failure you are.*

The phone in Bennet's hand vibrated, pulling her from her thoughts. She did not have to look to know who it was from; a glance confirmed that she was correct. Her boss had sent her a message; the fourth text from her this morning.

Bennet read the message with equal parts anxiety and irritation:

Staff meeting in 30 minutes!

We were scheduled to meet before!

Where are you?

Where are the coffees?

Don't forget my croissant!

Just once she could get her own coffee. A master's degree from NYU and this is what I've become; a glorified errand girl waiting in line.

7

"Um, I think I'll try that double mocha blended beverage," said the woman directly in front of Bennet who had finally made it to the register. A late twenty-something mom in knockoff designer yoga pants; she had obscenely large breasts that appeared to be struggling to be contained in her overly taut, bright pink tank top. Even more annoying than her outfit and her general sense of perkiness was that, as if unable to stop moving, the entire time she had been in line she had been lightly pushing one of those overly expensive, designed to impress runner's strollers back and forth as the toddler sleeping inside it remained oblivious to the mindless process in which he was peripherally involved.

Likely meeting friends for a relaxing morning, this woman—whom Bennet noted with a deep sense of irony was about her age—probably had no demanding nightmare of a boss waiting for her and so no need to rush. For Bennet, however, the speed at which she could place her coffee order would play a key role in determining the success of her morning as this woman pathetically now stood as the final impediment to her ability to maintain her sanity; not to mention, possibly, her job.

Seemingly confused over her order, the woman asked, "Wait. That's the one with the extra shot of espresso? And can I have it made with soy milk? Hold on. Never mind. I think I will try the caramel mocha with almond milk."

Make up your mind already! We have been in this line for twenty minutes. Couldn't you have decided by now? Bennet thought as she listened to the woman debate her coffee options as if it was her first time in a café.

Struggling to maintain her composure, as she waited Bennet had just begun scrolling through the morning emails on her phone when a frustrated barista's voice called out "Next" punctuated by an exaggerated sigh.

A surge of anger coursed through Bennet at the employee's insinuation that it was she who was holding up the line and not the ten people who had come before her. Still, refusing to show her frustration, she took a step forward and placed her order as calmly as she could muster.

"Three large coffees with room and one croissant."

"Sorry, no more croissants," the barista answered; the complete lack of interest clear in his voice.

"What do you mean? There's one in the case right…"

Bennet stopped speaking as she watched another worker pull the last of the French delicacies off the refrigerated shelf, place it in a bag, and hand it to the man at the register next to her.

"Wait, that's mine!" Bennet cried out as the man turned and started to move toward the exit.

"Son of a…" Bennet began to mutter as she quickly swiped her corporate card through the reader. Not waiting for a receipt, she grabbed the carrier tray filled with coffees and rushed to the condiment counter where she stashed a handful of creamers and sugar packets into her oversized black leather tote. Then, moving as quickly as possible, she maneuvered through the waiting crowd and used the weight of her body to push open the shop's door.

Oblivious to the coffee spilling onto her coat, once outside Bennet began to furiously look around trying to catch sight of the man who had absconded with her pastry. While still early, the sidewalks were already beginning to become populated with people, most of whom were either busy rushing to get to work or were part of the onslaught of tourists who every day traversed the streets of Manhattan, taking in the sights of the city.

Most mornings Bennet enjoyed watching these strangers as she walked to work, imagining their stories and wondering where they were heading; but today she had no time for any of this. Desperate as she was to find the man who had left with her croissant, they served simply as colorful obstacles obscuring her line of sight.

Scanning her eyes over the crowd, she was just about to give up hope when she glimpsed the back of the man as he was ready to turn the corner onto Fifty-ninth Street.

"Wait!" Bennet cried out as she began moving in his direction, bumping into people in the process as she tried to weave her way through the sea of bodies. All the while her pathetic attempt to keep her arm straight above her head to try to maintain the uprightness of the carrier tray filled with the freshly poured coffees made her a truly absurd sight.

Having lost him once more for a few seconds, as Bennet rounded the next corner she abruptly and forcefully slammed into the front of the man as he stood waiting at the crosswalk.

"Bloody hell. You should watch where you're going," he muttered angrily as he stepped back from her, struggling to keep his grip on his own coffee.

While she had been frantically chasing after him, Bennet was still somewhat surprised at her sudden face-to-face interaction with the stranger. She had been moving on instinct and guided only by her need to get that croissant; she had not thought through what she would do if she caught up with him since it was in fact his pastry that he had paid for and to which she had no claim whatsoever.

Having a moment to recover, she took a quick visual measure of the man. The cliché "tall, dark, and handsome" sprung to mind. At several inches past six feet, he had dark brown hair which, while trim, had enough length to give it a slight wave. In striking contrast, his eyes were so crystal blue that it reminded her of the color of the tropical water pictured in resort getaway advertisements that Bennet looked at but never seemed to take. He had a perfectly chiseled face with the slight angularity that often characterized the men in British period dramas and while thin, she could see he had the promise of an athletic build by the way his crisp white dress shirt lay with just the hint of snugness against his chest under his expertly tailored navy-blue suit. In fact, there did not appear to be a single inch of him out of place, down to his perfectly polished brown leather shoes.

Once again Bennet felt the ever-so-slightly out of place pang that had plagued her most of her life. She was not unattractive and when she put effort into it, she knew she could even be considered pretty. The problem was she rarely felt it and she did not need a high-priced therapist to identify the two main reasons. First, she lived in Manhattan; a city filled with model-level, beautifully coiffed and dressed women which could make even the most confident of females feel less than. This was something most women struggled with however, and could be managed if it had not been for the second reason. The fact was, Bennet's whole life had been spent being less than subtly reminded of her deficiencies by her well-intentioned but forever clueless and critical mother. Phrases like "Can't you do anything about your hair?" or "You sure that looks good on you? It's amazing how you don't care what you look like or what is in fashion," were constantly directed at her.

Even worse however, were her mother's comparisons of Bennet with her older sister. From as early as she could remember her mother had questioned why she could not be more like Jane. One of her favorite topics during Bennet's emotionally volatile and vulnerable high school years was her inadequacies in the dating department compared to that of her sister. "Can you imagine Jane had not one but three boys ask her to the dance?" was a question her mother seemed to derive great pleasure in asking of her second, less impressive daughter. It would usually be followed by the ever so helpful observation that "Maybe if you tried harder you could get yourself a good boyfriend." A statement that never failed to elicit an eye roll and mumbled "whatever" from Bennet.

While yes, the "good boyfriends" that Jane seemed to so easily attract and which were comprised largely of the high school's star athletes and prom kings were uninterested in Bennet, she was also wholeheartedly uninterested in them. It was a fact that she had sadly never been able to make her mother understand and who viewed it simply as another of her daughter's many failings.

In many ways, Bennet and her sister were complete opposites. Jane, two years older, had been born perfect. Besides her ability to seemingly without effort, remain a perfect size two, Jane had flawless skin that stayed with her even through the awkward teenage years. Her blonde hair, the color of golden honey, was the stuff of shampoo commercials and never looked out of place, not even as a child. Bennet, on the other hand, was plagued by a stubborn spattering of freckles across the bridge of her nose; brown hair with an everyday wave that could get downright curly when there was even the slightest hint of humidity in the air; and despite her best efforts to drag herself to the gym, had spent every day of her life struggling to stay at a size eight.

None of this was her sister's fault however, and Bennet adored her. It was just Jane forever seemed to have everything together whereas Bennet never did; a fact her mother seemed to relish in pointing out whenever the opportunity presented itself. Jane's role as prom queen and senior class president were followed by an accounting degree from Princeton. Her sister's crowning achievement, and the only thing that truly mattered to their mother, was a fabulous newspaper announcement-worthy engagement and marriage to a financial advisor at one of Manhattan's top firms. And now Jane was the perfect stay-at-home, charity supporting wife and mother to the most adorable two-year-old daughter that anyone had ever seen.

In contrast, while yes, Bennet had excelled in school academically, the popular crowd was never for her. Instead, she dwelled on the fringes of the high school hierarchy and felt more at home with the drama and art clubs than on the homecoming court.

Despite her mother's best efforts, Bennet rejected her plans to study business in college as her sister had done; which was according to their mother a suitable degree for a woman that allowed for job security until she could get married and have a family. Instead Bennet had chosen to study art and followed it up with a master's degree in art history.

Her current museum work and unimpressive yearly salary had failed to meet her mother's expectations and much to her horror had led Bennet to her current residence in a small apartment below Forty-fifth Street where she lived alone. But perhaps worst of all in her mother's eyes were her unsuitable and, truth be told, rather uninteresting boyfriends who had paraded in and out of her life over the last decade and who were barely worth mentioning.

All this was running through Bennet's mind, part of a never-ending loop of failures, when she was interrupted by a deep but haughty male voice with a slight British accent.

"You almost spilled hot coffee on me. This is a handmade Italian suit; not that you would even know. You can't just barrel your way around a corner. Are you even listening to me?"

Shaken from her thoughts, Bennet blurted out, "That's my pastry."

A look of shock spread across the man's face.

"What did you say?" he asked with genuine disbelief.

Suddenly the madness of the situation came crashing down on Bennet like a ton of bricks. She was standing on a Manhattan street corner accusing a perfect stranger of stealing the croissant that he had just purchased. She knew she sounded crazy. It was confirmed in the faces of the people gathered around them who stood waiting to cross the street and were watching their interaction with a great degree of curiosity. That she had managed to surprise and engage them, in a city population used to looking away from any form of odd street behavior, was actually quite impressive.

Embarrassed at what she had just done, Bennet was about to apologize when she saw the man snicker.

"Unbelievable. You're absolutely nuts lady. You can't just…"

As she processed his condescending words, a deep rage filled Bennet that went way beyond the pastry. The arrogance of this man, the cruelty of her boss, the demands of her mother, and the myriad of other unfair aspects of all pieces of her life came together in one intense affront.

Rather than explain herself or simply walk away, Bennet lost it.

"I'm unbelievable?" she blurted out, effectively cutting him off mid-sentence. "You've got real nerve you know that. You're the one who's unbelievable. I waited in line for more than twenty minutes just to have you leave with the last croissant. It was mine and I needed it. You can't just take what you want when you want it."

"That's exactly what I can do. This is America, in case you've forgotten, and that means since I paid for this croissant I get to keep it."

"I don't… I mean, you can't…" Bennet stammered.

Letting out a small grunt that reeked of disapproval, the stranger added, "You are certifiable, you know that lady? Maybe you should worry less about your breakfast and focus more on your sanity."

Feeling the sting of his words, as Bennet struggled with a reply, the man reached into the bag, pulled out the croissant, dramatically took a bite, and smiled.

"Mmmmmm, delicious," he murmured smugly before turning his back to her and proceeding to step off the curb and cross the street.

CHAPTER TWO

Bennet stood dumbfounded as she watched the stranger walk away. In that moment her sense of righteous indignation outweighed every other emotion. She should have been able to grasp the ridiculousness of the situation. Had she really just chased a man two city blocks for a pastry that he had legitimately bought in a café? Were things so unbearable at her job that she could lose control enough to actually behave that way? On the other hand, was it necessary for him to be so rude?

What an arrogant ass. Why do all the handsome ones have to be jerks? Bennet wondered as she caught the last glimpse of him disappear into the crowd of suits that was the morning work rush.

The sudden buzzing of her phone pulled her back to reality. Stepping away from the curb, Bennet rested the carrier tray on a sketchy looking newspaper box. Covered with stickers and chewed pieces of gum in a rainbow of colors; it was offering free copies of the neighborhood paper, which in this issue promised the juicy details of a scandal featuring a local councilman.

Pulling her phone from her bag, Bennet read the message on her screen:

> **Don't know where you are but you missed our appointment.**
> **You better have a good reason!**

Letting out a sigh, Bennet quickly fired off a reply:

Sorry.

I'm on my way.

Will explain when I get there.

Almost instantly, a response appeared:

It's too late now and I have no use for your excuses.

Just get here and don't even think about missing the
staff meeting!!!!

Great. This morning has been an absolute waste.

Looking up from her phone, Bennet glimpsed her reflection in the windowpane of the shop in front of which she now stood. She was a mess. Her frantic run through the streets had caused coffee to not only spill over and soak the cups and carrier tray, but also drip down the front of her coat.

No wonder the man thought I was crazy. I look like I just escaped from the mad house.

Trying not to think about how much her appearance as well as her behavior only seconds before would have proved her mother's point about what an absolute mess her life was if she could see her daughter at this moment, Bennet pulled a tissue from her bag and furiously blotted the stains on her coat. The action did nothing but deposit little bits of white cotton onto the fabric making it look worse. It was useless; nothing would help. Shaking her head at the lost cause that was this morning, she tossed the ruined coffees in a nearby trash basket and began to walk, as quickly as she could in two inch heels, the remaining blocks to the museum.

As she hurried, her thoughts once more turned to the stranger and his smug attitude. Bennet knew she would never be able to explain how he was the reason she was so late. The whole morning escapade had been for nothing; she had no coffee, no pastry, and her boss would be in a mood all day and probably already was given the abundance of punctuation marks she had used in her text. And now that she had missed their meeting, there would be yet another thing to be held against her. Not to mention the small matter of having just appeared like a deranged lunatic in front of an arguably quite handsome, though utterly infuriating man.

Even moving as quickly as she could, Bennet still had time to reevaluate her life. She knew she should never have taken this job. When the senior curator post had opened up with her predecessor's retirement, she had no intention of applying. Her job at the museum was only supposed to be a stepping stone; a chance to get some experience in the art world before she moved on to something she really wanted to do with her degree. Yet now, almost five years had passed and she was still working there.

It certainly did not help that her mother, who had never approved of her career choice, was at least excited by the prestige of the museum itself. It made it a little easier to say her daughter worked "in the arts" if she could throw around the name of the museum to her friends. The mere thought of telling her mother she was leaving was enough to give Bennet pause.

In her former position as associate curator, Bennet had enjoyed being able to work with the collection and had answered directly to Lionel the senior curator. A nice man, he had valued her input in the major exhibitions the museum had put on since she began working there. He had also given her free reign to pursue artists she thought were interesting and had even strongly encouraged her to curate her own first show of an up-and-coming South American artist. Bennet had enjoyed the process of conceptualizing and realizing the show and the exhibition had received good reviews in the press; something that had filled her with pride. Perhaps most importantly, in that role, her interactions with Katherine Hartis, the museum's conniving and belittling deputy director and head of development, and Brent Stromwell, the social climbing and small-minded director, had been limited. For the most part, Lionel had served as a buffer between them and their department of two. But now, as curator, she was in their direct line of fire.

After Lionel had retired, Bennet knew how important optics were and, thinking there was no chance that she would ever be promoted to fill his position but that it would look bad if she did not show interest in the role, had submitted her application. Six months passed and no one had been hired. Bennet had her suspicions that anyone they interviewed soon realized the gross incompetence of the senior administration and coupled with the ridiculously low salary they were offering had led every other candidate to pass on the job.

And so, eight months ago when the director had called her into his office and offered her the position, Bennet had reluctantly accepted. Offered was actually too strong of a word to describe what had taken place. In reality he had informed her, with smug Katherine Hartis sitting in his office to witness the humiliation, that while she would not have been their first or even second choice, they needed to move forward and so they were going to do Bennet the favor of letting her take on the position.

She should have run screaming from the office. Every fiber of her being told her to tell them to shove the offer. Deep down she knew her worth enough to know how qualified she was for the job and how her ideas would benefit the museum; but they were never going to admit that. She should have not only turned down the job, but also resigned right there on the spot. But as with everything in her life, at key moments when she needed it most, courage failed her and she had found herself accepting the position.

Every day since then had lived up to Bennet's fears. It was true, in a senior position, she had more direct contact with the art and artists and could advocate for what she felt was important-new acquisitions for the collection. She enjoyed that as well as the increased responsibility that came with the job, but this did not come close to measuring up against the constant criticism she had faced since becoming curator.

Nothing she did seemed good enough for her new bosses who managed to find something wrong with every project she worked on. There was no detail that was too small for their comment or criticism. And worse yet, when she did something that was well received publicly, like her newly developed lecture program focused on up-and-coming young artists that brought positive attention to the museum, it only seemed to threaten her bosses who reacted by finding new ways to hold things against her. Now, in what she knew was an attempt to watch her fail spectacularly, Bennet had been put in charge of organizing the new exhibition of the Winthrop Collection.

After years of cultivating a relationship with the extremely wealthy socialite Vivian Winthrop, the board of trustees and senior administration had succeeded in securing her private art collection as a gift to the Northhom Museum. Bequeathals of works are common in the art world and are considered to be the lifeblood of the acquisition process. While museums often purchase works of art, the prices for pieces by some of the most established and famous artists are often too expensive and can fetch tens, even sometimes hundreds, of millions of dollars at auction. That amount would be more than the endowment for purchases of a museum for several years; and so, the only real chance of obtaining some of these key art historical masterpieces is when a person chooses to donate them to the museum. Sometimes important collectors will even give their entire collections as a gift, which they view as a way of allowing their legacy to live on long after they are gone.

This is what Vivian Winthrop was doing in gifting her collection to the Northhom Museum. However, the fact that she was donating her artworks while she was still alive and not as a bequeathal as part of her estate, was a real coup for the museum as it meant immediate access to the collection.

Known by reputation as having a difficult and demanding nature but also as someone who relished social accolades, Bennet had a sneaking suspicion Vivian Winthrop had given the works now to soak up the lavish attention and praise that was sure to be heaped on her by the art world. It would also allow her to bask in the considerable press coverage that would inevitably follow such a donation while she was still alive to enjoy it.

A team led by Brent and Katherine had been assembled to deal with all aspects of the gift; and as curator, it fell on Bennet to be the point person to develop and mount an exhibition of these works which would showcase the collection to the world. She should have been excited about the prospect of working with the undeniably impressive paintings and sculptures that Vivian Winthrop was gifting to the museum. It was usually a curator's dream to have control over how such an exhibition of works would be organized. Bennet, however, was immediately wary of the task since she knew her bosses would be expecting, maybe even waiting for her to make a mistake so they could use it as evidence to support their belief that she was not the best person for the role of curator at the Northhom.

Still, Bennet had resolved to use this exhibition to once and for all prove Brent and Katherine wrong about her and had even begun to allow herself to become excited at the prospect of working with the collection. Having as yet only reviewed the files on the more than fifty works that comprised the donation, Bennet was eager to get started working with the actual artworks and conceiving the layout for the show.

Then last night, Katherine had emailed her that there had been a development with the exhibition and she wanted to brief her about it this morning before the monthly staff meeting. Bennet had spent the rest of the evening going from wondering to worrying about what had occurred. Unfortunately, now because of this morning's coffee shop debacle, she had missed her meeting with Katherine which meant she would have to wait until after the staff meeting to find out what was going on and how this development would directly impact her life.

This day had not started well and Bennet could not fight the sense of foreboding that it was only going to get worse.

Chapter Three

Bennet reached the Northhom Museum in record time. One of Manhattan's smaller art institutions, it was founded in 1937 as a legacy to one of New York City's most prestigious and wealthy families. Patriarch Henry Northhom had used much of his mid-eighteenth-century banking fortune to amass an impressive art collection, to which his son had added many of his own purchases. His only grandchild, a bachelor, had established the family home as a museum with the purpose of showcasing the collection. Intended to be a lasting memory to the family, the museum was formed with a sizable endowment and a mission to acquire new works that would promote important art and artists of the day.

In addition to a stellar collection, the museum's building itself was an almost equally impressive work of architecture. A grand fixture of the city's Upper East Side, the most impressive feature was the front veranda of the three-story former mansion with its ornate columns which now served as the public entrance to the museum. Almost as remarkable was the impeccably landscaped and gated garden, complete with benches behind the building, providing a welcome rarity in the urban jungle of the city. While usually a favorite spot for Bennet, she had no time this morning to take in its beauty as she rushed down the path to the staff entrance located on the east side of the museum.

Pushing open the glass doors, she waved to the security guard who responded with a blatantly obvious, "Wow, someone is really late this morning."

Gee, you think? Bennet thought, but simply nodded and smiled, barely making eye contact as she hurried past. After barreling her way through a second set of interior security doors, Bennet took a sharp left and headed down a flight of stairs.

Several years ago, the museum had gone through a substantial renovation project which involved the addition of a more modern set of office suites on the third floor. Many offices, however, were still in what was originally the mansion's servants' rooms in the basement, including those of the Curatorial Department.

With most of her colleagues already gathered at the staff meeting, the floor was deserted. When Bennet reached her office it took her a minute to find her key and then fumble her way through the process of unlocking her door. Knowing she had zero time to spare, once inside she ripped off her coat and flung it and her bag on the table next to the large file cabinet that filled the left side of the small room she called her own. Moving with urgency to her desk, she rifled through a pile of folders and papers she had readied the night before and grabbed what she needed for the meeting; the second of her morning responsibilities for which she was now late.

Preparing to leave, she risked a quick glance in the mirror she kept hidden on the wall behind her door.

"Just perfect," Bennet muttered, appalled at her reflection.

Slamming the folders down, she shut her door so she could take in a full overview of her appearance. Her coat must have been slightly unbuttoned this morning and so the coffee that had spilled on it while she ran through the streets of Manhattan had, just her luck, also spilled onto her blouse, causing several ugly looking brown stains including one directly in the middle of her chest.

Desperate, and with nothing to change into, Bennet did the only thing she could think of in the moment. Taking off her blazer, she pulled her arms through the holes of her sleeveless blouse and turned it around. Wearing it backwards would at least look better than the proper way where the stains were so plainly visible; and with a little luck maybe no one would notice.

Frowning at her makeshift fashion solve but resolved that there was nothing else she could do, Bennet picked up her files again and sprinted up the stairs and into the museum's galleries. Normally Bennet relished walking the halls of the museum before the public arrived when she could spend some quiet time with the works of her most cherished artists. Today, however, the paintings of Degas, Modigliani, and Monet were nothing more than blurs of color as she rushed by.

Finally, she reached the corridor of her destination. While the museum had a decent sized conference room on the third floor and a small meeting room in the administrative suite, for the monthly staff meetings when almost all employees were present, everyone gathered in the large assembly room which was where the public lectures and other heavily attended visitor programs were held.

Hoping to sneak into the meeting undetected, as Bennet rounded the corner she could hear finance director Neil Bates reviewing the new procedures for purchase orders.

Perfect. I'll just sit down in the back while everyone is focused on his slide presentation.

Using the open door on the left side of the room, Bennet hurried toward an empty seat she spotted only a few feet away and was just about to sit down, when she heard the grating voice of Katherine Hartis.

"Well how nice of you to join us Bennet," Katherine said with a smug smile on her face.

Neil stopped speaking as every head turned towards Bennet.

"Sorry I'm late," she began, painfully aware of the pink color rising in her cheeks. "I ran into a little trouble this morning."

"Oh my, a little trouble," Katherine continued in her most condescending of tones. "Well I hope you are okay now. Everyone else, it seems, was able to get here on time, but if you had a problem, I guess there was nothing you could do about it."

Turning back to Neil, she added, "So sorry for the interruption. Please continue."

An affable man, Neil had himself experienced the wrath of Katherine Hartis on more than one occasion and did not envy the spotlight in which Bennet now found herself. Feeling nothing but sympathy for her he replied, "Actually I think I'm about wrapped up here. Everyone should just begin experimenting with the new purchase order system on their own and anyone with questions can come see me directly."

Then, after sending a kind glance in Bennet's direction, Neil began the walk from the front of the room to return to his seat.

"Okay then," Katherine continued, failing to hide her annoyance at Neil for prematurely ending her bit of theater. "If that is all you have for us, I guess now that Bennet is finally here she can give us a Curatorial Department update."

Just perfect. Why the hell not with the morning I'm having.

Katherine's request was unexpected as she had made a point of telling Bennet just the other day that she would not be needing her to present anything at this meeting and wanted her instead to wait until more details were known about the new Winthrop exhibition. It had been a deliberate lie, Bennet now realized, and Katherine had been setting her up so she would look unprepared when called on to present in front of the entire staff.

Well, you might think you've won Katherine, but I won't let you get the best of me in front of everyone.

Rising to her feet, Bennet walked to the front of the room.

You can do this. Just a quick summary and you can sit back down.

Steadying her voice, Bennet began to address the group. "I would be happy to update everyone Katherine. In fact, I have prepared a few notes just in case you changed your mind and decided to have me present today," she lied.

Let everyone wonder what that means.

Glancing at her folder, Bennet pulled out a legal pad. Looking down at the blank page as if it contained brilliant paragraphs of text, she began to provide a rundown of the work she and her assistant Sara had been concentrating on for the last month.

As she cast a quick glance at Katherine, she could see her seething over the fact that her plan had not worked. She had not managed to trip Bennet up.

Pleased at how she had handled the curve ball Katherine had thrown at her, Bennet was starting to reconsider how bad this day might turn out.

"And finally, I'm excited to start really digging into work on the Winthrop Collection gift. The plan is to start physically going through the inventory of paintings and sculptures over the course of the next..."

"I am afraid I will have to stop you there Bennet, before you go any further," Katherine said as she got up from her seat in the front row and went over to stand beside her.

Flashing a fake smile, as Katherine spoke she projected her voice to be sure everyone in the room could hear her. "I had hoped to discuss this with you this morning, but as we did not meet I will have to tell you now that Mrs. Winthrop is very concerned that the exhibition of her works be absolutely perfect."

"Of course. I can assure you that everything is..." Bennet began before she was cut off again.

"Let me finish please." It was clear Katherine was loving every minute of this performance.

"Vivian Winthrop believes the only way to ensure the exhibition's success, and I and our director wholeheartedly support her in this plan, is that her nephew take on an active role by working with you to put the exhibition together."

Katherine's words had come as a complete shock to Bennet; so much so that she worried she might be physically sick. Her legs felt suddenly weak and the room was beginning to spin.

Stay calm. Do not let anyone see how much she has rattled you.

Struggling to maintain her composure, it took all of Bennet's strength to look Katherine directly in the eyes as she stated, "Well I look forward to discussing this with you and Brent so you can fill me in on the details."

Willing herself to keep it together, Bennet gave a small smile to the staff and began what felt like the longest journey of her life back to her seat; all the while praying no one saw her shaking hands.

Throughout the remainder of the meeting Bennet kept her gaze laser focused at the front of the room as she tried desperately to give the appearance that all was well. She hoped that anyone who looked at her would believe she was just really interested in the rest of the presentations. On the inside however, she wanted to scream. Katherine had managed to humiliate her in front of everyone. Not only did it look like she did not know what was going on in her own department, but it also now seemed like no one had confidence in her ability to put together this important exhibition. What other curator would have to work under conditions like this? Certainly none of her contemporaries at other museums in the city.

Over the course of the last week, Bennet had actually allowed herself to begin to get excited at the idea of working on this show. It was going to be her most important project since assuming her new position. Of course she had anticipated having to participate in periodic meetings with Mrs. Winthrop during the planning stages, but she had thought they would largely be of a symbolic nature. She had no reason to believe that as curator she would have anything but free rein to put the exhibition together the way she wanted.

Now, in this public way, Katherine had informed her that Vivian Winthrop had requested her nephew be involved in all stages of the exhibition and would be working directly with her to mount the show. An unwelcome development to be sure, Bennet was less than pleased at the thought that she would have someone wholly unconnected with the museum, and with presumably no knowledge of art, advising and directing her efforts.

CHAPTER FOUR

The rest of Bennet's day went by in a blur as she found herself stuck in back-to-back meetings until mid-afternoon. Even her plan to sneak home to her apartment at lunch to change her coffee-stained blouse had been derailed when Stella Thompson, public relations manager at the Northhom, had asked her to sit in on a round of interviews for her department's vacant assistant position.

Bennet could never resist a request from Stella as each was the person the other turned to for support when things became overwhelming at the Northhom. Having both started at the museum within a week of each other, the two initially bonded over the shared burden of trying to navigate their way through being new to the staff. Finding they had a lot in common, they soon began socializing outside of work, and now Bennet considered her a good friend.

Two hours later, interviews done but with no time for lunch, the pair walked into the breakroom hoping they could scrounge up a snack. A drab, sparsely furnished room with a lingering smell of burned popcorn, it offered nothing in the way of comfort, but at the moment it was their only option.

Opening one of the cupboards, Bennet retrieved two mugs and placed them on the gray laminate countertop. As she had suspected, the last person to use the coffeemaker had not bothered to fill up the water tank and so she had to take that extra step before loading in a pod and beginning to make a much needed brew.

Stella in the meantime had begun a search for food. Opening the door of the large refrigerator that was almost entirely covered with takeout menus, she scanned the shelves to no avail.

"Well there's nothing worth eating in here unless you want two-week-old Thai leftovers or an expired yogurt."

"Thanks," Bennet replied with a smile, "but that's a hard no."

"Wait," Stella called out after having moved her search to the cabinets. "I found a half full bag of chips. We could share those."

"Perfect," Bennet said as she went over to the table in the center of the room, bringing with her two mugs of fresh coffee.

Once Stella joined her, they began to dig into the chips and as they ate Bennet filled her in on the morning events at the café.

Stella had remained silent until Bennet finished her story and then burst out laughing.

"What I don't get," Stella began as she struggled to regain her composure, "was what was your plan. I mean did you really think he was going to give you his croissant?

"He must have thought you were absolutely crazy. Just the thought of you running through the streets waving a carrier tray of coffees makes you seem nuts to me and I know you."

"I honestly don't know what came over me," Bennet admitted as a fresh wave of humiliation washed over her at the recollection of her actions. "It wasn't like I planned what I was doing; I just reacted. I had been waiting in that line for what felt like forever for that stupid pastry which had made me late for work and then when I saw them give the last croissant away all I could think of in the moment was how miserable Katherine was going to be without it. I guess I just felt like the very least I could do was try and get it back so I could bring it to her.

"Really, who does something like that? It was like I was having an out-of-body experience or something. God Stella, I think this place is actually making me lose it."

Bennet took a sip of her coffee. Then, shaking her head as if still unable to believe her own actions, she added, "It would have been marginally less humiliating if he had been some gross-looking wierdo but of course that wasn't the case."

"Was he really attractive?" Stella asked; already knowing the answer by the look on Bennet's face.

"Please, attractive doesn't even begin to describe it. Drop dead gorgeous might be more accurate."

Stella sighed. "Oh, man; that perfect."

"But I'll tell you one thing," Bennet smiled at the recollection. "He might look like a movie star, but when he took that croissant out of the bag and took a bite I had never seen anyone less attractive in my entire life. It took all my strength not to throw what was left of my coffee right in his smug, self-satisfied face."

"Lucky you didn't." Then, turning serious Stella added, "Listen, I've been wanting to ask this all day. Are you doing okay after this morning? You know Katherine is a right cow to tell you about the development in the Winthrop gift that way. There is really no excuse for it."

While the mere mention of the staff meeting made Bennet start to relive her humiliation all over again she could not stop a smile from spreading across her face at the thought of Katherine as a large cow. Stella was nothing if not a master at spot on descriptions. It was one of her many gifts. In fact, Stella was the most unique person Bennet had ever met; not only in her take on situations but also in her entire persona. Bennet deeply admired her quirky sense of style, especially her ability to mismatch every piece of an outfit with the end effect of always looking perfectly put together; as if she were a walking Pop art painting. Her off-beat style was enhanced by her thick purple eyeglass frames and her short black hair that she wore either in pronounced spikes or slicked back depending on her mood.

Bennet had long thought that despite having no background in the field, Stella seemed more at home with the art crowd than in the corporate world of marketing and public relations. It had certainly helped to land her the job at the Northhom. But the thing she admired most was how incredibly kind Stella was and her uncanny ability to say just the right thing, just when one needed it. This was something Bennet had often benefited from during rough days at the museum, like the one she was having today.

"You know the worst part about all of this?" Bennet asked.

"What's that?"

"As horrible as Katherine was by announcing Vivian's demand in front of the entire staff—so that it looks like no one trusts me to do my job without supervision—that is not what truly got to me. She's so miserable and mean that sadly I've come to expect that kind of behavior from her by now.

"No, what was really awful was that I was actually starting to get excited about putting this exhibition together. The paintings and sculptures in that collection are amazing. It has become so unbearable here most days that I was just looking forward to working with all these new artworks."

"Well you will still get to do that." Stella was trying her best to sound reassuring while knowing she was failing.

"True, but now I have to share it with some rich entitled Winthrop relation who has probably been placed here as a spy to report my every move back to his aunt."

Bennet stood up and began to pace around the room. "He's probably one of those guys who thinks he knows everything about art when he actually knows nothing and he'll want to start mansplaining my own exhibition to me. I swear Stella, if he tries to tell me how I should arrange the layout I don't know what I'll do."

"Do you know anything about him?" Stella asked.

Stella had known Bennet long enough to recognize when her friend was in the beginning phase of one of her work rants and was trying her best to steer her out of it so she did not get any further stressed than she already was.

"Not really," Bennet replied. "I did some research on Vivian Winthrop when we first learned of the gift. I know she was widowed years ago and had no children, but there was mention of a nephew who is a businessman or something like that. I wanted to do an Internet search on him today to see what kind of nightmare I am in for, but I haven't been at my desk for more than ten minutes.

"I don't even want to think about how many emails and voicemails are waiting for me when I get back to my office."

Stella smiled. "Well after the events of this morning I was thinking of you, good friend that I am, and so I spent part of the morning in my office doing a little searching on the web for info on this mysterious nephew."

"Oh, yeah," Bennet said sitting down again and grabbing a few more chips. "Find out anything good?"

"I don't know if it's good or not, but it's certainly interesting at the very least. His name is Luke Dawlton and to say he is a businessman is a bit of an understatement.

"He is the founder of Dawlton Capital which has offices both in London and here in New York."

"No art background I'm sure." Bennet absolutely refused to be impressed with anything to do with this man.

"No, not that I could find; but Bennet…"

"What?"

"He might have other gifts."

Choosing to ignore Bennet's eye roll, Stella continued, "He seems to be an active player on the Manhattan social scene. There are photos of him with all sorts of beautiful women. There's even a rumored affair with some B-list actress a while back.

"And he's really sexy. Who knows, you might even have fun. Just think about all those long work sessions with just the two of you, late at night in the galleries."

"Yeah right because my life isn't already enough of a disaster that I need to add in some spoiled playboy trying to tell me how to do my job. As if I don't get enough of that from Katherine and Brent.

"Besides if he's as hot as you say he is then he's probably full of himself on top of everything else," Bennet said as she walked over to the garbage can to throw out the empty bag of chips. She knew Stella was only trying to cheer her up but it was not working.

Bennet sighed. "I remember when I thought I would do something meaningful with my career. Instead it's days like today that I'm painfully reminded that I'm nothing more than an underpaid and underappreciated decorator for rich Manhattan snobs. I really can't take this job somedays."

"I know and I'm sorry it's been such a horrible day." Standing up, Stella followed Bennet's lead and took the mugs over to the sink, rinsed them out, and put them to rest on the drain board.

"I'm not trying to minimize what you're feeling; honestly I'm not. And in an effort to try and make you smile, I'll just say that if there is no way to get out of dealing with this guy, then at least it might make it a little more bearable if he is easy on the eyes."

Despite her strong reservations about the situation, Bennet laughed.

"Stella's philosophy for a happy life right?"

"Right," Stella said putting an arm around Bennet's shoulders and giving her a squeeze.

Then, as she glimpsed at the clock on the wall, Stella added, "Look it's twenty minutes to five. Not long now and this horrible day will be over. You need to go home, take a hot bath, and forget today ever happened. Or better yet, we could go out for some drinks."

"Sadly neither of those options are possible. My nightmare of a day is far from over; I promised my mom I would come over for dinner tonight."

If Stella had not felt bad enough for Bennet before, now she felt ten times worse. Besides the countless stories shared by her friend, Stella had met Bennet's mother and therefore knew full well how intense a personality she was and would not wish a dinner with that woman on her worst enemy after a day like Bennet just had, let alone her best friend.

"How does that saying go? When it rains it pours," Stella asked.

"Oh, I'll manage," Bennet replied as she gave her friend a smile full of defeat and resignation. "Besides, when you think about it, it's actually a fitting end to a perfectly humiliating day. I'll see you tomorrow okay?"

"Definitely. But call me if you need to talk tonight. Or better yet, let me know if you manage to find a way to ditch your mother and want to get that drink."

"I will. Thanks," Bennet replied, laughing as they left the break room and began their separate treks; Stella to her office in the new staff wing and Bennet, she felt rather fittingly, back to the basement.

CHAPTER FIVE

Letting out a long sigh, Bennet walked into her office and reluctantly took a seat at her desk. As she had expected, she was swamped with messages. Knowing she should at least scroll through her emails before leaving or else be completely overwhelmed the next morning, she quickly fired off a response to five out of the thirty that needed an immediate reply. The rest she decided, could wait until tomorrow.

Turning her attention to her voicemails, Bennet listened to the seven lengthy messages that had accumulated since this morning. Six were related to work and Bennet dealt with them quickly. The other message was from her mother reminding her about tonight's dinner. She immediately deleted it.

All day Bennet had been fighting the dull throbbing in her left temple which she knew from experience marked the beginning of a major stress headache. Now as she sat at her desk with the sharp glare from her computer screen reflecting back at her, it seemed to have become noticeably worse and she forced herself to close her eyes and rest her head in her hands.

After a few minutes indulging in the quiet, Bennet was about to start packing up for the day when her desk phone rang. Glancing at the display screen she saw Katherine Hartis's name.

Great. What now?

Forcing herself to smile, as if she could somehow be seen through the concrete brick walls of her office, Bennet reluctantly picked up the phone.

"Hello Katherine," she began as she tried her best to sound cheerful. "How can I help you?"

"You can get yourself over to the director's office right now," Katherine barked. "Vivian Winthrop is here with her nephew. She wants you to meet him so that you will be prepared to start working with him tomorrow."

"Tomorrow? I had planned on at least another week of going through the paperwork and archive files and then I need to conduct a physical review of the works before we can even begin to think about conceiving a layout for the exhibition."

"Well plans change," Katherine snapped. "Her nephew is back in town earlier than she expected and she wants him to get started on the project now.

"I should not have to remind you of this, but what Vivian Winthrop wants she gets. If she wants you to mount the entire exhibition in a circus tent in the middle of Central Park and work with a team of acrobats to get it done you will do it."

"I understand. It's just I…"

"I do not have time for this," Katherine interrupted. "You seem to be operating under the assumption that you have some sort of say in this matter. I can assure you that you do not.

"So now that this is clear, I want you to get down to Brent's office immediately. Vivian can't stay long as she has another function to get to. You need to say hello and move on."

"Of course," Bennet sighed. "I'm on my way now."

Unbelievable. You would think Vivian Winthrop was gifting us the Holy Grail the way we're all expected to drop everything whenever she snaps her fingers, Bennet silently complained as she rolled her chair away from her desk, stood up, grabbed the file she had started for the project, and headed towards the door.

As was the case this morning, a quick glimpse of herself in the mirror as she was about to leave her office managed to stop her in her tracks. To say she was not looking her best would have been a gross understatement.

Putting down her folder, Bennet retrieved her cosmetic case from her tote bag. There might be nothing she could do about her coffee-stained blouse, which she was still wearing backwards, but she could at least work on her face a bit.

"It will have to do," Bennet said to her reflection after applying some lipstick and refreshing her mascara.

———————————

Given that it was only a few minutes until the museum closed for the day, Bennet's walk was a relatively quiet one.

Hopefully this will not take long, she thought; although if she were being honest with herself Bennet was no less interested in getting to her next obligation of the dreaded dinner with her mother. That was an event she knew from experience would be about as pleasurable as a root canal.

The museum's first floor consisted of one large main gallery, home to many of the key permanent collection works, as well as two smaller galleries on the east and west sides of the building. At the far end of the main gallery was also a hidden set of rooms that the staff referred to as the administration suite. It housed the offices of the senior staff and a small meeting room. Accessible by a door along the wall on either side of the gallery, it was designed to blend in with the space to cause as little distraction as possible to the museum visitors.

As Bennet reached the corridor's west entrance she was stopped short by a man's voice. Standing several feet away from the doorway with his back to her, she could see he was well-dressed in an expensive-looking suit. Gesturing with one hand as he held his phone to his ear with the other, it was clear that he was engaged in a heated conversation with the person on the other end of the line.

Over the years Bennet had witnessed a number of bad examples of museum visitor etiquette, but one of her biggest pet peeves was when guests used their phones in the museum instead of looking at the art. Having debated whether to remind him that cell phones were discouraged in the galleries, she decided against interrupting him, choosing instead to leave him to his conversation.

Having reached the door to the corridor, Bennet was about to use her staff badge to access the administrative hub when she overheard the next portion of the man's conversation.

"What do you want me to do? I know how busy we are right now, but she is demanding I do this. You will just have to reschedule this evening's conference call. Believe me, if there was a way I could get out of this ridiculous obligation I would but my aunt knows she has me right where she wants me. It's not worth it for me to even try to say no."

Realizing that this must be Vivian Winthrop's nephew, Bennet was desperate to avoid him seeing her or for him to realize that she was privy to this obviously private conversation. Deciding to retreat and use the entrance on the other side of the museum, she was about to turn around when she heard him say something that made her stop dead in her tracks.

"Look, I have to go back in now and meet this curator, whom I am guessing is some failed artist wannabe intent on proving herself by putting on this show."

How dare he think I don't know what I'm doing, Bennet thought as she tried to process the cruelness of his words.

He doesn't want to work with me? If anyone has the right to be unhappy about this arrangement it is me. I sure as hell don't want to work with him and I'm just going to have to make sure he knows it.

Fueled by her anger, Bennet no longer cared whether he saw her or if she disturbed him. Instead, she proceeded to boldly push her way into the corridor.

Brent Stromwell's office was at the end of the hallway and whenever she made this journey she always felt like she was walking the gauntlet to certain disaster. It reminded her of the one time she had been sent to the principal's office. She was in third grade and had got into a shoving match with a girl from her class named Stephanie who demanded Bennet let her cheat off her math quiz. When Bennet said no it had turned ugly.

Even now Bennet could remember the long walk to the office where she had to sit waiting for what seemed like ages for her mother to arrive to take her home. Of course, while she was glad her daughter had not cheated, her mother also had not hesitated to remind Bennet that she had never had to pick up her sister at the principal's office.

Now as Bennet reached the end of the corridor she could hear voices coming from Brent's office.

Here we go. Calm down. Just say hello and get out.

You will have time to put Vivian Winthrop's appalling nephew in his place later.

Squaring back her shoulders, she rounded the corner and walked into the room.

"Ah, here she is," Brent said upon Bennet's appearance.

Brent had been in the middle of a conversation with Vivian Winthrop and Katherine Hartis and as he spoke Bennet was quick to pick up on the hint of annoyance in his voice. She was sure Katherine had told him she was late, when in reality she had only learned of this meeting minutes before.

"Bennet you have met Mrs. Winthrop I believe," Brent continued.

You know I've met her. You were there when I did.

In fact Bennet's first impression of this woman was reinforced upon seeing her again now. In her mid-seventies, while pristine in her appearance, she was extremely thin which made her head look slightly too big for her body; a fact that was highlighted by the short pixie cut style in which she wore her gray hair. The word pointy sprung to mind as Bennet noted not only her sharp nose and chin but also her toothpick-like shoulder bones visible through the cream-colored sweater set she was wearing with a black pencil skirt and simple black pumps that, while plain, cost more than a week of Bennet's curator salary.

Vivian Winthrop gave Bennet a quick up and down stare looking none too pleased.

Well this is off to a good start, Bennet thought wondering how this exchange could get any worse.

"Yes, of course I have met Mrs. Winthrop," Bennet began, ignoring the icy reception she had just received. "It is nice to see you again. I am really looking forward…"

"Yes, yes," Vivian Winthrop replied with no attempt to disguise her disinterested tolerance of Bennet's presence. "There is no time for that. I am already late for another engagement."

"Of course," Brent hurried to add.

Anxious as he was not to annoy the great benefactress, Bennet was struck by just how pathetic her director looked in this moment.

"Bennet it is important you meet Mrs. Winthrop's nephew," Brent instructed.

As if on cue, Luke Dawlton entered the room.

All the anger Bennet had for this man and his rude comments about her that she had just overheard in the hallway were in that moment completely replaced by a wave of nausea that washed over her with the intensity of a tsunami.

To her absolute horror she realized, as she was now for the first time able to see his face, that the man walking towards her was the very stranger whom she had confronted on the street corner this morning and accused of stealing her croissant.

Feeling the color creep into her face, she prayed he would not remember her; all the while knowing the futility of such a hope.

"Ah, here you are," Brent continued to ramble, although Bennet could hear nothing but her own heart pounding so loud she was sure everyone else in the room could hear it as well.

"Luke Dawlton, allow me to introduce Bennet Reynolds. She is the curator who will be overseeing the exhibition of your aunt's most generous gift."

Say something now. Say anything. Just open your mouth and say something! The words echoed in Bennet's head.

"Mr. Dawlton, pleased to meet you," she finally managed to stammer.

Pausing for just the briefest of moments, Luke Dawlton extended a hand to her. "You as well."

While his outer appearance betrayed nothing of the morning's escapade, and the tone of his voice was as cold and as disinterested as his aunt's, the glint in those piercing blue eyes confirmed that he knew exactly who she was.

The image of this arrogant man smugly taking a bite of his croissant on the Manhattan street corner hours before flashed through her head as Bennet quickly dropped his hand and turned her gaze away, becoming intensely focused on an imaginary spot on the floor.

Katherine, who was eager to insert herself into the conversation, looked directly at Luke and stated, "Yes, well, we can assure you that Bennet is eager to have someone with your incredible talents help her in this endeavor."

Oh that's just great. Because this whole situation isn't humiliating enough why don't you tell him I'm a complete and utter incompetent.

"Well, my aunt feels strongly that she would like some input from our end," Luke Dawlton replied, "but I am sure the museum staff has everything well in hand."

Yeah I bet you do; you uptight jerk.

While his words were polite enough they were equally condescending and Bennet was not buying his act one bit having just overheard what he had said in the museum gallery. In fact, she found herself fighting the overwhelming urge to tell him off right there in Brent's office.

And just where do you get off calling me the museum staff? I am the senior curator at this museum and the person putting together this exhibition, Bennet thought as she reflected on his words.

As Bennet's mind struggled to process all that was happening, she was nevertheless aware that her ability to show him her worth had, she feared, been forever replaced by the image of her accosting him on the street this morning and accusing him of stealing a pastry.

At her nephew's remarks, Vivian Winthrop, who had been in conversation with Brent, cleared her voice and in so doing without saying a word made a firm statement regarding her lack of faith in Bennet's ability to accomplish this on her own.

"Oh your help would be ever so appreciated I am sure Luke," Katherine added, seeing an opportunity to draw focus on herself once more and ensure her relevance in the conversation.

Then to Bennet's shock, Katherine gave what she could only assume was her attempt at a coy laugh but to Bennet sounded like a cross between a hyena cry and a donkey baying.

Dear God is she actually trying to flirt with him?

Knowing she had to say something or seem like a complete idiot, Bennet tried her best to once more look him in the eye before adding, "Of course Mr. Dawlton whenever you would like to sit down and meet we can…"

"Oh my Bennet," Katherine said cutting her off, "I think there is something on your blouse. Yes, there is definitely something there by the neckline."

Much to her horror, Bennet realized that Katherine had caught sight of the tag which was, in this light, visible through her blouse.

Noooooooooooo!!!!!

"Bennet, is your blouse on backwards? Yes, I think that is your tag I can see." Katherine laughed, that haughty laugh that Bennet had come to despise. "My, my, someone must have dressed in a hurry this morning."

Bennet could have slapped her. Just one quick, hard slap to wipe that smug look off her face. Instead she mustered the last bit of strength and dignity she possessed and replied, "Leave it to your keen eye to notice Katherine. I spilled some coffee down my blouse this morning and had to improvise."

To her complete mortification, Bennet actually caught the slightest flicker of a smile cross Luke Dawlton's face.

"Yes, well the streets can be dangerous," he replied, his cold and uninterested tone betraying nothing of the personal meaning his words had for both him and Bennet.

Her face now beet red, Bennet lacked the strength to even attempt a response.

Katherine unsure how, but feeling as if she was being left out of a shared moment, hurriedly added, "Well, I think that is all for now Bennet. I am sure Luke will have his assistant call you to set up a time to meet."

"That will be fine," Bennet replied as Luke nodded. "I will wait for your call Mr. Dawlton." Then, trying not to gag on the words, Bennet managed to add, "Nice to meet you."

As Vivian Winthrop had returned to her conversation with Brent and seemed wholly uninterested in Bennet, she turned and walked as quickly as possible out of the office without any further goodbyes.

Bennet had almost reached the end of the corridor when she heard Katherine's grating voice echo through the hallway.

"And of course Luke, I will be happy to help you in any way you need. All you have to do is ask."

Chapter Six

Once back in the gallery, Bennet leaned against the corridor door, closed her eyes, and let out a deep breath she had not realized she had been holding. Not for the first time today she wondered how her life had become such a hopeless mess. Then, remembering the museum's cameras and not wanting to put on a show of her anger to the entire security department, she began moving as fast as she could back through the now closed museum and down the stairwell to her office.

Once inside the safety of her own room, Bennet slammed her door and let out a yell of frustration before sliding down to the floor in a heap.

"You idiot," she said to the empty void of her office before beginning a silent reflection on how things could not possibly be any worse.

With more than one and a half million people on the island of Manhattan, what were the odds that Luke Dawlton would be the horrible man from this morning. And now that she knew who he was, any hope she had of gaining the upper hand in her first meeting with Vivian Winthrop's nephew was gone. She feared she had lost any chance of taking the lead on the exhibition and asserting real authority over this project. There was no way now that this man could consider her anything but a complete incompetent.

In a day of humiliating moments and soul crushing insults, the worst however had to be the memory of what she had overheard in the hall only minutes ago. Luke Dawlton's comment about her being a failed artist was like a sucker punch to her stomach as he had managed to hit on the one thing that scared Bennet most.

Even as a child all she had ever wanted was to be an artist and had gone so far as to study art in college. But then her father and champion died, and Bennet began to doubt herself. She lost her confidence and had settled for museum work instead where, when she was not busy helping others' work get seen instead of her own, she spent the majority of her time building up and stroking the egos of elite patrons like Vivian Winthrop that the board and administration seemed so eager to attract rather than trying to ensure every person had access to art, not just the rich and entitled. Bennet wanted so much to use her art and her skills to make a difference and she knew that was not happening where she was now.

Bennet had shared little of her feelings and aspirations with the people in her life. She had only truly confided in her sister and Stella, sharing with them the insecurities she felt about her career and her belief that most of the time she believed she was failing at her job and wishing she could do more. Her mother, she knew, could never understand and instead would most likely view it as simply another of her daughter's little problems.

Of course, Luke Dawlton had no way of knowing any of this when he had referred to her as a failed artist. He knew nothing about her; but that did nothing to lessen the blow when she heard him disparage her out loud. This arrogant stranger, with his charming British accent and stunning good looks, had no right to make any such assumptions about her. Did he think for a minute that she was any happier with this arrangement than he was? She had a far greater right than him to be outraged. This was her job he was interfering with, and the inconvenience and indignation was hers alone to be felt.

She might have even been able to get past what he had said and welcomed the chance to prove him wrong if not for the events of the morning. How could she ever expect him to think of her as a professional after what she had done?

He must think I'm absolutely insane, Bennet thought, torturing herself as she replayed the details of their first interaction as well as what had just taken place in Brent Stromwell's office. The truth was she was mortified at the way she had acted.

As she was reflecting on her own behavior however, she could not help but be reminded of how rude Luke Dawlton had been.

Who the hell does he think he is saying that about me? He's as cold and dismissive as his aunt, Bennet thought angrily.

As if her shifting moods were anchored to a never ceasing pendulum, suddenly any regret she felt towards her actions was replaced by the firm opinion that Vivian Winthrop's nephew was a complete jerk. He did not even know her and he was already thinking she was some amateur.

Then, quite unexpectedly, her thoughts turned to the admittedly sexy flicker of a smile that had flashed across his face when she had been forced to make reference to her stained blouse.

He really is attractive. That jawline and my God those eyes. Were they that beautiful this morning?

"Well that's certainly not helping," Bennet said aloud as she struggled to shake these new, unwelcome thoughts from her mind. Standing up she began to pace around her office and give herself a pep talk.

"Pull yourself together Reynolds. There's nothing you can do now but find a way to move forward. You have no choice but to work with this pompous, arrogant jerk so you have to get control of yourself and start acting like you are in charge."

Unable to bear being in the museum one minute longer and suddenly overwhelmed with the desire to drown her sorrows in a big glass of red wine, Bennet grabbed some work she hoped to review tonight, her planner, and her phone and threw them all in her tote bag.

Having pulled her coffee stained coat off the door hook, she was in the process of putting it on when her thoughts returned once more to her appearance and a fresh wave of embarrassment washed over her. As if she had not given Luke Dawlton enough ammunition to use against her, he now had visual confirmation that she could not even dress herself.

Damn that Katherine. She loved pointing out my blouse. Just once I wish it was me who could put her in her place instead of the other way around, Bennet thought.

She knew however, that like everything else today, she would just fail at that as well.

———————————

A rush of fresh air hit Bennet as she stepped outside. At once she was reminded how much she loved that in early September one could feel the stifling heat of the summer beginning to give way to the hint of autumn's cooler breezes, and today there was just enough for her to see the gentle rustle of the branches of the small trees in the museum's gated park.

The serenity of the moment was quickly broken however when hearing the door to the museum close behind her, Bennet was struck by the thought that if only she could shut a door on her entire day and have a do over then it might be okay. But that would be too easy. There was no way that was going to happen. It was her life, so Bennet knew all too well things could only get worse.

As she began her three-block walk to the subway station Bennet allowed herself to get lost, if only for a few moments, in the barrage of street sounds as the city's inhabitants were engaged in rushing along as part of their end of the work day ritual. Most days this brief walk, followed by the twenty-or-so minute subway commute home provided an opportunity for the worst moments of her workday to dull and allowed her to let go of enough stress to reach her apartment in a reasonably relaxed state.

That was not the case tonight however, as she found herself trapped in a packed train car. With no chance of a seat, Bennet was forced to stand inches away from a man who clearly felt deodorant was an option rather than a necessity. Overwhelmed by the stench of his body odor, she had the additional misfortune of a view that was limited to the back of the woman in front of her, a toddler on his mother's lap to her left who appeared to be in a race to see how far he could jam his stubby finger up his nose before his mother caught him, and a man seated to her right who was engaged in a heated conversation with himself. While she could not hear what he was saying, from his expression it seemed as if the man was losing his imaginary debate and he grew increasingly animated and agitated with each passing minute.

Such as it was, the subway car's cast of horrifying characters left Bennet plenty of time to relive once more the humiliating moments of her day. As she did she found her thoughts kept returning to Luke Dawlton, his rude behavior this morning, and her horrible luck that he would be Vivian Winthrop's nephew.

Based on what she had overheard of his conversation in the gallery, he had as little interest in working on this project as she had in working with him. Could she have used that to her advantage and convinced him to play a minimal role in putting the exhibition together? Maybe. But there was a slim chance of that now. She had heard what he thought of her when he was speaking on the phone in the gallery and that was before he realized who she was.

She had never imagined that she would see the man from the café again nor could she even attempt to try and calculate the infinitesimal odds that he would be the man she would be forced to work with on the Winthrop exhibition. With what was sure to be his extremely low opinion of her behavior and perhaps even her mental stability based on her interaction with him this morning, how was she ever going to work with him now? It was almost too much to think about and yet it was the only thing running through her mind like an endless, anxiety-inducing loop, as she walked the remaining blocks home from the subway station.

Bennet's apartment building was one of those old city structures that lacked modern amenities such as a communal fitness room, central air, or a designer kitchen. Still any deficiencies were made up for in the building's overall charm, and most importantly in her case, decent rent.

Bennet had been lucky in securing the apartment four years ago. It had belonged to her father's aunt, who had moved to a retirement home in sunny Florida to be nearer her son and arranged for Bennet to move in and take over the rent-controlled space. She knew her aunt had left it to her because she felt sorry for her. Bennet accepted that her aunt was worried she might end up alone and needed the security the apartment would offer, but she did not care how pathetic her aunt thought she was because the apartment meant she could afford to live alone without roommates; something most people her age in the city and making the salary she did still needed to do.

An elevator being another of the building's missing luxuries, Bennet was forced to climb the three flights of stairs leading to her apartment; one of two on the top floor. As she reached the door, she could hear the excited clicking of Daisy's paws on the hardwood of her hallway.

"There's my girl," Bennet said by way of a greeting as she was met by the fluffy white, thirteen-pound ball of fur.

"And how was your day? Not as eventful as mine I imagine."

Bennet had long since resigned herself to the fact that she was fulfilling a stereotype by not only living with but carrying on one-sided conversations with a cat.

Dumping her bag and coat on the floor as she was too tired to bother to hang either up, she kicked off her heels, walked into her kitchen, grabbed a bottle of red wine, and poured herself a glass. But then, just as she was about to take her first sip she remembered her night's obligation.

"I just can't, Daisy," Bennet said before letting out an exhausted sigh. She knew after today there was no way she could face dinner with her mother and the inevitable barrage of questions and judgments she would have prepared solely for her younger daughter this evening.

Adelaide Reynolds was a force to be reckoned with; one that belied her petite stature. A mere five feet tall, thin with blonde hair that she had always worn in a perfect chin length bob, she had an uncanny ability of dominating any room she was in and would go head to head with anyone who dared disagree with anything she said. Her opinions, whether on politics, religion, or even something as mundane as what brand of peanut butter tasted best, were always considered right and she would challenge anyone who presumed to question her on any subject.

The formidable Adelaide knew what she wanted for herself and for others. While Bennet's father was alive she had spent most of her time doting on him, but now that he was gone this energy was focused almost entirely on her daughters; something that proved more often than not exhausting for Bennet, for whom Adelaide had made it her mission to shape the course of Bennet's life in the direction she wanted regardless, it often seemed, of what Bennet may have planned for herself.

Picking up her phone, she dialed her mother's number.

Let it be the machine. Please let it be the machine, Bennet silently pleaded.

"Reynolds residence."

Damn.

"Hello, Mom."

"Bennet, I hope you are phoning to say you are almost here."

"Actually, that's what I'm calling about. Something has come up and

I need to spend tonight preparing for an important meeting tomorrow," Bennet lied.

"Oh. Well that's no problem."

The ease with which her mother had handled this last-minute change in plan instantly alarmed Bennet. There was no way it could be this easy.

"Really? It's just I expected you to be a little more upset."

"Bennet please. You make me sound as if I am some difficult and demanding person." Her mother sounded shocked that her daughter would question her motives.

Well, I have had a lifetime of experience that proves you are, Bennet thought, grateful her mother could not see her rolling her eyes.

After a pause Adelaide added, "But I guess that if you did want to make it up to me, there is one thing you could do."

There it is. Here comes the catch.

"Your brother-in-law's firm has purchased some tables at this charity gala Saturday night and your sister needs help to fill one of them. You can attend the event and we will call it even."

Just kill me now.

"Saturday is kind of busy for me. I don't know if I can…"

"Listen Bennet," her mother cut her off. "This is important to Jane and since I have not had a chance to see you tonight, it would be nice if you could support her and spend some time with me by attending."

"It's just I…"

"It's just what, Bennet? It's not like you have a date for Saturday evening. What are your plans? Some all-night television binge with your friend Stella? Jane has worked hard on this and…"

"Fine, Mom," Bennet said in an act of surrender. Exhausted at the conversation, she knew from experience there was no way she could win. "Saturday is fine. I will call Jane and get the details."

"No need," Adelaide replied, the sound of victory clear in her voice. "I emailed them to you an hour ago."

As Bennet came to the realization that this had been her mother's plan all along, she could actually picture her mother smiling on the other end of the line.

Bennet let out a deep sigh. "Okay Mom, sounds good. I better go now. Lots of work to do."

"Sure, sure. And Bennet, so you are aware, I told Jane not to hold a second seat for you. I knew you wouldn't have a date. Who knows, you might even meet some rich, eligible men at the gala."

"Whatever Mom. Gotta go. I'll talk to you later."

Hanging up her phone, Bennet could not shake the feeling that she had traded one dreaded evening with her mother for another, far worse one. She would now have to attend a charity function this weekend without a plus one and sit at a table filled with couples and God help her, her mother.

Resigning herself to whatever was to come, Bennet decided she would worry about Saturday night later. Right now she had more pressing problems. Grabbing her glass of wine, she moved to the couch, turned on the television, and started up a saved episode of one of the several British dramas presently filling up her DVR queue.

Next she opened her laptop and typed in a search for Luke Dawlton. To say he led a privileged life would have been an understatement. From the bio on his company's website she learned that after earning an undergraduate degree from Columbia, he had gone on to receive his MBA from Oxford. He started his own finance company twelve years ago at the impressively young age of twenty-five and his firm had quickly grown to become one of the top fifty both in the United States and Great Britain.

So what, Bennet thought. *All those degrees certainly haven't made you a nice person.*

Bennet quickly saw that Stella had been right about his image as well. He actually seemed to become more handsome with each photograph she clicked on. There were of course the standard headshots from his firm's page and the several organizations on which he served as a board member. But there were also several "about town" photographs of him at various charity and society functions. The last of which, Bennet noticed, often placed him with a series of different beautiful women on his arm leading her to believe that he was just as superficial as he was obnoxious.

Bennet took a big sip of her wine.

"Well Daisy, I seem to have managed to screw this one up and I haven't even started yet, have I?"

Daisy nuzzled her head against her owner's leg and let out a soft meow before curling up and falling asleep.

Powering down her laptop, Bennet turned her attention to the television. The problem of Luke Dawlton would still be there in a few hours. For now, she would focus on what seemed like the far simpler problems of the British aristocracy.

CHAPTER SEVEN

Forced awake by the irritating buzzing of her alarm clock; as Bennet opened her eyes she was confronted with the cold, hard truth that the disasters of yesterday had not been just a bad dream. Not wanting to move she spent longer than she should buried under her down comforter, trying to convince herself to get up and go. Once she finally did motivate herself to leave her bed she spent the next twenty minutes rushing to get dressed, make coffee, and hurry out of her apartment to the subway station so she did not miss her train.

Her arrival at work had done nothing to better her mood. Instead as she spent the first part of her morning reviewing the Winthrop Collection files her anxiety level actually increased as she thought about Luke Dawlton's forced involvement in the project and what his next move was going to be. She had no idea how she was going to face him when inevitably they would finally have to meet to discuss the exhibition.

"Any word from Prince Charming yet?" Stella asked, startling Bennet with her sudden appearance in her office doorway.

"Jeez, Stella; ever heard of knocking?" Bennet replied with a smile as she looked up from her computer screen.

"If you mean Mr. Dawlton then no, I haven't heard from him. And please stop calling him that. There are a lot of names I can think of to call him but that sure as hell isn't one of them."

"Come on, tell me you didn't spend last night surfing the Internet trying to find out all about him," Stella teased as she took a seat next to Bennet's desk.

"It doesn't matter if I did," Bennet replied as she tried her best to avoid Stella's stare. "This entire situation is a nightmare."

"I know, but you can't blame a friend for trying to lighten up the serious mood, can you? Okay. Fine. Subject change here; how was the dreaded dinner with your mom?"

"I got out of it."

"Really? How on earth did you manage that? You must have lied something good to avoid dinner with Adelaide."

"Yeah, I did. And believe me, it's going to come back and bite me in the ass you can be sure of that. When I told her I couldn't make it, my mother was so eager and willing to accommodate that I knew something was up."

"Oh, I'm sure there was." Stella had survived enough interactions with Adelaide Reynolds to know her completely capable of manipulating a situation to her advantage. "What did you have to promise her, your first born?"

Bennet laughed. "Are you kidding? According to her if she made me promise that she would be waiting around forever. As she likes to remind me on an almost daily basis, she has given up any hope of me, her lonely spinster daughter, giving her a grandchild anytime soon.

"No, she basically blackmailed me into attending one of Jane's husband's charity dinners on Saturday night. Won't that be wonderful?"

"Oh yeah, all kinds of fun." Stella smiled. "Twenty bucks says she tries to set you up with every single man under the age of seventy-five."

As Bennet began to laugh, the sound of a throat being cleared interrupted her and Stella's conversation.

Looking up, they were shocked to see Luke Dawlton standing in the doorway.

"Apologies," Luke said, with the hint of that smile Bennet found so unsettling tugging at the corners of his mouth. "I don't mean to interrupt."

Mortified just thinking about the fact that he might have heard their conversation and confused as to his sudden appearance in her doorway, Bennet was quick to reply, "You are not interrupting, I assure you, we…"

The sudden ringing of her desk phone caused Bennet to stop speaking.

After a quick glance at the ID display, she fixed Luke with a firm stare and said, "Excuse me, it's security so I have to answer."

Striving to sound as professional as possible, she answered the phone, "Bennet Reynolds, here… Yes, well thank you but he has already reached my office."

Hoping Luke could not sense her irritation and embarrassment, she quickly added, "No problem. Thank you."

Then to her further humiliation, as she tried to hang up the phone, Bennet accidentally dropped the receiver. Bouncing against the hard surface of her desk before falling, only the cord prevented it from slamming onto the floor as it began to bob up and down like a yo-yo.

For the last several seconds Luke had watched in amazement as Bennet had become increasingly frazzled. Now, as she struggled to pick up the phone, he actually had to try hard to stifle a laugh.

Stella, wanting to help her friend who at this moment she feared might be beyond any possible assistance, stood up and walked towards Luke with her hand extended.

"I don't believe we've met. I'm Stella Thompson. I handle public relations at the museum."

Luke shook her hand. "Nice to meet you. Luke Dawlton."

"Yes, I know."

Having finally managed to properly hang up her phone, Bennet caught the slight inflection in her friend's voice and shot her a warning glance. The last thing she needed was Stella letting Luke think he had been the subject of any discussion between the two of them.

"Well I'm sure you both have work to do. I will leave you to it." As Stella walked past Luke, she turned back and gave Bennet a wink. "Call me," she mouthed before disappearing from view.

"I have some paperwork that my aunt's lawyer needs to be reviewed by your director as soon as possible. I had a meeting in the area so I thought it would be best to drop it off with you so you can see that it gets to the appropriate people," Luke began once they were alone.

"I had no intention of disrupting your day but the guard at the door directed me to your office."

"I assure you, you are not disrupting anything," Bennet said rising from her desk and walking towards him.

Even while she was making a mental note to have a firm conversation with security over whom they just let wander down to her office, she had enough presence of mind to attempt to make the effort to get back some of the control in this conversation with Luke Dawlton even if it killed her. And, if dying of embarrassment was actually possible, there was a good chance it just might happen.

"I was under the impression that your office was going to call to schedule an appointment," Bennet began, unable to completely keep the irritation from her voice. "I have materials I would've liked to have had prepared to start going through with you, and..."

"Yes, I understand," Luke began abruptly cutting Bennet off mid-sentence, "but as I explained this paperwork needs the museum's immediate attention. I could have easily messengered it over at much greater convenience to myself I might add, but I thought you might like the opportunity to clear the air regarding yesterday's meeting. I appreciate that this working situation is probably not ideal for either of us."

You can say that again, Bennet thought as she tried to control her rising anger over the audacity of this man suggesting that his being here in her office should be seen as some kind of generosity on his part. As far as she was concerned, the only person who needed to clear the air was him for his rude behavior both yesterday morning and for what he said about her later that afternoon.

"Look Mr. Dawlton," Bennet began, "I think if..."

"Luke, please."

Wow he just can't stop interrupting. He probably loves the sound of his voice so much that he never even stops to consider that anyone else might have something important to say.

"And may I call you Bennet?"

"What?" Bennet asked as Luke's question served to pull her back from her thoughts.

"I asked if I can call you Bennet," Luke replied.

Not waiting for an answer, he continued, "I must say, it is quite an unusual name."

Here we go. Every time I meet someone new it's the same thing.

Bennet had lost count how many times in her life she had been called upon to explain her "unusual" name. Every time she did, she reflected on why parents could not simply stick to lovely, common names like Mary, Jennifer, or even Kate. The irony had not been lost on her that despite her mother finding her almost painfully normal, she had burdened her with a name that was anything but.

"Does it have a story behind it?" Luke asked.

Regretting that once again she would have to share the origins of her name with a nosey stranger, Bennet nevertheless felt compelled to explain.

"My mother picked the name. She's a literature buff. My sister is named Jane for Jane Eyre and I'm named after the main character in Jane Austen's *Pride and Prejudice*."

"Your mother didn't want to go with Elizabeth?"

"So you know your classics," Bennet replied.

Despite her best efforts not to be, Bennet was impressed. Most men she met had no idea who Jane Austen was let alone her most famous character, Elizabeth Bennet.

"No, not my mother. Using the heroine's first name would have made things too easy to be my life. She thought it would be more intriguing to use the character's last name instead." Bennet sighed. "And because of it, I have spent my entire life explaining my name."

"At least tell me you like the novel since you're named after it?" Luke asked, ignoring what Bennet had hoped had been her less than subtle hint that she no longer wanted to discuss the subject of her name with him.

She was confused as to what his game was and what he was hoping to achieve with this line of questioning.

Bennet could not believe he was really interested in any of this. And yet she found herself still having to explain.

"Despite my best efforts not to like the novel for the sheer pleasure of annoying my mother, I have to admit that it's actually one of my favorites. I'm a bit of an Anglophile really."

As Luke smiled at her comment, Bennet realized how what she had just said could have been misinterpreted. Since he had a British accent, she did not want him to think that she meant she might like him too. The truth was his accent was a bit of a mystery. While it was slight, she found herself wondering how he had come by it and what his background might be. She had also hated herself for noticing that when he smiled his entire expression changed from the cold, judgmental one she had most often seen on his face to one that brought a sparkle to his piercing blue eyes. The last thing she needed to be thinking about was how attractive he was.

Reminding herself that Luke Dawlton's looks and accent were completely irrelevant to the jerk she knew him to be, she hastened to add, "What I mean is I have a strong interest in British literature and films."

The smile reappeared on Luke's face as if he could read her thoughts. This time however, thinking he might be mocking her, she found herself disliking the expression more than if he had actually snickered. She did not want him to think that he had any effect on her whatsoever.

Mad at herself for letting this conversation move away from the business of the Winthrop Collection, Bennet was desperate to regain control of their exchange.

"We have a lot to do with this exhibition Mr. Dawlton and I think it is really important that we take the time to establish what needs to be done and how you see your role in this process progressing."

"I am starting to think you don't like me very much," Luke replied as he noted the irritation in her tone.

Well I don't like that smug attitude of yours; that's for sure, Bennet thought as the image of him taunting her while he took a bite of his croissant on the street yesterday morning popped into her head. It was followed by the memory of him insulting her in the museum's corridor later that afternoon when he referred to her as a failed artist.

"It doesn't matter what I think of you. All that matters is that it seems we will have to work together and so that is what I am trying to do."

Bennet knew she should be making more of an effort to stay civil but there was something about the cocky way he was standing there, uninvited, in her office and questioning whether she liked him or not given how he had treated her thus far that was getting on her nerves.

Luke visibly stiffened at her words and his expression turned hard once more.

"Really I think you should at least appreciate the fact that I am willing to even attempt to work with you on this project," Luke replied, his annoyance clear in his voice. "I am sure you are embarrassed at your frankly crazy behavior when we first met and I thought I would be generous enough to allow you to see I was willing to move past it."

"Your generosity?" Bennet asked incredulously. "Am I supposed to thank you? Thank you for what I wonder. Is it for being rude to me when we first met; or showing up at my office unannounced; or the condescending way that you are right now implying that I should somehow feel grateful to you over your willingness to work with me?

"We both know you are only here because your aunt wants you to be so what I feel about the situation or even you, for that matter, is irrelevant. And you can be sure that I couldn't care less what you think about me. Besides, you are certainly in no position to pass judgment on my behavior or attitude," Bennet snapped.

Luke was rarely in a position where he felt at a loss for words but in this moment, he found himself staring at Bennet, unsure what to say next. Her hostile tone had come as a surprise and while at first he had found her flustered reaction to his presence at her office slightly amusing he was quickly becoming angry at her attitude. He wondered just who this woman thought she was and knew that if she were seriously waiting for an apology or for him to attempt to placate her then she would be in for a hell of a long wait.

"Listen, I don't mean to be rude," Bennet was becoming uncomfortable with how quickly their exchange had deteriorated. Like it or not he was Vivian Winthrop's nephew and she was stuck with his involvement on this project. The last thing she needed was him making trouble for her or complaining to Brent and Katherine.

Trying to regain some professionalism she added, "The truth is just what I said; we have a lot of work to do and I want to make sure it all goes smoothly."

Then, unable to resist it, she found herself throwing his own words from yesterday back up at him. "The general impression of me might be that I am some failed artist wannabe struggling to put this show together, but I can assure you I know exactly what I'm doing. I am completely invested in my job and making this an impressive exhibition. So what I need from you is…"

The sudden buzz of Luke's phone startled both of them, causing Bennet to stop speaking mid-sentence.

Luke looked at his screen.

"Excuse me, but I have to take this call."

"It's no matter to me," Bennet replied brusquely as she directed her focus to the stack of papers on her desk.

Despite her best efforts not to listen to his conversation, it was easy enough to see he was quickly becoming frustrated.

"No, I am in the middle of a meeting here and I… What time is he leaving for the airport? Well then I have no choice do I? Tell him I will meet him at the office in twenty minutes."

Ending the call, Luke turned to Bennet and added, "I have to go."

The nerve, Bennet thought while still struggling to control her temper.

"Mr. Dawlton, you are here at your aunt's request," Bennet began, her annoyance now palpably clear in her tone. "If you have to go, then go. But before you do, I feel I should remind you that it is you who showed up uninvited to my office and it is you who stood here just now demanding that I take care of making sure your aunt's paperwork gets signed as if I were some intern rather than the curator of your aunt's exhibition.

"I was made to understand by my bosses and your aunt that your presence on this project was nonnegotiable. So I guess that means it is up to me to schedule a meeting so we can get the project moving forward. I am free tomorrow morning at 10 am. We will meet at the museum so I can review with you the plans I have for the exhibition. And don't worry, I will make sure your papers are signed and ready for you to take back then."

As she was speaking Luke struggled to understand the audacity of this woman who seemed to be implying that he was guilty of doing something wrong. Right now she seemed more like the crazy woman who had accosted him yesterday morning than what he had expected of the curator of a respectable museum such as the Northhom.

The fact that Bennet Reynolds made no attempt to hide the hostility she felt towards him had also come as a surprise. He had believed things might be a little awkward considering their first interaction on the street yesterday morning, and because of that he had already decided as he arrived at the museum today that he would not raise the subject of the incident to spare her any further embarrassment. Feeling it was a magnanimous gesture on his part, he firmly believed that the least she should have done was appreciate it. But she actually seemed more annoyed than embarrassed and he found himself wondering just who she thought she was to have such feelings. She was the one who had behaved like a crazy woman that morning, not him. If anything, he should be the one annoyed at the ludicrousness of this entire situation. He was the one with no desire to be here; the one who was stuck working on this project which was neither a part of his job nor something he was even remotely interested in.

Luke's anger was clear when he next spoke. "I will have my assistant check my schedule. Your meeting is far from the most important item on my list of things to do. In fact this entire situation is, I assure you, the very last thing I want to be doing."

Unable to help himself he added, "Just see to it that these papers get reviewed and signed by your director. That is, if you think you can handle such a simple task and it is not beneath your station as curator of the great Northhom Museum."

Grabbing the document envelope from his hands, Bennet placed it forcefully on the stack of papers in her inbox.

"Oh I will just have to try my best to manage," Bennet snapped back at him. "In the meantime, I will continue to do what is my actual job and prepare your aunt's exhibition. Now, since you found my office with no trouble, I assume you don't need me to walk you out."

"No, I will be fine," Luke replied haughtily as his phone rang again.

Letting out a sigh loud enough to ensure her disgust was clear, Bennet turned her back to him and tried her best to appear to be focusing on something on her computer screen.

About to say something more, Luke suddenly changed his mind and instead began to answer his phone while storming out of her office.

While all too glad to see him leave, Bennet was unsettled by their conversation. It was all his fault as far as she was concerned, beginning with the fact that he thought he had the right to just show up at her office. She was sure he did not meet with just anyone who turned up at his firm without an appointment. It was a power play, plain and simple. He had to know that by arriving unannounced he would be catching her off guard. And by giving her papers to be signed he had to be trying to make it clear he was in charge.

He's as arrogant now as he was yesterday morning, Bennet thought. And yet, for just the briefest of moments she allowed herself to consider that he had seemed actually genuinely interested, almost even nice, when he asked about her name.

Had I overreacted to his stopping by? Maybe he really did just mean what he said that he was nearby the museum and needed to get these papers signed and so decided to drop them off.

But then just as quickly Bennet remembered his conversation in the hallway yesterday where he accused her of being incompetent. That was the real Luke Dawlton; she was sure of it. Besides, she reasoned, being smooth and schmoozing people to get them to do what he wanted was probably all in a day's work for someone like him.

The only thing that mattered, Bennet reminded herself, was that right now Vivian Winthrop's appalling nephew had the upper hand. Since he thought she was an amateur she would just have to prove him wrong by putting together the best exhibition this museum had ever seen.

She might not be able to undo what had already happened or change his clearly biased impression of her but she could promise herself, right here and right now, that she was never going to let him surprise her again. From this point on she was going to take charge. This was her project and she would make sure the insufferable Luke Dawlton knew it from the very start of their next meeting.

As he stormed out of the museum, Luke could not help but think about all that had just taken place with Bennet Reynolds. Nothing that had happened had been expected and he was actually shocked at her attitude. Thinking back to their first interaction yesterday morning, he realized she had some justification in having reservations about him. He knew he could have handled the exchange better, and if he were honest he had behaved like a bit of a jerk. But then who was she to run after him like that? At the moment she had seemed crazy; certainly not the respectable curator of the Northhom Museum who was in charge of handling his aunt's multi-million-dollar art collection.

What were the odds that this would have been the same woman he was now being forced to work with. Once more Luke found himself cursing his aunt for her attempts to control him. She had emotionally guilted him into doing her bidding and not for the first time. When would it be enough? When would he be able to stop feeling like that little boy who had to do everything she asked to please her so she would know how grateful he was to her for taking him in?

Luke had thought nothing about showing up at Bennet's office this morning. Surely, he had every right to deliver the paperwork to her. Who did she think she was to question his motives. As far as he was concerned the museum worked for his aunt. That meant they also worked for him by extension. The museum staff would do well to remember that fact if they wanted to get their hands on her artworks.

Still, she seemed so annoyed by it that it had him rethinking what he had done. Was she right in questioning his motives? He had certainly flustered her showing up the way he did. Even now, despite how angry he was, he had to try not to laugh at the ridiculous way she tried to grab that phone as it just kept bouncing up and down against the side of her desk. Her ability to become both so easily riled and flustered at the same time had the effect of making her seem strangely endearing.

There were even a few minutes when they had been talking that the conversation seemed to be going well. For a moment he thought he saw a different side of her, but just as quickly she had turned angry again.

Still, there was also something about what she had said that was nagging at him. What was it about the turn of phrase she had used to describe the impression others had of her as a failed artist that seemed so familiar? Why did it bother him so much?

Suddenly it dawned on him. During his conversation with his assistant the previous afternoon, he had referred to the curator that way. He had been so angry about his aunt's need to once more exert her control by making him participate in this exhibition.

Was it possible that she had overheard him? He had no way to be sure; but if she had it would certainly help to explain her open and blatant animosity towards him.

Luke shook his head as if attempting to push the thoughts out of his mind. So what if he had voiced concerns about her. He didn't even know who she was and in a way he had been right anyways, given she was the woman who only hours earlier had accosted him on a Manhattan street corner.

Luke was frustrated with himself. He was spending too much time thinking about this woman. What did he care about any of this anyway. He had no interest in working on this project. More importantly, he did not care about what some museum employee thought of him. The city's wealthiest residents trusted him to invest their fortunes. He certainly did not have to prove himself through some art exhibition.

And yet, if he had nothing to prove and this curator was no one he should be bothered to care about, why had she managed to annoy him the way she did.

CHAPTER EIGHT

Bennet's morning encounter with Luke Dawlton had left her unsettled, and as a result she had found it difficult to focus the rest of the day. She could not figure him out and for someone who needed to be in control, this was more than a little troubling.

Fortunately Bennet had plenty of work to keep her busy and before she knew it she was walking out of the museum. Her bag was loaded down with files on the Winthrop Collection and she knew she had hours of work ahead of her at home if she wanted to be prepared and at her best for her meeting with Luke tomorrow morning.

Besides the work, the stress of the day had left her wanting nothing more than to go home but it was Tuesday and so, despite zero desire to do so, she found herself heading to the yoga studio to meet her sister.

Bennet failed to see the point in yoga. It hardly seemed like a workout and all the benefits one was supposed to derive from it, namely the increased flexibility and centeredness of mind and spirit, had never seemed to come her way. It also did not help that she had zero aptitude for it whatsoever, but it was something Jane loved and the class gave them a chance to spend time together once a week, just the two of them. She knew her sister needed this break from her husband and even from her adorable yet demanding two-year-old daughter Charlotte. And they both certainly needed the time alone, away from their mother who dominated every moment when they gathered as a family.

Walking into the studio, Bennet was confronted with the overwhelming scent of lavender. While it was a flower known for its relaxing properties, that had never been her experience. Every time she entered this space the intensity of the smell brought on the start of a headache and today had the added effect of serving to ratchet up her already substantial stress level.

Not unusual for her, she was already late and so not wanting to disturb the class that was just beginning, Bennet rushed into the changing room to quickly switch into her workout clothes before joining her sister who had held open a spot next to her at the back of the studio.

Jane had laid out their two mats and of course looked perfect and ready to go as Bennet joined her. She, in sharp contrast, already looked exhausted and had not even begun the class yet.

"Rough day?" Jane asked in a whisper.

"You have no idea," Bennet replied. "I just found out that I'm going to be stuck working with Vivian Winthrop's nephew to put on the exhibition of her collection. He did a surprise drop-in at my office today and I have to meet with him again tomorrow. I am absolutely dreading it."

"Now we will transition from warrior one to warrior two," the instructor said, continuing her sequence.

Just perfect, Bennet thought as she looked up and noted the identity of the instructor.

Of the three teachers who rotated weeks leading this class, Kayla was her least favorite. Her model perfect appearance never failed to make Bennet feel like a fat, sweaty pig by the time they were halfway through the routine and her cheerleader style perkiness was almost impossible to stomach. Every request for a position change was called out like a verse from a song while the entire time she had a smile permanently fixed on her face, so wide Bennet wondered how it was even possible to achieve it.

At least when Javier was the instructor Bennet could take some pleasure from watching him demonstrate the poses, and his sexy Columbian accent as he called out the moves in the sequence made even the most ridiculous of positions seem somehow more intriguing.

"Is it a bad thing having to work with this guy?" Jane asked, knowing how important the exhibition was to her sister. "How terrible is he?"

Bennet sighed as she was forced to return from thoughts of Javier.

"Believe me, it's going to be an absolute nightmare. He's completely arrogant; some big finance guy."

Jane laughed. "Oh sure, you know those finance people; they are the worst."

"Sorry Jane," Bennet replied quickly. "Of course you know I don't mean your husband. Trust me though, Luke Dawlton is a total jerk; nothing like David."

"And now downward facing dog," the instructor continued. "And breathe deeply. You can do it. Come on you in the back row; let me see those smiles."

As she switched positions, Bennet fought back the overwhelming urge to flip Kayla off. Already struggling to keep up she noticed how effortlessly Jane transitioned through the routine's movements. She, on the other hand, was already out of breath and her thighs felt like they were on fire.

"Wow. Luke Dawlton," Jane said, impressed. "I've never met him myself, but I know him by reputation. He's a really big deal. His company, Dawlton Capital, is one of the top firms in the city. David could only dream of working at a place like that."

"Great," Bennet replied after blowing back a stray strand of her hair that had escaped from her ponytail and fallen into her face.

"And now let's all move into three legged dog," Kayla continued but not before Bennet caught the look of annoyance she sent in her and Jane's direction regarding their conversing; a blatant violation of the class's no talking policy.

Undeterred, Bennet whispered to her sister, "What is it with yoga and dogs? I mean really can't they think of something more inspired as names for these positions? It might make it more fun."

When Jane chose to ignore her sarcastic questions, Bennet switched the topic back to Luke. "Working with the nephew would be bad enough. It's like having a babysitter who is going to be watching everything I do with this exhibit. But that's not the worst thing about the whole situation. The morning of the day I found out I had to work with him I kind of accosted him in the street over a croissant."

At her words Jane actually laughed out loud, causing a nearby participant to shush her and a second, more threatening glare to be directed at them from their usually unflappable instructor.

"Oh whatever," Bennet hissed back to the woman on the neighboring mat. "Do you really need absolute silence to lift your leg in the air? I mean come on, it's yoga not surgery we're doing here."

Jane shook her head as she tried desperately not to laugh again.

Speaking in a whisper, Jane added, "Bennet please. This is the only chance I get for real physical exercise all week. Let's just get through the class and then I am going to make you tell me absolutely everything."

"Okay," Bennet replied, struggling to keep herself from toppling over, "but you know there are so many other more fun ways to burn calories. We could be shopping, or drinking, or..."

"Shush Bennet," Jane pleaded while appearing to be struggling to hold back a smile.

Thirty minutes later, Bennet and Jane were seated in the Japanese restaurant next door to the yoga studio, drinking sake and sharing three rolls of sushi.

"Now see, this is my kind of exercise," Bennet said before popping a California roll into her mouth. "Just think how many calories we are burning with each bite, and it's delicious."

As they ate Bennet relayed the events of yesterday morning.

Jane had worked hard to maintain her composure as she listened to her sister, but as Bennet finished giving a full account of her exploits she burst out laughing.

"I can't believe you did that. What on earth were you thinking?" Jane asked after taking a sip of her drink.

"That's just it. I don't think I was thinking at all. I just reacted in the moment and it's me so of course I reacted badly."

"And he remembered you when he saw you later that day?" Jane asked.

"Would you forget the crazy woman who crashed into you on a street corner and accused you of stealing her pastry?"

Jane laughed again. "Wow Bennet, you really don't do anything halfway do you?"

Bennet shook her head as she absently used a chopstick to swirl the flecks of wasabi around in her soy sauce.

"Maybe it won't be so bad," Jane said encouragingly. "I mean you said he seemed to be unhappy about being forced to work on the exhibition so maybe he won't want to be that involved."

"Maybe. But I'm not going to hold my breath. We couldn't manage a civil conversation with each other today and we haven't even begun to work on the exhibition itself. I feel like we are locked in a power struggle in which I am losing spectacularly. How am I going to work with him tomorrow?"

"By being Bennet Reynolds; that's how," Jane said smiling. "This is your exhibition. You are in charge. Not him and not your horrible bosses."

"You know what bothered me most?" Bennet asked. Without waiting for a reply, she added, "It was the comment about me being a failed artist."

"He didn't even know who you were when he said it, Bennet," Jane said reaching out and giving her sister's hand a squeeze. "Believe me, the only place you are a failure is in your own mind." Jane smiled. "You know what I think?"

Bennet sighed. This was not the first time she had engaged in this conversation with her sister.

"Yes. You think that I should just do it."

"Exactly. You will never be a true artist unless you try. Have you sent out those illustrations like we discussed?" Jane asked, referencing a potential freelance project Bennet had told her about a while ago and had been actively avoiding.

Bennet shook her head. "No. I'm just too busy with this exhibition. Besides I can't handle any more rejection right now."

"You should send the drawings. Not trying is the only true way to fail."

"Wow, and here I was thinking fortunes were only given out in Chinese restaurants. I didn't know they were available in sushi bars too." Then smiling at the kindness of her sister's words, Bennet added, "Thanks Jane. I know you are only trying to help."

"I am. But now sadly I must say good night because I have stayed out way longer than I should. I better go relieve David of his Charlotte duties before bath time."

"How come whenever it's the father staying home with his children everyone says he's watching his kids as if he's the babysitter and not the parent. What I'd like to know is, who relieves you?"

"I don't know. It's just the way it is I guess."

"Well, all I know is that you are a saint. Anyways, I better go too. I've got to prepare for my meeting with the nephew tomorrow," Bennet replied.

Bennet placed money down on the table and shook her head as Jane tried to pull out her credit card. "No. Let it be my treat tonight."

The minute they stepped outside the restaurant Jane was able to hail a taxi. It was yet another of her many skills that Bennet admired as even the cabs seemed to rush to accommodate her perfect sister.

As Jane was about to get into the car, she turned back and called out to Bennet, "Hey you never said; what does this guy look like?"

"Don't ask."

"That good huh?" Jane said with a smile before waving goodbye.

Bennet stood for a few moments watching as the cab merged into traffic before it disappeared from sight. Then, since her apartment was only ten blocks away, and feeling the fresh air would do her good, she began her walk home. As she did, thoughts of Luke Dawlton and her preparations for tomorrow's meeting weighed heavily on her mind.

CHAPTER NINE

Bennet sat at her desk, sipping her coffee as she nervously reviewed her notes on the Winthrop exhibition. Glancing at the clock she knew she only had thirty minutes before Luke Dawlton was set to arrive. Having done her best to remember all her sister had told her last night at their post-yoga sushi dinner, she had made a promise to herself that no matter what he did to try to insult her or antagonize her, she was going to remain professional, get through the meeting, and focus solely on her job.

The sudden ringing of the phone shattered the silence of the office.

"Bennet Reynolds," she said absently into the receiver.

"Ms. Reynolds, my name is Tara. I am calling from Luke Dawlton's office."

The mere mention of Luke's name made Bennet sit up and take notice.

"How can I help you?" Bennet asked, wondering what could possibly be this woman's reason for wanting to speak to her.

"I am calling to let you know that Mr. Dawlton will be unable to make your meeting. He has been delayed at another appointment and will not have time to travel over to the museum today. We will need to reschedule and he has asked me to review his calendar to select some times that might work for you so we can get something on the books. He would prefer that the two of you meet before the end of the week."

Oh well, if he would prefer it then we should just make it happen right? If it was so important we meet then why the hell couldn't he have got here today?

Bennet struggled to comprehend the weight of what Luke's assistant was telling her. She was furious that not only had he canceled their meeting, but he had even more despicably waited until the absolute last minute to do so.

Knowing she had to remain calm, Bennet reminded herself that none of this was his assistant's fault. If anything she felt sorry for this Tara, whoever she was, if she had to work every day for Luke Dawlton.

"The only time I have available for the remainder of this week is tomorrow morning at 10:30 am," Bennet lied. "If Mr. Dawlton cannot make it at that time, we will all have to suffer his displeasure and he will have to wait until next week." Bennet made no attempt to hide the sarcastic tone in this last statement. She might be forced to work with this man but she was certainly not going to make it easy for him. He was going to find out she could be just as difficult as he was. If he could not make this meeting tomorrow than he would have to wait until next week. Hell, he could wait until next year for all she cared.

"That will be fine," Luke's assistant replied, unaware of any issue on Bennet's part. "I will let Mr. Dawlton know."

Wishing for nothing more than to end the call so she could have the proper meltdown she felt on the verge of having at this very moment, Bennet was about to say goodbye when Luke's assistant spoke again.

"Sorry, Ms. Reynolds, I almost forgot but Mr. Dawlton asked that I make sure to remind you to messenger those documents he left with you yesterday back over to his office this morning. He needs to have them returned to him by no later than noon today."

Bennet had no recollection of her reply to Luke's assistant but she must have agreed to send over the documents and said goodbye because next thing she knew her phone was back in its receiver and she had moved on to lightly banging her head against her desk.

Furious did not begin to explain how she was feeling; there were no words she could think of to accurately describe how angry she was. Bennet knew there was no possible way she could excuse Luke Dawlton's behavior even if she had wanted to. She was unable to see his canceling of their meeting as anything other than another attempt to get the upper hand. It was the same stunt he had pulled when he showed up at her office yesterday unannounced. He wanted to make sure she knew that she worked for him and his aunt, not the other way around.

Unwilling to give him the satisfaction of knowing that he had angered her however, Bennet quickly put the documents she arranged to be signed for him as he had requested in a large mailer and prepared them to be sent.

I hope he gets the world's largest papercut when he opens the envelope, Bennet thought as she left her office and headed in the direction of the mailroom to arrange the messenger service.

As hard as she tried to shake it off, Bennet's anger at Luke had stayed with her throughout the remainder of her workday. While for most of this time she was able to keep it at a simmer, it had flared up again as she tried to restrain herself from confronting the head of the IT Department who, at the last moment, had insisted she attend a two hour training session that afternoon on one of the museum's software programs. It was nothing more than an incredible waste of her time, which she had politely tried to communicate to him based on the fact that she had never once used the old version of the software nor did she have any plans of using the new one. Her reasoning had fallen on deaf ears however, and so she had been forced to sit shoulder to shoulder with several other staff members unlucky enough not to find a reason to get out of the training either.

As she pretended to listen to the presentation, she was unable to stop her mind from replaying all her miserable interactions with Luke Dawlton over the course of the last few days. She could see his smug face and hear his haughty tone as he criticized her actions and directed her as to what she needed to do for him.

As if the training had not been painful enough, late in the day Brent had called to inform her that she would have to give a tour to some prospective donors. Friends of one of the museum's board members who he undoubtedly wanted to impress with his status at the Northhom, Bennet knew what was at the heart of this tour. As curator she would be expected to do her best to schmooze and suck up to this group of people by walking them around the museum and making them feel special by pointing out artworks in a way that allowed them to feel that they were being made privy to some private view of the museum that everyday visitors would never get to see.

These types of tours were one of Bennet's least favorite things to do at the museum; and yet she found she had to do them more often than she would like. And so today at five o'clock, as most of the rest of the staff was preparing to go home for the day, Bennet found herself standing in front of one of the museum's most popular Impressionist works explaining how the movement helped to usher in the birth of modern art and make Paris the center of the art world.

While the guests seemed kind enough, they had no qualms about making it clear they were more interested in socializing then in listening to what Bennet had to say. It was as if she were simply a tour guide serving as background noise to what was really important to them, the act of being seen on an exclusive tour with the museum's curator. The behavior of these three couples brought Vivian Winthrop and her nephew back to the front of her mind as that was how he made her feel, like she were simply some employee he had to deal with and could order around so as to further his aunt's agenda.

For thirty minutes Bennet gave an overview of key works as the participants, blissfully oblivious to her feelings, joked with each other and carried on whispered conversations. Describing a painting depicting a café in 1920s Morocco led one of the women in the tour group to tell another about a new tapas bar they had ate at on Saturday night that had just opened on Fifty-third Street. Later, as Bennet discussed the influence that a well-known artist had on the development of twentieth century landscape painting in America by pointing out elements of his painting of Long Island, one of the men in the group actually felt it was the appropriate time to launch into a diatribe over the construction on the main route into the Hamptons and how the detour added an extra forty-five minutes on the weekend commute to their summer home.

Worse than their lack of attention however was the fact that of all the board members for whom she could have given a tour, this man was the absolute worst. One of the more obnoxious members of the board, he was secretly known as "Handsy Harry" among a select group of the staff because he always seemed to find a way to stand just a little too close and flirt a little too hard with the museum's younger female employees. Bennet herself had been forced to deal with his unwanted attention on more than one occasion when she had been seated next to him at some of the museum's many formal dinners. Fortunately his wife was with him this evening and so he had to at least pretend to behave.

The fact that Katherine had decided to join them for part of Bennet's tour had only served to increase her overall annoyance with the proceedings. It was something Stella surely noticed as she walked by Bennet and her group in the main lower gallery as she was making the trek over from her office on her way out of the building for the evening. Stella motioned to Bennet to call her by making a gesture of a phone by holding her thumb and pinky finger to her ear and lips.

Smiling at her friend to let her know she had seen her, Bennet took it as her cue to start wrapping up. However, as if realizing she wanted to leave them, the group suddenly started peppering her with questions, delaying her ability to conclude the tour for another twenty minutes.

While that should have been the end to her workday from hell, Harry had thrown in the added surprise of inviting Katherine and Bennet to join him and his group for drinks before their dinner. As these were prospective donors with deep pockets and it was a well-connected board member making the ask, it wasn't really a request as much as a requirement.

Still, Katherine had managed to excuse herself as she claimed to have a prior dinner engagement. This meant that Bennet would have zero possibility of being able to get out of joining the group without the risk of causing offense; something she would only pay for later by being reamed out by the director when the slight would inevitably be reported to him.

Explaining that she would meet the group at the bar in twenty minutes, Bennet now found herself outside the museum taking in her first breaths of fresh air all day. As she stood listening to the orchestra of sounds that made up the Manhattan evening rush hour she was, not for the first time, reminded of the fact that spending all day in the museum could get her so involved in the minutia of all the problems of her work world that she could almost forget there was a big, exciting city right outside, full of people with their own sets of daily concerns and problems. Standing outside as she was now, Bennet was able to remember that the Northhom Museum was not the center of the universe, no matter how much Katherine and Brent wanted everyone to think it was and despite the fact that it often felt like it when she was up to her elbows in the muck of the institution's problems and petty dramas. It was a feeling that, if only temporarily, made her mood improve.

She had never wanted this museum world to become her life and recently Bennet had been thinking more and more about what it would be like to take a real leap and try to do something else. What would happen if she just decided one day that she had had enough and was going to take a chance on herself and her art. Could she really be brave enough to try and do something more with her life, she wondered.

The last few days had certainly not helped to improve her outlook on her present state and where she stood in her career, that was for sure. Leading this tour had exhausted all that remained of her energy and while she had been looking forward to a fun dinner with Stella tonight, now, because of this last minute drinks invite, she had been forced to cancel her plans. It was yet another sacrifice she had made for the institution; one that she was sure would go unnoticed and unrecognized. So, instead of dinner with a friend or even just a leisurely walk home after which she could have indulged in a good stress cry on her sofa, Bennet was instead heading to a trendy new bar and restaurant that had opened three blocks from the museum.

On her short walk to the establishment, Bennet had tried to mentally prepare herself for having to make small talk with her tour group one last time tonight. She knew it was expected that she try to help them see the importance of being a part of the Northhom's great legacy of donors while they all sat sipping thirty dollar cocktails.

Just as Bennet was about to enter the restaurant, her phone beeped, alerting her to a text.

Looking down at her screen she saw that the message was from Stella:

> **Just got hit on by a weirdo with a handle bar**
> **moustache while waiting for takeout!**
> **Seriously what's up with the men in this city???**
> **See what happens when you ditch me**
> **and I'm on my own for dinner!**

Still it's better than being stuck
having drinks with Handsy Harry!

Despite everything Bennet smiled at the message. She had been so busy today she barely had time to fill Stella in on the details surrounding Luke's canceling of their meeting. She couldn't wait to call her tonight and tell her everything.

Knowing she needed to go inside and join her party, Bennet quickly texted back a reply:

I'm just about to go in now.
I'm staying for one drink and then leaving.
Who knows, maybe moustache guy is your
prince charming!
LOL

Not waiting to see if Stella would reply, Bennet quickly stashed her phone in her tote and walked into the restaurant.

The space was already crowded even though it was early for dinner, and a cursory glance around the room was all she needed for Bennet to know that while it was trying to be trendy, the restaurant would never get there. The majority of its patrons were wealthy couples in the mid to late stages of middle age and that was not the crowd a place needed to attract to reach true trendy status. What you needed was the younger, hipster crowd, who would post about the bar on social media making it the place to be for at least a few months before they moved on to their next find.

Spotting her group seated around one of the bistro tables in the back of the restaurant, as Bennet began to walk over to them she realized that three more people, two men and a woman, had joined the group. She would have thought nothing of it but as she was just about to reach the table, one of the men turned, revealing himself to be Luke Dawlton.

What the hell is he doing here? Bennet thought as her feelings of anger at his standing her up this morning came surging back.

Upset as she was with his presence, Bennet also, much to her annoyance, could not stop her hand from reflexively moving to the top of her head to check her hair and from wishing she had taken the time to double check her makeup before walking into the restaurant.

Knowing there was no way she would be able to avoid dealing with Luke if he was now with her tour group, Bennet struggled to maintain her composure and walk calmly to the table.

"Ah, here she is," Harry said as he stood and began pulling out a chair for Bennet. Even his voice gave Bennet the creeps. "We were just about to order a round of drinks. What's your poison?"

"A gin and tonic, thanks," Bennet answered refusing to make eye contact with Luke and quickly taking a seat.

As Harry motioned for their waiter and began placing their order, one of the women from the tour turned to Bennet and began speaking. "We are so glad you could join us for a drink. We had invited some other friends to join us for dinner and I was explaining how you had given us such a lovely tour at the Northhom. Imagine my surprise when Luke said he already knew you. How lucky you are to be able to work with his aunt's collection. I hear it is wonderful."

My God, does everyone feel the need to suck up to this miserable man?

"Yes, it's an amazing collection and the Northhom is fortunate to have been gifted it," Bennet replied, trying her best to appear pleasant and keep a smile on her face.

As she spoke, Bennet could feel Luke's eyes on her but refused to give him the satisfaction of meeting his gaze. Instead she was intent on making it clear she was ignoring his presence. She had not had a word from him since this morning when his assistant rescheduled their meeting. It had also not escaped her notice that his office did not even have the decency to reach out to her to acknowledge the receipt of the package and thank her for messengering over the documents earlier in the day.

"And you get to work with Luke on the project. That must be nice for you," the woman continued.

What's her obsession with Luke? Why can't you let the subject drop already?

Realizing it would be rude not to answer Bennet did her best to calmly reply. "Well it is unusual to get such outside assistance; but I am sure the exhibition will be wonderful."

Bennet hoped her answer was enough to satisfy the woman and end her incessant questions. Still as she finished speaking she could not help but send a quick and what she hoped was a withering glare in Luke's direction.

Somehow Bennet managed to make it through a round of drinks, engaging in light banter focused on talking up the Northhom Museum. She also did her best not to acknowledge Luke or include him in her conversations. Still, when she did glance in his direction twice during the thirty minutes she was trapped in this hellish round of small talk, she noticed he was looking at her with an expression she could not read. Whether it was smug amusement, irritation, or haughty superiority, it was an expression she wholeheartedly wished she could wipe off his perfectly chiseled face.

Having served her time, Bennet eagerly said her goodbyes and left the restaurant as quickly as she could, weaving her way around the now even more crowded tables. Once outside she only walked a few feet away from the restaurant's entrance before she stopped and pulled out her phone to call Stella.

Within seconds, she found herself deep in conversation with her friend, relaying the details of the morning and her unbelievable round of bad luck to find herself stuck with Luke among the guests at her table for drinks.

"I mean really; only I would be so unlucky as to have him be a part of Handsy Harry's entourage. Stella, I swear it's like I can't get away from him. First he purposely cancels our meeting this morning and then he has the nerve to sit here tonight all smug."

"Don't get mad," Stella began, knowing she had to tread lightly with her clearly incensed friend, "but I'm just saying maybe he did honestly have to cancel the meeting this morning."

"Yeah right," Bennet replied. "It was a power play, nothing more. I have had it with people like him. They get a little bit of money or some prestigious job and they think they can boss everyone around. Who the hell cares about Dawlton Capital anyways. This city's full of investment firms; what makes his—or him for that matter—so special. I swear my two-year-old niece behaves better than he does. Besides, how do you explain his presence here tonight?"

"Well, I'm sure he didn't know you were coming. You said Handsy Harry invited you at the last minute after the tour ended. So really how could he have known."

Bennet was having none of Stella's attempts to be rational.

"No, he is playing games and I've had enough. The way I see it, Luke Dawlton has three choices. He can tell his aunt he doesn't want to be a part of this project; or he can get his aunt to get me removed from her exhibition; or he can get his head out of his ass and get on board with the fact that we are stuck having to work together and let me do my job. At this point I really don't care which option he chooses but he…"

The sound of a man clearing his voice caused Bennet to stop speaking mid-sentence.

"Excuse me, but I think you left your jacket inside. I offered to see if I could catch you before you left the restaurant."

Shit. Shit. Shit. Shit.

"Holy crap, is that him?" Stella asked as she strained to hear the conversation from her side of the line.

Bennet knew there was nothing she could say in this moment that would restore any of her dignity. Shaking slightly and knowing her face must have been red with embarrassment she was only glad it was too dark for him to see it.

Turning around, Bennet found herself face to face with Luke who, at the moment, was wearing a smirk which she could not determine whether it was one of anger or amusement. Fearing she would lose what little remained of her control if he actually began to laugh at her, she instead forced herself to look him straight in the eye.

"Yes, it's mine, thank you," Bennet said as if she had not just utterly humiliated herself by having been overheard talking about him.

Grabbing her coat from out of his hands, Bennet turned back around and started to walk as quickly away from him as she could without breaking into an actual run.

She had almost made it around the corner and out of his sight before she heard him call out, "I'll see you tomorrow morning, Bennet. Should I bring some croissants?"

Luke's comment, a blatant reference to the first time she had embarrassed herself in front of him, was like a bucket of cold water suddenly being thrown over her head. Freezing in her tracks, she felt her entire body tighten. If it were possible she wished the sidewalk would simply open up and swallow her whole but as she knew this would be impossible, she summoned the little strength she had left and, refusing to give him the satisfaction of looking back at him, she forced herself to begin walking again, not stopping until she was around the corner and out of sight.

"Are you still there?"

Stella's voice made Bennet jump as she realized her friend was still on the phone.

"You mean am I still alive or did I actually die of embarrassment already?" Bennet asked.

She could not believe what had just happened. She had let her anger get the better of her yet again and managed to make an absolute fool of herself once more in front of Luke.

"I can't believe I was so stupid. I didn't see him behind me. Why couldn't I have just kept my mouth shut."

"Because he has treated you horribly and he has behaved like a jerk to you and because you have had a horrible day," Stella said, trying to make her friend feel better.

"Yeah, maybe that's true but it's really no excuse. How the hell am I going to meet with him tomorrow after what just happened? I'll be lucky if he doesn't take me up on option two and get his aunt to have me fired."

"Well at least you would be done with Luke Dawlton." Then, trying to cheer her friend up Stella added, "Did you really tell him to get his head out of his own ass?"

"Yep. That was option three." Despite the bad situation she now found herself in, Bennet actually laughed. "You know if just for one second I knocked that smug, arrogant smirk off his face it might even have been worth it. What am I going to do tomorrow morning when we have to meet?" Bennet asked, as the reality of her situation settled back over her.

"You are going to say good morning and then you are going pretend like none of this happened," Stella replied. "If he is really angry he will surely complain to Brent and Katherine tonight or first thing tomorrow morning. You will know about it even before you get into work tomorrow."

"I'm sure Katherine would love that," Bennet said, wanting to kick herself all over again at the foolishness of what she had just done.

"Right, but if you don't hear anything from them," Stella began, "then I guarantee he isn't going to say anything. So then you just meet with him tomorrow, act like the professional curator of the Northhom Museum that you are, and pretend nothing even happened."

"I really don't have any other choice do I," Bennet replied, already dreading what fresh horrors tomorrow would bring. "I think I might actually despise him, Stella."

"Well then use it. Take your anger and channel it into putting on the best exhibition of your career," Stella suggested. "Now go home, go to bed, and try not to think about it until tomorrow."

Bennet knew her friend was right, but as she said goodbye to Stella she was sure she would not be able to follow through with her advice. She would have bet money on the fact that there was a long, sleepless night waiting for her, one in which she would be unable to keep the detestable Luke Dawlton from her mind.

Luke stood on the sidewalk watching as Bennet turned the corner and disappeared from view. He had not been able to help himself when he called out after her with that final remark intentionally reminding her of the last time she had appeared absolutely ridiculous in front of him. What was it about that woman that made him want to behave like a fifth grade boy he wondered.

Seeing her walk into the restaurant this evening had been a shock. The clients who had invited him to dinner did not tell him that they had also invited a board member and staff from the Northhom Museum or he would have made some excuse to get out of it. He had had enough of that museum to last a lifetime.

But he also knew it wasn't the museum so much as the idea of having to be at the beck and call of his aunt that was really annoying him. She was the true source of his frustration. Vivian had always been demanding but recently, ever since she had come up with the idea that he needed to supervise the exhibition of her gift to the Northhom, she had become relentless. The last thing he needed or wanted to do was indulge her vanity by making the events surrounding her gift even more extravagant then they would already be. Still every time he had attempted to deny her request she had laid on the guilt in that passive aggressive way she had until it became less hassle to just agree to helping than to continue fighting her.

Luke knew he should try harder not to let his frustration with his aunt impact how he interacted with the Northhom staff. He especially needed to try to remember that it was not Bennet Reynolds's fault that his aunt had roped him into this project. Still it had not helped that she seemed to annoy him with an increasing intensity every time they met.

The truth was Luke had just endured a horrible day and he was in no mood for anything remotely social this evening. He had been stuck in back-to-back meetings all morning, followed by a conference call with one of his most demanding and difficult overseas clients. Then to top it off, he had spent the last hour being forced to sit with his firm's human resources manager terminating the employment of one of his junior associates for poor work performance.

Seeing Bennet was the last thing he had expected or needed this evening. He gathered from her openly hostile attitude towards him tonight as well as the conversation he had just overheard that he had offended her by canceling their meeting this morning. His assistant had said nothing other than that she had spoken to her and that the meeting had been rescheduled for the next day. But still, she must have been more upset than either of them realized.

Luke failed to see how she had any right to be offended. The truth was he had not given it a second thought when he had instructed his assistant to call to reschedule. After all it was Bennet who had made the meeting the day before while she was behaving so rudely to him at her office and without allowing him to consult his schedule first; so what had she expected would happen. He was a busy man and he certainly had more important things to do than talk about an exhibition. Surely she should have understood that.

Still while it was true he did not want to be involved in this project, the collection had meant a great deal to his uncle and for that reason if for no other he had convinced himself he could rally enough to help make sure it was as fine an exhibition as possible. Now however, having met Bennet, the prospect of having to work with her had made him question his ability to make even that happen. She had managed to get under his skin from the minute she first confronted him on the street with the absolute nerve of accusing him of stealing her pastry.

Luke had to assume that she was knowledgeable or she would not have the prestigious position she did at such a fine museum. Besides he had done his homework after their first introduction in Brent Stromwell's office and knew she had a good reputation as a curator and that she was well educated in the field. It was just her attitude that had left a great deal to be desired. He found it hard to reconcile her erratic behavior with how a curator should comport herself with patrons.

Still, as he stood outside the restaurant, remembering her words as she described what he could do and the look of utter shock and embarrassment as she turned around and realized he had overheard her, Luke found he had actually begun to smile. She certainly needed to learn how to think before she spoke. It was like she had a crazy switch that seemed to be turned on anytime they were together. And yet there was also something intriguing about her. She was certainly not like any other woman he had ever met.

Despite everything that had happened, and much to his own surprise, he found that he was actually looking forward to seeing her again tomorrow; if of course they could manage to go ten minutes without screaming at each other.

Chapter Ten

The night's humiliation was fresh in Bennet's mind as she rushed into her apartment to answer her ringing phone. While her sister Jane had said she was calling for a quick chat, Bennet liked to believe their familial bond had somehow allowed her to sense she was needed.

Knowing only what Bennet had told her the other night at yoga about the Winthrop exhibition and her being saddled with the patron's nephew, Jane supportively listened as her sister explained her anger and what a fool she had made of herself that evening. As always Jane had offered a metaphorical shoulder to cry on as she tried to assure her things were not as bad as they seemed, and Bennet had ended the call promising her sister that she would take her advice and just calmly go about the meeting tomorrow without getting worked up or letting Luke Dawlton aggravate her into saying anything additional that she would regret.

As Bennet heated up some questionable leftover pad thai and sat alone at her kitchen counter eating the congealed noodles she could not help but question her ability to do as she had promised her sister. She had often been fascinated by the fact that living in such a big city meant there would be hundreds of people that you passed by each day as you went about your daily life and you would never know them and they would never know you. She had always found that anonymity amongst a crowd strangely comforting, and yet she also knew that there was the chance that some of the people you passed might become involved in your life in some way in the future. There was always the chance that maybe one of those strangers—the ones you bumped shoulders with in the subway or stood behind in line at the drugstore or sat next to on a bench in Central Park on a lazy Saturday morning—had the potential to become someone important in your life; it was just you had not met them yet.

If all this were true, Bennet wondered what the universe was trying to tell her about Luke Dawlton, thrusting him into her life the way it had. Of all the millions of strangers in her beautiful city that she could potentially meet someday, why did the one man who she was beginning to actually loathe keep popping up in her life? It was bad enough that she was going to be forced to work with him but if tonight were any example, it seemed everywhere she went he was there; like a bad cold that stays with you on and off for the entire winter.

Trying her best to forget Luke and stop agonizing about how she had embarrassed herself yet again in front of him this evening Bennet threw out the largely uneaten container of pad thai and went to bed early, hoping to at least get a good night's rest. This was not to be however. Maybe it was the unappetizing leftovers that had settled like a lead balloon in the pit of her stomach or maybe it was her anxieties about what tomorrow would hold, but whatever the cause Bennet spent the night tossing and turning, unable to get more than forty minutes of uninterrupted sleep at a time.

Hours later Bennet woke up to find her embarrassment over the previous evening's events had been firmly intertwined with anger over Luke Dawlton's behavior. She rushed through her morning routine getting ready for work, convinced this whole situation was his fault since if he had behaved better in the first place she would never have felt compelled to say the things she had said outside the restaurant yesterday night.

As she took more time than usual figuring out what to wear, trying on several outfits before settling on a pair of black dress slacks and a fitted gray cashmere mock turtleneck sweater that she usually liked but today found drab and boring, she reviewed everything that Luke had done that was out of line since they had first met. Even though she had tried her best to convince herself that she had been the wronged party, she did not succeed in lessening her worries that she had overstepped yesterday evening. She knew if she was going to make it through this exhibition she was going to need to find a way to control her temper and not let Luke get to her.

When Bennet arrived at her office she was convinced there would be a message from Brent or Katherine demanding she come to their offices so they could fire her. When that did not happen, Bennet had to concede that Stella had been right and Luke had not reported anything about her and her behavior the night before to her bosses. Unsure whether that meant he was waiting to humiliate her until he could see her face to face or, like Stella believed, he was just going to let it drop, Bennet decided she no longer cared.

No matter what happened she refused to spend one more minute worrying about Vivian Winthrop's nephew. She may only have a few more hours left in her role as curator of the Winthrop exhibition depending on what Luke's next move would be but while that was her job she was going to do it the best she could. The only thing she knew for certain was that she had to meet with Luke this morning and when she did, she resolved to keep it strictly professional and treat him like any other person she had to interact with on behalf of the museum. What happened after that would be entirely up to him.

The phone rang as Bennet was sitting at her desk trying her best to focus on reviewing a registrar's file and not on her quickly approaching meeting with Luke Dawlton.

"So, how are you doing? Is the nephew there yet?" Jane asked by way of a greeting.

"No, not yet and I don't think my nerves can handle the waiting. Is everything okay?"

"Yes, it's fine. I'm just calling for moral support. You didn't sound good last night and I wanted to check in. Seriously, are you all set for your meeting?"

"You mean I didn't sound good after making an ass out of myself in front of a loathsome man who now sadly appears to hold my entire professional career in his hands; hard to imagine why I might be stressed."

Jane laughed. "Okay, let's start again and answer me this; are you ready for your meeting?"

Despite everything, Jane's call had made Bennet relax just the slightest bit.

"I'm as ready as I can be I guess. I mean I have the materials I want to review ready. But I wish I didn't have to deal with him at all and that I could do this project on my own. I have humiliated myself in front of this man twice already and I feel like now I have not only Katherine and Brent but this guy all waiting for me to fail. If I can't…"

"Now wait just a minute," Jane interrupted. "The Bennet I know would not let anyone stop her from doing the best work she can do. Certainly not that nightmare boss of yours and not some pompous nephew.

"So what if you said some nasty things about him. You didn't know he was standing there and he shouldn't have been listening. It sounds like it was just the reality check he needed anyway. Seriously, who cares what he thinks. You are the best curator for this job and you are going to do great things with this exhibition."

"I guess," Bennet said in a tone that held zero conviction.

"No. You do not guess. You know," Jane was becoming increasingly animated. "You have bigger dreams than this place. Don't let this derail you. You take control of this meeting and don't look back."

"Aye aye captain," Bennet laughed, holding back the sudden urge to give a mock salute. Once again, Jane had managed to say just the right thing and at just the right time to make her feel better. "And I guess wiping the smug look off Katherine Hartis's face when the exhibition is a big success will be worth it."

"There you go," Jane cheered. "What time is your meeting?"

Bennet glanced at her clock.

"Oh crap, it's in fifteen minutes. No time left to worry I guess. Jane I better go. Wish me luck."

"You are going to be great."

Bennet gave a shrug that did not imply she one hundred percent believed it.

"One can only hope. Besides he didn't cancel the meeting so I guess he hasn't decided to try to get me fired yet."

"Hey and word of advice; maybe, if you think you can manage it, try not to go all crazy lady on this guy today, okay?" Jane added.

"Oh you're so funny," Bennet replied, laughing despite herself. "I will call you later with a debrief."

Bennet remained at her desk for a minute more after hanging up the phone and imagined what might happen next.

"All right Bennet, you can do this," she said as she stood up quickly, knowing if she waited any longer she might lose the courage to do what she needed to do.

Grabbing her files, Bennet left her office and headed to the museum's public galleries. She had an appointment to meet Luke at 10:30 am. With no desire to repeat the events of yesterday when he had caught her off guard by showing up at her office, she promised herself she would be waiting at the front visitor's desk so she could be there to greet him. This time Bennet was determined to get the upper hand.

Luke Dawlton sat in the back of his car working on some papers while his driver did his best to weave through the city's heavy traffic. This exhibition was nothing but an unwanted distraction for which he had no time, and yet despite his busy schedule he now found himself once more heading to the Northhom Museum.

He had made his feelings on the subject clear to his aunt on more than one occasion since she had decided to gift her collection. However she had insisted that he be a part of the process; reminding him how she had been there for him throughout his childhood. Every time she mentioned this fact, Luke had to fight back the urge to in turn remind her of how this support had been in terms of accommodations and physical needs but emotionally it was an entirely different story. He never vocalized this however, which allowed her to continue to stress how now it was his turn to be there for her. She made it clear to him that it was her and his dead uncle's legacy on the line and she refused to entrust it to incompetent museum staff. His aunt had absolutely insisted that Luke be there to oversee the exhibition to ensure that the Winthrop name was protected and represented appropriately.

Once he had finally resigned himself to this obligation, Luke had hoped that he would have to do as little as possible and had planned on making only one or two obligatory appearances at the museum; that was all. But then he had met Bennet Reynolds. He had to admit, the feisty curator had been a complication he had not anticipated. Stranger still was the fact that she was not an entirely unwelcome one.

He should have simply written her off. But what had surprised him was the fact that despite how much she infuriated him and how irrational she was most of the time, he couldn't seem to get her off his mind. Even now as he prepared to see her for their meeting at the museum, he found himself thinking about what she had said as she described her dislike of him outside the restaurant yesterday evening. He could have been gracious and not let her see him but instead he had been unable to stop himself from adding to her humiliation by letting her know that she had been overheard. He had been angry in the moment. She seemed to do that to him. Really she had no right to talk about someone connected to such a generous gift to the museum and she certainly needed to learn to control what came out of her mouth in public. Still he knew he had taken the low road and in that moment he couldn't control himself enough to not gloat at her embarrassment. It had been a momentary victory and he liked watching her squirm.

After his initial anger subsided and as the evening wore on however, he found that the whole situation had amused him more than anything else. She had nerve and he liked that about her. Most people would never tell him what they thought of him. In fact, he was used to people sucking up to him. Bennet Reynolds clearly had no intention of doing that.

The truth was he found her interesting and different from most of the women he met. She was pretty and obviously smart or she wouldn't have the job she did at the Northhom. But he could have his pick of attractive and intelligent women who were not also irrational, quick to anger, and infuriating like she was. So why couldn't he get Bennet Reynolds off his mind?

Much to his surprise, Luke now found himself in the unexpected position of looking forward to the challenge of this morning's meeting.

"Mr. Dawlton, we're here," the driver said as he skillfully brought the large black sedan to a stop at the curb in front of the museum.

"Thank you, Charles," Luke replied as he was pulled back from his thoughts.

Grabbing his brown leather satchel, Luke hurried to step out of the car to ensure he would not be late for his meeting. Certainly the last thing he wanted to do was incur Bennet Reynolds's wrath again.

Whatever else he might be feeling about this project, the beauty of the museum's building impressed him every time he saw it. An avid art enthusiast, albeit a novice one, he had been in many museums in numerous countries, but there was always something about these converted former mansions that struck him as the perfect home for the old masterpieces. He wondered what it must have been like to be a Northhom living in this house a century ago.

Despite the fact that his aunt's gifting of her collection, something his uncle had taken great pride in cultivating, was a manifestation of her vanity; it still pleased him that the artworks would have such a good home. He liked the idea that future generations would have a place to come and view them long after his aunt was gone.

Once inside the museum, Luke announced himself at Guest Services and was informed that Bennet Reynolds was on her way and would meet him momentarily. He had to smile as he realized she was not going to let him surprise her again at her office. Yes, there was no denying that he was definitely looking forward to their meeting.

Having opened fifty minutes before, the museum was already crowded when Bennet began her trek to the visitor's desk to meet Luke. Even though the Northhom was one of the city's smaller museums, by sheer virtue of its location in Manhattan there was never a day of the week or hour of the day when the main galleries were not filled with visitors, many of which were tourists.

On weekdays at this time of the year the museum was also often heavily populated with children on school field trips. That was the audience that Bennet liked best; so much so that whenever she had a spare minute she would volunteer to lead a tour. The joy it brought her to watch the young children's eyes light up when they discovered something hidden in a painting or heard a fascinating tale about an artist and how he created a sculpture was beyond calculation.

As Bennet was just about to reach the museum's entrance, she overheard a docent speaking to a group of second graders.

"Now what do you think the artist might have been trying to show in this painting?" the docent asked.

"I don't see anything," one boy announced.

"It's just a bunch of colors," another replied, seemingly bored and ready to move on to the next painting.

These were the typical responses for that age group when looking at an Abstract Expressionist painting. For that matter many adult groups she had worked with over the years often responded the same way. This was especially true with the museum's more contemporary works where the most frequent and most insultingly negative response she had to deal with was how even a child could paint something better.

Depending on the audience, Bennet would sometimes try to steer them towards a better understanding of what the artists were trying to achieve. Most of the time though, the argument fell on deaf ears and she had to admit she often grew tired of trying to make her point.

Children were different however, and Bennet had found them to be much more open to accepting and exploring new possibilities. So, while she was about to pass the group by, her attention was diverted by a young girl who said something out of the ordinary.

A colorful work of art herself, she wore a pink raincoat over black leggings with purple polka dots and rainbow striped bows in her long blonde pigtails. Standing on her tip-toes, she was peering intently at the painting as she boldly announced, "I think I see a flower."

"Don't be stupid, Emily," one of the girls in her class remarked as many of the children began to laugh.

What makes children so cruel? Bennet wondered as she remembered how it felt to be that girl's age and be singled out as different. The truth was, she had felt like that for most of her life.

Undeterred by the smirks of her classmates, this little girl spoke again.

"No, I see a flower," she insisted with a passion and unabashed certainty that seems reserved only for the young.

Unhappy with the others' inability to see what she recognized so easily, the girl spotted Bennet who had stopped to listen to the conversation and was standing just a little distance from the group.

"Excuse me; but do you see the flower?"

Bennet, who had been watching the exchange, was amazed at the adult sounding tone of this precocious child. Giving her a smile, she walked over to the group.

"Sorry Ms. Reynolds, but I wonder if you would mind joining us for a minute?" asked the docent leading the group's tour.

Bennet recognized her as a dedicated member of the museum's volunteer core with whom she had shared a few passing conversations and who always asked thoughtful questions during Bennet's trainings of new exhibitions, which was a requirement before the guides could give tours. She knew that this woman had been volunteering for decades and probably knew more about the museum than most of the people who were presently employed as staff.

As Bennet nodded, the docent added, "Boys and girls, Ms. Reynolds is a curator at the museum. That means that it is her job to put all the works you see here onto the walls and to take care of all the museum's paintings and sculptures. Maybe we should ask her what she sees."

"Can you show me where you see the flower?" Bennet asked.

Excited to be singled out, the little girl enthusiastically and rather dramatically pointed out the flower, rising once more on her tiptoes to do so.

"I do see how that could look like a flower," Bennet began as she pointed a knowing smile in Emily's direction. She was aware she had caught the group's attention and that they had become interested that this new adult had seen what Emily did. "But do you know what is the most important part about this painting?"

As Emily shook her head no, Bennet continued, "It is that you see it. That is the beauty of a painting like this with all its shapes and colors. Each person gets to see in it exactly what he or she wants to see."

"Like when you look up at the sky?" Emily asked. "I always see things in the clouds."

"Just like that."

"Thank you," Emily said with a smile, enjoying the fact that she had been vindicated among her less than kind classmates.

Giving an appreciative nod to Bennet, the docent then refocused her attention on corralling the group back into order so they could continue on their tour.

"Okay, what do you say we look at some more paintings?" she asked as she began to lead them further down the hall.

As she watched the class begin to gather in front of a new painting, Bennet caught a glimpse of Luke Dawlton standing in front of the visitor's desk. Just the sight of him filled her with a rush of nerves; not only because it triggered a fresh memory of all their embarrassing interactions and his infuriating behavior flashed through her mind once more like the trailer to a really bad movie but also because, she would have been ashamed to admit, she could not help but notice how undeniably handsome he looked.

"I apologize for my lateness, Mr. Dawlton. I'm sure you are busy." Bennet was aware that her voice held more of an edge than it should have, but she was mad at herself. She had wanted to be in control from the moment their meeting began which meant being there at the front desk to greet him when he arrived. But now, because she had stopped to spend time to speak with the students, she had unfortunately become late for their meeting.

"How could you not be late, when you had such an inquisitive visitor asking you questions."

Expecting there to be, but not finding any sarcasm in his tone, Luke's response allowed Bennet to realize that her lateness had given him the opportunity to observe her interaction with the group. The last thing Bennet wanted was to put on another show for this horrible man but as she looked at him, she was surprised to see that his usual air of haughtiness had been replaced with what appeared to be an expression of genuine interest.

"You seemed to really enjoy that," Luke continued.

"Best part of my job actually," Bennet replied. "Seeing that spark of interest that you can nurture. Helping them to understand that with art all things are possible. It's not just with the young children either.

"Take this text here," Bennet began pointing to the signage on the wall to her left that served to introduce a selection of Cubist works from the museum's permanent collection. "I try my best to make sure the materials that visitors read are as accessible and engaging as possible; otherwise how can we expect the viewer to understand and hopefully get excited about a work of art. This is how you make visitors want to see more."

Having begun a discussion on a topic important to her, Bennet continued on as if she were unaware of who she was speaking to and answered her own question.

"But most of the time I feel like I am the only one who realizes how important this is. And with children especially, if we can engage them while they are young and get them excited about art then they have the potential for a lifetime of loving art ahead of them. They might even become future artists, patrons, or collectors. That is what I think is really necessary to do as a…"

Suddenly Bennet stopped talking as she realized Luke was staring at her. She did not understand what could have possessed her to say all that in front of him, of all people. She was not about to start sharing with him her philosophies on the art world or any of her other thoughts or hopes and dreams for that matter; she had just gotten carried away.

Bennet knew she needed to pull it together. She was not going to let someone like him think she was anything less than one hundred percent focused on this job.

"I apologize. That certainly is not why you are here today, Mr. Dawlton so I think..."

"Luke, please."

It had not been his intention to interrupt her. And yet, realizing he had, Luke found himself wondering what was it about her that made him react so wholly opposite to the way he intended. It was just watching her interact with that group of children made him see her, for the first time, in a different light and in his overeagerness to make sure the conversation stayed cordial he was afraid he may have already annoyed her.

"Fine. Luke then," Bennet said as she tried her best to ignore his interruption and hold true to her promise to herself to remain cool and calm no matter what this man said or did.

Bennet knew she had already made a wreck of her first three, and, thanks to her behavior outside the restaurant last night, fourth interaction with this man. And, worried she would make another bad impression, she found herself wondering how she should start the meeting. She knew the right thing to do was come clean and address what had happened last night and for that matter the morning they first met as well. But she did not know how to raise the topic without the fear of starting something up again. The last thing she needed to do was lose her temper or put her foot in her mouth once more.

"As I was saying," Bennet began deciding to just plow ahead as if nothing had happened, "since I assume you must be as busy as I am, I think it is important that we get started. Shall we?"

Without waiting for an answer, she continued, "If you follow me, I have reserved the conference room for our meeting."

Luke nodded. "Lead the way."

As Luke walked with Bennet down the hallway he once more found himself at a loss to understand this woman. She was a bundle of contradictions. He had always prided himself on his ability to be unflappable in any business situation and in interactions with adversaries he always remained in complete control. And yet here, with this woman, he struggled to figure her out. She had been so animated when she was talking with that child about the painting, and then just now with him she had once more turned cold and distant.

As they walked together in silence they passed several groups of students and one child caught both their attention. As a docent stood talking about a landscape painting by one of the great Hudson River School artists, one of the boys in a group of third graders, having lost interest in the discussion, had let his eyes wander. They of course landed on a painting of a nude woman that was hanging on the far side of the gallery.

While the docent had quickly passed by the painting, the boy, like a moth to a flame, had still managed to find it. Bennet and Luke watched as when he realized what he was seeing he began to stare at it with eyes open as wide as possible. He struggled to force himself to pull away just long enough to get his friends in the group to look too.

"Eyes here," the teacher ordered as, once the laughter started to spread among the group, she was able to catch on to what the boys were up to.

The docent, now also aware of the situation, quickly led the group on to the next painting—which was located a much safer distance away from the distracting work—all while doing her best to hide a smile at the boys' immaturity.

Despite their best efforts at professionalism, Bennet and Luke both laughed.

"Some things never change," Luke said giving her that smile that despite her best efforts to withstand it, seemed to always unnerve her.

Then, struggling to regain her own composure as they reached the administration corridor, Bennet used her staff ID badge to let them inside and directed Luke to follow her through the first open door on the right which housed a small meeting room.

Walking along in silence with Luke, she had come to the realization that being with him was like taking a stroll through a minefield. One wrong word or look and everything might blow up again. She did not trust her temper and yet, so far everything had gone well. In fact, the tour group and the boy's comical response to the painting had served as a nice diversion and helped to break the tension of the start to their meeting without either of them having to figure out how to awkwardly broach the subject of what had happened in the restaurant last evening.

Not wanting to risk the fragile calm that they seemed to find themselves in at this moment, once in the room, Bennet instead decided to launch right into a discussion of the exhibition and hope that he would follow along.

Having prepped the space when she first arrived at the museum this morning, she had a number of files relating to the Winthrop gift spread out on the large table that dominated the room. After directing him to a seat, Bennet spent the next forty minutes going through the technical requirements of the exhibition space. She reviewed with him all of the pieces that comprised the gift and allowed his answers to fill in some missing bits of information from the sparse files that had been passed on to her from Vivian Winthrop. She also importantly informed him of what still needed to be done and how she would proceed with the next steps in putting the exhibition together.

Half expecting him to rudely interrupt her with comments or judgements on what she had done so far, Bennet had been pleasantly surprised that throughout the entirety of her presentation Luke had appeared to be listening to what she said, paying complete attention and not speaking other than to provide her with any information she requested from him.

She was not the only one who had been surprised by the way the meeting had progressed. As Luke listened to Bennet discuss the exhibition he had to admit he was impressed. It was obvious she knew her stuff and he could tell that what she had already conceived of the layout for the exhibition was well thought out; she clearly possessed a thorough understanding of the artworks and how they fit together as a cohesive whole.

It was also while listening to Bennet explain her vision to present the collection to the public that he realized that how the exhibition was received actually did matter to him. While he had no interest in stroking his aunt's ego or encouraging her vanity, these artworks had been important to his uncle who had meant so much to him growing up. These works were, in a way, a part of Luke's childhood too and he wanted to see them respected and valued by the Northhom Museum who would now forever own them. Whatever else he might have thought of this woman, Luke now felt confident that Bennet Reynolds could do that.

Luke was actually trying his best to remain professional and not do anything to anger her again. Still as he listened to her make her presentation, he found he had to work hard to fight back the urge to laugh at the memory of her face yesterday when she had realized he was behind her and overheard her scathing description of him and her unflattering assault on his character. He actually found it rather refreshing that she seemed not to care one bit what he thought about her and was certainly not making any effort to disguise her feelings about him. He liked her brutal honesty.

He had also noticed last night how pretty she looked when she was riled up and annoyed by him. It was a confusing and uncomfortable development and he had promised himself on the way over to the museum that he would do his best to ignore such thoughts to stay true to his plan of doing the bare minimum for this exhibition so he could return to more important work. This had not proved an easy task however and as he listened to her now, he found himself working hard not to become distracted by how beautifully her face lit up when she was focused on describing her vision for the exhibition. In fact for the last five minutes he had seemed unable to concentrate on anything other than how she was absently playing with a stray lock of hair which had slipped from behind her ear; twirling it around her long, elegant finger as she detailed potential themes for the different galleries which would be used for displaying the collection.

Unaware of the effect she was having on him, Bennet checked her notes one final time to make sure she had addressed everything on her agenda for the meeting.

"Well I think that covers everything I had to review at this time. Do you have any questions or thoughts about anything I've done so far?"

Bennet's question pulled Luke back from his thoughts.

"No, that was a very thorough overview. You clearly have everything in hand," Luke replied, hoping his voice did not betray the flustered feeling he was experiencing at the moment.

Luke's positive response had surprised Bennet since she had feared that he might try to fight her on some of her ideas. She was also slightly taken aback at how attentive he seemed to be and how focused he was on what she had been saying; something which at times had begun to make her feel slightly self-conscious.

Whatever else he might be—arrogant, aloof, smug, self-righteous— she could not deny how unbelievably sexy he was; a fact that she had found increasingly hard to ignore as she was making her presentation. He dressed well, that was for sure, as today's ensemble proved. The charcoal gray suit he was wearing with the light blue shirt that almost perfectly matched the color of his eyes certainly did not help to keep her from becoming distracted. But he also had an inherent attractiveness, something in his eyes and mouth, and the outline of his features which no amount of good tailoring could achieve; one either had it or they did not, and Luke Dawlton certainly had it.

"So you think this concept for the exhibition will be in line with what your aunt wants for the show?" Bennet asked quickly, trying to move away from any thoughts on his appearance.

Luke smiled. "I will make sure it is. I like what you have planned and I think it will present well with the public."

His smile had done little in the way of making Bennet less distracted.

"The works speak from themselves really. I just group them together on the walls. It's the collection that is truly amazing," Bennet hurried to say.

"Well, I think there is a little more to your role in the exhibition than that."

Bennet was unsure whether Luke was being sincere. The meeting had so far gone well; almost too well, and based on their previous interactions she could not help questioning what game he might be playing or wondering if he was being sarcastic in some way.

"You don't believe me?" Luke asked picking up on Bennet's hesitation in responding and the skeptical expression that had briefly flitted across her face.

"No it's not that," Bennet said shaking her head. She was unsure if she should continue and risk the peaceful setting in which they now found themselves. Still, eventually she decided she had no choice but to continue. "I am just glad we will be able to move forward on this."

"You mean you're glad I decided to, how did you phrase it last night, pull my head out of my own ass and just get on board with everything?" Luke replied.

Luke could not help but smile as he watched Bennet's face turn a deep shade of red.

At first he had wondered if he had gone too far in making the remark and was about to curse his need to always push things, but then much to his relief Bennet laughed. The effect of which was to light up her whole face and make her beautiful hazel eyes sparkle.

"I guess I deserve that. Seeing you at the restaurant yesterday evening was a surprise, that's all, and I was truthfully still annoyed from the morning. You have to know I had no idea you were behind me when I said what I did last night or I would never have said anything."

Luke cockily raised his left eyebrow as if he doubted the veracity of what she had just said.

Bennet smiled. "Well at least not then, and definitely not to your face."

Returning the smile, Luke replied, "So let me get this straight, if you only share your true feelings about me when I'm not around; then when we met face to face for the first time and you had no problem accusing me of being a thief on a crowded street corner that was you holding back? I can't even imagine what you really thought of me."

They both laughed.

"I promise you I am more professional than I seem," Bennet replied. "Certainly more than you have every reason to believe based on our limited interactions."

"I don't know, I find it kind of refreshing actually," Luke began. "Most people just want something from me so they would never say how they truly feel. You, on the other hand, I think would actually happily tell me to go away if you could. I'm sure my presence on this project is nothing you desired and I can understand how upsetting it must be for you."

Bennet was more than a little surprised by his honesty.

"The way I see it," Luke continued, "we don't have to like that I am stuck being involved with this project but we have to find a way to work together. For reasons I have no desire to get into right now I have to be involved with this exhibition. I assure you this was not my idea.

"More importantly, I know this is your job and I have no interest in interfering with your process; nor do I feel I have any right to question the decisions you make regarding this exhibition. I promise you that I have no illusions as to who is in charge."

Bennet was impressed with his assessment of the situation and his ability to empathize with how she was feeling about his role in this project.

"Thank you. I understand the situation you are in and will keep you updated on everything. I do appreciate what you…"

A knock interrupted Bennet and startled both of them.

As they simultaneously turned towards the sound, they watched as Katherine Hartis opened the door.

"A little birdie told me you were here, Luke," she said as she walked into the room; without being asked Bennet was quick to note.

There are few people for whom the word duplicitous could be better applied. To those that did not know her, Katherine could appear to be a well-intentioned member of the museum's senior staff simply checking in to see how the exhibition preparations were progressing. But Bennet knew differently and on several occasions had witnessed firsthand Katherine's superficiality. She might exude an air of generosity and kindness to some, but it was all a pretense. When one truly got to know her there was a realization that there was nothing sincere about her person whatsoever.

She liked to present herself as a mentor to Bennet and the other younger women on the Northhom's staff, but the whole time she would be working systematically behind the scenes to thwart their chances of success or any ability they might have to rise in the institution. Bennet had herself experienced two instances when Katherine had actually taken credit for something she had first suggested.

Worse yet, Katherine and Brent Stromwell were thick as thieves and locked in some bizarrely codependent relationship. Bennet knew that while they had no option but to give the planning of this exhibition to her since she was the senior curator, both were unhappy about it and she knew that Katherine especially was sincerely wishing she would fail. And now it seemed Katherine had made it her mission to attempt to insert herself into every interaction she could between her and Luke. Bennet was even beginning to suspect Katherine was jealous of her need to work with him on the project. This moment was a case in point. Having walked into the room for no legitimate reason and determined to interrupt their meeting, she stood there looking ridiculous in her royal blue pant suit, overly large tortoise-shell glasses, and obnoxiously chunky silver mesh rope necklace that knotted a few inches below her neck before breaking off into two long, hanging strands that actually looked like her head was struggling to support the weight of it.

"Good morning, Katherine," Bennet said, hoping the tone of her voice did not reflect her severe irritation. "I believe I emailed you and Brent that we would be meeting this morning. We have begun reviewing the logistics for the exhibition."

After directing a withering stare in Bennet's direction, Katherine focused her attention squarely on Luke. "I hope everything is going well. I certainly do not wish to interrupt."

Oh yeah, I bet, Bennet thought, wishing more than anything that Katherine would leave them alone.

"I just wanted to take a moment to let you know on behalf of Brent and myself how pleased we are that you will be helping Bennet with this very important exhibition."

Bennet physically tensed over her words and the implication to Luke that she would need help. Their meeting had gone surprising well so far and she did not want Katherine to do anything to undermine the progress they had made this morning.

Luke sent a charming smile in Katherine's direction. "Well thank you for your kind words."

Luke had instantly sensed Bennet's unease with the appearance of her boss and wished to help alleviate her clear discomfort.

"While we have had a productive morning, I do think it is important that I take this moment to assure you, Katherine, that I feel strongly that this is completely Bennet's exhibition. I am simply planning on following her lead.

"Truth be told, I am only here at my aunt's insistence. Without it, there would be no need for me to be involved in the preparations whatsoever. That being said, I must add that the pleasure of Ms. Reynolds's company has made this a far less disagreeable task than it could have been with what is my incredibly busy schedule."

As Luke spoke, Bennet watched Katherine. While she had been surprised and pleased with what he had said in defense of her, it had certainly had the reverse effect on her boss. Bennet had never before seen the look that Katherine wore on her face at this moment. Her smile looked glued on and she seemed to be struggling in her attempt to keep it there. She was clearly at a loss for words as she tried to maintain her façade of congeniality.

Luke, having waited a few moments to let his words sink in, now diplomatically added, "But I do thank you for checking in on us, Katherine. This is going to be quite the exhibition I am sure. I know my aunt is so looking forward to it, as am I."

"Yes, certainly you are right," Katherine said trying to regain some of her composure. "If all is well here then I guess I will let you two get back to work."

As she began to back out of the room Katherine added, "I almost forgot. I wanted to tell you that I am looking forward to the reception your aunt is hosting for the Board in a few weeks."

"As am I," Luke replied.

Sending a quick glance in Bennet's direction, Luke returned his focus to Katherine and added, "Actually I am glad you brought that up. I wanted to make sure you knew that while of course Bennet should be included as curator of the exhibition, if there are any other key museum staff besides yourself and Brent that you feel should also be invited just let my office know. I will make sure the information gets to my aunt's event planner."

"Yes of course. I will have my assistant get those names over to you right away," Katherine replied before leaving the room as quickly as she could; shutting the door behind her.

Once alone again in the conference room, Bennet suddenly felt awkward in Luke's presence. While the silence hanging between them was palpable, it did provide her with the opportunity to take stock of what had just occurred and as she did, she found herself struggling to hold back a smile. Whether intentional or not, Luke's words had served to bring Katherine down a peg, and the look on her face as he did so was priceless.

"I will wager you knew nothing about the party," Luke said breaking the silence.

"No. Not yet. I'm sure I would have learned about it only at the very last minute." Bennet knew she probably should not have made such a derogatory statement about her boss but at the moment she did not care.

"She is quite something, isn't she?" Luke asked, unphased by her statement. "She certainly seems intent on putting you in your place."

"Only every day and in every possible way."

Luke laughed. "I deal with people like that all the time in my line of work. Katherine perceives you as a threat, so she tries to assert her authority over you as publicly as possible."

Bennet was impressed by his ability to get the full picture of her boss in just the few brief interactions with her he had had so far.

"It was for her, you know," Bennet blurted out.

"What was?"

"The croissant that morning," Bennet replied, embarrassed at her outburst. "I figure one of us has to acknowledge the giant elephant in the room. It might as well be me. In fact, it probably should be me since I am the one who behaved so abominably."

Not waiting for Luke to say anything and afraid she would lose her nerve if she actually stopped to consider what she was saying, Bennet continued, "I was late for a meeting with Katherine that morning because I was stuck in line waiting for her breakfast order. Why it is my responsibility to fetch her morning coffee and croissant is beyond my understanding and I know I should refuse as it is not part of my job duties as curator, but I never do.

"So there I was standing in line and while I was waiting I had received a text from her questioning where I was. When I finally got to the front of the line and placed my order, it was at the exact same second that a barista was handing the last croissant to you. In that moment I could think of nothing but how miserable she would be all that day if I showed up late for our meeting and without her breakfast."

Feeling a flush of heat spread across her cheeks, Bennet kept talking, eager to explain.

"You have to know how thoroughly mortified I am at my behavior that morning, but it was like something in me just snapped. I found myself chasing after you without really even knowing what I was doing. I promise you I have never done something like that before and I really don't know what came over me."

Luke appeared to be trying not to laugh. "Well yes, I can imagine it wasn't your finest hour, and I must admit in the moment I did worry you might be some sort of deranged woman."

It was now Bennet's turn to laugh. "I would be lying if I said that when I saw you take a bite out of that pastry, I didn't have to fight the overwhelming urge to throw my coffee at you."

Luke smiled. "Yes, I'm sure you did. I assure you I don't normally make a point of antagonizing perfect strangers even when they do accost me on a street corner accusing me of being a thief."

"Good to know," Bennet replied.

Again an awkward silence filled the room and they were once more left staring at each other. It was as if they were both afraid to say something that might disrupt the fragile peace that they now seemed to find themselves in. Still, Bennet knew she had no choice but to move forward with this project and it would be better if she and Luke could at least get along.

As if he had been reading her thoughts, Luke broke the silence first. "What do you say we forget about everything and start over again?"

"A clean slate? I like that." Bennet was relieved at his words. She could never imagine they would be friends, but at least they might be able to get through this project without killing each other.

Wanting to make sure they stayed on track, Bennet was quick to add, "Now regarding next steps, I usually have several months to put together an entire exhibition. This is not the case with your aunt's gift and so I will be moving fast to make sure everything is done on time for the opening. If it is alright with you, as I continue to go through all the files and move forward with everything I will keep you posted on my progress. Does that sound good to you?"

"Yes, that's fine." Luke was just as relieved that they would be able to work together now.

Just then Luke's mobile rang and Bennet noticed how, unlike before, he now silenced it without looking at the screen.

Bennet was about to suggest they end the meeting when Luke began to speak.

"Actually, this might be a good place to break for today. I have to be at a lunch meeting downtown in thirty minutes."

As Bennet nodded and both of them began to stand up, Luke added, "I did mean what I said to Katherine. I have confidence in your abilities with this exhibition. Just keep me posted for my aunt's sake and do let me know if she becomes too difficult. I know what she can be like."

"Well I guess that's that then. It all sounds good. Thank you, Luke."

"You're welcome, Bennet."

After escorting him out of the museum and beginning her walk back to her office, Bennet found herself both surprised and pleased with the outcome of their meeting.

CHAPTER ELEVEN

"Well good morning my sweet Daisy," Bennet said sleepily as she reached out from under the comfort of her duvet to stroke her cat's head.

After the long and certainly not uneventful work week she had just had, Bennet was is no rush to get up and so allowed herself another twenty minutes in a state of cozy half-sleep before several deliberate paw swipes by Daisy to get her attention forced her to start moving.

Bennet threw back the covers and climbed out of bed. "All right miss. I get the hint. Let's go get you some breakfast."

Walking into her kitchen Bennet was struck again by how much she loved her apartment. She had come to think of it as an oasis of calm in her often-chaotic life. In addition to her bedroom, she had a decent sized kitchen with a counter island and a large open studio space with three windows, which allowed for an abundance of natural light to flood the room. It was not only spacious enough to accommodate a living area and table for dining but also a corner nook in which she had placed a drawing table. The favorite feature of her apartment however had to be the large clawfoot porcelain tub in her bathroom, where more times than she would care to admit, it had been used as an escape after a long day. She would relax in it, surrounded by bubbles, while indulging in reading a book and drinking a glass of wine.

Much of the apartment's appeal was due to Bennet's own creative flourishes which occurred not long after taking it over from her aunt; she had done some serious redecorating to make it look just right. A tedious amount of time had been spent removing the orange floral wallpaper and cumbersome antique brass lighting sconces. In its place she had selected a pretty shade of light gray paint for the walls and had painted the moldings a soft white, which brightened the space and made it feel larger. The installation of track lighting in the hallway and living room provided the apartment with a more contemporary feel, as did the art she had hung on the walls.

While Bennet lacked the funds to purchase art as seriously as she wanted, over the years she had slowly begun to fill her apartment with pieces. Some were by artists she had come across in her various gallery visits and others by friends whom she had gone to school with and who, unlike her, had committed to making a go of it no matter how difficult the life was to live. The most important factor to influence each purchase was whether the work made her feel something and so now as she looked at the paintings and drawings hanging on her walls they evoked a variety of emotions. Some brought her joy, others made her contemplative, while others filled her with longing; all of which helped to make this cluster of rooms feel like a home.

As Daisy meowed loudly in an attempt to hurry her owner along, Bennet went to the cupboard under the sink where she kept Daisy's food and poured her a bowlful of kibble. Only once the cat was happily eating did she move on to making herself a pot of coffee which she was eagerly watching percolate when the buzzer sounded announcing she had a visitor.

Walking over to the hallway's intercom, she pressed the button.

"Hello."

"Morning, sunshine. Just popping over for a minute. Let your older sister in, would you?"

"Come on up. I just made coffee," Bennet answered as she buzzed opened the building's exterior door.

Jane's visit, while unexpected, was certainly not unwelcome.

Having already unlocked the door for her sister, Bennet was back in the kitchen and pouring two mugs of fresh coffee when Jane walked in and took a seat across from her at the kitchen island.

Once they were both settled, Jane began to laugh.

"What's so funny?" Bennet asked.

"It's just every time I come here to visit I can't help but think of Mom having to climb those three flights of stairs to get to your apartment. It has got to be the first thing she complains about when she reaches the door."

Bennet smiled. "She just loves to tell me how uncivilized it is to live in a building without an elevator. Then she takes great pleasure in reminding me how you and David live in an upscale apartment building with not only a roomy lift but also its own doorman."

"Sorry. She never lets up does she?"

"No. But that's not your fault." Bennet smiled in an attempt to show Jane everything was fine. "Now, I must ask, not that any visit from my sister isn't lovely, but I have a feeling you have a reason for stopping by."

"I was having my dress for tonight altered in a shop not too far away and I had to pick it up, so I thought I might stop in and see you while I was in the neighborhood."

A look of disbelief appeared on Bennet's face. She knew her sister would never go to a tailor this far from her apartment building.

Knowing Bennet was not buying her story, Jane added, "Really I did have to pick up my dress; but actually, since we are speaking of Mom, there is something else."

"I don't actually think we were speaking about Mom," Bennet replied, letting out a sigh as she could only imagine what was coming next. "You might as well come out with it. What is it?" Bennet asked before taking a sip of her coffee.

"Well, I thought I should warn you she does have matchmaking plans for this evening."

"Great, that's just what I need," Bennet said, her voice heavy with sarcasm. "I figured she had some agenda when she didn't get moody after I canceled on dinner the other night. Seriously, who is he? How bad is it this time?"

"He's a nephew of one of her bridge friends," Jane replied.

Bennet rolled her eyes. "Just great. Nephews seem to really be my thing lately."

"Speaking of which, you never told me. How did the meeting with Luke Dawlton go? Was it as awful as you thought it was going to be?" Jane asked.

"I don't know. It was kind of strange; definitely not what I thought it would be. He actually seemed to be trying to be nice. I'm willing to admit that he might not be quite as bad as I first thought."

"Aha," Jane said with an air of superiority. "So the big, bad finance guy isn't as diabolical as you imagined. Interesting."

"Yeah or he might just be legitimately afraid of me and is trying to patronize me so I don't go all crazy on him again.

"He didn't go into any details of course but during our meeting I got the sense that he wasn't happy with his aunt for making him work on this project. That doesn't mean we are going to become friends or anything, but I might just get lucky and he will leave me to work on the exhibition pretty much by myself."

The truth was her meeting with Luke had left Bennet unsettled. His entire manner seemed so different to the man she had interacted with previously. It had certainly left her thinking that perhaps there was more to him than she first thought. Regardless of her feelings however, she was not going to share any of this with her sister who would want to do what she always did and analyze every moment of their interaction and review the conversation word by word.

Jane laughed, "Well either way, we will definitely be discussing Luke Dawlton further later, I promise you.

"But as for this guy tonight; Mom invited him as her guest. She used the excuse of needing to help me fill the table, but he is definitely meant for you. Bennet, I'm not going to lie to you…"

"How bad is it?" Bennet asked. There was an edge of suspicion in her voice as she interrupted her sister.

"Well, let's just say if he ends up being your soulmate it will not be for his looks. I saw a picture." At that Jane, despite her best efforts, started to laugh.

"Oh sure, it's funny for you. You're married to Mr. Wonderful."

"Yeah, Mr. Wonderful."

"What is it Jane? Is everything okay?" Bennet asked, noting the sudden change in her sister's demeanor.

"Yes of course. Everything is fine," Jane answered quickly as if trying to brush off the seriousness of her previous words. "David has just been very busy with work lately. He is so distracted all the time."

"Your face doesn't look like that's it."

"Leave it Bennet. It's just boring married stuff. Honest. You wouldn't understand."

Bennet stiffened slightly at her sister's words. "Right. I couldn't possibly understand. I'm not part of your little club. I don't think I should have to apologize just because I don't have the same life as you do."

"Oh Bennet, I didn't mean it that way. Honest I didn't," Jane replied looking crestfallen. "I'm sorry. Really I am. David and I are fine. He just seems distracted lately, but who the hell isn't right? Really Bennet, I didn't mean what I said. I'm just all over the place today."

"It's okay," Bennet said and meant it when she saw the distress visible on her sister's face.

Despite her words, she found herself wondering, and not for the first time, why married people always seemed to feel that they had to speak to single women like they were some alien species which they would never understand. Still, it was completely out of character for her sister to have said something like that to her. For her to be so insensitive as she had been just now led Bennet to believe something was really bothering her.

There had to be something more going on with Jane, but she also knew her sister well enough to know she was not going to talk about it at this moment and Bennet knew better than to push the subject with her now. If she was stuck going to this awful dinner with her mother's horrible fix up then at least, she reasoned, she would have the opportunity tonight to see how they seemed when Jane and David were together at the gala.

Glancing down at her watch Jane got up, walked over to Bennet, and gave her a hug.

"I better get going. Lots to do before tonight. Are you sure we're okay?"

"Yes, we're fine. I promise." Bennet smiled. "Besides, I have to get ready for my fix up with Mr. Right. I swear Jane, he and Mom both better keep their distance from me tonight. I have had an intense week and I'm in no mood to deal with this. I promised Mom I would come to the dinner, but that is all I promised."

"There's my feisty little sis," Jane said laughing. "And don't go thinking I am letting you off the hook about the other nephew in your life by the way. We are going to talk about Luke Dawlton again."

"Sure, sure. You better go, Jane," Bennet replied with a smile as she guided her out of her apartment.

Chapter Twelve

Seven hours after being warned by her sister about what was sure to be another of their mother's legendary matchmaking fails, Bennet was seated in the back of a taxi on her way to the gala. The cab was an expense that normally this early in the evening she would not have allowed herself, but she found the idea of riding alone on the subway in a black cocktail dress too sad even for her independently-minded spirit.

As the driver expertly wove his way through the city traffic, Bennet was finding it difficult to fight back the gnawing feeling in the pit of her stomach as to what this night would hold. Even in the best of circumstances an event like this would be painful. She had been dragged to enough of these functions with her brother-in-law's business acquaintances to know the presentations would be long, the food overly rich and proportionally challenged, and the small talk at the table stifling. But tonight, with her mother playing matchmaker, it had the potential to be truly dreadful.

Bennet could not remember when it had actually begun, but for as long as she could remember, she felt like she had been locked in some undeclared battle with her mother regarding her relationships. Adelaide Reynolds was a unique breed of woman who would have fit better in the 1950s than the present day. While no one could debate her devotion to her offspring, the way she showed it had always seemed to Bennet to be misguided. She was one of those mothers to whom it was especially important that her daughters have boys like them and as they were growing up she had spent countless hours on what she felt were the beauty necessities of life which would help aid them in their quest to gain attention from the opposite sex. From an early age, Bennet and Jane had been shown the proper way to wash their faces so as to better prevent wrinkles and were encouraged to use lotion on their hands first thing in the morning and right before going to bed at night because as Adelaide was keen to repeatedly say, "No boy is going to want to hold hands with a girl whose palms feel like the scales of a fish." It did not matter that in the fourth grade Bennet had no interest in holding a boy's hand, finding them nothing more than a classroom annoyance; Adelaide Reynolds still felt it was essential she be prepared.

While some of Bennet's friends had to fight with their mothers to get their ears pierced or to be able to start using their first shade of lipstick, her mother was forcing her to do these things long before she had any interest. Jane of course always did as her mother asked and it was her mother who took credit for the fact that the boys swarmed around her like bees to a jar of honey. But Bennet, on the other hand, fought her mother every step of the way. She preferred to sit with her father, reading the comics as he perused the business section of the newspaper; or to go with him to his office on Sunday mornings when the firm was nearly empty and wait patiently until he finished reviewing his work so they could have lunch together or go on a nature walk through Central Park.

When Bennet finally did start to take notice of boys, instead of making her mother happy, none of the ones she liked were of the sort that met with her mother's approval. Their first full blown teenage knock-down, drag out fight between mother and daughter occurred when for the eighth-grade dance Adelaide wanted Bennet to attend with the son of one of her friends from church. Already aware of him by reputation, Bennet knew him to be a real jerk; one of those leering jocks who only stopped talking about football long enough to stare at a girl's chest and whose stocky frame included a head and broad shoulders but seemed to be missing a neck. When Bennet adamantly refused the arrangement, instead choosing to go to the dance with a group of her girlfriends, a set of imaginary battle lines were drawn and it seemed they had been warring with each other on the subject ever since.

Tonight was just another page in their mother-daughter saga. Fifteen years after the eighth-grade dance and in her mother's eyes Bennet had failed spectacularly in that, at twenty-eight-years old, she not only had no husband but she lacked even a single decent prospect in that department. And so now, once more it seemed, Bennet found herself dreading another fix up. This time however, since the forced date had been arranged through emotional blackmail, the refusal of which would have disappointed her sister, Bennet had no choice but to go along with it. The entire situation helped support her belief that her life was like one of those sappy romantic comedies that she secretly enjoyed watching. Although, as she was painfully aware, the similarities always stopped right before the moment where the female lead gets her happy ending.

Ten minutes later the cab came to a stop in front of the hotel in which the gala was being held. Knowing there was no way to turn back and there was nothing for Bennet to do but accept her fate, she paid the driver, reluctantly left the cab, and began the slow march up the flight of stairs to the hotel's entrance.

After checking her wrap, Bennet headed towards the direction of the ballroom, but stopped before entering. Standing in the doorway, peering into the grand space she instantly saw that it was as bad as she knew it would be. The room was already nearly full to capacity with people, many of whom were walking around or standing in small groups chatting. Others were seated at the elaborately decorated tables on each of which stood a short vase filled with a tightly wrapped bunch of what she guessed had to be at least thirty lavender roses. The whole room was dripping with elegance from the crystal chandeliers to the chairs and tables covered in silver silk organza. As she took it all in, Bennet found herself thinking how much additional money could end up in the hands of the evening's charity if these type of events were less lavish and less expensively run. Sadly this crowd, she suspected, were more inclined to give if they were beautifully dressed and surrounded by opulence.

Unable to delay the inevitable any longer, Bennet reluctantly began her journey across the crowded floor to her table. As she got closer, she caught sight of her mother in the process of switching two name tags.

Here we go, she thought at what she was sure was her mother's maneuvering to seat her next to her arranged date for the evening.

As Bennet began calculating her chance of making it back through the crowd and out of the room before they began seating for dinner, her mother caught her eye and gave her a glare that made it seem as if she had been reading her daughter's mind.

Letting out a frustrated sigh of resignation, Bennet grabbed a glass of champagne from a passing server, took a long swig, and continued towards what she was sure to be her impending doom.

Bennet reached her table at the same time Jane and her husband David returned from their pre-dinner mingling. As usual, her sister looked absolutely stunning in a sapphire blue one shoulder dress that, slightly fitted, hugged her slender frame perfectly. David looked equally handsome in his tuxedo and Bennet was struck once more as to how easily the pair could be one of those glamorous couples seen walking an award show red carpet.

Jane had met David when she began her career working at the firm where he was then an associate. While she had done well for herself and had begun to rise in the ranks, she had given it up to have her daughter, choosing instead to stay at home and take care of her child and simultaneously support her husband's career. While Jane usually seemed happy about the arrangement, as much as Bennet loved her, she could never understand how her sister was able to spend her days constantly building her husband up. Bennet liked David, she really did, but the arrangement was something she could never see for herself. Not that anyone was asking anyway.

Maybe it was because of the conversation they had had this morning, but as she looked at her sister just now Bennet could sense that there was something about her that was the slightest bit off. On the surface she looked the same as always and no one would be able to notice if they did not know her as well as she did; but it was clear to her how Jane's eyes lacked their usual sparkle and she looked just the littlest bit uneasy, almost as if she were trying a little too hard to make it seem that everything was perfect. Bennet also thought David appeared stressed, but it was harder to tell with him under the plastic veneer of an expression he saved for all his finance clients and which was now firmly fixed on his face.

"You okay?" Bennet asked Jane when she reached her side.

"Of course," Jane replied unconvincingly.

Bennet stared at her as if she was questioning her answer.

Realizing what Bennet was referring to, Jane quickly added, "Honestly, if this is about what I said this morning, don't worry. I was tired and anxious that everything go well tonight. David's just working too hard and I'm making too much out of nothing; that's all."

Jane squeezed Bennet's hand in reassurance as she added, "Things are good, I promise."

Bennet was not at all sure she believed her sister. "Okay, if you say so. You look beautiful by the way."

"So do you," Jane said as she took in the sight of Bennet in her simple black capped sleeve dress with flared calf-length skirt and black embroidered overlay.

"Milton Winer is sure to think you are lovely."

Bennet, who had been mid-sip, began to choke on her champagne. Coughing and laughing at the same time she finally recovered enough to ask, "Dear God, that's not his name is it?"

"Afraid it is, sis. Remember, it's just one night."

"Yep. Just one night," Bennet replied, taking another big gulp of her drink. "One long, miserable night."

Just then David, who had been talking to a colleague, gave Jane a slight nod. It was one of those gestures between couples that made words unnecessary that had always fascinated Bennet and yet simultaneously seemed to her so foreign as her relationships had never seemed to reach that point of mutual comfort and ease.

"Time to take our seats," Jane said. Wanting to be encouraging, she added, "Remember, you can do this. Besides he might be funny or really interesting."

"Oh yes, I can't wait to discover the hidden depths of Mr. Winer," Bennet added stepping away from Jane to take her seat which was positioned across the table.

Besides family, the rest of the twelve dinner companions were a mix of David's finance colleagues and in some cases their significant others. A few she recognized from other work functions she had been dragged to, but most were strangers.

It appeared her mother had worked her magic, as Bennet could tell from a quick glance down at the table cards that she had been conveniently trapped between her and the infamous Milton Winer.

Trying to make it impossible for me to escape, are you, Mom? Well we will just see about that.

"Ah, you're finally here," Adelaide Reynolds said, the impatience clear in her tone.

While Bennet was left to wonder how she could possibly already have managed to annoy her mother, she smiled at her and replied, "Hello

Mom. Actually, I've been here for a while as you are well aware, since I know you saw me enter the room."

Ignoring her, Adelaide continued, "I would like you to meet Milton Winer. He was nice enough to be my guest this evening. You know his aunt, my friend Barbara Haines."

Oh yes, I know Barbara Haines; the pointy-nosed busybody who never hesitates to point out my faults whenever I see her.

Having at first been largely obscured from view behind her mother, at that moment Milton Winer stepped forward providing Bennet with her first glance of the man. To say he lived up to her expectations would have been an understatement. Severely balding, he was easily four inches shorter than Bennet's five feet seven inches. A bit of a caricature, his pasty complexion had the effect of transforming into a canvas of blotchy red spots at her mother's introduction, and he was plump enough that in his black suit the first thing that sprang to Bennet's mind was the image of a penguin. In particular his white shirt beneath his dinner jacket was so tight across his mid-section that the space between each button was spreading slightly giving the effect that they might pop off at any moment.

Bennet was afraid to look anywhere for fear that if she caught Jane's eye she would be unable to keep a straight face. So instead she focused on the man himself and while she was imagining the many ways she would deal with her mother later, she knew for now her problem was getting through this evening.

"Mr. Winer, nice to meet you." Bennet's words, while civil, lacked any trace of enthusiasm.

"Please, call me Milton," he began with a voice that was, Bennet noted, appallingly both high and nasally and seemed to perfectly fit his last name.

"It was so kind of your mother to invite me. But Adelaide, are your sure this is your daughter? She could easily be your sister."

Just kill me now, Bennet thought as she found herself fighting back the urge to gag.

"Actually Milton, since you are my mother's plus one for the evening, I insist you sit next to her."

"Bennet, I think Milton is fine where he…"

Ignoring her mother's threatening look, Bennet cut her off, "No. I insist."

Moving quickly, Bennet switched the name cards so that Milton was now in the middle between the two of them.

If I have to suffer dear mother, then so do you, Bennet thought as she resisted sending a gloating smile in her mother's direction.

Across the table, Bennet caught David's eye as he gave her a wink. He had been at enough functions with Adelaide to know her game.

Point one, Bennet, she thought as she sent a smile back in her brother-in-law's direction.

The next fifty minutes, from the salad course through the entrée, were some of the longest of Bennet's life. Rather than exchange a few simple pleasantries as would have been appropriate, Milton Winer instead bombarded her with a litany of mind-numbing questions including what she did for work, where she completed her schooling, and whether or not she had any pets. Her favorite however was when he asked if she had ever been to the Bahamas and when Bennet said no he proceeded to ask if she wanted to go some time.

Bennet did her best to sit patiently and try to answer his questions with the minimal amount of words necessary, careful not to say anything that he may wrongly take as encouragement. With the personality of a wet mop, however, she found she had never wanted anything more than this meal to be over so Milton's questions might end. The worst part was he never seemed to pause between his rapid-fire questions. Instead, he proceeded to move from one subject to the next so fast that one stood the chance of developing whiplash.

"Do you like plants?" Milton asked.

"Excuse me what?" Bennet was beginning to fear she would be unable to take much more of this.

"I asked if you liked plants? I have what they call a little bit of a green thumb you see," Milton said with a nasally chuckle that made it clear he thought himself highly amusing. "I guess you can say it is a passion of mine."

The leering look he gave Bennet at the word passion caused her to fear she would be unable to hold down her salmon en croûte.

"Do you know much about plants?" Milton continued, unabated.

"Plants? Um, no, I can't say I do. I usually end up killing anything green and based in soil," Bennet replied, hoping this would end the conversation.

"Well, I consider myself an amateur horticulturist."

"Mmm hmm," Bennet said absently.

"There is a show currently on view at the botanical gardens that is supposed to be excellent. Perhaps I could show you some of my..."

Oh no. There is no way that is going to happen, Bennet thought as it suddenly became clear what he was saying and where he was hoping to go with this conversation.

Unable to take it any longer, Bennet refused to give him the opportunity to ask her out and so rushed to stop him from finishing his sentence.

"Actually, it is my mother who loves gardening. Perhaps she would like to know more about the show."

Luckily Milton Winer's obsession with plants made him oblivious to the brush off.

"Well I would love to tell her about it," Milton replied smiling, face beet red, as he turned to direct his smothering attention on her mother.

"Adelaide have you ever heard of a tracheophyte?"

"A what?" Adelaide asked with a look of confusion on her face.

With her mother now pulled into what promised to be a dreadfully dull conversation with Milton, Bennet was able to experience her first few seconds of long desired quiet since the start of dinner. At the thought of what she had just endured during the meal, she rolled her eyes; a gesture which caught the attention of a man sitting across the table.

Bennet returned the smile he aimed at her. She had noticed how attractive he was the minute he joined their table right before dinner had been served and had made a mental note to ask Jane about him later. Impeccably dressed in a black tuxedo and straight black tie; he had dirty blond hair and as he smiled she could not help but notice how a most charming dimple appeared on his left cheek. She had felt his eyes on her a few times while they had been eating and she could only imagine the show Milton Winer was putting on for the rest of the table.

As dinner was ending and there would be a break before dessert and the closing presentation, some of the guests had begun to get up and wander around the tables to once more mingle and socialize with other attendees. Having watched the couple seated on her right vacate their seats, Bennet was surprised and pleased to see the man get up and make his way over to her.

"Wow, your boyfriend is quite the talker," the stranger said as he sat down in the empty seat next to Bennet.

Bennet laughed. "Oh God, he's definitely not my boyfriend."

Extending his hand to her, he added, "Well, Ms. 'he's definitely not my boyfriend', allow me to introduce myself. Jeremy Burlow. Nice to meet you."

"Bennet Reynolds," she replied shaking his hand. "Nice to meet you too."

"So how did you manage to find yourself at this utterly boring event?" Jeremy asked.

"I'm a guest of my brother-in-law David Setton and his wife, my sister, Jane. His firm bought this table."

"David's a wonderful guy."

"Yes, he is. Do you work with him?"

"No, but we are both in finance. We are actually in the beginnings of putting a deal together that looks to be quite promising."

"Well there isn't anyone better than David at what he does," Bennet replied.

As they enjoyed the next several minutes of pleasant conversation, Bennet could not help but note how different this exchange was from the one she had just endured with Milton Winer. Jeremy Burlow seemed to ooze charm while Milton—who sadly would not know how to be charming if he tried—was at the moment, she noted with amusement, still holding her mother hostage to his musings on horticulture and one could only guess what else.

In fact, Bennet had become so engrossed with her conversation with Jeremy that she was startled at the sound of David's voice.

"Sorry to interrupt, but Jeremy I'm afraid I need to steal you away for a few minutes. There is someone I think it is important you meet."

"Yes of course," Jeremy said as he rose and began to step away from the table.

Turning back to Bennet, Jeremy flashed her a smile in which she could see two rows of perfectly straight and gleaming white teeth.

"I'm very much looking forward to continuing our talk later."

"I'd like that," Bennet replied just before he walked away.

Throughout her conversation, Bennet had noticed her mother's thinly veiled attempts to eavesdrop on what they were saying. Now seeing the stranger who had been speaking with her daughter walk away with David, Adelaide sensed the opportunity opening up for her to free herself from what by this point even she had to admit was the oppressive weight of Milton Winer's conversation.

"Bennet, perhaps you and Milton..." she started to say but was stopped short at the sight of her daughter turning her back to her and rising from the table.

Sorry Mom. You started this and you will have to finish it, Bennet thought as she grabbed her clutch and moved as quickly as she could away from her mother.

There was no way she was going to get pulled into another discussion with Milton Winer, the chatty amateur horticulturist. At least not without another drink first.

After a quick trip to the bathroom to refresh her makeup, Bennet reentered the ballroom where even from across the crowded room she could still make out her mother deep in conversation with Milton. Even with the sympathy she was beginning to feel for her mother at this moment, she could not prevent a smile from spreading across her face; Adelaide had brought this on herself.

Deciding it best to avoid the table altogether for as long as she could, Bennet instead proceeded to the bar.

"One glass of champagne please."

As the bartender handed her a glass, she heard a voice coming from behind her, "Excuse me, but I think that's my drink."

An unsettling rush of warmth spread over Bennet at the sound of his deep voice with just the slightest hint of a British accent. Trying to appear composed she turned around to find Luke Dawlton looking down at her.

In that moment Bennet was struck by the realization that while there were many handsome men in the ballroom tonight, Vivian Winthrop's nephew was in a class all by himself. His tuxedo must have been made just for him; it fit him so perfectly. And as she met his gaze, he gave her a slightly cocky smile that with the twinkle in his blue eyes made it clear to

Bennet that he was enjoying the moment and his reference to their first exchange.

The slight thawing of the animosity between them that had begun to occur in their meeting the other morning had allowed her to relax, even joke about the humiliating reference he was making.

"I am sorry, but you must be mistaken. This glass belongs to me."

"Well, if you are absolutely sure, then who I am to question you," he continued as he flashed her another smile.

"I wouldn't want you to take this the wrong way, but you are possibly the last person I would have expected to see here this evening."

"Why? Are you saying I do not seem the high finance gala type?" Bennet said giving an expression of mock offense.

Luke laughed. "No, absolutely not. It's actually one of your better qualities."

Was that a compliment?

Finding it surprisingly difficult to concentrate, Bennet quickly broke the silence by adding, "Well, thank you; I think. I'm here as a guest of my sister. Her husband's firm bought a few tables and they had some seats to fill so here I am." Smiling, she added, "Well that and, if I'm being totally honest, my mother used emotional blackmail to get me here tonight; but that's a longer and far more pathetic story."

Luke gave a little laugh. "What firm is your brother-in-law with?"

"He's a junior partner with Smith, Walters and Banks. His name is David Setton."

"That's a good firm. I've had dealings with them before but I've not had the pleasure of meeting your brother-in-law. So now that you are here, maybe you can help me out with something."

Bennet shot him a skeptical look.

"I've been wondering how this type of event compares to art world soirees?"

Despite herself Bennet laughed, relieved that the question was a lighthearted one and that they could continue in whatever this jovial banter was that they seemed to be engaged in.

"Surprisingly similar," she began, "just ours usually involve a bit funkier dress code. Think less black. Probably guests that are a bit less clean-cut too and definitely more facial hair."

"On the men, I hope," Luke replied with a smile.

Bennet laughed. *Damn he can be quite charming, can't he?*

"So what do you think the reception for our exhibition will look like?" Luke asked.

Did he just call it our exhibition? While it should have annoyed her, the subtle reference to their pairing was having quite the opposite effect.

"Well with your aunt involved I think tonight's event might be like Mardi Gras in Brazil compared to what we will be allowed to offer."

A sudden rush of panic filled Bennet at what she had just said and the realization that she may have both offended him and insulted his aunt at the same time.

"I am sorry. I didn't mean to imply anything about your aunt I just…"

Luke's burst of laughter interrupted her rambling.

"If anything, I can assure you that you are being too kind. Don't worry about it. My aunt has mastered the art of conservative entertaining, that's for sure. But the truth is, with you at the helm, I think the event will be a success."

At his compliment, an awkward silence fell over them. Bennet was surprised by his words and wondered why he had said it.

Luke was equally unsure of what had possessed him to flirt with her the way he was. The truth was he had been taken aback by how excited he was to see her tonight. He found that he was enjoying talking with her like this. Not wanting to let any uncomfortableness settle over them he hurried to get the conversation going again, choosing his next words carefully so he would not say something that might inadvertently cause either of their tempers to once more flare.

"There is something I have been meaning to ask you but didn't get a chance in our last meeting when your overeager boss interrupted us."

"And what would that be?" Bennet asked with a hint of apprehension in her voice.

"Well you spend every day surrounding yourself with all this beautiful art. You must have a favorite. I'm just wondering what it is."

"That's your question?" Bennet found herself unable to suppress a smile. "Well that is definitely a question easier asked than answered. I could never have just one favorite. For me it's kind of like picking your favorite movie or book. It's hard to name just one.

"There are so many artists I like from many different periods. I love the sculptures of Michelangelo and I think all the Impressionists are wonderful. I have always been wild about Edgar Degas's dancers, Amedeo Modigliani's portraits, and could look at Claude Monet's garden paintings all day. I have also always been drawn to the energy of the Abstract Expressionists and their use of color. And I haven't even included any artists who are working today. That's an entire other group where I have too many favorites to name."

Luke was fascinated at how Bennet's whole demeanor changed as she spoke about these artists. She had become animated to the point of excitement when speaking about something she so clearly loved. He found himself wondering if she had anyone in her life she looked at that way; then just as quickly he pushed the thought from his mind and chose not to question why it should matter to him if she did.

"But if I absolutely had to pick a favorite artist," Bennet continued, oblivious to the direction of Luke's thoughts, "it would have to be Sébastian Reno."

Luke smiled. "He's one of my favorites too. Why him?"

"You first," Bennet countered.

"All right then, I would say it is because among other things, I have always liked how he pushed boundaries. He imagined new ways to see the world around him and brought those things to life on his canvas. Now your turn."

There was no denying that Bennet had been pleasantly surprised by the direction of their conversation as well as being impressed by his knowledge of art, something she had up until now had no idea he possessed.

"Well sure, I admire Reno for what you said as well; but for me there is also a personal attachment."

Not sure why she was about to share this with a man who was basically a stranger and up until yesterday she could safely say she detested, Bennet began telling him the story anyway.

"One day, I couldn't have been more than eight or nine years old, I was with my family spending a Sunday in Manhattan. We had all gone to see a matinee and then we began wandering the sidewalks looking in all the fancy store windows. My mother took my sister Jane into a shop to try on a dress she liked. I, of course, wanted nothing to do with shopping and so my father and I went instead into this small gallery that was in the building next door. It was one of those old master galleries on the Upper East Side. It's not even there anymore, a testament to how this city is always changing I guess, but on that day when we went in it was my first trip inside a gallery and I was just in awe of the entire space. They had this small exhibition of drawings on view including one by Reno which immediately caught my eye.

"I had never seen anything like that drawing before and I remember being fascinated by this little sketch he had made of a bird from only a few simple lines. Years later I would study Reno's work and learn of his importance and now I even get to work with his paintings on a daily basis. But despite all his wonderful works that I have studied and seen since then, that simple sketch will always be my favorite and the most special to me.

"That day, when we got home from our adventure in the city, I remember sitting in my room for hours and trying to draw my own bird just like he did. Of course I wasn't anywhere near as good, and it took me several tries to even come close to creating something I liked. Still when I had finished it, I took my bird drawing and I remember making up a whole story about it and creating all the drawings to accompany the text. I think that simple sketch was what caused the first spark of interest in me towards wanting to make art."

"So you want to be an artist."

Luke's statement had caused an ache in Bennet's stomach and all at once she was overcome with the usual sense of failure she felt whenever she thought about how she was not doing what she really wanted to do.

"Yes I do; at least in some capacity."

"What led you to a job as a curator at the Northhom then?"

A few days ago, this question would have put Bennet on edge, thinking that he was questioning her qualifications. But there was no judgement in his words.

"You mean how did I end up a failed artist wannabe working in a museum?" Bennet asked with her eyebrow raised.

"So you did hear me that day in the hallway. I had wondered about that."

Luke was clearly uncomfortable, and if Bennet was honest with herself, she was enjoying watching him squirm a little more than she should have.

"It's fine really. I guess that's what I am technically."

"No," Luke hastily replied, and on instinct reached out as if to grab her hand before stopping himself, having realized to do so might cross some line.

"It's not fine at all. I didn't even know who you were when I said it. I was angry with my aunt for her manipulating me into this project. My issues with her run deep and are certainly complicated, but I had no right to take that frustration out on you."

"Well you're forgiven. The truth is, I'm aware that I have a tendency to be a little oversensitive about the topic."

"Almost as much as your feelings about pastries?" Luke asked.

Choosing to ignore his playful jab at her behavior during their first encounter Bennet added, "Besides, it's not like I haven't been caught saying things out loud that shouldn't have been overheard as well."

Luke could not help but smile as he remembered what she had said about him outside the restaurant the other night and the look on her face when she realized he had overheard her. "Yes, I guess we should both be more careful to check who is standing near us before we speak."

Bennet laughed. She hoped that this relaxed atmosphere between them would last as they worked together on the exhibition. But she was also starting to feel like there might be something more to it than just that. Here in the glamorous setting of a charity dinner she had dreaded coming to, she was actually enjoying talking to this man whom she had just days before despised. She honestly did not know what to make of what was happening.

"Here you are. I was wondering where you got off to," Jeremy Burlow said, surprising both of them as he came to stand right at Bennet's side.

Bennet had been so engaged in her conversation with Luke that she had failed to see Jeremy approaching and for the briefest of moments she felt regret that he was there.

"I should have known you would be here. Any important finance event could never be complete without the great Luke Dawlton making an appearance. Seriously though, it is good to see you mate," Jeremy said as he extended his hand to Luke.

It was as if Jeremy's appearance had completely broken the pleasant atmosphere between Bennet and Luke, the way a pebble thrown in the water shatters the still, mirror-like surface of a lake.

Bennet noticed a complete change in Luke's demeanor. Refusing to shake Jeremy's hand, he instead looked at her directly as he stated, "I was not aware you two knew each other."

"Actually, we've just met," Bennet quickly replied as she was suddenly overwhelmed with a compelling need to try to alleviate the tension that for some reason unbeknownst to her had suddenly developed.

"That's right. We had been having a lovely conversation at our table until I was reluctantly called away," Jeremy said as he reached out his hand and rested it lightly on the middle of Bennet's back.

Taken aback by the intimacy of the gesture, Bennet was even more concerned by the quick flicker of anger that she saw momentarily appear on Luke's face.

"Excuse me but I see a colleague I must speak to. Besides I have neglected my date for far too long already," Luke stated as he quickly turned and walked away without another word.

Bennet had watched in wonder as the engaging and dare she say even interesting Luke Dawlton of the last few minutes changed back into the haughty, judgmental, and arrogant man she had originally thought him to be.

Once more finding herself alone with Jeremy, Bennet stepped back creating a space between the two of them.

"I don't know what just happened. He was so rude." Bennet was confused as to what had taken place and the complete shift in Luke's demeanor.

"What, that?" Jeremy asked casually. "Well I'm not one for gossip, but let's just say just because someone is good at business, it certainly does not make him a good man or ensure that he always plays fair."

Bennet was surprised by Jeremy's words. While they had had their differences what he was talking about was Luke's behavior in the business world. She found it hard to believe he could be as successful as he was if he was as bad as Jeremy described. But then again she reminded herself, she really did not know him at all and she had not forgotten how detestably he had behaved in their first few meetings.

Distracted by her own thoughts, Bennet had failed to realize that Jeremy had just asked her a question.

"I'm sorry what did you say?"

"Well I don't know if I should repeat it if I can't hold your interest in a simple conversation," Jeremy joked. Unlike Bennet he did not seem phased by the exchange that had just occurred.

"I suggested that we not waste another second talking about Luke Dawlton and then I asked if you might want to go out sometime."

"Oh. Yes, that would be nice," Bennet replied as, forcing herself to push all thoughts of Luke from her mind, she chose instead to focus on the handsome man in front of her who had just asked her out.

"Good, why don't you give me your number and I will call you sometime," Jeremy said, clearly pleased with himself and with Bennet's interest.

"Actually, why don't you just give me a call at the Northhom Museum. I work as the curator there."

"Impressive," Jeremy replied.

Despite her best attempts to focus on what Jeremy was saying, Bennet was unable to keep from looking across the room. While she could not be sure, as she was speaking with Jeremy she thought she saw Luke watching them, but then a few guests moved and obscured her view and she could no longer see him.

Bennet suddenly felt the need for some fresh air and so decided it was best to end her conversation with Jeremy.

"No, not impressive at all I assure you." Smiling and trying her best to focus on their conversation, Bennet added, "I am looking forward to hearing from you, but I think for now, if you will excuse me, I've had just about all the small talk and fine dining I can handle for one evening so I think I'm going to leave."

As she walked away from Jeremy a myriad of thoughts were racing through her mind. Staring across the room she once more spotted Luke Dawlton. It did not escape her notice that he was now standing near his table and next to a stunningly beautiful woman who Bennet found herself hoping was not his date.

What are you thinking; of course Luke Dawlton would not be here alone. He told you himself he was eager to get back to his date. He was probably only talking to you to be polite anyway.

Mad at herself for caring at all about Luke Dawlton or his date, Bennet continued to mentally berate herself. *Knock it off Bennet. What difference does it make anyways?*

Desperate to look away, she once more scanned the crowd, this time searching for her sister. Eventually she spotted her and after catching Jane's eye, Bennet tried to motion for her to meet her outside the ballroom.

Seconds later, Jane found Bennet at the coat check.

"Are you okay?"

"Yes, I'm fine," Bennet answered unconvincingly. "I've just had enough for one night."

"I mean really? How long does it take to find a simple wrap?" Bennet asked impatiently, waiting for the attendant to return. She was holding on to the stub of her claim ticket as if it held the winning lottery numbers instead of simply the means to get her away from this evening.

"Who was that you were talking to?" Jane asked.

"His name's Jeremy Burlow. I thought you would know him. You sat next to him during dinner."

"No, not Jeremy. Of course I know him."

"Well, he just asked me out. I don't really know why I said yes, but I was a bit flustered and it all happened so fast."

Letting out an overly loud sigh of frustration at the fact that the attendant had not yet returned with her wrap, Bennet added, "Tell me he's not a pervert or anything like that; because I'm telling you that would be just my luck tonight."

Jane smiled. "No. He's not even a little bit of a pervert as far as I know and before you ask I have no reason to suspect he is an ax murderer either. My God, you just made a date with a smart, good looking guy. Only you could look miserable after a moment like that. It's not a bad thing that Jeremy asked you out Bennet. I mean really, did you see how fine he looked in his tuxedo tonight. I will try to find out some details about him on the sly from David. But seriously he has to be better than Milton Winer."

Despite herself Bennet laughed.

"That's not who I meant by the way," Jane continued. "I wanted to know who the other man was you were talking to at the bar."

"Oh him? That was the nephew."

"You're joking. That's Luke Dawlton? He's absolutely gorgeous."

"And he has a British accent," Bennet said, unable to stop herself from smiling despite her confusion and irritation at his attitude this evening.

"You're kidding me. That's who you chased down on the street? That's the man you have to work with to put together the Winthrop exhibition?"

"Yep," Bennet sighed. "Welcome to my world. And I think he might be crazier than I am based on what happened tonight."

Knowing her sister was not going to let the conversation end without a further explanation, Bennet began to provide an overview of what had just taken place.

"I bumped into him at the bar and we were actually having a nice time talking. We had already agreed in our meeting yesterday at the museum that we were going to try and be civil and work together to get through this exhibition. And honestly, that was the best I thought I could hope for; that he would not interfere with my work. But then tonight we were having a nice conversation, or at least I thought we were. But then he completely changed. It was like he flipped a switch or something when Jeremy came over. He couldn't wait to get away from me. He really is kind of a jerk I think."

"A jerk maybe, but sexy definitely," Jane replied.

"Ours is a business arrangement, nothing more; thank you very much," Bennet snapped.

"You sure about that?" Jane asked, refusing to let her sister off the hook.

"Yes, I'm sure." Bennet hoped she sounded convincing enough to shut down this thread of conversation.

Having finally been able to retrieve her wrap from the attendant who had suddenly returned, Bennet added, "Listen, you can harass me about this later. But right now I'm leaving. I've had just about enough drama for one night."

Bennet laughed, despite all that had happened this evening. "Do you think Mom is still stuck talking with Milton about plants? Does it make me a horrible daughter that there is a part of me that hopes she is?"

Jane could not help but smile at the thought of her mother trapped in a conversation with Milton since she really had no one to blame but herself. How in the world she thought Bennet would ever want to be with someone like him was something Jane would never understand.

"I really have to go. Make my excuses for me okay?" Bennet asked. "I promise I will call you tomorrow."

"Oh sure. Leave it to me to deal with Mom."

Bennet gave Jane a quick hug. "What are big sisters for?"

Then, giving her sister a smile she added, "You know you could stop having these functions and we wouldn't have this problem anymore."

As Bennet began to walk away she stopped for a moment. "Love you," she called back over her shoulder to Jane who nodded in agreement before she started her walk back into the ballroom.

Having moved as quickly as possible without running towards the lobby exit, Bennet was relieved when she was finally outside the hotel. Surprisingly the night air had a slightly dizzying effect on her which she realized might have been aided by the abundance of champagne she had drunk which she felt had been necessary to get through her meal with Milton. The confusing thoughts about Luke Dawlton and the handsome new acquaintance, Jeremy Burlow, were also not helping to keep Bennet from feeling more than a little off balance.

Initially she had worried it might be difficult to hail a cab at this time on a Saturday evening, but fortunately for her, a queue of taxis had already begun to form with drivers anticipating the end of the gala. Rushing down the hotel's exterior stairs, Bennet quickly secured one.

Once seated in the backseat of the cab, Bennet made one final glance back up at the entranceway to the hotel. For a fleeting second she thought she saw Luke Dawlton staring out at her, but she easily convinced herself she must have been mistaken.

Standing in the lobby of the hotel, Luke watched as Bennet stepped into a cab. As he observed the vehicle merge into traffic before disappearing from view he had time to replay their conversation. That she was different from any woman he had ever met was clear. Even now he knew he should be heading back into the ballroom and back to his date for the evening. But the truth was he found her utterly boring. An acquaintance he had met through one of his clients, she had spent the entire duration of their dinner either talking about something she had seen on social media or, much to his horror, actually taking pictures on her phone of the crowd and even several of her dinner plate to post on her own page so her so-called friends could reward her with a thumbs up sign or a smiley face that they approved of her meal. This woman was just one in a string of vapid and shallow women who had flitted in and out of his life in the last decade.

He knew he was as much responsible for the position he found himself in as anyone else. It had always been the easy way out to date women with whom he knew there was no future. He would have a little fun and then move on and he had always liked it that way. It was just lately he had begun to find he needed something more. He knew most of the women in his social circle liked him for what he did and how he made his living because he was the right kind of man for the Manhattan lifestyle they wanted to build for themselves. He also knew that this was not the kind of life he wanted for himself. The thought made him all the more angry with himself for mentioning to Bennet the need to return to his date when he stormed away from her at the bar.

Having tried at conversation with his date and failed, as the meal was ending Luke had made an excuse of needing to speak to a colleague and had planned on spending a few minutes of quiet peace at the bar when he had spotted Bennet. It had been the last place he would have expected to see her. And just the sight of her had been like a breath of fresh air in an otherwise stifling evening. He also could not help but notice how enchanting she looked standing there in her black dress. There was something in her manner that, try as he might, he could not actually articulate how but it made her stand out amongst the more conservative attendees that always seemed to populate these functions.

He had been relieved that only the other day they had managed to establish a kind of truce so they could get along together in their working arrangement. It had allowed him to speak to her at the bar and they had been having a surprisingly interesting conversation. The banter between them had seemed effortless and was so different from their first few interactions that Luke had found himself truly enjoying their exchange.

But then he had shown up. Jeremy Burlow's mere presence at this function would have been enough to make his blood pressure rise but that he was with her was unthinkable. To be fair, Bennet had been quick to tell him that they had just met and really what reason would she have to lie, but it was obvious how comfortable Jeremy had seemed around her. Even now the thought of Jeremy touching the small of her back the way he did sent a wave of anger coursing through him.

Annoyed at the direction of his thoughts, Luke made an effort to get control over his emotions once more as he reminded himself that who Bennet Reynolds saw or did not see was absolutely none of his business. He had to work with her on his aunt's exhibition, nothing more. Theirs was purely a professional relationship and he would do what he needed to see this project through and once more get his aunt off his back for a while. Then he would move on with his life and things would get back to normal.

Resigned to this plan, Luke began the walk back to the ballroom. As he did, he found he could not stop thinking about what had just happened. He was getting mad at himself for even caring, but he convinced himself that it was because he knew the kind of man Jeremy Burlow truly was that the thought of him with Bennet unsettled him so much.

Honestly he did not like the fact that any of this would bother him. Bennet Reynolds was beginning to take up too much space in his thoughts and he was going to have to work hard to change this. She could do what she wanted and he resolved not to think about it anymore. Still he had the sneaking suspicion that it would not prove to be an easy task.

CHAPTER THIRTEEN

Bennet found herself so swamped with work that, much to her relief, she had little time to think about anything but exhibition preparations since the gala the weekend before. Usually, there would have been several months between the conception of a show and its opening at the museum but that was not the case with the Winthrop gift which was just another complication to this already frustrating project. In this instance, the museum board and Vivian Winthrop herself had felt strongly that the momentousness of the donation of her collection meant that they wanted to bring this to the public as soon as possible and so from the announcement of her gift and the exhibition's debut, Bennet only had a little over three months to put the show together. It was an enormous task in the best of circumstances, and nothing about this project had proved easy thus far.

Despite the work however, Bennet found much to her annoyance that she was unable to stop her mind from periodically wandering back to her conversation with Luke at the gala. There had been an easy way between them that she had enjoyed. She just wished their exchange had not ended so poorly as she still struggled to understand what had gone wrong after Jeremy Burlow's appearance, something she hoped would not impact their ability to move forward on the exhibition.

A ding emanating from her computer pulled Bennet from her thoughts. It was a calendar alert reminding her of the Publications meeting that was to take place five minutes from now.

Good, just the boring distraction I need to get my focus back on my work, she thought as she grabbed her file and phone, locked her door, and began the trek upstairs to the meeting.

The Communications offices, a suite of rooms in the newly remodeled staff wing, had a large conference table in the center along with partially walled off cubical desk spaces for the Publications, Public Relations, and Marketing staff. Today, as she arrived, Bennet saw that the room was mostly filled and just as she was resigning herself to having to stand in the back of the room, Stella called her over to the open seat she had saved between her and the marketing assistant, a young woman named Beth.

"How's your day going?" Stella asked.

"I'm completely swamped with work on the Winthrop exhibition and could have used the extra time in my office instead of having to be here, but I'm finding it hard to concentrate so maybe this distraction will be good."

Stella smiled. "I think that might be the first time someone has ever found a good reason for this meeting."

Bennet laughed as these bi-monthly meetings were often a subject of complaint between her and Stella. While some of the items discussed were necessary, it was the structure of the meetings that they took issue with. These meetings were supposed to be held in order to discuss current projects and how the department team as well as the social media and digital platforms of the museum could be employed to help those efforts. However, at almost every one, the legitimate topics quickly dissolved into a complaining and gossip session about various other issues; something that had caused her on more than one occasion to wonder whether the incessant need to overthink and endlessly discuss a topic was unique to the museum world or if in fact it was a hazard wherever there were large office gatherings.

Bennet had already met with the head of publications, Lettie Waters, to directly discuss the Winthrop exhibition and what was needed in terms of signage and reading materials. Because of the quick turnaround time for the exhibition, the usual catalogue would not be ready in time to purchase at the opening. Instead the decision had been made to release it at the show's closing. It was a smart move since it encouraged those wanting to own a catalogue to return for a second visit and view the exhibition again at the end of the show's four month run. And as the Winthrop artworks would now become part of the museum's collection, the catalogue would feature works that would be a permanent part of the Northhom which would give the publication a longer shelf life in terms of appeal to visitors; something that pleased the gift shop manager as well.

For Bennet it meant she had another two months at least, maybe three, after the opening to get the catalogue ready. Still, she and Lettie had pitched the concept and received approval for the printing of a smaller booklet about the exhibition to be ready for distribution beginning the night of the opening. While it added to both of their already heavy workloads, they felt it was important that there was something printed about the Winthrop Collection gift available to all visitors.

Even with these two major decisions made, there were other smaller group issues to contend with and so when it was her turn on the meeting's agenda, Bennet presented a quick review of the progress she had made to date on the project. She also outlined some social media ideas she had formulated regarding possible ways to promote the exhibition.

"One other thought I had," Bennet began, "was that it might be fun to launch a teaser campaign in the weeks leading up to the exhibition opening. Maybe we could use our social media platforms to discuss a work that is part of the gift and give clues about it each day. We could encourage followers to submit their guesses before the big digital reveal of the piece. Maybe one a week with the work being made public on each Friday?"

As there were some nods of agreement and interest, Bennet continued. "I was also thinking there would be better buy-in if we could get Vivian Winthrop to agree to provide some personal stories or anecdotes about her paintings that we could incorporate into the campaign."

"We make them part of the clues," Beth said.

"Exactly."

"I like it," Sam Lennon added. As social media coordinator, his interest was essential if there was any hope of the campaign being implemented. "Maybe Bennet and I and a small group of others could sit down next week and start mapping out how this will work."

As Bennet was about to agree, the all too familiar grating voice of Katherine Hartis, like fingernails across a chalkboard, filled the room. "Well I don't know if it is necessary to bother Vivian Winthrop with such a trivial project. I am sure she has better things to do than participate in your social media games, Bennet."

Having walked into the meeting late, Katherine had of course chosen this moment to make her presence known; the perfect opportunity to belittle Bennet in front of the group.

"I think her participation would be important if we can get it," Stella said, intending to save her friend from Katherine's efforts to shut down the project. If it had been anyone else suggesting it, Stella knew this would not have been an issue.

"Bennet, do you think Mrs. Winthrop could be coaxed into participating?" Stella asked. "Because I think from a public relations standpoint her input would be of added benefit."

Grateful to Stella, Bennet was encouraged to keep pressing her idea.

"I don't know, but I can run it by her nephew and see what he thinks first. If he doesn't like it we will let it drop; but if he does, then we can ask if he will raise the idea with his aunt. I think if he presents it to her she would be more likely to want to participate."

"Sounds great," Sam added. "Why don't you reach out to her nephew before we meet next week and see what he thinks?"

"Okay; thanks, Sam."

Bennet smiled. She knew Katherine had to back off now or her reputation as the supportive administrator would be in question as people would begin to wonder why she was shooting down such a well-received idea.

It was only as Bennet took her seat once more that she realized that she had just volunteered herself to reach out to Luke, something that after the events of the gala she was more than a little hesitant to do. Still, she knew the scoring of a minor victory over Katherine was more than worth it.

After the meeting formally concluded, as was the usual routine, people sat clustered in small groups and the conversation transitioned from final recaps of relevant topics to casual discussions unrelated to Publications whatsoever.

Feeling she had enough work to do that she could not waste any further time chatting, Bennet was about to head back to her office when Beth leaned over to her and said, "Before you leave there is one thing I want to ask you. I want to know how you can even concentrate working with someone as sexy as Luke Dawlton? I mean really. When Stella showed me his picture on the Internet I about died."

Bennet laughed. "I'm sure Stella couldn't wait to show you."

"Listen, all I did was just happen to mention that Vivian Winthrop's nephew was not bad looking and one thing led to another," Stella replied. "Can I help it that before I knew it, the entire Marketing Department was drooling over his picture?"

"And you are going to have to work together," Beth said almost wistfully. "How come it's always the curators who get all the best assignments? All I'm saying is if I were you, I wouldn't say no to some after-hours meeting time at the museum."

Noticing Katherine glaring at her, Bennet felt a strong urge to end this conversation. While Beth was only joking, Bennet did not like the idea of any reference to Luke and her becoming part of the museum's gossip mill.

"There is nothing going on between me and Luke Dawlton other than working together to make sure this exhibition goes well," Bennet replied, her tone all business again.

Not wanting Beth to think she was angry at her however, she gave her a smile before adding, "And that is regardless of what you or Stella think about his looks. Now, as fun as this has been, I should probably be heading back to my office."

Bennet had just stepped out of the room and begun walking down the hallway when she heard her name.

"Bennet, wait a minute please," Katherine called out.

Why can't she just leave me alone, Bennet thought as she realized her boss must have followed her and that she now had no choice but to turn back and join her in the hallway right outside the Communications meeting room.

"I feel it is my job to remind you of just how important Vivian Winthrop's gift is to this museum," Katherine began in her most judgmental of tones.

"Your job title means you are in charge of the exhibition and yet, with your relative inexperience, you might not fully understand just how necessary it is that the exhibition be perfect."

Bennet mentally counted to ten before answering and hoped she had calmed herself down enough to respond. "Thank you Katherine, but I keep a copy of my job description in my office so I really don't need you to explain my responsibilities to me. I promise you I know perfectly well how to do my job so if you have a question about the exhibition then ask it; otherwise I have work to get back to."

Katherine flashed one of her condescending smiles that Bennet had grown to despise. "Bennet, I don't know why you insist on questioning my motives when I only have the best interests of the Northhom Museum at heart. You would do well to remember that if you fail it will be your job on the line."

"If that's the case," Bennet replied, fearing she was on the verge of losing her temper, "then I can't help but wonder why you made such a big show of trying to reject the idea I presented at the meeting. The social media campaign idea is a good one and you know it."

Unable to help herself, Bennet added a final dig to her boss. "I know it's important to you what people think so I'd be careful or the staff might start to wonder about your motives. They might even start to question your dedication to the Winthrop exhibition and you wouldn't want that."

Knowing her comment about Katherine's reputation, something she cared more about than anything else, had hit home, Bennet turned and walked away, leaving Katherine staring after her with her mouth wide open.

Back in her office Bennet was intent on shaking off her exchange with Katherine and so she went about returning to her work. Earlier in the day she had set up the layout model of the museum galleries that would be used for the exhibition. Early on in the design process she liked to move around little miniature versions of the paintings on the plastic model so she could visualize what they would look like in various places on the walls. While there were computer programs that could do this more efficiently, Bennet had always preferred the old school method. It was probably the artist in her who favored the tactile element of moving miniature copies of artworks onto the model's walls that this approach offered; and she had always found that it was the best way for her to think through potential arrangements of paintings by themes and to best visualize how visitors would interact with the exhibition.

Considering the option of groupings by movement, she was in the process of arranging the order of some Minimalist paintings in the smallest of the exhibition's five galleries when her phone rang.

"Bennet Reynolds," she said absently as she picked up her phone.

"Bennet, how are you?"

There was something familiar about the voice on the other end of the line, but she was struggling to place it.

"It's Jeremy Burlow. We met Saturday evening." Laughing, he added, "Don't tell me you have forgotten me already. I hoped I had made a better impression than that."

"No, of course not," Bennet replied, but in truth she had been so busy with work since the start of the week that she had almost forgotten; well, at least anything about him other than the reaction his presence had caused in Luke which was proving far more difficult to push from her mind. "How are you?"

"I'm good," Jeremy began, "but I was worrying that I might have missed my chance and you are already deep into a relationship with your dinner guest."

Bennet could not help but laugh at the memory of Milton Winer. "Not quite yet."

"Very good. Well in that case, I was hoping you might like to meet me for dinner?"

Bennet knew she had more on her plate right now than she could handle, but the thought of an evening out with an attractive and up to this point normal man did not seem like something she should pass up.

"That sounds great."

"Perfect. How about tomorrow evening. Let's say Florenzonos in the Village at seven. I guess I should have asked first; do you like Italian?"

"I love it; and seven is good. I'll meet you there."

As Bennet hung up her phone she smiled. Even with all she had to do, and with Katherine Hartis breathing down her neck waiting for her to screw up, the thought of a night out made her feel a little excited.

Chapter Fourteen

While having debated whether to cancel more than once, as Bennet walked into Florenzonos Italian Restaurant she was glad she had not listened to her inner monologue of self-doubt and decided to give the evening a chance. She had spent her lunch break that day with Stella discussing the contents of her wardrobe and had finally decided that tonight she would wear one of her favorite dresses, a navy-blue sheath which she had accessorized with a pair of perfectly worn brown leather boots that hit just below the knee and a simple silver cuff bracelet and small hoop earrings. Overall she was happy with her ensemble selection. It was dressy but still comfortable.

She had never been to the eatery Jeremy had selected and, as she stepped inside, she found it to be a modest space with only ten tables along with a mahogany bar running the length of the left side of the long, narrow room. The gray walls created a cave-like effect which was enhanced by the addition of minimal lighting and a single candle placed in the center of each table. Bennet's initial impression was that it was a bit too much of a romantic setting for her liking for a first date venue but she had promised Stella she would not follow her usual pattern and overthink everything. Instead she would try to give the evening a real chance. With that in mind she stepped further inside and quickly spotted Jeremy seated near the back of the room.

As she headed to his table, Bennet had the opportunity to get a closer look at her date. Jeremy was easily one of the most attractive men in the restaurant; exuding a sort of all-American male charisma mixed with classic good looks. Yet there was something about his manner both as he sat at the table this evening and when he had first spoke with her at the gala that made Bennet think he was the type of guy who knew just how attractive he was even though he pretended not to.

As far as first dates went, it began well. From the moment she sat down and the first glass of wine was poured, Jeremy was nothing but charm which allowed them to fall into an easy conversation that continued throughout the meal. They covered the full range of "first date" topics; lightly touching on the subjects of their jobs, family, schooling, and hobbies while avoiding the danger topics of politics and religion.

It was when the entrée dishes were being removed from the table and the after-dinner coffees were being poured that things changed. It was then that Jeremy, out of nowhere, decided to bring up the subject of Luke Dawlton.

"I was surprised to see Luke at the gala last weekend," Jeremy said casually.

"Really?" Bennet asked. "He runs one of the top firms in the city and it was a finance-related charity event. I wouldn't think it would be that surprising."

"No, I guess not."

Bennet noted an edge to Jeremy's voice that had not been there before. Thinking he might end this thread of conversation, he instead continued to broach the subject.

"It's just, I make it a rule to try my best to avoid places where I think he might be."

When Bennet did not respond, Jeremy pressed on.

"How do you know him?"

"I don't really," Bennet replied. "We only met a few weeks ago. I'm the curator in charge of putting together the exhibition for his aunt's art collection which she is gifting to the Northhom Museum. Luke is involved with the exhibition at his aunt's request."

Jeremy smiled. "Ah, the formidable Vivian Winthrop. She is quite something; or at least so I've heard. I'm sure she is almost as unpleasant as her nephew."

What does that mean? Bennet wondered.

While she knew from firsthand experience that Vivian Winthrop was certainly difficult to please, Bennet did not feel comfortable acknowledging it in front of Jeremy or anyone for that matter as she was of such importance to the museum; it seemed unprofessional somehow.

Bennet's confused expression must have given Jeremy pause as he quickly added, "Sorry. I shouldn't have said that. I wouldn't want to offend you."

"You're not. How could you really since I don't know either of them well enough to be offended."

Despite her words, Bennet was uncomfortable with his bringing up of the subject which seemed completely off topic from the rest of the evening's conversation. Still, while she should not have been, she found herself a little curious as to what he could possibly mean.

"Well, in that case," Jeremy began, "I would be remiss if I did not warn you to watch your back with Luke. He is not one to be trusted."

While Bennet said nothing to encourage him, Jeremy had no reservations about launching into what was beginning to feel to her like a character assassination.

"Of course, my assessment of Luke is solely based on my own experiences but what I have learned of him has shown him to be a man of questionable character, that's for sure. I first met him several years ago, when I was just getting started in business here in New York. I had just moved to the city from Chicago and was working on an important investment deal. Luke went ahead and bad-mouthed me to the client and then stole the client for himself.

"While these things sometimes happen, I was really disappointed that he would have been so duplicitous. You see, he was already highly respected in finance circles and I was looking to grow my reputation; get started on the right foot so to speak. Needless to say, it came as a crushing blow when he undermined me.

"Still, over the years I tried to be the better person and put the past behind us. I have even made several attempts to extend the proverbial olive branch so we could at least remain on good professional terms. He has wanted none of it however and has always gone out of his way to reject my overtures. I mean, you saw for yourself how rude he was to me at the gala."

"Well, I'm surprised he has made it as far as he has in his career if that is how he behaves," Bennet said as she struggled to process what she had just heard.

"Some men just get all the breaks I guess," Jeremy continued.

"Yes, but it's not fair," Bennet replied. She was genuinely upset for Jeremy over the way he had been treated by Luke.

Jeremy flashed her a smile. "Oh don't worry on my account. I admit I was concerned for a while that he would try and steal more clients from me. However, I pride myself on the fact that I have done just fine on my own despite Luke Dawlton's best efforts to thwart my success."

Bennet was glad that Jeremy seemed to not have been overly troubled anymore about what Luke had done to him. Still it had unsettled her and so eager to move away from this topic and not waste any more of their date discussing him, she quickly changed the subject.

Much to her relief they spent the rest of the evening discussing lighter topics and once they had moved on from any further discussion of Luke, the evening went well. And while she had refused Jeremy's suggestion that they go to a bar for after-dinner drinks, they shared a brief and not unpleasant kiss at the door of the cab, which he helped her hail before they said goodnight.

It was not until she was in the taxi pulling away from the restaurant that Bennet allowed herself to think about everything that Jeremy had said. She had to admit most of the date was fine. He was nice enough and she had found it easy to talk with him. Instead of focusing on that however, she found she spent most of the ride trying to reconcile Jeremy's description of Luke and what were, if what he said was true, his despicable actions with the man she had met. It was an undertaking which left her both frustrated and less sure of either man's character than before the start of the evening.

Bennet was surprised and confused by the story Jeremy had just relayed. She had started to soften slightly to Luke and had actually enjoyed talking to him at the gala but in truth she did not know Luke Dawlton well. And there was no denying how rudely he had behaved during their first few meetings. But that would have been nothing compared to what it said about his character if what Jeremy told her was true, which would have made him a truly reprehensible person.

Why would Jeremy lie about something like that? What would the purpose be? Bennet thought as she found herself becoming angry at Luke on Jeremy's behalf.

What would be so wrong about someone else trying to be a business success? Surely Luke has enough clients that he does not have to poach more from other hardworking people.

Bennet was still thinking about what Jeremy had told her during their date as she climbed the three flights of stairs to her apartment and let herself inside. She knew Luke was capable of being a jerk and she should have left it at that, but there was also another element to the evening that was nagging at her. She could not help herself from wondering why Jeremy felt the need to bring the topic of Luke Dawlton up in conversation in the first place. The truth was he seemed eager to relay to her how horribly Luke had treated him and to see her reaction, but she reasoned he might have genuinely been concerned for her and wanted to warn her to be careful around him.

While she should not have cared, the truth was Bennet was curious to know more about what had happened between the two of them. Still, what Jeremy had shared was enough to sour the evening for her.

Exhausted, Bennet decided to call it an early night and having gotten into bed, just as she was about to drift off to sleep her last thought was how ironic it was that tonight she had found herself on a date with an otherwise seemingly nice guy full of potential and yet she had spent the evening during and after unable to escape thoughts of Luke Dawlton. She would be relieved when this exhibition was over and she could be done with Luke once and for all.

CHAPTER FIFTEEN

"So, what do you think?" Bennet asked Stella as they sat across from each other at one of their favorite coffee shops on Saturday morning. She had been so busy the last two days that this was her first opportunity to fill her friend in on what Jeremy had told her during their date earlier in the week.

"Believe me I know Luke Dawlton is capable of being a jerk, but to mess with a person's career like that? You've got to admit that's pretty cruel."

"Yes, it is," Stella replied. "Providing it's true."

"You don't think it is? Why would Jeremy lie?" Bennet asked before taking a sip of her vanilla latte.

"I'm not saying that he's lying. There would be no way for me to know whether what he is saying is true or not. I just think you need to consider that he brought the subject of Luke up without you asking about it. That's kind of odd isn't it? I mean it's not really first date conversation."

"I guess you're right," Bennet replied, sounding unconvinced.

Since her date, she had gone over and over what Jeremy had said, and the more she did the more she felt sympathy for him. She struggled to understand how someone could be that mean, but why would Jeremy lie about it? The truth was, other than her most recent conversation with Luke, there was no denying he had been more than a little unpleasant so it was not that inconceivable that he could be as awful as Jeremy described.

"Okay, so let's leave Luke out of it for a minute. Other than the whole Luke thing, did you enjoy your evening with Jeremy?"

"He was nice."

"Was he a good kisser?" Stella asked. "Did anything else good happen?"

"Oh please," Bennet said, rolling her eyes.

A relentless Stella continued with her questioning, unwilling to let her friend off the hook. "Really, how was the date? Did you like him?"

"I said, he was nice. The date went fine," Bennet replied, sounding less than convinced.

"But?"

"But nothing."

Stella stared with an expression that implied she was waiting for her friend to elaborate.

Letting out a sigh, Bennet began to explain. "Seriously, the date was fine and if you must know the kiss was fine too. I mean the earth didn't move or anything but it was nice. Still, if you're asking if we're ready to go shopping for an apartment together and to start discussing what our children's names will be; I don't think so."

Stella laughed.

"I mean, what can you really learn from one date anyway," Bennet continued. "It's nowhere near enough time to get to know anything real. Everyone's on their best behavior and trying not to say the wrong thing. It's not until weeks, sometimes even months later when you find out the truly horrible stuff like he has an unhealthy obsession with his mother or he always sleeps with his socks on."

Stella shook her head. "Yeah, you've had both of those type of guys in your long list of bad boyfriends. God, do you remember that guy you dated who collected dolls?"

Bennet smiled. "That would be Christopher. And they were action figures not dolls thank you very much. He was still better than the one you dated who liked to let his three dachshunds shower with him."

"Yeah, I should have known right then that Simon and I were never meant to be," Stella replied as they both burst out laughing, causing an elderly couple at a nearby table to shoot them a dirty look.

Once she had managed to compose herself again, Stella added, "Well, you must have had a nice enough time with Jeremy if you've agreed to go out with him again tonight."

Bennet did not know why she had agreed to a second date. If he had not called again she would not have lost any sleep over it. The truth was, there was something nagging at her about their date which was preventing her from fully letting herself engage with Jeremy. It was hard to articulate to Stella or for that matter even to herself, but it was just that he seemed a little too eager to flatter. If it was possible for one to be so, Bennet thought he was just a little too charming. More than that, she had spent more time over the last few days thinking about what Jeremy had said about Luke Dawlton than about Jeremy himself. His comments had come out of the blue and he seemed too willing to describe to her all about how Luke had done him wrong. Why even bring the subject up, she had wondered more than once.

However, this morning Bennet had made the mistake of picking up the phone when her mother called. It had been the first time they had spoken since the gala as Bennet had done her best for the last week to dodge her calls.

True to form, after a quick greeting, Adelaide Reynolds had started in with her usual criticisms expressing her general dismay over her daughter's behavior towards both Milton Winer and herself at the gala. The conversation had the effect of allowing her mother to get into Bennet's head which led to her feeling insecure about spending another Saturday evening alone. So, when twenty minutes after ending her completely demoralizing talk with her mother, Jeremy called to ask if he could see her again Bennet decided to give him one more chance. She told him about an art gallery opening she was planning on attending later in the evening and when she asked if he would like to join her he had readily accepted.

"I think you should give me some credit here," Bennet began. "I am trying to take your advice and not overanalyze every little thing to death or be too quick to give up on something. I figured there isn't any harm in a second date."

Stella laughed. "Especially if he's as easy on the eyes as you say."

"Seriously, is that all you think about?"

"Well you have to admit that it's important."

Bennet smiled. "I figure, what's wrong with a little carefree fun. I'm tired of overthinking everything. Maybe he will turn out to be a nice guy."

Taking another sip of her coffee, Stella added, "Well if you want my advice..."

"I'm sorry, I don't remember saying I did," Bennet said laughing.

Smiling, but ignoring her friend, Stella continued, "If you want my advice, I say go out with Jeremy. Do something wild for a change and channel your inner Stella. But I'm being serious about this bit here; just do me a favor and don't be so quick to completely write off Luke Dawlton."

"We'll see," Bennet replied. "All I know for sure is that considering I only met Luke Dawlton a few weeks ago and I really don't know anything about him, he seems to be playing way too big a role in my life."

Chapter Sixteen

Nine hours later, despite the lukewarm attitude she had conveyed to Stella about her evening plans, Bennet found herself enjoying walking into one of the leading Soho art galleries on Jeremy Burlow's arm. She was usually stuck attending these functions with coworkers as part of her job which greatly decreased the enjoyment of the event. But tonight she was with someone who had come for no other reason than to be with her and it felt nice for a change.

Gallery openings in Manhattan are a completely different experience from visitors attending an exhibition on any other day of the show's run. As much as art viewing and buying opportunities, an opening was an event where people went specifically to be seen. Bennet usually tried to avoid them altogether and, when it was not required by her job, she would prefer to quietly view gallery exhibitions on her own on lazy Saturday afternoons or on her lunch break during work. Without a crowd, she could spend her time looking at the artworks instead of being jammed into the space where she was forced to take part in small talk with people she barely knew.

Despite her preferred method of viewing exhibitions Bennet knew there was no other place she would possibly rather have been this evening than here at the opening, showing her support for her friend, Terrance Lorder. An up-and-coming artist, he was recently branded one of the city's top young artists under thirty to watch by one of the industry's key art publications and had begun to make a name for himself with his large-scale sculptures made of found and recycled materials.

Bennet had known Terrance for years. A former classmate of hers from art school, they had instantly clicked during orientation at the start of their freshman year. Bennet was proud of the fact that they had remained friends even as their paths went in different art world directions and she was actively trying to support his work by having a piece brought up for consideration at the museum's next quarterly acquisitions meeting early next year.

While there was no question of her being here tonight to show her support for Terrance, Bennet had only been in the gallery a few minutes before the intensity of the crowd began to make her feel claustrophobic and she had to work hard to fight the urge to turn around and walk right out of the building. Fortunately, as she knew it would be, the art was amazing and she quickly became so distracted looking at one of Terrance's pieces that she almost managed to forget about the crowd.

At the moment her focus had been directed to an impressively robust and colorful, five-foot sculpture constructed of painted car fenders and other pieces of crumpled metal. Bennet had just begun to explain the piece to Jeremy when she heard a voice cry out.

"Finally, Ms. Reynolds is here."

At the sound of her name, Bennet turned to see Terrance waving to her from across the room. Just the sight of her friend made Bennet smile. She had always admired Terrance's slight flair for the dramatic and wonderfully eccentric style as well as his refreshing ability to somehow not take life too seriously and she honestly could not imagine her life without him in it.

Waving back at him, Bennet watched as Terrance began to cross the room making his way towards her. Sensing his importance, the crowd collectively began to part to allow him to pass; an action so theatrical that it caused Bennet to think of the scene from that old Bible movie where Moses crosses the Red Sea. While he would never admit it, Bennet knew that Terrance loved every minute of the spotlight this would direct towards him and such a scene served to elevate his importance and emphasize for anyone who might not know it that he was the star of the evening.

"There's my favorite curator," Terrance said as he made a show of giving her a big hug. "And just who is it you've brought with you this evening?" he asked, looking at Jeremy.

Bennet could not help but laugh. Terrance was one of those people who on the surface seemed one way, a mixture of elitism and fantasy that was the embodiment of the city art scene; but she knew that was simply a character he was playing. The truth was that beneath his exterior veneer was a sensitive soul who was one of the kindest and truest people she had ever met. Very few people were privy to that side of him however, and she absolutely treasured him for the unique creature he was.

"This is my friend Jeremy Burlow."

"Nice to meet you," Jeremy said as he extended his hand to Terrance. "Your artwork is ah, I guess interesting is the right word here."

Bennet cringed knowing just what her friend was thinking about her date's attempt at art critique.

"Well thank you," Terrance said giving Bennet a quick look that let her know he was less than impressed with Jeremy's response.

Despite the outgoing persona he often displayed in public settings such as this, Terrance could not abide insincerity. If one did not understand his art, he would prefer the person say so outright or even better say nothing at all rather than what Jeremy had just done which was to recite trite answers that had no weight behind them. Still, Bennet knew Terrance well enough to know on a night like this, in his gallery opening mode, he would willingly soak up any attention he received; sincere or not.

Just then Bennet caught sight of a tall man with gray hair and thick black spectacles clad in a pencil-thin black suit heading towards them. She recognized him as the gallery's director, a cold man who had a reputation in art circles for his arrogance and aloofness, but who she also knew had a good track record in terms of his ability to elevate his clients' careers. Terrance was fortunate to have secured his representation.

A dealer was always about business and so, as he approached them, Bennet knew he was on a mission to ensure Terrance made the rounds of the important people that evening. When he reached them, Terrance made the introductions at which point Bennet was able to witness once more one of the things that never ceased to amaze her about art world interactions. Upon first look, the director had nothing for her but a polite yet indifferent nod, but then when Terrance said her name and that she was the senior curator at the Northhom Museum his entire demeanor changed.

"Ah, Ms. Reynolds," he began with eagerness in his voice. "Of course. I thought I recognized you, but there are just so many people here tonight one can never be sure. I am so glad you were able to attend this evening. Please look around and if there is anything I can help you with it would be my pleasure to do so."

Now Bennet knew there had not been even the slightest stirring of recognition when he first saw her. Rather it was the knowledge of where she worked and the buying potential that such a position brought with it that made her a contact the director would now make every effort to nurture. She also knew for certain there would be a follow up call from him to her at the museum next week in the hopes of beginning a more intense dealer relationship between his gallery and the museum's curatorial department. It was all part of the game, and as Bennet thanked him for his offer of assistance, she also praised Terrance's work which pleased both the artist and dealer.

Knowing he was about to be dragged away, Terrance added, "Look around, and don't you dare think of leaving without speaking with me again first."

"Of course. Seriously Terrance, these pieces are amazing," Bennet replied.

Just as he was about to turn away, Terrance surprised her by whispering in Bennet's ear what she knew he had been dying to ask.

"Who's the new guy? I bet he couldn't tell a Michelangelo from a cheap piece of hotel room art. Seriously, what bad dating app did you find him on? I hope for your sake he has some real hidden depths because he is certainly no wordsmith."

Doing her best not to encourage him, Bennet simply smiled as a pleased Terrance gave her a wink before heading off into the crowd with his dealer.

Jeremy grabbed two white wines from the tray of a passing waiter and handed one to Bennet.

"Well we are certainly in your world now," Jeremy said as they found themselves once more on their own. "I must say I am impressed."

"Don't be," Bennet replied. "Nothing is real; everything going on tonight has been orchestrated purely for show. It's nothing more than theater really."

Savoring a sip of her wine, Bennet smiled before adding, "In fact, I would wager a good seventy percent of the people here have no interest in the art on view or even know what the artist looks like. I would much rather be here when the gallery is empty. That way you can really look at the pieces and not have to be interrupted by the people standing around chatting and taking selfies who don't care one bit about these interesting sculptures."

"That may be, but I was hoping you could show me a few of them now despite the crowds," Jeremy replied.

Pleased with his request, Bennet began to direct Jeremy over to one of the nearby pieces; an impressively sized six-foot sculpture Terrance had constructed out of recycled glass bottles and jars which he had then embedded with tiny LED lights. The lights radiated through the materials and onto the floor in an interesting patterning of colored specks. She had always been fascinated by the sense of movement his pieces could evoke, especially considering the utilitarian objects he used as materials. Many had a sensual quality that she enjoyed which had been the case even with his earliest works from back in art school when his pieces were considerably less refined.

While it had only taken a few moments for Bennet to become completely engaged with the sculpture, Jeremy it seemed was far less interested despite his request that she show him some of the works she liked best. It had not escaped her notice that since arriving at the gallery several women had been looking in his direction, and now as she moved her focus away from one of the works she realized Jeremy was no longer standing next to her, but was instead chatting with a young woman.

Tall, thin, with long blonde hair and equally long legs, the significantly younger woman was making quite the show of hanging on to whatever words Jeremy was saying. It also did not escape Bennet's notice that he in turn seemed to be thoroughly enjoying her efforts. Bennet watched as Jeremy leaned into her and said what one must assume to have been an extremely clever witticism based on the blonde's reaction and how she touched his arm in a flirtatious gesture as if he was the most interesting person in the room.

Annoyed, Bennet walked over to them and made a show of clearing her throat causing Jeremy to look at her once more.

"Ah, here you are," he said guiltily in the voice of a man who had clearly been caught in the act of doing something he should not have been doing.

"Where else would I be?" Bennet asked, liking the idea of seeing him squirm. She felt suddenly compelled by some repressed middle school code of behavior to make clear to this twiggy female that she was Jeremy's date for the evening.

Attempting to recover from any social misstep he may have committed, Jeremy rushed to explain, "Bennet this is Julie Smythe. She was just telling me how she is in art school and while interning at the moment at this gallery, what she really wants is to gain some experience in the museum world. She loves the Northhom Museum so I thought you two should meet."

What is it with the art world that ensures gallery interns all look like cheerleading prom queens? Bennet wondered.

"You managed to learn all that in just a few minutes; I'm impressed," Bennet replied her lack of enthusiasm clear in her tone.

Bennet had no doubt that the woman had zero interest in applying to work at the museum. And even if she did and it was not simply a flimsy excuse on Jeremy's part to lend a sense of altruism to his flirting, Bennet was certainly not going to bend over backwards to help her obtain one of the coveted positions in the Northhom's intern program; not for someone with the poor social graces to hit on someone else's date.

"Well Miss Smythe," Bennet began making a point of heavily emphasizing the formality of her use of the woman's last name, "we have a fine internship program that is administered through our Education Department. You should go online and check it out."

Jeremy was quick to sense Bennet's irritation and to note the coldness of her reply, although to be fair she had made no attempt to disguise it. Wishing to improve the situation and worm himself back into Bennet's good graces he quickly added, "I guess that is what you should do then, Julie. Good luck with everything."

Once the intern had walked away, but not before giving Jeremy one last brief but pointed look, he turned to Bennet and added, "There is so much art I need you to explain to me Bennet."

"Really, I thought maybe you had found other things you found more interesting than the artwork this evening," Bennet replied.

Jeremy smiled. "Maybe we could start with this piece here," he began, choosing to ignore Bennet's comment and hoping to get their date back on track. "I am just dying to know how someone goes about making such a fascinating piece."

While annoyed with what had just happened, Bennet decided to give Jeremy a break and allowed herself to be directed over to the sculpture. It was obvious that he hoped he had gotten her to move on from any need to discuss his conversation with the young blonde and yet for Bennet, she found she could not stop thinking about how slick he had just been. Even though Jeremy now seemed focused and eager to try to show an interest in the art around them, she found her radar was up and she was less than impressed.

Firmly planted in front of one of Terrance's sculptures, Jeremy had begun peppering her with questions in an attempt to soothe any bruised feelings. As he did so he moved his hand to rest on the small of Bennet's back.

Still irritated at his behavior, Bennet was not willing to let it be that easy and so stepped forward slightly so that his hand no longer connected with her before beginning her discussion of the piece.

"In this sculpture, I just love how he lets the metal speak for itself. See here how he guides the shape of the…"

"My God, I think I see Luke Dawlton over there," Jeremy said, interrupting her. "Well that will bring the party mood down for sure."

A wave of nervousness rushed through Bennet at the mention of his name. Looking over to where Jeremy had indicated, she caught Luke staring at her. Their eyes locked for a brief moment before he quickly looked away; not, however, before she could see the flash of hostility in his expression.

Jeremy once more reached out to her, putting his hand on her arm in an attempt to guide her to the next sculpture. But while he asked her more questions, Bennet found it almost impossible to concentrate on what he was saying.

What are the odds that Luke Dawlton would be here tonight? Bennet wondered before mentally chiding herself for even thinking it. He had every right to be at an art opening and Bennet reminded herself it should not matter to her one bit if he were in the gallery or not. She was here with Jeremy after all.

Forcing herself to bring her attention back to her date, Bennet was about to start discussing the merits of the next sculpture when Jeremy's phone beeped alerting him to an incoming text message.

Without a second's hesitation Jeremy reached into his jacket pocket, pulled it out, and silently read the message on his screen.

"I don't believe it. I am so sorry, Bennet but I am going to have to leave."

Bennet must have looked like she was struggling to understand what Jeremy had just said as he quickly added, "I hate to do this, really I do, but I have to dash off. There is an emergency at work."

"It's Saturday night. What kind of emergency happens at this hour?" Bennet asked as she made no effort to hide her annoyance.

"I know, I can't believe it myself, but it happens sometimes," Jeremy replied looking upset at the interruption of their evening. "I would normally try and put it off until Monday but an important client is having a bit of a meltdown and I need to go to the office and retrieve a file so I can call him back."

Bennet did not know what to think. She had no reason to doubt what Jeremy was saying, but more than anything she suddenly found herself very tired and disappointed in the entire evening.

"Well, if you have no other choice then I guess you have to go."

"I really am sorry," Jeremy said, sounding and looking both frustrated and contrite for abruptly having to now prematurely end the evening. "How about you let me make it up to you tomorrow?"

Bennet was in no mood to think about tomorrow.

"No, it's fine. You better go."

"No, I insist," Jeremy replied. "How about we meet up for brunch tomorrow. There is this new restaurant in the Village I have been dying to try. I'll text you the details later tonight. What do you say?"

Then flashing her a smile which reminded Bennet of just how charming and handsome he was, Jeremy added, "Unless of course you wanted me to stop by later at yours for a drink? I should be done with this client nonsense in a few hours."

Bennet knew exactly what a drink in a few hours in her apartment was code for but in this moment, as annoyed and disappointed as she was at the thought of having their date cut short, all she wanted to do was go home, alone.

"Maybe brunch. I don't know. I'll give you a call tomorrow."

Jeremy clutched his chest in dramatic fashion. "You are breaking my heart Ms. Reynolds. But I guess I will have to settle for whatever I can get and count myself lucky."

Despite herself Bennet found that she was smiling once more.

He is smooth and he's definitely got nerve. I'll give him that.

"Would you like me to get you a cab before I leave?" Jeremy had taken her expression as a positive sign and was clearly pleased at what he believed to be an indicator that he had managed to get back in her good graces.

"No, you're fine. I really should look around a bit more. There are a few pieces I haven't had a chance to see yet and besides, I still need to talk to Terrance again before I leave. You go."

"Okay, but I will be looking forward to your call tomorrow," Jeremy replied. Then unexpectedly, he gave her a quick kiss before turning and heading for the gallery's exit.

Bennet was surprised and slightly taken aback by his expression of public affection. It was not so much the kiss itself that had given her pause but rather it was the fact that before he had done so she saw him look across the gallery in the direction of where Luke was standing.

For a moment, as Jeremy was in the process of stranding her in the gallery for his work emergency, Bennet had managed to forget that Luke Dawlton was also in the gallery. Now, however it was all she could think about.

Did Luke see our kiss? she wondered before asking herself why it would matter if he had.

Jeremy's actions had annoyed her as much as his having to leave so abruptly. In fact, a good deal of his behavior since entering the gallery had been rubbing her the wrong way and Bennet found herself growing tired of what was quickly becoming a disappointing evening. The fact that Luke was here only made things more complicated.

Despite wanting nothing more than to go home, Bennet needed to make sure she saw every one of Terrance's sculptures as she knew he would call her, probably tomorrow morning, expecting a full accounting of what she thought of his show. He valued her opinion just as she did his, and so she wanted to be able to give him a rave review which meant her having seen everything he had on exhibit.

Knowing the task called for fortifications, Bennet helped herself to another glass of white wine from one of the reception tables before beginning to move around the gallery taking one last look at every work. Desiring to avoid any accidental interaction with Luke Dawlton, Bennet was being extra careful to make sure she was nowhere near him before moving on to each new piece. The last thing she needed tonight was to have to talk to him especially after she now found herself pathetically alone.

Bennet had not seen Luke since the night of the gala but, per Katherine and Brent's directive, she had sent him regular email updates on the progress relating to the exhibition. He had been true to his pledge to try and keep things professional between them and so thankfully these exchanges, albeit brief, had been perfectly congenial without mention of anything other than issues relating to his aunt's collection.

Still, as the days passed in her office working on Vivian Winthrop's exhibition, Bennet had been surprised by how often her thoughts turned from the art to Luke as she tried to reconcile the horrible things that Jeremy had said about him on their date with what she knew of him. She wondered how and why he would be so cruel and his presence in her thoughts had made her uncomfortable as she knew there was really no logical reason she should be focusing on him. While she tried to reassure herself that she was thinking about him because they had to work together and she wanted to do a good job on this exhibition, she knew if that were only it then she had no reason to be bothered by how mean he had been to Jeremy.

What was even more unsettling was the knot in her stomach which had formed when she first noticed him here tonight. She had not expected to see him but why be as bothered as she was? Bennet had to admit, it was not only his presence in the gallery but also the fact that he was standing next to a beautiful woman who seemed to be listening intently to whatever he was saying. While not the same woman as the night of the gala she was equally attractive and possessed the physical attributes of being rail thin, big breasted and leggy; three things Bennet was painfully aware she was not.

It is none of your business who he's with; even if she is a six foot tall blonde-haired goddess who looks like she just stepped off a runway, Bennet reasoned, mad at herself for even caring about Luke's date.

Still if it did not matter, Bennet wondered why she could not hide the sense of disappointment she felt when she stole another glance across the room and saw Luke whisper something to his date which she received with a smile. The whole scene made her annoyed at Jeremy all over again for leaving her stranded alone at the gallery like some kind of loser.

Forcing herself to continue her final walk around the exhibition, ten minutes later Bennet had stopped in front of the last work she had yet to see. It was one of Terrance's smaller sculptures which had been positioned on a pedestal and tucked away in the back corner of the room.

As she stepped back to allow herself a better look, Bennet felt herself bump into someone.

"Oh, excuse me," she said automatically.

Turning around, to her surprise and dismay, Bennet realized it was Luke. Instantly aware that their bodies were now so close that there was less than an inch of space between them, she had to strain her neck to look up and see his face. Her first thought as she did was how good he looked, something she instantly hated herself for thinking.

"I thought that was you," Luke said by way of a greeting.

Bennet was quick to note the lack of friendliness in his tone and that something in his voice seemed almost strained.

"Uh-huh; it's me," Bennet replied while mentally berating herself for not having something more engaging to say as an opening phrase.

"Nice to see you, Luke," she added, attempting to recover. "Considering just a few weeks ago we had never met, we do seem to run into each other quite a bit." Bennet knew she was beginning to ramble but she could not help herself.

Why couldn't you have just stayed across the room?

"Yes, well this is an art gallery so it's not so strange I would think," Luke answered coldly.

Do you always have to sound so smug? Bennet thought as she noticed how easy it was for him to revert back to the jerk she had first met on the street several weeks ago.

Tired, and not wanting to engage with him any further and risk losing her temper yet again, she quickly added, "Yes, I guess you're right. I'll leave you to look at the sculpture."

"Are you here on behalf of the museum?" Luke asked, the words rushing out as he attempted to stop her from leaving. While he had purposely come across the room to talk to her, as he stood in front of her now, Luke actually seemed unsure of what to say next.

"No. Purely a social outing tonight. I'm friends with the artist," Bennet replied somewhat nervously as she glanced across the room rather than look him in the eyes.

"Well, I should let you go. I wouldn't want to keep you from your date," Luke said coldly. He had misinterpreted Bennet's gaze at the other side of the gallery as an attempt to locate Jeremy, an action that had frustrated him more than he knew it should.

"My what?" Confused, it took Bennet a moment to realize that he meant Jeremy.

He had seen us. I wonder if he saw the kiss?

Bennet's mind was full of conflicting thoughts as the brief interaction had already completely unnerved her. But his attitude quickly replaced her worries with angrier thoughts.

What difference does it make if he did see us? It's none of his damn business who I'm with tonight.

Luke is the one who has been awful to Jeremy so he doesn't get the right to think anything about me being here with him, Bennet thought as her anger towards him grew by the second.

"Actually I'm sure I'm keeping you from your date," Bennet replied, matching the coldness of his tone as the sudden image of the beautiful woman she had seen him with earlier popped into her mind.

The moment she spoke, Bennet instantly regretted her words. The last thing she wanted was for Luke Dawlton to think she noticed or cared who he was with this evening.

"I'm sorry, my what?" Luke asked, the confusion clear in his voice. "Oh, you mean Gabriella? No. You are not keeping me... I mean she is not my date or rather yes, I brought her here but she is the wife of one of my firm's largest clients. They are both here tonight as my guests."

Shit, shit, shit!

"Oh, my mistake," Bennet stammered as she was struck by the thought of how typical it was of her life that she could not have spotted the woman's husband standing with her when she had first noticed Luke speaking with her earlier.

Then to make matters worse, Bennet found herself trying to explain.

"Well you're not keeping me either. I mean Jeremy had to leave; something with work."

As Luke simply stared at her, Bennet knew the last thing she wanted was to have to go into details about how Jeremy had left her stranded alone at the opening as she knew how pathetic that would make her look.

Frazzled, Bennet said the first thing that popped into her head. "He said you know each other from way back. You even had business dealings a long time ago."

Luke visibly stiffened. When he next spoke, the tone of his voice had altered completely. While before he had seemed annoyed, now he seemed incensed.

"I can assure you Jeremy Burlow is no friend of mine."

Looking at her with an expression of haughty judgement, he added, "To tell you the truth, I am surprised he would be a friend of yours. I would have thought you had more sense than that and that you were a better judge of character. But then again, I don't really know you at all do I?"

For a few seconds Bennet found she could do nothing but stare at him. *Did he really just say that to me? Who the hell does he think he is?*

Both his words and the way he delivered them, instantly reminded Bennet of the arrogant Luke Dawlton she had first encountered and so once more, as had become their pattern, he had managed to trigger her anger, causing her to instantly react without thinking about what she was doing.

"You're right; you don't know me at all. A fact that I assure you I am in no hurry to change. I fail to see what business it is of yours who I am with. More importantly I couldn't care less what you think of me.

"You just stand there in your suit, looking all smug and thinking you are better than everyone else but I can assure you you're not and I will thank you not to presume to comment on my sense."

Bennet knew she was speaking without considering what she was actually saying but in the moment she was so angry she could not stop herself.

"You are certainly in no position to judge anyone's character, not after the way you treated Jeremy. Now he's a man with both sense and class. If he can move past whatever attempt you made to steal his client from him, I fail to see why you can't at least be civil to him."

Now it was Luke's turn to look shocked. In that moment he believed that if she had actually struck him it would have had less of a sting than her words. For a moment he simply stood there staring and leaving Bennet to begin to wonder if he had even heard what she had told him.

But then, when he finally spoke his voice was ice cold, making it clear he had heard every word. "It's almost unbelievable really; once more you have managed to speak before you have time to think about what you are saying. I have never met a woman less able to censure herself than you."

Knowing he should stop talking but unable to help himself, Luke continued, "I would appreciate it if you not embarrass yourself by commenting on things you know nothing about. Clearly you and Jeremy Burlow are made for each other. Now if you will excuse me, I have people waiting for…"

"How wonderful," Terrance exclaimed, his appearance surprising them both so much that Bennet jumped slightly, almost causing her to spill her wine.

"Two of my favorite people together at my exhibition. I do love when good things happen to good people, and by good people I of course mean me."

Having appeared unnoticed in front of them as he had just done, Terrance must have realized that he had interrupted a heated conversation. The animosity was so obvious between them it was almost palpable.

Wanting to diffuse the situation, as Luke and Bennet remained speechless and glaring at each other, Terrance continued to speak as if nothing was wrong.

"Until now I had not connected it, but of course Bennet you would know Luke because of the Winthrop exhibition. Luke, isn't Bennet just the most amazing curator? Believe me when I say you could not have a finer person working with your aunt's art collection."

Luke made a huff of disapproval.

Terrance recognized that the look on his friend's face at Luke's response made it clear she was about to lose it. Hoping to prevent this, he quickly added, "I think Bennet is just marvelous. Do you know she was a spitfire even back when we were in art school together? I sometimes wonder how we managed to stay only friends."

While Bennet should have been wondering how it was possible that Terrance knew Luke, at the moment she could think of nothing but fighting back the overwhelming urge she had to throw her wine directly in his face.

"Yes, well, you and I would never have worked out Terrance and I will be happy to tell you why since Mr. Dawlton here has been so quick to enlighten me to my personal defects this evening," Bennet snapped.

Sending a withering stare in Luke's direction, Bennet continued, "It is because of my poor judgement in the opposite sex, my inability to control what I say, and my overall lack of sense. Character deficiencies which apparently are so obvious that even arrogant, pompous men whom I barely know can easily identify them. But then at least I'm not the type of person who is so insecure and treats other people so despicably that I will try to stop others from achieving a modicum of success."

Her anger mixing with exhaustion, Bennet suddenly found herself fighting back the urge to cry. She knew she had to get out of this room before she actually screamed. The last thing she wanted to do was make a bigger scene than she already was or do anything that would ruin her friend's big night.

Willing herself to remain calm, Bennet turned to Terrance and gave him a tired smile. "Anyway my darling friend, your show was absolutely wonderful as I knew it would be. I will talk to you later, but suddenly I'm not feeling very much like socializing so I'm going to leave. Congratulations again."

Reaching out to Terrance, Bennet gave him a quick hug before turning away from them without giving Luke so much as a passing glance.

As they both watched her walk away, it was Terrance who first broke the uncomfortable silence.

"Sorry, but I feel like the homely girl left sitting on the bleachers at the school dance. You must tell me what I missed?"

"Nothing worth mentioning," Luke replied curtly.

Unwilling to say anything further on the matter, Luke struggled to regain his composure. When next he spoke, there was a false sense of calm in Luke's voice which was fooling no one.

"Now Terrance, tell me about this piece here. I have not been able to take my eyes off it all night."

"Haven't you?" Terrance asked, clearly referring to the exchange Luke had just had with Bennet.

When Luke refused to respond, Terrance laughed. "Come on, let me show you. Talking about art is my second favorite topic after talking about me."

Despite Terrance's animated description of his sculpture, Luke only pretended to listen as he found he could focus on nothing but his horrible interaction with Bennet. Why had he come here tonight he wondered, as he cursed the fact that everywhere he turned lately she seemed to be there. More than anyone he had ever met, she, it seemed, had an unexplainable power to get his back up and before he knew it he was losing his temper.

Tonight was a perfect example. He was sure he had been the injured party and there was no way he could have helped what happened this evening. He tried his best to rationalize that there would have been no other way to respond but with outrage over the fact that she had actually tried to insinuate that he was somehow the villain when it came to the history between him and Jeremy. Luke tried to comfort himself with the reasoning that if Bennet could date someone like Jeremy Burlow then he had been wrong to have changed his initial impressions of her and to think she was anything more than the irrational crazy woman who had confronted him on the street weeks ago.

This did nothing to stop the disappointment he felt that she would have such a wrong opinion of what had taken place. Certainly his actions tonight would do nothing to disprove all the things he was sure Jeremy had said about him. Angry all over again at what had taken place as well as his inability to control his temper, Luke was surprised to find what upset him most was the fact that it seemed to matter so much what Bennet Reynolds thought of him.

Chapter Seventeen

Feeling as if she were struggling to breathe, Bennet pushed her way out of the gallery as she forced herself to draw in some deep breaths of fresh air. She would not have believed it possible, but right now she was angrier with Luke Dawlton than she had been the first time they met. Once more she found herself wondering what gave him the right to speak to her that way. At least the first time she had approached him she had been in the wrong and while he did not have to be so arrogant about it, he did have a right to be annoyed; but tonight was a completely different story. While they were admittedly forced to work together by unconventional circumstances, theirs was purely a professional relationship. Luke Dawlton had absolutely no business attempting to pass judgment on who she spent time with. It was none of his concern who she dated; not Jeremy Burlow or anyone else for that matter.

Since Jeremy had described Luke at dinner the other night, there was a part of Bennet that had found it difficult to reconcile that version of him with the one she had begun to see emerge. She had acknowledged to herself that she did not know either man well and was willing to forget about it all just to be able to finish the exhibition in peace. But now with the way Luke had behaved tonight, in her mind it all but proved Jeremy's story.

She began to walk down the crowded sidewalk with no clear destination. While still seething in anger over Luke's actions, after a few minutes Bennet was able to compose herself enough to realize she was walking in the direction of Jeremy's apartment. He had told her where he lived earlier this morning when they had made plans to meet, as he had been surprised to find he lived only a few blocks from the gallery. Thinking about Jeremy changed her mood drastically, from one of anger to disappointment as she remembered his having to leave so suddenly. It made her look pathetic to be abandoned by him in front of Luke of all people. But she knew she should be understanding and that he could not help it if he had a work emergency. So, while he might still be out dealing with the matter, if he had arrived back home already then she decided she would stop by and surprise him. She might even stay the night.

Why not have an evening of uncomplicated, no strings attached sex? Bennet reasoned. She knew it was what Jeremy wanted when he had suggested he stop by her apartment later for a drink when he finished with his client. It was a possibility she considered as she walked along while trying to ignore the nagging thought at the back of her mind that her anger with Luke might be influencing this impromptu decision.

Bennet had even begun to fantasize about what Jeremy might be like in bed as she rounded the corner and reached the street on which his apartment building was located. Full of anticipation, in an instant her excitement turned to shock as she saw Jeremy at the top of his steps locked in an embrace with none other than Julie Smythe, the trampy blonde from the gallery.

Without the proof right before her eyes, Bennet would never have believed that he could ditch her at the opening for a random hookup or how quickly he would have had to have moved in the short time they were talking at the gallery to arrange the rendezvous. Still, the disgustingly passionate kiss they were in the process of sharing left Bennet no way to misinterpret what was happening.

Feeling the crushing weight of disappointment mixed with embarrassment settle over her, all Bennet wanted to do was to leave before either of them noticed her presence. Backing up, she started to turn away when she tripped and stumbled into two metal garbage cans which, to her horror, fell over with a loud banging sound and began to roll along the sidewalk.

"Dammit," she muttered.

Distracted by the noise, Jeremy looked over in time to see her stumbling to pick up the cans.

"Bennet?"

Unable to find any words, she simply glared at him before righting herself and beginning to hurry away.

On instinct, Jeremy began to chase after her.

"Bennet wait," he cried, as he reached out and, grabbing her arm, pulled her round to face him. "I didn't realize you would be stopping over. If I had, I would have…"

Wrenching her arm free of Jeremy's grasp, she cut him off, "You would have what? You would have waited to screw the blonde intern until some other night? My God, you just met her an hour ago."

The words were spewing out of Bennet's mouth as if it were poison she was trying to expel from her body.

"We've only been on a few dates. You can't really have thought I wouldn't see other women."

As he had made his statement, Bennet noted that Jeremy had the audacity to give her a patronizing smile as if to imply she was the one who was somehow overreacting.

For a moment Bennet actually thought she might throw up as a wave of disgust washed over her. Then, just as quickly, the feeling morphed into one of burning rage.

"Don't flatter yourself. You can sleep with whoever the hell you like. I just assumed you would at least give me the courtesy of not lying to me and abandoning me on our actual date so you could hookup with some other woman on the same night. Don't ever think of calling me again," Bennet added, knowing full well how pathetic she sounded.

Bennet walked away as quickly as she could, never once looking back. As the tears filled her eyes she refused to allow them to spill over, even as she began to berate herself for her stupidity. The further she walked, the more she realized that she was less disappointed than she was embarrassed and angry.

Jeremy Burlow was a jerk, but she had known plenty of jerks. The truth was she did not even care enough about him to worry she would miss him. Rather, it was the way he had lied to her about his needing to leave, and that the twit of an intern had witnessed her embarrassment that made it hurt the way it did.

And then of course to make matters worse, the most humiliating thing was that Luke Dawlton, that infuriating man who had no business to speak to her the way he did tonight, had been right. The thought that she had defended that jerk in front of Luke made her sick. As much as she hated to admit it, she no longer thought Jeremy was telling the truth about Luke. He was a liar, plain and simple and she was glad to be rid of him.

More than anything that had happened tonight, Bennet wished Luke had never seen her with Jeremy.

Having lost her battle with self-control, by the time Bennet reached her building the tears were streaming down her face. Eager to get inside so no one else could witness her humiliation, she slammed her door behind her as she walked into her apartment, kicked off her ridiculously high and extremely uncomfortable shoes, and collapsed in a mess on the hallway floor.

As Daisy bounded over to her, Bennet heard the door to the other apartment on her floor open.

"Are you okay, dear?" a woman called out.

The voice belonged to her neighbor, Mrs. Morateli. A widow in her late seventies, she had lived in her apartment for the past five decades, the first four of which were spent with her husband before his death. While kind, she was equal parts busybody and meddler, and Bennet had spent many an hour trapped either on the landing or seated at the woman's kitchen table drinking tea while she regaled her with the gossip of the building and stories of her past, including her life as a girl growing up in Italy.

Usually Bennet found she enjoyed these conversations. She even tolerated the numerous occasions when their talk veered to her love life or lack thereof. Being old school, Mrs. Morateli could not understand how in her words, "a nice girl like you could still not have a husband. You better hurry up and meet someone before you become an old maid, my dear." But tonight Bennet found that she lacked the patience or strength for her well-intentioned neighbor.

"Yes, I'm fine, Mrs. Morateli. I just stubbed my toe when I walked in," she called out, her voice slightly muffled as it had to travel through her closed door.

"Do you want to come over for some tea or a late-night tipple? I have some brandy."

Despite her mood, Bennet smiled at the use of the word "tipple" as it made it sound like they were back in the 1950s.

"Thank you, Mrs. Morateli, but it's late. I'm really tired but I promise I will stop by tomorrow for a chat."

"Hope you spent tonight with a nice gentleman caller," she prodded.

Actually no. I spent the night with one obnoxious jerk and another lying, cheating ass.

"I had a nice evening, Mrs. Morateli," Bennet lied. "Good night."

"Night, dear."

Hearing Mrs. Morateli shut and bolt her door, Bennet let out a sigh as she closed her eyes. She could have stayed there until morning if it were not for Daisy's pawing at her leg and demanding her attention.

"You don't judge me, do you girl?" Bennet asked, to which Daisy let out a loud meow of agreement.

Getting up, the pair walked into the kitchen where Bennet poured some milk into the cat's bowl and herself a glass of red wine. Then she grabbed her oversized purple fuzzy cardigan from the back of her kitchen stool and put it on, wrapping it around her tightly as much for comfort as for warmth.

Despite everything that had happened tonight, a smile crossed Bennet's lips for just the briefest of seconds at the knowledge of how much her mother hated when she wore what she referred to as that "ridiculously hideous-looking rag." Raising her glass, she gave a silent toast to her mother and the disastrous evening of failed romance which she knew would only help to validate her mother's opinion of her daughter's lack of a love life if she were ever to know the details of what had taken place tonight.

Bennet had planned to wallow in the misery of the evening curled up on the couch, but on her way into her living room space her eyes wandered over to the drawing table in the corner of her apartment. It stood there, a silent reminder of her failures, like a statue erected to her lack of courage and her unwillingness to take risks. A utilitarian object without an owner who would allow it to perform its function, it had become a collection site for magazines and clothes she never seemed to bother to put away.

How many times have I promised that I would sit down and spend a few hours at this table working on my drawings? Bennet wondered as she stared at the table, hating herself.

No wonder Luke Dawlton has such a low opinion of you. He can probably see what a coward you are, Bennet thought in an act of silent self-torture.

Looking at the drawing table, Bennet knew she had no excuse not to be working at it every spare hour she had. A month ago Terrance had even tried to force her hand and push her into creating when he told her about an author friend of his who was working on a children's book and wanted to try out some artists to possibly hire to illustrate for him. Terrance had given him Bennet's name and, based solely on her friend's description of her talent and potential, the author had emailed her a working draft of the story and asked her to get back to him with some sketches.

Bennet had read the story and liked it immediately. It was about a boy who spent the night locked in a zoo and had an amazing adventure as all the animals began to speak to him. She could imagine the characters coming to life and how she would render them on the page. She knew this was the perfect project for her; it had been her desire for so long to be a real artist, and the idea of illustrating a children's book and helping art come alive for young readers was like a dream. And yet something had prevented her from sitting down and working on the drawings. She had easily reasoned that it was due to all the stress at her job. Moreover, the work of the Winthrop exhibition was so demanding that she had little time for anything else at the moment. But deep down Bennet knew it was more than that. She was reluctant to take the risk and just try it.

The truth was, there was a big part of Bennet who was just scared. Until now, the idea of being an artist one day was still a hope but if she submitted her drawings and they were found to be not good enough, then it would be devastating. It would be another thing she had failed at and another way she would disappoint everyone again, including herself.

The author had given her eight weeks to get him some samples. A month had already passed and she had nothing to show for it.

Sure Bennet, blow this chance too, she thought as she curled up on the couch.

Her eyes bloodshot and her face puffy from crying, she allowed herself to remember the image of Jeremy Burlow kissing that horrible blonde.

Good riddance to him.

After taking a sip of her wine and pulling her sweater tighter around her, Bennet could not help but think once more of her exchange with Luke Dawlton. She realized that it bothered her more than anything Jeremy had done. He had no right to speak to her that way and to presume he knew anything at all about her. Still, the look on his face when he called her out for her lack of sense made her more sad than angry. She wished she could say good riddance to him too, but as they still had to work together, she knew that was impossible.

Exhausted as she was, it did not take long for Bennet to fall asleep.

CHAPTER EIGHTEEN

Bennet woke to the sound of her phone doing a vibrating dance across her coffee table. Feeling the early morning sun shining on her as a beam through her window, she realized she had spent the night curled up on her couch; still in her clothes from the night before and with her purple fuzzy sweater wrapped tight around her like a security blanket.

As she slowly emerged from the fog of sleep that was only partly wine induced, she was reminded once more of the humiliation she had suffered the prior evening at the hands of not one, but two men.

While Bennet had zero interest in interacting with anyone at the moment, just to stop the incessant buzzing of her mobile which felt like a jackhammer inside her skull, she made herself read what was now a succession of three text messages; all of which were sent within the last two minutes.

Morning gorgeous.

You up?

Continuing to read, the second text stated:

What was the drama with Luke Dawlton last night?

And seconds later; the most direct text was basically delivered in the form of an order:

I want details.

Call me!

Only Terrance would be texting me with this so early in the morning, Bennet thought as she fired back:

Exhausted.

Have a splitting headache.

I'll catch you up later.

Terrance's reply was almost instantaneous:

No way.

It's not going to be that easy!

Just as Bennet suspected; only a few seconds after she received his last text, her phone rang.

"You can't get rid of me that fast," Terrance said by way of an introduction.

"Well good morning to you," Bennet replied sarcastically.

As she knew Terrance was nearly impossible to resist, Bennet resigned herself to this debrief happening now.

"Give me a minute. I think this conversation calls for coffee," she said with a sigh.

Reluctantly and slowly Bennet got up from the couch and began moving in the direction of her kitchen.

"Why don't you tell me first about how the rest of the opening went after I left."

As Bennet busied herself with making a pot of coffee, Terrance regaled her with details of the night's event. It had been a successful evening with the exhibition having been well received by the critics as the morning papers attested, and he had already sold three works which had pleased his dealer immensely.

Only after he had finished his recap and she had fed Daisy, poured herself a large mug of coffee, and settled down on her couch once more did Bennet finally begin to fill Terrance in on how she had met Luke. She described their spirited interactions thus far and what he had said at the opening that had made her so angry.

Then despite her mortification, she also recounted the events that had taken place outside Jeremy's apartment which caused a fresh wave of humiliation to wash over her.

"Well that's a lot of drama," Terrance said as he attempted to process all she had told him. "First off, let me just say that the Burlow character is not worth your effort no matter how handsome you think he is. A good time is not so hard to find that you have to stoop to his level."

Bennet smiled. "Maybe not for you."

"Please. If you only put some effort into it, you know you would be unstoppable."

"That's debatable," Bennet replied. Letting out a sigh of exhaustion, she continued, "Anyways, moving on; how do you know Luke Dawlton of all people?"

"He handled some investments for my father not long before he died."

Bennet should have guessed as much but Terrance's bohemian lifestyle often caused her to forget that he came from old money and a conservative family.

"I don't want to make you feel any worse than you already do," Terrance continued, "but I feel like I should tell you that from what I know of him, Luke is a really nice guy."

"Well not according to Jeremy. And don't forget how rude he was to me when we first met."

"You chased him down the street like a mad woman all because of a French pastry. I can just picture you accusing him in that way you get when you are all riled up about something; you get so intense and focused. I bet you were scary as hell," Terrance teased, doing his best to lighten the mood.

"I will have you know that I was the picture of dignity and grace," Bennet replied just before she burst into a round of laughter which did nothing to help her pounding headache.

Letting out a long sigh, she added, "I hate that he was right about Jeremy."

"I think what you should really be asking yourself is why Luke cared enough to say something about Jeremy in the first place?"

"That's obvious. He hates Jeremy. They have some kind of history."

"Oh come on, Bennet. I don't think that's it at all." Knowing he had to choose his next words carefully, Terrance added, "Trust me; a person does not get that worked up unless they are at least a tiny bit jealous."

Bennet could just imagine the smug look on Terrance's face.

"Oh please," she said, rolling her eyes.

"Don't you go rolling your eyes at me," Terrance replied, as if he could see right through the phone.

Bennet smiled at how well her friend knew her. "I'm sorry but I don't think you know what you're talking about. You're not exactly an expert on relationships either."

Terrance laughed. "Whatever. Expert or not, jealousy is jealousy and all I'm saying is that Luke Dawlton had a little visit from the green-eyed monster last night."

"Now who's the one being crazy? All I know is he acted like a total jerk and I can't just forget about him because I am stuck having to work with him. I have no choice but to deal with him as I put together this exhibition and now I'm back to not being able to stand the sight of him.

"You don't know how I wish I had never invited Jeremy to the opening. Then I would have avoided all of this. I feel like such an idiot for being wrong about him."

"And all I'm saying is I don't think you should be so quick to write off Luke Dawlton," Terrance countered.

"Careful. Keep talking like that and people will figure out you're a romantic at heart," Bennet teased.

"That's me; a big softie. Now, on to more important things. You need to be distracted. What are you up to today? Come to my studio and we will hang out. We can review all the good press I received this morning from my show."

"You know there's nothing I would like more than to bask in your spotlight for a while but I have a pile of work to do. And later I have to go to dinner at my mother's house with Jane and her family."

"How absolutely awful. What a perfect waste of a Sunday.

"I hope at least the work you're doing includes those illustrations."

"I've got some sketches down," Bennet lied.

"Uh-huh. I'm sure," Terrance replied sounding unconvinced.

"You know you cannot blow this off Bennet. This is your chance. You don't have much more time until the deadline. Don't you dare waste this opportunity."

"Okay, Mom."

"Now you don't have to get mean. You know your mother scares the hell out of me. I think she could make a nun nervous."

Bennet laughed. Terrance was definitely one of the things in her life that her mother struggled to understand. For his part, besides being afraid of her mother, Bennet always felt whenever Terrance and her mother were in the same room together he studied her as if she were some sort of alien species.

Shaking off any thoughts of Bennet's mother, Terrance added, "Well in that case since you're abandoning me after my artistic triumph, I guess I'll be off.

"Remember what I said about Luke Dawlton. He was not that worked up just over some jerk guy who, by the way, knows nothing about art. Don't go all Bennet on me and overthink everything to death."

"I don't know what you mean," Bennet said while wondering why it was everyone seemed to feel the need to tell her that. "Love you. Gotta go."

"Love you too. And finish those illustrations. I mean it," Terrance reminded her before ending the call.

Once alone again, Bennet spent a few minutes thinking about what

Terrance had said. She knew her friend liked to stir up trouble and loved a good drama more than anyone else she knew. Try as she might she could not believe that there was anything more to Luke's words beyond his strong dislike of Jeremy so Terrance was simply trying to wind her up.

Bennet knew it was none of her business but it did not stop her wanting to know what had gone on between the two men. The only thing she knew for certain was whatever had really happened to make the two men despise each other, she had learned enough of Jeremy Burlow on her own in the last twenty-four hours to know his character was not trustworthy or reliable. At least Luke Dawlton had been right about that.

While Luke had been totally wrong to speak to her the way he did and to say the things he said, Bennet could not help wishing she had learned what she now knew about Jeremy earlier so as to have prevented herself from bringing him up to Luke in the first place. After their argument at the gallery she had no idea how they were going to make it through the several more weeks of working together they had left before the exhibition opening.

The rest of Bennet's weekend had been spent in a downward spiral of self-pity and regret. Desperate for any kind of distraction and not wanting to spend any more time thinking about Saturday evening, after ending her phone call with Terrance, she had decided to go to the museum and had spent most of the day working in her office.

Unfortunately, focusing on the Winthrop Collection was all it took to keep Luke Dawlton fresh in her mind. And of course, there was the bitter memory of how her date had ended that evening with her falling over garbage cans and looking the complete loser as she tried to get away from Jeremy and the leggy, blonde intern. The humiliation was still so fresh in her mind that she could not bring herself to tell her sister about it when Jane asked about her date with Jeremy when they were together at their mother's Sunday dinner. Wanting to avoid an analysis of everything she had done wrong, Bennet brushed off her sister's question by telling Jane the date went fine, but that there were not enough sparks for it to go any further. Having accepted the answer, Bennet was forced to listen to Jane's well-intentioned but somewhat insulting encouragement that there were other men out there waiting to be found. Jane had thankfully stopped short of actually telling Bennet there were "other fish in the sea" which in her state may have actually caused Bennet to lose it.

The only saving grace about the entire depressing weekend was that she had never told her mother, who was still annoyed with her over her behavior towards the now infamous Milton Winer, that Jeremy had asked her out. Since her mother did not know about her dates with Jeremy, at least Bennet had been spared her disapproval and what would surely have been the focal point of their Sunday dinner conversation, complete with a lengthy commentary on what she would have considered to be yet another example of her daughter's disastrous love life.

Chapter Nineteen

If Bennet thought the start of a new work week would offer her the opportunity to move past the events of Saturday night, she soon learned she was greatly mistaken. Humiliation it seemed was still on the menu and in a reminder that her professional and personal life were becoming inextricably linked, Monday morning had begun with her being forced to attend a meeting with Katherine and Brent during which they informed her that Vivian Winthrop had decided to keep fifteen of her favorite paintings on display in her home until the week before the exhibition opening.

This decision had seriously complicated Bennet's job. To be able to finalize the layout of the exhibition, it was essential she be able to physically inspect the works and now they would not all be in the museum. Knowing this, Brent had taken it upon himself to schedule a time on Wednesday for Bennet to go to the Winthrop home and look at the paintings. Katherine had then proceeded to inform Bennet that Vivian Winthrop had arranged for Luke to be there with her to oversee her work.

Bennet grew queasy at the mere suggestion that she would have to meet with Luke again so soon. She refused to betray any of her feelings to Katherine or Brent however, and so instead sat quietly throughout the meeting, only speaking when necessary to agree to everything they discussed in the hopes of bringing the conversation to a swift conclusion.

After the meeting ended and Brent was about to leave her office, Katherine asked Bennet to stay back a minute.

"So, how is everything going with the exhibition?" Katherine asked as she fixed Bennet with a hard stare.

"Everything is just fine." Bennet could not help but wonder where the conversation was heading.

Bennet was always uncomfortable when she was forced to be in Katherine's office as the cold, almost clinical appearance of the room seemed to be a reflection of her boss's personality. If someone wanted proof that one's environment could echo one's personality then they need look no further than Katherine's office. At first glance everything seemed perfect with not even a paper clip out of place, but it was staged, part of an image she wanted to project to others. Katherine had taken time to decorate the room with little touches that included a miniature Zen garden on the corner of her desk next to a Tiffany-style lamp and an expensive brown cashmere throw resting on the back of her leather desk chair. Even the framed photograph of her smiling family was an illusion as Bennet knew for a fact that she and her husband, a doctor at one of the city's elite rehab clinics, had been having marital troubles for years and that her seventeen-year-old daughter barely spoke to her. But it was the surface appearance for Katherine that mattered, and here in this office, one would think her life was exactly how she wanted it to be perceived: perfect.

"Are you sure?" Katherine asked with an air of condescension in her voice.

Bennet sighed. "This is not my first exhibition Katherine. I know what I'm doing."

"While it might not be your first exhibition Bennet," Katherine began, throwing her words back in Bennet's face, "you are certainly no expert."

"Well I haven't had any complaints so far. In fact I've had some pretty decent reviews of my previous exhibitions, as you are well aware," Bennet answered, trying her best to stay calm and not rise to Katherine's negative remarks. "They've also driven up the museum's attendance numbers so I'm sure you'd agree that's a good thing."

Katherine smiled. "That may be, but this is a different type of exhibition all together. I am sure Vivian Winthrop had imagined someone more experienced and accomplished than you would be working with her important collection when she made the decision to give this gift to the Northhom Museum."

"And do you know that for a fact? Because if there is an issue on Vivian's part then I should address it with her directly. Or perhaps I could ask Luke Dawlton how she feels," Bennet added, wondering why she had brought his name into the conversation.

"Watch yourself, Bennet. I feel I must warn you that you are not nearly as clever as you think. Theirs is a world that you will never be a part of and do not think that just because you are working with the family on this exhibition that you will be welcomed in."

"I don't know what you mean, Katherine. I'm just doing my job," Bennet replied. "The job, might I add, that you assigned to me."

Bennet knew she had to remain calm and that what Katherine wanted more than anything was for her to lose her cool. If she did lose her temper than her boss would have something to hold against her and bring up with Brent, which was the last thing Bennet needed.

Continuing in her assault, Katherine stared directly at Bennet as she added, "I assure you that Vivian Winthrop will not tolerate your attitude. You would do well to remember that she would not have felt the need to put her nephew on this project if she had had any faith whatsoever in your abilities, especially as I was not able to offer her my assurances that you would be completely up to the task."

Katherine's words were like a slap in the face and Bennet found herself reeling from what she had just heard. If she was to be believed, then Katherine had contributed to Vivian Winthrop's lack of confidence in her work on this project. More than that, Bennet realized that Katherine had wanted her to know that to shake her confidence.

"You screw this up, Bennet, and we might just be forced to rethink your viability in this position," Katherine added as she delivered her final low blow.

Refusing to let Katherine know how much her words had stung, Bennet looked her straight in the eyes and said, "I should thank you. I was confused as to why you were so focused on what I was doing with this exhibition but this little conversation has helped me understand what's really bothering you. You can't stand that I have to work with these people and you have no ability to control my involvement in this project.

"If I've figured it out than you're not as subtle as you think you are. You should be careful because someone might just catch on. Now if you will excuse me," Bennet continued, standing up and heading to the door while doing her best to ignore Katherine's glare, "I have work to do."

Katherine's words were still nagging at Bennet two days later when she was dropped off by a cab at Vivian Winthrop's townhouse.

One of those grand establishments that serve as a vestige to Manhattan's wealthiest, it was an Upper East Side four-story gray stone wonder. Given its occupant, there was a part of Bennet that expected to see two stone gargoyles perched somewhere on the roof looking forebodingly down at her as she approached the house. It would have supported what she was feeling at this moment; a combination of anxiety and dread at the thought of not only having to see Luke again, but because of her task, their having to spend time together as she followed him around his aunt's house inspecting the paintings she had chosen to keep in her home until right before the exhibition. It was a thoughtless decision on Vivian Winthrop's part but as she was the patron and Bennet only the lowly curator there was nothing she could do to prevent it.

Having walked up the front steps, as she tentatively employed the use of the ornate golden knocker, fashioned in the shape of a lion's head in the center of the solid oak door, Bennet tried to call upon the resolve she knew she would need for the uncomfortable situation in which she now found herself. She had spent time thinking about it over the last two days since she was informed by Katherine and Brent that she would have to do this horrible task but she still had absolutely no idea how she was supposed to act around Luke or what he might say given their last disastrous encounter at the gallery opening. Just the thought of seeing him made her angry all over again. It was an anger that was mixed with an overwhelming sense of embarrassment and nervousness, all of which at the moment had resulted in making her as stressed as she had ever been.

Eventually she had to be content with reminding herself that it was her job to examine and assess these works so she could put together her exhibition, and she was not going to let Luke Dawlton's arrogance or opinions about her impact her ability to do her job. She promised herself she would remain absolutely professional and would not say anything to him unless it directly related to the artworks.

Bennet's knock was answered by a young woman whose uniform made it clear she was a housekeeper.

"Hello. My name is Bennet Reynolds. I have an appointment with Mrs. Vivian Winthrop."

The woman motioned that Bennet should step inside. "Please wait here," she ordered, barely making eye contact before disappearing down a long corridor.

As Bennet stood alone in the large foyer, she took in the grandeur of her surroundings. A round, white marble table rested in the center of the room, which matched the similarly colored marble staircase to her left. On the other side of the stairs she could see into an open room—a lavishly furnished parlor complete with a baby grand piano in the far corner. The whole scene looked as if it belonged in an architectural magazine, and Bennet realized it probably had been photographed for that exact purpose in the past. As a child whenever she would travel into the city with her parents from their home in Brooklyn, she would look at houses like this in wonder, creating stories about the lives of the inhabitants. Yet even her active childhood imagination could never have brought to life someone such as Vivian Winthrop.

The sound of heels clicking on the floor pulled Bennet back from her thoughts as she looked down the long corridor to the right of the stairs where a woman was walking towards her. In her late fifties, she was wearing a dark green pantsuit with a crisp, white blouse beneath which reminded Bennet of the outfits worn by the wives of old conservative politicians; all that was missing was a paisley pashmina wrapped around her shoulders and tied at a knot in the middle of her chest. The severe expression on this woman's face was made more pronounced by the way she had fashioned her graying hair into such a tight bun that it made Bennet's head ache just to look at it.

"Ms. Reynolds," the woman said in a tone that was more command than statement while she simultaneously gave her a quick once over that implied she was less than impressed. "I am Nora Mason, Mrs. Winthrop's personal secretary. She asked me to escort you around this afternoon and guide you to each of the paintings you need to see."

"I'm sorry," a confused Bennet began, "but I thought Mr. Dawlton would be here to work with me."

"Yes, well, he informed Mrs. Winthrop that he was being called out of town unexpectedly for a few days and did not know if he would be back in time to keep this appointment. So now she has had to rearrange my schedule so I could assist you. I can assure you that it is a great inconvenience." The last words were uttered in such a way as to imply this was somehow Bennet's fault.

"Well, I would be fine on my own," Bennet offered. "If you just point out where the paintings are hanging I can review them myself."

Nora Mason gave a slight but distinct huff.

"I am afraid that will not be possible," she said, her voice dripping with condescension. "Mrs. Winthrop cannot be expected to just allow people to wander freely throughout her home."

Bennet was mortified that she was being treated as if she were a stranger who could not be trusted instead of the curator of one of New York's finest museums. More than that, while she should have been glad that she would not have to deal with Luke today her initial feeling after being told he had canceled this meeting was anger that he could not remain professional and be here to assist as his aunt had requested. Once more, his actions were impacting how she did her job.

While annoyed, Bennet refused to let Luke, Vivian Winthrop, or her stodgy secretary make her feel inadequate and so instead she looked Nora Mason directly in the eyes and in as authoritative a tone as she could muster she stated, "If you insist on accompanying me, then fine; lead the way and we can begin."

As she began her work moving slowly from room to room, examining the paintings and documenting details about each of the fifteen works still on display in the Winthrop home, Bennet felt the secretary's silent hawklike presence staring over her shoulder to be disconcerting. Merely out of politeness, as she worked she tried to engage the woman in some small talk. Beginning with what she thought was the neutral topic of the weather; she described how nice it was to start to lose the heat of summer.

Nora Mason's reply was a simple grunt.

Undeterred, a while later as she was creating a condition report on a small but beautiful landscape painting by a well-known sixteenth century Dutch master, Bennet once more attempted a conversation.

"This is a truly breathtaking work. Most people know this artist for his portraits, but I think the way he captures the natural light in his landscapes is really something. Wouldn't you agree?"

This time Nora Mason gave no reply.

"You must be sorry to see these paintings leave. I can't imagine what it would be like to wake up surrounded by such masterpieces," Bennet said after another twenty minutes when she found she could no longer stand the woman's silence.

"No, I imagine you cannot," Nora replied.

Choosing to ignore her rudeness, Bennet continued, "Do you have a particular favorite that you…"

"Look, Ms. Reynolds, I have a lot to do today. I would suggest you focus on the work at hand rather than interjecting your own opinions every five minutes so we can both move forward and get on with our very busy schedules."

Okay. That's just fine, you miserable thing, Bennet thought.

Deliberately choosing not to utter another word, for the next two hours, Bennet finished her review of the remaining paintings in silence.

During her work as she tried hard to ignore the beady-eyed stare of Nora Mason, her mind returned once more to Luke. While she was relieved that she had not been forced to spend three hours with him here in his aunt's house after what had happened at the opening and with Jeremy's humiliation still fresh in her mind, she could not stop thinking about the fact that he had ditched his responsibility of being here to assist her as his aunt had requested. While it was possible that a work conflict really had developed, Bennet had her doubts, believing it was more likely that there were no meetings out of town and he just did not want to be in the same room with her because he thought she was a horrible person.

The more time that passed working in the Winthrop home, the angrier Bennet became.

Maybe it was more than him not wanting to see me. Maybe he is deliberately trying to make things as difficult for me as possible. Is he really capable of that?

This is my job. I needed to see these paintings and his aunt had insisted he be here so in a way he is putting my professional career on the line by canceling the meeting. How dare he be so rude.

Does he think I wanted to be around him anymore than he did around me? I couldn't stand the thought of seeing him today but I am here doing my job; something he clearly doesn't have the decency to do.

By the time her train of thought had reached its conclusion, Bennet had convinced herself that Luke's actions were just another clear example of his self-entitlement and arrogance.

So much for a clean slate and trying to work together for the sake of the exhibition. Well he can't just simply refuse to work with me; not completely anyway, and I am not going to let him prevent me from doing my job.

Figuring she had wasted enough time thinking about Luke Dawlton, Bennet reached the conclusion that the only thing she could do was to continue to put together this exhibition and he could either help or not. She was not going to let such an insolent and unpleasant man get in her way and she did not care if she ever heard from him again.

———————————

Bennet was still fuming an hour later when she walked back into her office after what could only be described as an extremely frustrating and exhausting few hours at the Winthrop house. With the intention of simply depositing her files and leaving for the day, she made herself instead sit down and check her emails.

It always amazed Bennet how everyone seemed to not only have a problem when she was out of the office but also that the issue was so urgent it demanded her immediate attention. Today was no different.

As she went through her inbox she responded to the education director confirming her presence at a docent training tomorrow morning, clarified details about an item she had included on a purchase order she had submitted to the Accounting Department, and did a final review of the text for the labels of five paintings that were scheduled to be installed in the main gallery next week. All matters which in her opinion could have waited to be addressed until tomorrow but were considered important by the senders and so she was forced to reply before leaving for the day.

What she had not expected to see in her inbox was a message from Luke Dawlton. The fact that he had sent it thirty minutes after she had arrived at Vivian Winthrop's house instantly filled her with anger. She was convinced he had done so deliberately.

Nervous at the thought of what the email might contain, Bennet stared at the heading with the simple "Meeting Today" as a subject line. She could not even begin to imagine what Luke Dawlton could possibly have to write to her that would explain his absence at his aunt's house. It took her several minutes before she was able to work up the courage to click on the message and read it:

To: Bennet Reynolds
From: Luke Dawlton
Date: October 3 - 01:31:45 EST
Subject: Meeting Today
Bennet,

I regret that I was unable to meet you at my aunt's house today. Don't hesitate to call my office if you have any questions about the paintings.

Regards,

Luke

Once she had read the message, Bennet simply stared at the screen as her mind tried to process what he had said. As she did she felt her anger rise in intensity with each passing second.

Well aren't you just the picture of politeness, Luke Dawlton? Bennet thought as she reread the email for the second time.

You wait until I am firmly at your aunt's house to send a message.

I certainly did not, and do not, need your help. I can promise you that.

The mood she was in, Bennet knew she should ignore his email. She even got up from her desk and started packing up her things to leave for the day. But the email remained on her screen, the words so pronounced it was as if they were being projected off the monitor in big, bright lights. Finally she found herself returning to her desk and reading it once more.

Despite knowing better, Bennet was so incensed that before she could stop herself, she found herself composing a reply, her fingers angrily flying across the keys as she typed a response:

To: Luke Dawlton

From: Bennet Reynolds

Date: October 3 - 04:42:31 EST

Re: Subject: Meeting Today

Mr. Dawlton,

I must admit that I find myself at a loss as to how to understand you. I thought despite anything else that had happened that we had established how important this exhibition is to not only your aunt's legacy but to the Northhom Museum as well. I thought we had agreed to be professionals and to attempt to civilly work together.

I was prepared to work with you today despite your unforgivably rude behavior towards me the other evening. I see however, you are incapable of that level of maturity.

This might simply be an obligation for you, but this is my job. I will not let anything interfere with that, not even your attempts to undermine me with what seems to me to be nothing more than childish behavior.

I handled the review of your aunt's work today on my own just fine and I assure you I was not in need of your assistance. Besides, I had the lovely and highly chatty Nora Mason to stand over me for three hours keeping watch in case I decided to turn my hand to thievery and run off with one of your aunt's valuables.

All has been handled to what I believe will be your and your aunt's mutual satisfaction.

Bennet Reynolds

A few seconds after hitting send Bennet felt a tightness in her chest as she began to realize the full weight of what she had just done. She knew better than to commit anything to writing in the heat of anger, but she had done it anyway.

If Luke reacted to this, which he had every right to do given the hostile tone in which she had composed her reply, and it was shared with his aunt or even Brent and Katherine, she could be in real trouble. Worse yet she had put in writing a reference to the gallery opening the other evening which she had no desire to explain to her bosses.

More unsettling was the fact that after rereading Luke's email for the fourth time, she realized it had been nothing but polite. Even if he had deliberately avoided their meeting because he was angry with her about previous events, there was no proof of that in his email. He, unlike her, had been smart enough to make himself look both professional and forthright in his correspondence.

Bennet should have realized this but she had read and responded to his email message on instinct while upset at his prior behavior and while still feeling the sting of humiliation over the events of Saturday evening.

Looking at the sent message taunting her on her computer screen, Bennet knew there was nothing more she could do now. The ball was in Luke's court and she would just have to wait and see what he would do next. She would have no one to blame but herself if he decided to make her life miserable by sharing this email.

Once more she found herself wishing she could break free from this man's unwanted presence in her life.

CHAPTER TWENTY

Somehow Bennet had managed to keep the contents of her email to Luke to herself for more than a week, a task that was accomplished in large part because she was completely swamped with work for the Winthrop exhibition. It did not, however, prevent her from remaining in a state of nervous limbo waiting for some sort of reaction from him. Any response, even one that brought her professional world crashing down around her, would have been better than not knowing what would happen next.

Unable to keep it to herself any longer, the following Friday morning she found herself sitting in her office confessing all to Stella.

"Maybe it doesn't sound as bitchy as I think it does," Bennet said as her friend sat reading a copy of the email she had printed out for her. She had reread it so many times that Bennet found she could not bear to look at it again on her computer screen, taunting her; a visual reminder of how she had once more lost her temper and acted without thinking first.

"Oh no. It's definitely that bad," Stella replied. She knew where her friend's head had been when she sent the email but they were both aware it had not been her finest hour.

Stella had arrived at Bennet's office early that morning with the excuse of having to review some press releases for the Winthrop exhibition and needing some quotes from Bennet. What she really wanted was to spend a few minutes drinking coffee with her friend and trying to psych her up for Vivian Winthrop's cocktail reception which she would need to attend nine hours from now. After having just read Bennet's email, however, she now realized that was going to be a more difficult task than she originally thought.

"I can't believe I'm going to have to go back to that house tonight and face this man. I mean really, when does my humiliation end?"

"Maybe he hasn't read it yet. You could still recall it," Stella suggested, trying to sound reassuring.

"I already tried. It didn't work." Bennet shook her head. "No, he's definitely read it."

"Maybe he's just going to ignore it," Stella said. "I mean he was horrible to you at the opening and then he found a way to get out of seeing you when you had to review the artworks at his aunt's house. It is possible he just wants to avoid you and is waiting for this project to finally end as much as you."

"Yeah he was definitely a total jerk that night and I know I wish the whole thing had never happened; so maybe you're right and he just wants to forget about it and get this whole project over with. But then, this is my life we are talking about so I don't know if I get to be that lucky."

After taking a sip of her coffee, Bennet added, "Don't forget he has the advantage. Thanks to my stupidity, he has my unprofessional bitchy email to hold over my head and really he could use it any time he wanted to make trouble for me."

"Have you decided what you are going to say to him tonight?" Stella asked.

"Nothing if I can help it. I'm going to do my best to just avoid him."

Stella laughed.

"What's so funny?" Bennet asked.

Stella shook her head. "Nothing really. It seems like a great plan. You can just spend the entire evening ducking and weaving in and out of the crowd trying to avoid the man whose aunt is hosting the reception. That won't seem weird at all."

Bennet let out a loud sigh of frustration.

"Well what other choice do I have? I mean, I couldn't have been more direct in my email about my feelings for him and his not showing up at Vivian Winthrop's house that day and he sent no reply. I haven't had one word from him in days so I certainly can't confront him again on it.

"Besides, it seems every time we are around each other either I lose my temper or he does and I don't want that to happen again. So, the way I see it the only real choice I have is to just try and blend into the crowd and leave the reception as soon as I possibly can without appearing rude or like I am neglecting my job."

Stella had serious doubts as to her friend's chances of making her plan work, but not wanting to make her more nervous than she already was, she decided to change the subject. Standing up, she began inspecting the garment hanging on the back of Bennet's door. She knew the pale blue dress with fluttered sleeves was one of Bennet's favorites to wear to work functions since it was professional while also making her feel pretty at the same time.

"For a woman who wants to blend in, there is no doubt you are going to make a statement."

"The last time I saw Luke Dawlton I absolutely humiliated myself. Just because I am going to try to avoid him does not mean I can't look good doing it." Bennet smiled at her friend before making an attempt to look busy once more.

"All right now. I have wasted enough of my time on that man. Don't you need quotes from me or something?" Bennet asked. "We probably should at least try to do a little work this morning."

Bennet felt a strong sense of déjà vu as several hours later she found herself once more walking up the steps of the Winthrop townhouse. This time, however, she would not be alone with her paintings as tonight was the long-anticipated reception Vivian Winthrop was hosting for the museum's board of directors and most elite donors.

As she walked into the foyer and saw the crowd of people, Bennet became painfully aware that this would not be the subdued affair for which she had been hoping. With what she estimated to be about seventy people present, it was clear that in addition to those linked to the museum, Vivian Winthrop had also invited many from her high society circle of friends; no doubt so that they would lavish her with praise for her magnanimous gift to the museum.

Bennet's presence at the reception was a requirement of her job, and so despite it being the last place she wanted to be, she had no choice but to make the rounds and represent the Northhom Museum. While she would do her part, she had formulated a plan on the way over to the event that included her making small talk with a few of the key board members to make sure her presence was noticed and saying a quick hello to the hostess, although she doubted she would care. Once those two tasks were completed she would leave the reception as quickly as she could. Most importantly her plan hinged on the fact that she would try at all costs to avoid any interaction whatsoever with Luke Dawlton.

After twenty minutes of mingling, Bennet found herself once more on her own and had begun the trek to the far corner of the room with the pretense of grabbing a drink from one of the two discreet bars that had been setup in the space. What she really wanted, however, was a few minutes on her own without being forced to make any further small talk.

Just as Bennet was about to reach the bar, a group of guests who were standing nearby broke apart, revealing that Katherine Hartis was standing directly in front of her path. While that would have been enough to make her want to turn and run, she realized that her boss was in conversation with one of the museum's trustees and Luke.

Overcome with nerves at the sight of him, Bennet could not help but notice his appearance. Wearing what she now recognized as his normal outfit of expensive, expertly tailored dark suits, tonight he was also sporting the slightest bit of stubble growth on his chin, the effect of which was to make his face look more perfectly chiseled than ever.

Turning away as quickly as she could, Bennet was just about to make her escape when she heard Katherine's annoying voice call out.

"Ah, Bennet, is that you?"

Knowing she had no choice now but to join them, Bennet turned back towards the trio with a smile plastered firmly on her face, and went over to stand with them.

"Hello, Katherine."

"I do not believe you know Nella Burke, one of our trustees," Katherine stated as if trying to impress the group with her own knowledge while simultaneously making it clear that her subordinate was nowhere near as well connected.

What is she playing at? Bennet wondered.

Bennet was about to clarify that she did in fact know the board member when she spoke first.

"Of course I know Bennet," Nella interjected, her tone implying that she was slightly confused at Katherine's remark.

"Yes," Bennet agreed. "We work together on the curatorial committee. It's nice to see you again Nella."

"You as well. I was just telling Luke how much I am looking forward to seeing your exhibition."

"Thank you," Bennet managed to mutter. She was finding it hard to concentrate on what was being said; she was so focused on avoiding making eye contact with Luke.

Then to make matters even more uncomfortable, Nella added, "Katherine, I think I see Mabel Rivers from the hospital board. I would love for you to meet her. Would you mind coming with me so I can introduce you?"

"It would be my pleasure," Katherine replied.

Bennet knew this was a lie as she was sure Katherine did not want to leave her conversation with Luke but was trapped as she would never refuse a trustee's request.

Knowing that she and Luke would now be left standing awkwardly alone together, Bennet was almost sorry to see Katherine leave.

But then of course, her boss managed to make matters even worse.

Just as Katherine and Nella Burke began to walk away, Katherine could not help but turn back, adding with a laugh, "Oh by the way, Bennet, I received your email this afternoon that you will be bringing one less guest to the opening reception. I hope that does not mean you are having any relationship troubles."

Bennet willed her face not to turn red. While Katherine had no way of knowing anything about Jeremy or the tension her association with him had caused between her and Luke, she had still managed to say the one thing that could make the moment even more unbearable.

As mortified as she was, Bennet refused to let Katherine see any distress on her face so instead she replied as calmly as she could with what was in fact the truth, "None whatsoever Katherine. My cousin wanted to attend but will be out of town so I need one less reservation for the opening reception. But thank you as always for your attention to detail."

Katherine flashed her a knowing smile before walking away. If she had wanted to cause embarrassment, she had succeeded.

Having watched them disappear in the crowd, Bennet instantly became aware that she was left standing alone with Luke. Stuck in the one situation she had desperately been trying to avoid since she arrived at the reception, she knew the best thing she could do was make an excuse and get out of his presence as quickly as possible. However when she opened her mouth to speak, her words and tone were anything but congenial.

"I see your pressing business didn't keep you from attending this event."

Why would you say that? Bennet reasoned with herself.

"If I had business I wouldn't be here, but I don't, so I am." Luke hated the haughty tone he could hear in his voice as he had snapped back his reply, but once more this woman was beginning to get under his skin despite his vow to himself to try and rectify his behavior towards her the other evening.

"Well then I should probably go before I say something else that falls into the category of commenting on something I know nothing about," Bennet said, throwing his words from the gallery opening back up at him.

"You know you make things impossible, don't you?" Luke asked, his frustration clear. "I was going to apologize but now I don't know if I even want to."

"Well by all means, Mr. Dawlton, don't do anything you don't want to do," Bennet replied.

Suddenly Luke laughed, surprising both himself and Bennet. It was a gesture that miraculously broke the tension between them.

"What's so funny?" Bennet asked, unable to stop herself from starting to smile.

"Nothing, it's just I have never met someone who makes me go from calm to outraged in such a short amount of time."

It was Bennet's turn to laugh. "I think we have finally found something we have in common."

Seeing this as an opportunity to rectify his past wrongdoings, Luke decided to try again.

"I really did want to apologize for my behavior."

Luke's words had taken Bennet completely by surprise. She had been convinced that if she did manage to find herself alone with him tonight then he would certainly begin yelling at her at the first moment of contact.

When Bennet said nothing, Luke continued, "I had no right to question you about your personal life the night of the gallery opening. Who you date is absolutely none of my business."

Bennet noticed that as he was speaking Luke now seemed nervous; it somehow managed to make him look more attractive than he had just moments before, if that were even possible.

Damn. Does he have to look so sexy?

"You're right, it isn't any of your business. But for the record, I am not dating Jeremy Burlow."

Why does he have the power to make me feel so flustered all the time? Bennet wondered.

Unable to stop herself, Bennet began to explain, "We actually only ever went on a few dates and I'm sure you will be pleased to know you were right and I quickly found out that he was a jerk."

Why am I telling him all this, Bennet wondered, hating herself for her lack of ability to once more control her incessant rambling. It was an action she seemed only to do when she was around him and found it incredibly frustrating that he had such an effect on her.

"Well, if that is the case then, besides all the other defects in his character, I can now add that he is a complete idiot if he was in any way foolish enough to treat you poorly."

Luke's comment threatened to make Bennet blush as she wondered if he had really just said what he did or if she had imagined it.

When she finally spoke the words seemed to come out in a rush. "You're not the only one who feels they should apologize. The email I sent you last week was completely unprofessional. I'm afraid I was still angry over the events of the weekend and I let that come out in my message to you. I hope that you will not hold that against the Northhom or let it interfere with…"

"Bennet, please," Luke began, cutting her off, a habit he had noticed he seemed to do far more often when talking to her than he wanted. "You had every right to be upset. I see how it could have appeared that I purposely missed the meeting. I assure you though that I really did have a meeting out of town. I only got back to the city yesterday."

Luke's words were true. While he had no idea how he was going to make things right, from the moment Bennet had left the gallery opening that evening, he had wanted to find a way to apologize and show her that he was nothing like all the horrible things he could only imagine Jeremy had said about him. Then, when he was forced to cancel the meeting at his aunt's house where he might actually have been able to try and make things better and he had read her reply to his email he had known he had only made matters worse. Rather than be angry at her message as she had clearly thought he must be, it had only made him more embarrassed and regretful over his actions at the opening.

Smiling, Luke added, "Although I must say that on more than one occasion I, too, have enjoyed the sparkling wit of Ms. Mason that you described in your email. She is quite the conversationalist."

Bennet laughed, which Luke took as a good sign that he should continue. "Have you noticed how we seem to spend a lot of time apologizing to each other?"

"Yes, I'm afraid we do," Bennet replied, giving him a smile.

Once more a silence developed between them which, she noted, this time lacked any sense of uneasiness; so much so, that the pair failed to notice a man approaching them.

"Luke, pardon the interruption, but I was hoping I might bump into you this evening."

"Ian, good to see you," Luke said recovering quickly. "I can honestly say that you are one of the few people I can stand to make more than small talk with at my aunt's functions."

As the man laughed, Bennet had a moment to take his measure. Middle-aged and balding with thin silver wire glasses, he was well dressed in a navy suit. He had a pleasant air about him and she found that she had taken an instant liking to him, most notably because of what she felt was his kind face and seemingly genuine smile.

"Ian, allow me to introduce Bennet Reynolds. She is the curator responsible for my aunt's forthcoming exhibition at the Northhom Museum."

Then, turning to Bennet, Luke added, "Bennet, this is Ian Bristle."

"Nice to meet you," Ian said warmly as he extended his hand to Bennet. "It must be quite an undertaking bringing Vivian's works to view like that. I do not envy the task."

His smile left Bennet with the impression that he knew a little about Vivian Winthrop's difficult nature.

"It has been an interesting process; that's for sure," Bennet began. "But the paintings and sculptures in her collection are amazing. The Northhom is fortunate to be on the receiving end of such an impressive gift."

"Yes, they certainly are."

"How do you know Luke?" Bennet asked, her curiosity getting the better of her.

"Ah, well we go back a long way. I'd say probably ten years when he made his first donation to my foundation," Ian explained. "His generosity, in my opinion, in many ways outshines his aunt's. Although he rarely lets anyone know it."

"You don't mean the Bristle Foundation? You're not that Ian Bristle?" Bennet asked, noticing how uncomfortable Luke had become at the praise from his friend.

Ian laughed. "I'm afraid that's me."

"I have to tell you, I have long been an admirer of your foundation and the work you do in so many important areas including the arts. I believe so strongly that everyone should have access to arts and culture."

"I agree," Ian said with a shift in his tone that implied a focused interest on what she had just said. "Tell me, Bennet, I wonder which of our programs you feel are most important from your perspective?"

Bennet was flattered by his interest in her opinion. She had not been exaggerating when she had said she admired the work of Ian's foundation.

"Well I've always been impressed by the impact your refugee immersion programs have had in helping immigrants assimilate to life in their new communities. But, I also think your music access program that brings inner city school children into contact with music and theatre organizations is so important."

Debating whether she should continue and deciding to risk it, Bennet added, "I've always thought there could be room for the visual arts to factor into such a program. It's so important to instill in children the power of art at an early age. My father began taking me to museums in the city when I was a little girl and it had such a strong effect on my life. I feel every child should have that chance."

Bennet realized she was gushing, but it was easy to do when she meant every word.

As the pair continued their conversation, Luke was able to quietly observe their interaction and had quickly become mesmerized by Bennet and her sudden animation. It reminded him of their talk at the gala that night that now seemed ages ago, when she had described the Sébastian Reno drawing she saw as a young girl. While her passion for her field was impressive, as he listened to her speak with his friend about a topic clearly important to her, he was equally struck by how she appeared even more enchanting than when he first noticed her walk into his aunt's parlor earlier this evening in that stunning blue dress; looking determined as ever to take control of the room.

Not wishing to upset her any more than he already had between his behavior at the gallery and the effects of his email canceling their appointment, before he had arrived this evening he had promised himself that he would give Bennet space tonight. But then fate had seemed to transpire and Katherine Hartis had called her over. While he had little respect for that woman, he was grateful that she had been the catalyst for bringing them together. And after what had seemed to begin with the potential for another hostile exchange between them he had thankfully been able to steer their conversation back on track. The fact that they had ended up laughing just now hopefully meant that he had cleared the air between them enough that they could work together to finish this project. He would just not mention Jeremy or anything personal again.

While he more than anyone knew the horrible depths of Jeremy Burlow's character, he also knew he had no reason to comment at all on her relationship with him. More than once since the gallery opening he had tried to convince himself his behavior that evening had been his attempt, albeit a clumsy one, of trying to warn her off Jeremy so she would not get hurt. He could almost make himself believe that was all there was to it, but deep down he knew that he had also felt a pang of jealousy at the sight of her walking in on that disgusting man's arm. Of course as had become their pattern, whenever he was around Bennet all his good sense and judgement was transformed into completely inappropriate statements which he rendered in the haughtiest tone possible just as he had done that evening, and he had been regretting it ever since.

Then minutes ago, when she had said she was no longer with Burlow, he had been filled with relief. Why did it matter so much he wondered. She was nothing more than the curator of his aunt's exhibition and yet he could not seem to keep her from his mind.

"Well Bennet, this was a real pleasure," Ian said shaking her hand again. "Sadly, I have to leave and need to say hello to Vivian before I do so. Luke, let's talk soon; it has been good to see you again."

Ian's last words pulled Luke back from his own thoughts in which he had been so lost he had no idea how much time had gone by.

"Absolutely," he replied.

Having watched Ian walk away and disappear into the crowd, Bennet became aware that she and Luke were once more alone together. While the tension had definitely been lifted between them she did not want any awkwardness to return and figured it was best she make her own exit.

"Well, I should get going too, I think."

"I wonder if you would allow me to show you something first?" Luke asked. He had not planned on making this request, and yet, as he spoke the words he was filled with anticipation for her answer.

Intrigued, Bennet nodded and followed Luke as he began to make his way through the crowd.

Chapter Twenty-one

Once out in the foyer, Luke led Bennet down the same long corridor from which on her last visit Bennet had seen the formidable Nora Mason emerge.

While she had no idea why she had agreed to go with him and was more than a little afraid she might put the wrong foot forward again with him or worse yet, lose her temper once more, she was too intrigued by Luke's request not to follow him when he asked.

Passing a series of rooms, Luke stopped at the last one on the left. Opening the door for her, as they stepped inside, Bennet found herself in a large study. Two walls were lined floor to ceiling with shelves filled with leather-bound books of the type that always seemed to Bennet like they were there to be looked at as much as read. An impressively grand mahogany desk with a large green leather chair edged with antique gold buttons dominated the room, next to which stood a huge globe.

"You told me about your favorite artwork. I was hoping you would permit me to show you one of mine."

A slight current of nervous energy passed through Bennet at his words. While innocent enough there was something about the request that made her excited as it seemed to possess an air of intimacy that she had certainly not been expecting when she accompanied him out of the reception.

As she followed Luke to the far side of the room she was surprised to realize that he was gesturing to a small sketch by Sébastian Reno. Roughly rendered, it featured a figure drawn in a Cubist style whose entire body was a configuration of geometric shapes in various shades of gray. Stunning in its simplicity, the artist in Bennet was instantly attracted to it.

"My aunt wanted me to select a work to keep before she donated her collection to the museum. I'm sure she assumed I would take one of her large paintings and I know I surprised her when I asked instead for two small sketches; this being one of them.

"Of course, she was not pleased with my choice and could not understand why, if it was a Reno I wanted, that I did not instead select one of his large paintings. She repeatedly reminded me that not only would they be worth more, but that they would be more impressive as part of my own collection.

"I refused to give in however, and she finally agreed. I'm afraid I have always been a mystery to my aunt. The way she sees it I have let her down on more than one occasion."

Bennet found herself wondering how this successful man could ever be considered a disappointment to anyone. Knowing more than a little about letting down a parent, she failed to see how anything Luke did would qualify.

"This sketch has always hung in this room, which was my uncle's study. My aunt has left everything just as it was before he died over two decades ago. She never comes in here. Truth is, she rarely did when he was alive either. It was his sanctuary. I guess you could say it was his version of a man cave."

"It's certainly a very upscale version," Bennet replied.

Luke smiled. "Yes, well that was the only type my aunt would allow. But it was the place I believe he felt most at peace. And in a way it became my sanctuary too.

"My mother died when I was still young and my father threw himself into his work. He spent very little time with me and reflecting back on it I think I reminded him too much of what he had lost. I understand now that it wasn't that he did not love me. I just don't think he knew how to be with me. It was too painful for him. Still, it was hard to take as a young boy; so I basically spent all my time here with his sister Vivian and her husband Richard.

"Age has softened my aunt and if you can believe it, she was even colder and more distant then than she is now. Showing love and affection to a ten-year-old boy, especially one that was not her own child, certainly did not fit into her plans. She had told me more than once growing up how she lacked any maternal instincts, and so, when my father died a year later she wasted no time shipping me off to boarding school. I was only eleven.

"My uncle was a different story. He was a highly successful and busy lawyer, but he always made time for me. When I would come home on breaks I used to hide out here in his study for hours while he worked. You know I think I have read nearly every book on these shelves. And I remember our favorite game was for him to spin that globe and I would put my finger out to stop it and where it landed he would teach me about the place and we would plan what we would do if we went on an adventure there.

"He died of a sudden and massive stroke when I was fifteen," Luke added. The sadness present in his voice made it clear how much he still missed the man.

For the first time Bennet wondered if the cold, stoic exterior Luke always exuded could have been more than just a haughty sense of entitlement. Maybe some of it was an act of self-preservation; a mask he wore to cover a childhood of loss and loneliness.

"After he died," Luke continued, "I threw myself into my studies since

I felt like it was all I had left. It was only then, when I started excelling in the last years of boarding school, that my aunt began to truly take notice of me. It was never for my benefit though, I knew that. Rather it was the fact that my academic accomplishments could make her look good that was the cause of her interest. I became one of her social achievements.

"Even now, whenever I am in this house, I still try to spend as much time as I can in this room. This sketch is linked to the good memories I have of my uncle and when I look at it they always come flooding back. My aunt would never understand that, nor would I even attempt to try and share it with her.

"Still, I know you like Reno, and the artist's work had a strong impact on you as a child. I thought perhaps, you would appreciate seeing it."

"I do. Thank you for showing it to me." Bennet had been moved by the honesty with which Luke had shared this personal part of his life.

Somewhat overcome by the moment and what he had so unexpectedly shared, Bennet struggled with what to say next. As always, however, art provided the vehicle for her to continue the conversation.

"I've always been interested in drawings like this; I think because it is really all about the process."

"Well, when I was young, I just liked the figure," Luke began to explain. "He seemed alone like I was. I guess I related to it."

Watching him as he spoke, Bennet became overwhelmed with the image of Luke as a sad, lonely boy. She was struck by how while some children have to deal with the loss of a parent, Luke had been forced to come to terms with the death of both his parents and a beloved uncle. The weight of that must have been almost unbearable.

"As you know, my aunt had other paintings by Reno in her home," he continued. "They were so different with their bright colors and when I was young and knew nothing of art, I could scarcely believe they could have been created by the same person. When I felt overwhelmed after my uncle's death I told myself if Reno could have so many different versions of himself, then I did not have to be defined by all the losses I had experienced in my childhood. I could reinvent myself too."

Luke shook his head. "Sorry, it must sound ridiculous. It doesn't make sense, I know." Luke seemed embarrassed by what he had just shared. "All I know is, it inspired me."

"It makes sense to me," Bennet replied softly. "The power of art to shape your life, believe me I understand that all too well."

"I thought you might," Luke said as he gave her a smile that literally made Bennet's knees feel like they would buckle.

"I have never shared that before. I just brought you in here to see the sketch. I honestly don't know what came over me, but I guess I just wanted you to know."

"I'm glad you did. I want to…"

"Luke, are you there? Luke?"

The voice of Vivian Winthrop rang out, the effect of which was to destroy their moment as suddenly as if someone had turned the lights on in a dark room.

"Sorry," Luke whispered, before calling out. "Yes, Aunt Vivian; we're in here."

"We? Who is we?" Vivian Winthrop asked as she walked into the room.

"Ah, Ms. Reynolds. What is so important, I wonder, that it has taken both of you away from my reception?"

If she was surprised to find them alone in her deceased husband's study, Vivian Winthrop had too much respect for societal constraints to vocalize it. However, the frosty stare she briefly fixed on Bennet made it clear her presence in this room with Luke was very much an unwelcome sight.

"I was showing Bennet the Reno sketch," Luke replied in a tone that Bennet was quick to note was all business again.

"I will never understand your obsession with those two drawings," Vivian stated with a distinctly cold edge to her voice. "Why you so admire a simple sketch of a figure and a…"

"Aunt Vivian, I assume you need me to return to the party," Luke blurted out the words, cutting her off so abruptly that he had actually managed to startle his aunt.

"Ah, yes, yes, that is correct," Vivian said, swiftly recovering her composure after his outburst. "If you will return back with me, I want you to meet someone. Unless of course, there is something else you feel you need to show Ms. Reynolds." The coldness in her tone was more than enough of a warning that she did not consider this a viable option for her nephew.

"We would be happy to come back with you," Luke said as he began moving towards the door.

Vivian took Luke's arm so that he could guide her back to the reception. Since the corridor through which they traveled was narrow, Bennet had no choice but to walk behind them. It was a move she was sure Vivian had done deliberately and which was confirmed for her when, as they reached the parlor, she wrapped her arm around Luke's and swiftly led him back into the room, leaving Bennet standing alone at the doorway without so much as a glance back in her direction.

Bennet was surprised to find that as she stood there watching Luke disappear into the crowd of Manhattan's who's who she was actually sorry to see him go. Two hours earlier she could have never imagined having such a feeling. She had dreaded seeing Luke again and yet the conversation they had just had and what he had shared with her had been so heartfelt and honest that it left her seeing an entirely different side to the man who, up until that moment, she had convinced herself she detested. The truth was she had never met a man who had confused her or challenged her as much as he seemed to do. What would have happened, she wondered, if they had been allowed a few more minutes undisturbed.

Sensing she would not have the opportunity to see Luke again this evening, Bennet was overcome by the sudden urge to leave the party, get into the fresh air, and think about all that had taken place.

Just as she was starting to make the move to leave however, Bennet was once more accosted by Katherine Hartis.

"Bennet, you can't be leaving so soon?" Katherine asked as she came to stand beside her.

What is it with this woman? It's like she appears out of nowhere. Why can't she just leave me alone?

Bennet was just about to answer that she was in fact leaving when Katherine began speaking again.

"Were my eyes playing tricks on me or did I just see you walking back into the foyer with Vivian and Luke? Just where have you been hiding yourself?"

"Well hello again, Katherine," Bennet began speaking as calmly as she could. "Are you enjoying the reception?" Bennet asked, choosing to ignore her boss's question.

Standing there in her overly expensive black suit and leopard print stilettos, Katherine stared at Bennet as if trying to make her uncomfortable.

"Perhaps you did not hear me. I asked where you had gotten off to with Vivian Winthrop."

"Don't forget Luke Dawlton. I believe you also asked about him," Bennet replied.

The look Katherine aimed at her left no doubt as to her annoyance.

"I fail to see how this is any concern of yours," Bennet stated, trying to remind herself to not get riled up.

While Bennet did not want to extend her conversation with Katherine any longer than necessary, she felt compelled to give her boss some sort of response to her question and so added, "If you must know, Luke and I were discussing a piece of art. Then Vivian came to retrieve him because she needed Luke to meet someone, and so we returned to the party. Did you need to ask them something? I'm sure I could pass it along for you."

As Katherine stared at her, Bennet could almost feel her boss's hatred. She had never understood why Katherine disliked her so much and she had always tried to get along with her but now, in this moment, Bennet realized she simply no longer cared whether her boss liked her or not. She knew she would never be able to change her feelings since they were not based on any rational foundation.

What was clear, however, from the expression on Katherine's face was that she did not like this newfound confidence Bennet was displaying.

Katherine glared at Bennet. "Let me remind you that you are on very thin ice," she replied, the words uttered so intently they almost sounded like a hiss. "We all have serious concerns over whether you will be able to put this show together. I would seriously keep your attitude in check and not get cocky. There is a lot of time before the exhibition and many moving parts. You would not want to mess up."

Whether it was the wine she had drunk earlier or the high she was feeling from the shared conversation with Luke moments ago, Bennet felt empowered to continue speaking when common sense would have dictated she simply walk away.

"You know Katherine, I've always wondered why you work so hard at trying to put me in my place. I can't believe I matter that much to you. I am however, well aware of your lack of faith in me and my abilities. In fact, I don't believe there has been a single day since I have assumed this position that you have not strove to make that clear to me.

"As always, your concern is noted. I do recommend however, that you get better at faking your confidence in me. If you seem worried it might cause Vivian and Luke to start to worry about their exhibition too and that certainly would not be good for the Northhom.

"Now if you will excuse me, I am going to say goodnight. Feel free to say goodbye to Luke and Vivian for me if you get a chance."

Bennet was about to turn and leave when she glanced once more into the room. To her surprise, she saw Luke staring at her. Engaged in a conversation with his aunt and a middle-aged couple, she knew he would not be able to get away and so she gave a slight smile; a gesture he immediately returned.

Unbeknownst to Bennet, Katherine who was already furious at Bennet's remarks, had witnessed the exchange. Had she seen the look of jealousy on Katherine's face she might have realized she should watch her back as she knew how dangerous her boss could be, especially when she felt threatened.

Bennet however, was too heady over her exchange with Luke to see anything.

Bennet barely noticed anyone on the subway ride home from the reception or during the three-block walk from the station to her apartment building; her mind was so filled with the events of the evening. It now seemed ridiculous that she had ever thought Luke had purposely missed their meeting at his aunt's house.

Walking into her apartment, Bennet was still in the process of mentally reviewing their exchange. First there was the rush of pleasure she had felt when he called Jeremy Burlow an idiot for treating her poorly. While that was undeniably a good moment, it was what he had shared with her while they stood together in his uncle's study that gave her the most to think about. It meant a lot to her that he had opened up about the drawing and his childhood. His story had made her start to see him in a whole new light and despite knowing such an exercise would get her nowhere, she found herself beginning to wonder what might have happened if Vivian Winthrop had not interrupted them.

Then just as quickly Bennet chided herself for entertaining such thoughts. He had shared something personal with her; that was meaningful, but Bennet reasoned that he was probably simply being kind and wanted to smooth things out between the two of them so things would no longer be uncomfortable. The thought even crossed her mind that what he had said was a peace offering of sorts for his rude behavior the night of the opening. Theirs was still a professional relationship and she would be foolish to think it anything more than that and so she vowed she would not allow herself to read more into it. Instead, she would settle for being grateful that she could at least now be at ease working with Luke as she prepared the exhibition. It would certainly make her job more enjoyable.

Having fed Daisy and changed out of her dress and into her comfiest joggers and oversized sweatshirt, Bennet curled up on her sofa with a cup of tea and began to go over the other part of the evening that had been an unexpected pleasure. She had thoroughly enjoyed her chance meeting with Ian Bristle. While she had long admired his foundation and the work that it did in the city, she was surprised that he was nothing like what she had imagined someone of his stature and prestige would be. For such a wealthy and powerful businessman, he seemed both down to earth and approachable. She had enjoyed their conversation and had felt at ease with him while they were discussing the foundation's work. She had often wondered how it would feel to effect real change like that and to realize he was as nice a man as he was a philanthropic one had served to restore some of her faith in mankind.

Lest she forget the evening also involved the presence of Katherine Hartis who, as usual, had behaved miserably. But tonight she had not got to Bennet the way she usually did. While she did not know where her forthrightness had come from this evening, she realized it was the first time since working at the Northhom that she had really stood up for herself with her boss. Even though she knew it was petty, Bennet found that she enjoyed the idea that Katherine had actually been jealous of her being alone with Luke and Vivian Winthrop.

Picking up Daisy, she gave her a kiss on the top of her furry head and was able to manage a quick snuggle before the animal squirmed out of her arms and ran across the living room in search of a new adventure. It was certainly true that a cat's affection was given rather than forced; everything was done on its terms.

To be so free and in control of one's life, Bennet thought as she watched the cat bound across the room before settling in a ball under her drawing table.

For so long just the sight of the table was enough to fill her with self-doubt and overwhelming feelings of failure, but now as she got up from the sofa and walked across the room to stand in front of it, Bennet found she possessed a strong desire to create.

Taking a seat on the highbacked swivel chair, Bennet ran her hands across the cold surface of the large square table. She had it tilted up at just the right angle to best absorb the light that filtered through the large window nearby, and she noticed with a smile how tonight the glimmer of the street lights outside seemed to sparkle and dance across it. It was as if the table itself was beckoning her.

Resting on the table was the copy of the text to the children's book that Terrance's friend had sent her. She had printed it out and read it when the author first emailed it to her with the request that she submit some sample illustrations. She had not touched it since.

Now, as she sat there and began to read it again, the images of the boy's overnight adventure in the zoo began to once more come alive in her head. Excited, she pulled some clean, crisp sheets of drawing paper from the drawer located on the left side of the table and began to sketch.

Suddenly, the idea of working on drawings for the story proposal did not seem so daunting. Emboldened by the night's events, Bennet soon found herself swept away in a wave of creativity as she began to sketch in earnest, rushing to capture with her pencil all that she was seeing in her mind.

Chapter Twenty-two

The early morning light roused Bennet from sleep as a sensation of warmth caressed the side of her face. Disoriented at first by the hard surface on which her head was resting, she soon realized she had fallen asleep at her drawing table surrounded by the sketches she had spent most of the night working on. Eager to look at them again with the fresh eyes of a new day, she began to comb through the sketches; as she did, she found she absolutely loved them. She had brought to life the words of the author's story, depicting the smiling giraffes with their long, spotted necks; a family of gorillas including a baby riding on his father's broad shoulders; and two proud peacocks with dazzling sapphire blue and emerald green plumes who wandered freely on the path that wove throughout the zoo. She had also captured the young hero of the story; a ten-year-old boy in his striped red and gray shirt, short spiky brown hair, and a spattering of freckles across the bridge of his nose.

After brewing a pot of coffee and subjecting herself to a brief but invigorating shower, Bennet found herself back at her drawing table, surprising herself at how eager she was to get back to work and put some finishing touches on the sketches she had created the night before.

Three hours and several mugs of coffee later, Bennet pulled back from the table, satisfied with her drawings. Whether or not the author liked them did not matter in this moment because she knew that with these works she had jumped some imaginary hurdle of her own making, which had been preventing her for so long from taking this chance of putting herself out there with her art.

After scanning the images and reconfiguring them into downloadable files, she composed a brief email to the author informing him of what she was attaching for his review. Then, after closing her eyes for a moment and saying a quick prayer, she took a deep breath and hit send. A swoosh and a ping from her laptop and her drawings were out there and ready for someone else to see; proof that she was an artist.

Overwhelmed by what she had accomplished this morning, Bennet felt the day held limitless potential. Deciding not to spoil it by thinking about all the work she had left to do on the exhibition, she instead decided to do something she loved. Lately it seemed like a luxury she never had time for, a few hours just wandering around the city and doing whatever she fancied in the moment, no set plans, no list of items to check off.

Thirty minutes later, after treating herself to a vanilla latte with a double shot of espresso, Bennet found herself headed to one of her favorite galleries to take in the exhibition of a young New Orleans based artist she had been following for a while. It was nice to walk around the gallery looking at each painting simply because she wanted to and not because she was obligated to do so for her job.

Bennet next decided to do a little shopping and while in one of her favorite consignment boutiques she fell in love with a vintage dress that she thought would be perfect for the Winthrop exhibition opening. A designer label, it cost nearly as much as a week's salary so Bennet hurriedly put the charge on her credit card before she could talk herself out of it. Then, as it would need a few alterations, she decided to drop it off at the tailors just a few blocks away so it would be ready in time for the opening.

Pleased with all she had accomplished this morning and satiated from her art viewing and shopping excursions, Bennet was about to head home when she received a text from her sister.

What are you up to?

Mom wants me to bring Charlotte over for a visit.

Be a good sister and come with me!

Bennet had been having what she could only describe as that rarest of perfect days and the absolute last thing she wanted to do was ruin it by visiting with her mother.

Without hesitation she texted her reply:

I've been out all day.

I'm planning on heading home now.

A text from Jane appeared almost instantly:

Come on.

Be a good sister and come along.

Bennet shook her head as she texted her reply:

Sorry but not in a "Mom" mood.

You'll have to deal with her on your own this time.

Unfortunately for Bennet, her sister refused to give up and another text appeared seconds later:

Don't you want to see your beautiful niece?

The niece who loves her Auntie Bennet!

Don't leave me to deal with Mom alone.

Please!!!

XX

Bennet had to smile because even as she had pressed send on her last text reply, she knew it would not be enough to deter Jane who would continue to pester her until she agreed.

Besides, Bennet was still worried about her sister. Despite several efforts to raise the subject of her and David, she had quickly been shut down by Jane's insistence that all was fine. Maybe, Bennet reasoned, she could get something out of her today if she could get her alone and talking while her mother was distracted with Charlotte. It also occurred to Bennet that if she did join her sister there would be an added benefit that, though she should have been ashamed to admit it aloud, if she spent time with her mother now she could blame work for the next two weeks and maybe not have to visit again until after the opening.

Bennet let out a sigh of resignation as she fired back a text:

Fine.

You win.

But only because your daughter is so adorable!

I'll catch the train now.

See you there in a bit.

XX

Once the text had been sent, and knowing there was no way she could back out now, Bennet set out for her mother's house with the promise that she would not let Adelaide put a damper on the good mood she had been in since yesterday evening.

Forty minutes later, Bennet resurfaced aboveground from the subway station. The air had seemed to develop a slight chill to it since she left Manhattan and she was struck once more by how much she loved the fall. Besides the colder weather which ushered in the opportunity to show off a whole new aspect of one's wardrobe including chunky sweaters, light scarves, and great hats, Bennet loved the season's ability to excite her artistic sensibilities. There was nothing like autumn in New York as it allowed her to revel in the explosion of colors that the changing leaves brought to the landscape, like the first dabs of watercolor on a clean sheet of paper. Today she noted how all around her this was beginning to occur on the trees lining the streets as she walked the four blocks to where her mother lived in the Brooklyn neighborhood of Park Slope.

Adelaide Reynolds still lived in the family brownstone after all these years, the last eight of which had been spent on her own since her husband's death.

The walk from the subway station to the front door of her parents' house was always a bittersweet one as it brought a flood of memories of her father back to her; first good ones filled with times spent together and then sad ones as she remembered his death. In that moment she would always feel once more the acute pain of losing him. His sudden death had come as a shock to all of them when, at the young age of fifty-two, he died of a heart attack while sitting as his partner's desk at one of the big law firms in Manhattan.

A kind, compassionate man, Bennet had loved her father dearly and he had held the same feelings for his two daughters. While he was often busy, he always had time for his girls. Her favorite memories of him involved the Sundays he would take her and Jane to visit the many different art museums in the city. They would spend hours walking around, making sure that they always included a visit to each of their favorite paintings. He would then take them out to their favorite diner on Forty-sixth Street where they would have lunch followed by ice cream sundaes. A few years ago, Bennet had sat with her sister having one final lunch at that very diner before the restaurant closed its doors. She was surprised how much that moment felt like she was losing their father all over again. One of the great things about the city was how it was always changing and there were always new exciting things to do and see; and yet sometimes she found herself wishing just a few things could stay the same.

When Bennet was in college, she and her father had started a new tradition which involved him sneaking out of work on Wednesday afternoons when she had a break in classes and they would meet for a late-day snack. It was there, sitting at a table, just the two of them, while sharing a plate of French fries or a slice of pie, that he had encouraged her to follow her dreams and study art. He had told her time and again how, while he was grateful that his job allowed him to provide a good home and life for his family, he did it because he loved it and he wished more than anything that she would find what made her happy. He wanted her to pursue that with all her heart even if other people, and by that she knew he meant her mother, could not understand.

He had died eight months before she graduated and she had missed him every day since. While he never saw her achieve it, it was his words, long after his death, that gave Bennet the confidence to pursue a career in the art world.

As always, Bennet's thoughts were on her father as she used her key to open her mother's front door.

"Mom? You here?"

"Bennet? Is that you?" Adelaide asked. "I'm in the kitchen."

As she walked through the foyer, Bennet's eyes were drawn to the rows of framed photographs on the wall opposite the stairs that led to the house's upper floors. In two dozen images she could see a visual summary of her family's life. A wedding portrait of her parents was surrounded by pictures of Jane and her as children, teenagers, and later adults, all of which documented key milestones in their lives like birthdays, graduations, and Jane's wedding. There were also several pictures of her niece.

Adelaide Reynolds was standing at the kitchen counter, pouring just-boiled water into a porcelain tea pot as Bennet walked into the room. On the counter rested a tray along with three matching cups with delicate blue forget-me-nots painted on the rim; part of a service that had once belonged to her great-grandmother. In that moment Bennet was struck once more at how perfect her mother always appeared. Just like the perfect tea service, there was never anything about her mother that was out of place from her pristine ballerina flats, to her crisply ironed tweed trousers and cranberry blouse, to her graying bobbed hair that had never been allowed to grow more than an inch below her chin.

"Well this is a surprise," Adelaide said as she looked at her daughter.

"I called you and told you I was on my way. When Jane said she was coming over with Charlotte I thought I would visit too."

"I know, but it was still a surprise. You don't usually come without me guilting you into it."

"Can we please not, Mom?" Bennet asked, failing to prevent the irritation from manifesting itself in her voice.

"Honestly, I don't know what you mean. But to avoid an argument with you Bennet, sure.

"By the way, your sister called, and she is running late. Something about Charlotte and not being able to find her stuffed rabbit. You know, the one she will not go anywhere without. She said she should be here in about thirty minutes. I thought we could have some tea first."

"Okay," Bennet answered, silently wishing her sister would have texted to let her know she was running late. If she had Bennet would have walked around and not arrived so soon to spare herself from what was sure to be an inquisition now that she would be stuck alone with her mother.

"Why don't you go ahead and bring the tray into the garden. I'll slice the pound cake and be right out."

Following her mother's instructions, Bennet smiled as she entered the backyard and took in the view. Over several decades the rough patch of grass had been painstakingly transformed into a thoughtfully designed garden. It was truly her mother's domain, and whenever she was not tending to her daughters' lives, she lavished that attention on her flowers.

Standing here among Adelaide's creation, Bennet could not deny that her mother had a talent for gardening. Surrounding a wrought-iron table and four chairs were an explosion of colors coming from impressive blooms that included large chrysanthemums in various shades of pink, purple, and red; rising towers of delphinium blossoms in a rich indigo blue; and her mother's favorite flower, roses, of which there were seven varieties in a full range of colors and sizes.

"Your garden looks beautiful, Mom," Bennet said as her mother joined her outside, placing her freshly baked raspberry pound cake, plates, and silverware on the table.

"You know, everyone loves spring and early summer for all the flowers, but I have always liked the blooms of autumn best of all. I think it is because that is when my roses look their best."

"Well, there are some Impressionist garden paintings that would pale in comparison to what is on view right here," Bennet replied.

Just as Bennet found herself wishing all their conversations could be this easy her mother spoke again, shattering the peacefulness of the moment.

"You know, if you had actually sat and listened to Milton Winer at the gala instead of running off and leaving me alone with him, you could have learned a little about flowers."

"Learned a little?" Bennet said as she rolled her eyes. "I have a difficult time believing that he would be capable of saying just a little about anything. Come on, Mom; even you have to admit he was painfully boring."

"Well regardless, it was incredibly rude of you to leave me with him," Adelaide snapped.

Despite her words, Bennet saw her mother trying to hold back a smile.

"You know you deserved it. No one asked you to play matchmaker that evening and if I had I would certainly have fired you on the spot for your completely underwhelming selection."

Seeing that her mother was about to reply, while trying her best to stay calm, Bennet hurriedly added, "I have been here all of five minutes. Do we really have to start already? Besides, I didn't come here to talk about all my failures."

"Oh, I know that. I am sure you are only here because your sister called you and twisted your arm to get you to come along."

When Bennet provided no response, Adelaide continued.

"See. I knew I was right. You girls can't take being here unless I guilt you into it."

Bennet sighed.

"Well, you don't make it easy, Mom."

What the hell, Bennet thought as she silently made the decision to push this conversation further. *It can't make things any worse.*

"I'm sorry I'm a failure to you," Bennet began. "I really am, but you know what, I don't think I'm a failure and that is all that should matter. Do you know what happened today?"

Not waiting for her mother to answer, Bennet continued, "I submitted a set of illustrations for a children's book. It is a really big deal for me. I've been excited all day and I should be able to tell you about it. You should be happy for me. But I don't tell you these things because I don't want to hear yet again how I have let you down."

Adelaide grew quiet. For a few moments she sat staring out at her flowers, still but for her forefinger slowly tracing the outline of the rim of her dainty porcelain teacup.

Bennet had begun to fear she had gone too far. She had never really pushed her mother on this subject, figuring it was always easier to just internalize her feelings and avoid confrontation; but something about making those drawings and taking that chance this morning was making her feel brave now.

Just as the silence was beginning to grow unbearable for Bennet her mother spoke again.

"Do you really think I believe you are a failure?" Adelaide asked with sadness in her voice.

Bennet made no attempt to answer.

"If it feels like I am always judging you, I am sorry. The truth is that you are a mystery to me most of the time, Bennet. I know you were your father's girl and you think of me as some outdated meddling mother. But let me tell you something. You may have loved your father, but your father was my whole life; him and you girls. We met in college and married as soon as we graduated. And when we did I instantly became his wife and his champion. I spent my time running his home, raising his children, and helping him by supporting him in his career. I loved every minute of the wonderful life he built for us and that I shared with him.

"Then he died, and that is when I lost everything. I realized after his death that I had no identity of my own. I had no idea who I was without your father. I was lost as to what to do with him gone from my life, and so I focused all my energy on you and your sister.

"Jane is a lot like me I think. But you, Bennet, you fight the entire life I have known and would want for you. And when you do, it is like you reject me as well."

"It's not that I don't want everything you had with Dad; it's just I..." Bennet began before her mother reached out and gently touched her hand, effectively cutting her off.

"I know. It is just that you don't need it the way I did and probably even the way Jane does," her mother replied. "You are your own person and you know who you are.

"The truth is, I think I am a little envious of the life you have built for yourself. You have your circle of friends and your own career and you've shown that you are happy just being you. That makes me proud, even though I had nothing to do with it. I even admit that maybe I have not always found a good way to show it."

Bennet was both surprised and touched by her mother's words. She could not remember ever having had such a frank conversation with her before.

"You have had as much a part in shaping who I am as Dad. You have to know that."

Adelaide smiled. "Well, I just want you to know I am happy you are submitting your illustrations. I am glad you told me about them. I might not understand how that can be a career, but I do know you are incredibly talented and I am proud of you."

"Thanks, Mom," Bennet said softly, overcome by her mother's words.

Then, just as quickly as her mother had shared her feelings the moment passed.

"Yes, yes, well that is enough of that for now," Adelaide said as she placed her teacup down on the table.

"And don't for a minute go thinking that this means I understand why you reject every nice young man I send your way. I fail to see why it would be impossible to do your drawings and date an eligible man."

Bennet smiled at the return of the mother that she knew. Still, there was no denying the importance of their conversation. It would not change much in their daily interactions; her mother would be her mother. And yet, while somewhere deep down on a fundamental level she knew her mother was proud of her, hearing her mother actually say it aloud had effected a chip in the metaphorical wall that had existed between them, one that no one had deliberately built but had been erected nonetheless. Now, Bennet felt that she could maybe start being a little less guarded about sharing things important to her, like the illustrations, with her mother.

Bennet laughed at her mother's words. "And you wonder why I don't let you know I'm coming over too soon in advance. I'm always afraid there is another Milton Winer waiting."

"God, he was awfully boring, wasn't he?" Adelaide asked, unable to hide a smile.

They were both laughing when Jane called out from inside the house announcing her and Charlotte's arrival.

Chapter Twenty-three

Walking into the Northhom Monday morning, Bennet was full of optimism and eager to get down to work. The two weeks before an exhibition opening were always her favorite part of the preparation process. There was a kind of frenetic energy that ran through every one of her tasks and she got an overwhelming thrill of satisfaction when she could check off an item on her extremely long list of things to do.

That positivity had carried her through the first four days of her week, which she had spent primarily holed up in her office working and reworking the design of the show on the scale model of the museum's exhibition spaces and reviewing final drafts of the show's wall text and labels. Today she had finally been able to start doing what she loved most about putting together a show: getting out into the galleries and physically overseeing the beginning of the layout of the works. This was an important final step before the art preparation team could begin to actually start hanging the paintings.

Despite the demanding work, Bennet had found she could not stop smiling all day. Early this morning she had received an email from the author she had sent her drawings to, informing her that he loved her concepts for his characters and that he was interested in having her illustrate his story.

After rereading the email three times just to make sure she was not imagining it, Bennet had called him and immediately accepted his offer. They had engaged in a brief discussion of preliminary details and had made plans for a lengthier phone conversation the next morning, followed by a meeting scheduled two weeks from now to sign a contract and discuss next steps.

Bennet knew she would have a lot of work ahead of her in the coming month but she was too excited to mind. It was the first time she would be recognized as an artist. More than just that amazing prospect, her drawings would be part of a book that might become a favorite of young children for future generations, like the treasured books from her childhood had been for her. That fact was almost more than she could stand. It was so much to think about that several times today she had found she had to actually remind herself that what had happened was real and not just some wonderful dream from which she would soon wake.

Naturally she was eager to share the news with her sister, Terrance, and with Stella, all of whom she knew would be thrilled for her; but she had been so busy today that she had not yet had the opportunity. What had come as a surprise was how often today she had caught herself wondering what Luke Dawlton would think of her becoming a published illustrator. There was no logical reason for her to share the news with him and yet she wanted to. In fact, since the reception he had been a frequent visitor in her mind as she had often found herself thinking about what he had shared with her at his aunt's house and how nice it felt to be there with him in his uncle's study.

Doing her best to rationalize these thoughts, Bennet tried to convince herself it was because they still had to work together on the exhibition. She was absolutely sure that was all he was focused on, a fact which was supported by the email he had sent her this morning asking if there was anything further she needed from him or his aunt in regards to preparations for the opening. It was the first communication they had exchanged since their conversation at the reception and she would have been embarrassed to admit to anyone that she had read the email twice trying to analyze each word as if there would be some hidden subtext or second layer of meaning. Of course there was not. Rather, while cordial, it was purely professional and accommodating. Chiding herself for trying to find something more in the message, Bennet had settled on the fact that at least there was no doubt as to the friendly tone and could be content that it held none of the animosity that had once so clearly existed between them. That was at least something good to have come out of their exchange at the cocktail reception.

Having spent far longer than she should have in crafting her reply, Bennet hoped that her response matched his tone as she informed him that all was moving along nicely with the exhibition and that she would probably be working late tonight and over the course of the weekend on the layout. Knowing it would be good if he could assure his aunt that all was running smoothly, Bennet also wrote to him that if he wanted to stop by tomorrow while the crew was installing the works she could arrange to meet him there to take him through the galleries. She even suggested that he bring his aunt if he wanted, although the idea of spending any time with the judgmental and dismissive Vivian Winthrop was about as appealing as a tax audit.

As she had hit send on her message, Bennet had mentally tried to convince herself that her motives were purely for the betterment of the Northhom and that there was not even a small part of her that wanted to talk with him again. She knew it was pathetic, and completely unwise, but even as Luke had still not replied to her email when she last checked her computer at lunchtime, she found herself looking forward to the possibility of seeing him.

"I think we need to move this painting over here. What do you think Steve?" Bennet asked the head art preparator as she tried her best to focus on the work at hand.

"You're the boss," he replied smiling. "It's your call."

"Well then, I say let's move it," Bennet began after returning his smile. "There is both a better supporting wall here for a painting of that size and more importantly it will make a strong impact as the first thing visitors see when they enter this space."

"Exactly," Steve agreed.

"Do you have time now to help me try switching them out?"

"Sure. Better to have it ready for my crew in the morning."

Noticing he had hesitated just the slightest before answering, Bennet glanced at her phone. Her suspicions were confirmed when she saw the time.

"Steve why didn't you tell me it was after 5:30?" Without waiting for his answer, Bennet continued, "You go now and we will deal with everything in the morning."

"Bennet, it's fine. Let's finish this now before I leave."

"No, I'm good, really."

Bennet knew the art prep team would be putting in a long day in the museum on Saturday and at least a half a day on Sunday so there was no reason for Steve to work late tonight.

"I'm going to be here for a little while more. You go home. We've got a full day ahead of us tomorrow."

"If you really are sure, then I won't say no. Don't stay too late," Steve added as he started to walk out of the gallery.

"And remember, I'm bringing the donuts for you and the crew tomorrow morning," Bennet called out after him.

Steve turned back for a moment and smiled. "I love it when a curator knows the right way to bribe her team. You have a good night."

"You too," Bennet said, laughing as she watched him leave. Now, as so often when she had worked with him in the past, she was struck by Steve's easygoing manner. There was a delicate dance that existed between a curator and the art preparators as they worked together to bring an exhibition to life. Without good personalities from both parties and a willingness to be open and flexible it could often be a difficult process. Bennet did her best to be patient and value everyone's opinions; and thankfully for his part Steve never seemed to get stressed no matter how many times she wanted to switch things around, which she often did in the last days of her show preparations. More than that she had always found Steve to be a steady and calming influence. Bennet knew it was better he go home now and get some rest as she would need his help this weekend and in the coming week when they would inevitably be putting in extra hours and have a few long nights before the opening next Saturday evening.

But just because Steve and most of the museum staff had gone for the day did not mean Bennet would be heading home just yet. Having already informed security that she would be staying late, she was determined to do some more work in advance of the weekend. Finding herself alone and relishing the quiet, Bennet began reviewing her sketches for the layout which she had spread out on the floor of one of the second floor galleries.

Working with models in her office was one thing but once in the physical space she often rethought where certain works might look best. After some consideration, Bennet decided to play with switching the placement of two of the Cubist paintings, and so walked to the back corner of the smaller gallery to retrieve one of the paintings. Safely nestled in its packing crate, she gently carried the work, container and all, to the side wall of the main gallery.

"Could you use some help?" a voice echoed through the empty gallery space, shattering the silence.

Even though her back was to the entranceway, Bennet instantly recognized that it was Luke. As a flustered feeling settled over her, she found she needed to take a few seconds to compose herself, and so she took her time slowly and gingerly placing the crate against the wall before turning to face him.

Standing there, in front of Luke, Bennet became instantly aware of how much of a mess she must look. She mentally berated herself for her choice from a few minutes prior to pull her hair into a loose knot and kick off the heels that had been killing her feet and left her now standing barefoot on the cold marble floor.

Resigning herself to the fact that there was nothing she could do about it now, she made an effort to meet his gaze with as much dignity as she could muster. "What are you doing here?"

If Luke had any knowledge of his effect on her, his smile did not show it.

"I just ended a meeting with your finance director. Of course, I was acting on my aunt's behalf as she felt the urgent need to review some contractual issues with her gift; although not so urgent that she would miss her dinner engagement, which is why I was sent instead."

The truth was, only a few weeks ago, Luke would have complained and done anything he could to avoid having to make another trip to the Northhom; but when his aunt called his office a few hours ago and insisted he handle this matter today, he had readily agreed. While he tried to convince himself he was simply being helpful he had hoped he might run into Bennet again. She was becoming a bit of a distraction as he had found her to be a recurring presence in his thoughts since that time spent together in his uncle's study at his aunt's reception. He had found himself wondering where the conversation might have gone had his aunt not interrupted them and he had been eager to talk with her again; but now that he was with her alone in this gallery he found, much to his surprise, that he was slightly nervous.

"Since I was here I thought it would be good to check in with you as well," Luke added by way of an explanation for his presence at the museum. "I was just starting to head in the direction of your office when one of the guards informed me you were up in the galleries."

Smiling, Luke asked, "I hope my stopping by is not unwelcome?"

Damn that smile.

"No, not at all," Bennet replied as she silently pleaded with herself not to show anything other than professional indifference with his presence here before her. "I was just reviewing the layout for the exhibition and was debating switching the location of two works. I should be waiting for the art prep team tomorrow morning to do it, but I know if I don't try to see what it might look like now before I head home I will spend all night thinking about it."

Bennet sighed before adding, "Pathetic, I know."

Luke laughed. "Not pathetic at all. I'd say dedicated would be more the right word. Since I'm here why don't you let me help. Besides, I think as a Winthrop relative I would have permission to handle the paintings."

"I definitely think you have clearance," Bennet smiled as she replied, hoping she looked more at ease than she felt. The truth was his unexpected presence next to her in an otherwise empty gallery had unnerved her more than a little.

Motioning for Luke to follow her across the large gallery room, Bennet began to explain what she was doing. "I already moved one of the paintings but if you can help me move this Juan Gris to over here we can see if it works."

They each took one side of the frame and brought it closer to where they had first been standing.

"Thanks. Now if you don't mind, just help me lean it here against the wall."

Once it was in place, Luke followed Bennet as she stepped back a few feet and looked at the painting in the new location.

"I like it," he said as he observed how her seemingly small and simple decision to move the piece made it, in the new location, seem to be perfectly situated between two other works of a similar muted color palette.

"Me too," Bennet agreed. "It's like the three works are now in conversation with each other. And I think it makes a stronger impact on viewers as they round the corner from the first gallery."

"Since most of the paintings are already leaning on the floor below where they will be hung; would you like me to give you a preview tour?" Bennet asked. "There may be some changes, but you will get the general idea."

Luke spent the next several minutes walking from gallery to gallery, looking at how Bennet had arranged the paintings for the exhibition.

"Impressive," Luke said when they had finished the tour. There was genuine respect in his voice as he added, "I've been around these paintings for most of my life, but to see them all here in one place, grouped together like this is really something."

"Your aunt might be many things, but she certainly has amazing taste in art and a great eye."

Suddenly, much to her horror, Bennet's stomach let out a grumble. While low and soft, it was magnified by the empty vacuum of the gallery space.

"Oh God, sorry," Bennet began, hoping that her face had not actually turned red. "You know, I've been so busy that I haven't eaten all day."

Luke laughed, "Actually, for a second I was worried it came from me. I'm starving myself."

After a slight pause, as if weighing the wisdom of his next words, he asked, "You wouldn't like to get something to eat, would you?"

"Well, we are both hungry, so it's probably not a bad idea. Sure. I mean, if you want," Bennet rambled.

What the hell is wrong with you? Just say yes.

"Sorry, long day. Let me start again. Yes, that would be nice."

Luke tried his best to keep a straight face as he noted, not for the first time, how absolutely charming she looked when flustered.

"Do you like Chinese?" Luke asked.

Knowing his ability to easily rile her temper, he was being extra careful not to do anything to risk shattering the peacefulness of the moment.

As Bennet nodded in affirmation he added, "Great, because there is this little place in Midtown that has the best Chinese in the city. It's called Stew's Garden Palace."

At the mention of the restaurant, Bennet's eyes widened in surprise.

"I know, I know, it's a weird name, but the owner's wife is Chinese and does all the cooking. It seriously is the best."

"Oh, I know. I go there all the time. The restaurant is actually just a few blocks from my apartment. I can't believe you know it though."

Luke raised an eyebrow, "Really? And why is that?"

"I just mean… Well, at the risk of offending you, let's just say it doesn't seem your type of place."

"Oh, I see; it's not glamorous enough for someone like me? Just what kind of guy do you take me for?" Luke asked with an exaggeratedly hurt look on his face.

Enjoying the playful banter, Bennet added, "Those are your words, Mr. Dawlton, not mine. Anyways, I don't think I've ever heard of Stew's referred to as glamorous before, that's for sure."

"I will have you know as an undergrad I just about lived at that place," Luke began to explain. "Later, when I went to study at Oxford, it took me months to find something even half as good. England's really not known for its cuisine."

Bennet found herself smiling at the image of him combing the streets of that old academic city for somewhere to eat and tried but failed to imagine what the British equivalent of Stew's Garden Palace might look like.

"Besides, Ms. Reynolds," Luke continued, "despite what you think of me, I assure you my tastes are as bohemian as yours."

At that Bennet laughed. "I sincerely doubt it, but I guess I'll have to take your word for it.

"I just have to run down to my office and close up for the day. Should we meet at the restaurant in thirty minutes?"

"Perfect," Luke nodded.

Having descended together to the first floor, they were standing at the foot of the stairs in the main gallery space finalizing their plans when Katherine Hartis rushed out of the administrative corridor. Clearly in a hurry, besides her briefcase, her arms were burdened down by a stack of large binders she was attempting to carry, which, despite her tall height and thin frame, seemed to be causing her to struggle to maintain her balance.

It would have been an understatement to say that she was shocked to find them there, but recovering quickly, she broke into a broad smile.

"Luke, what a treat it is to see you. Whatever could you be doing at the gallery so late?"

"Katherine, it's lovely to see you as always," Luke replied. "I was just going through some final exhibition layout plans with Bennet. It really is going to be an amazing show. You must be as excited as I am."

"Oh I am, believe me," Katherine said, dripping charm.

Bennet found herself fighting back the urge to puke.

"Actually, if you don't mind Katherine, I have to get back to my office." Giving Luke a quick wink, Bennet added, "Perhaps you wouldn't mind walking Luke out?"

"Of course. It would be my pleasure," Katherine replied.

Bennet had done her best to keep her distance from Katherine since the reception. But in this moment she could not resist asking her to do something. It made it seem that Bennet were in charge and it was a move that was sure to annoy Katherine. Bennet knew she would probably pay for it later, but at the moment, she simply did not care.

"Good night, Ms. Reynolds. See you soon," Luke said, cool as could be.

"You too, Mr. Dawlton," Bennet replied with a smile.

Chapter Twenty-four

Thirty minutes later, having made her best effort at a hair and makeup refresh that involved expertly wielding a mascara brush across her eyelashes with a steady hand as her cab wove in and out of the rush hour traffic, Bennet arrived at the crowded restaurant. Everything she had said about Stew's Garden Palace was true. Despite its uninspiring name and the building's plain exterior, once inside, she knew firsthand how patrons became privy to a hidden treasure of culinary delights, which in this case was some of the best Chinese food in the city.

Luke had already arrived and as she walked into the restaurant he spotted Bennet and stood up, gesturing towards her with a slight wave.

"So, you survived your exchange with Katherine then," Bennet said with a smile as she reached the table.

"Yes but it did not escape my notice how quickly you were willing to throw me to the wolves. Thanks for that by the way," Luke replied, returning to his chair only after Bennet was seated.

Luke flashed her a smile, which he hoped hid the wholly unexpected rush of nerves he had experienced as he watched her walking into the restaurant. It was something he reckoned had not happened to him since his school days.

They could register that smile as a weapon, Bennet thought, completely unaware of Luke's nervousness.

"I assumed you would appreciate the whole every man for himself thing. You're supposed to be a cutthroat businessman after all, right?"

As the waiter came over with the menus, he also placed an open bottle of red wine on the table.

"I hope you don't mind," Luke began, "but I ordered a bottle before you arrived."

"Not at all. Should we just order a few dishes and share?" Bennet's question was a test which Luke unknowingly passed when he agreed that it was a good idea.

As a single woman of a certain age, Bennet subscribed to the theory that there was much to be learned about a man through his food preferences. First dinner ordering habits was a case in point. While the meanings changed depending on the type of eatery, in a Chinese restaurant, a good man would never order his own dish and would instead choose to share a variety of items. Such a gesture meant he most likely tended towards selflessness, had the potential to be a giver, and was often willing to try new things. It was one of her and Stella's rules to date by, and she made a mental note to remember to tell her friend about it later.

During their meal, Bennet and Luke quickly fell into a comfortable conversation that easily flowed from one topic to the next. Considering how much she had despised him upon their first meeting and their several disastrous interactions thereafter, Bennet was surprised at not only how easy it was to talk with Luke now but also how much she was enjoying it.

"There is one thing I have been wondering about," Bennet began as she helped herself to a spring roll.

"Just one? I'm surprised."

Bennet smiled. "Well, one for now at least. What I can't quite make out is how you came to have your accent. It's subtle, but it's definitely there. You said you attended Oxford but I would think it would've been too late for your accent to develop by then."

Luke laughed. "So you have been trying to find things out about me."

"That's what you took away from my question?" Bennet replied, once more enjoying their easy banter.

"Absolutely. Since you're so eager to know, I lived in London until I was almost ten years old. My mother was British but after she died, my father could not bear to be there any longer so he arranged a job transfer and we returned to New York. I had enough of an accent from my formative years that it stayed with me slightly. It's strange but when I returned to England to attend school years later, I think it actually grew a bit stronger once I was back around people talking the same way.

"I lived in London for another five years after I finished school before starting my firm here in the city. It's funny because my British friends and clients think I'm too Americanized, but it's the first thing New Yorkers notice. It's a big attraction with all the Anglophiles."

"I bet," Bennet said with a laugh. "You're a regular Mr. Darcy."

"Well I am having dinner with a Bennet," Luke replied giving her a wink, "so I must be doing something right."

Bennet felt her stomach do a somersault.

"You know, in a way you seem to have lived up to your heroine's namesake."

"Oh really, and how do you figure I've done that?" Bennet asked.

"Well, you were completely wrong about me in the beginning just like Elizabeth Bennet was wrong about Mr. Darcy."

"I was wrong?" Bennet asked, doing her best to look incredulous at his remark. "You were the one who wronged me by stealing my pastry. Besides, if we follow this theory of yours than I believe that would make you prideful."

"Who, me? Never," Luke replied. Smiling, he added, "It's funny but I don't seem to remember that part of the novel so well. I guess it's proof that the literary analogy only goes so far."

"Although maybe you have a point," Bennet began as much to herself as to Luke, "since I seem to have dated more than my fair share of Mr. Collinses."

Luke could not help but laugh at her comment. As much as his decision to invite Bennet to dinner had been a spontaneous one, he had instantly been glad that he did. Then waiting for her to arrive in the restaurant he had second guessed whether it had been a mistake; he knew he had the habit of saying the wrong thing around her which resulted in her becoming angry and he did not want that to happen again. The truth was she had an effect on him that he found both interesting and unsettling.

Much to his relief however, things had gone well so far. He had been thoroughly enjoying their evening and unless he was totally wrong, so was she. In fact, as the restaurant staff suddenly appeared and began clearing their plates, he found it hard to believe that they had been sitting together, enjoying each other's company for more than an hour.

When the waiter returned with the check, Luke grabbed it quickly and, despite Bennet's protests, insisted he pay.

While they waited for the server to return with Luke's receipt, Bennet picked up the plate on which rested two fortune cookies and offered one to Luke before taking one for herself.

Luke cracked his open and began to read the fortune.

"Wait," Bennet said as she reached out and put her hand on his arm to stop him. Letting it linger there a second longer than the gesture warranted she suddenly realized that they were touching and quickly pulled her hand back.

"You have to read the fortune first," Bennet instructed.

"I've never heard that before," Luke said, trying hard not to focus on the jolt of electricity he had experienced at the touch of her hand.

"It's Chinese gospel, I'm afraid," Bennet said, smiling.

"All right then; shall we?" Luke asked.

Only after they both broke their cookies into pieces and ate them did Bennet return once more to the fortunes. "You first."

"Okay, but I warn you, I never get a good fortune," Luke replied.

Looking at the small slip of paper, he shook his head before reading the fortune out to Bennet.

"The color of your rainbow depends on the color of your rain. See, what does that even mean really? It's a dud. I'm telling you it happens every time."

Bennet laughed. "You're right. That's pretty bad as far as fortunes go."

"Okay then. Let's see how you do."

Having glanced at the fortune first, Bennet smiled as she read it aloud. "Those who take great risks gain big rewards." Bennet looked up from the paper before adding, "I hate to break it to you, but mine already came true."

"Really?" Luke asked, sounding intrigued.

Unsure whether to share her news, Bennet found herself telling him anyways.

"No one knows this yet, but I just learned this morning that a set of drawings I submitted to an author were well received and I am going to be illustrating his next children's book."

"Congratulations," Luke said as he broke into a broad smile. "Seriously, that is great news."

"Thanks. I think so too. As excited as I am about it though, I have to admit I'm having a hard time believing it's real."

"Well, I think it's the perfect way to start this next week of what is sure to be filled with Bennet Reynolds achievements. I think you will…" Luke began before the waiter returned to the table with the receipt, interrupting whatever he was going to say next.

Silently cursing the waiter for his sudden appearance, Bennet reluctantly found herself speaking the words that would inevitably mark the beginning of the end for their evening.

"Well, we should probably go. I'm sure they want the table."

"Yes, I think you're right," Luke replied as they stood up and began making their way to the door.

While the night air that hit Bennet as they exited the building was a welcome feeling from the crowded space of the restaurant, Bennet found herself sorry to be leaving.

"You know, I can't help but remember the last time we both stood together on a city sidewalk," Luke began looking down at her. "You are much less scary now."

"And you are definitely less arrogant," Bennet replied with a smile.

Luke laughed, after which a silence settled between them as they remained standing on the sidewalk facing each other.

"Well, this was nice. Thank you," Bennet said as she found herself wondering what might have happened next had she not broken the silence.

"My pleasure," Luke replied.

"Please, let me call my driver or hail you a cab," Luke added reluctantly, sorry to see their conversation end.

"Thanks, but there's really no need. My apartment is just a few blocks from here."

"Then I'll walk with you," Luke insisted and, as Bennet nodded, they began to set off in the direction of her apartment.

In only a matter of seconds, their steps synched up as they took in the sights and sounds around them. As they walked along Bennet found herself wondering what other people passing by might think when they looked at them. Did they seem like a couple, like two people who belonged together? Or did they appear to everyone as what she reminded herself they truly were: two business acquaintances who had simply enjoyed a nice evening.

"This is me," Bennet said with a twinge of regret as they reached the steps to her building. "Well, this was nice," she rushed to add. While she hoped she did not sound as lame as she felt, she did not trust herself to say anything more for fear she might say the wrong thing.

"It was," Luke agreed.

Taking a small step forward which had the effect of slightly closing the space between them, he looked down at her. "Bennet, I…"

Suddenly a voice called out, "Bennet, is that you?"

Dear God no.

Hoping she had imagined it, Bennet turned to see her neighbor, Mrs. Morateli, walking towards them. Struggling to carry an overflowing shopping bag in each hand she gave the impression of a waddling duck and lent the moment an almost comical air.

"Is that a nice young man I see you with?" she asked.

Why me?

Without realizing it, Bennet and Luke both stepped back from each other.

Knowing she would now never know what Luke had been about to say to her, Bennet gave him an apologetic smile in advance of whatever was going to happen next at the hands of her well-intentioned but unpredictable and meddlesome neighbor.

"Yes, Mrs. Morateli, it's me," Bennet called out. "Here, let me help you with your bags," she added as the old woman came to an abrupt stop in front of where they stood on the sidewalk.

"What a nice girl you are. And who is this handsome man with you?"

Bennet let out a sigh and rolled her eyes at Luke as an attempt to apologize for whatever her neighbor might say.

"This is Luke Dawlton. He's a friend from work," Bennet said unsure of how else to describe him.

"Hello, Mrs. Morateli," Luke said, extending his hand to her as Bennet grabbed her shopping totes. "Lovely to meet you."

"My, what a delightful accent. And so tall too," the old woman added as she looked him not so subtly up and down. "Nice to see you with a fellow on a Friday evening Bennet instead of alone all the time."

Luke cleared his throat in an attempt to stifle a laugh.

"Isn't it a little late to be shopping?" Bennet asked quickly, trying to prevent her neighbor from making any further embarrassing statements.

"I just wanted a little ice cream so I went to the deli. And then you know how it goes, I thought of ten other things I needed when I was in there."

Never having taken her eyes off of Luke, Mrs. Morateli grinned and asked, "Maybe you and your friend would like to have some dessert with me. I was just going to turn this ice cream into a sundae. I have loads of fixings already at home."

Bennet was mortified. She could not have dreamed of a more embarrassing situation than Vivian Winthrop's nephew standing at her doorstep being offered an ice cream sundae by a geriatric matchmaker who was looking at him as if he were a prized cut of meat.

"I am afraid I have to go, Mrs. Morateli," Luke replied with a wink to Bennet. "But perhaps another time."

"I do hope so," she replied in a voice that Bennet feared was her neighbor's attempt at sounding coy and flirtatious.

"Goodnight, Luke," Bennet said quickly, grateful that at least Mrs. Morateli would be unable to say anything further to humiliate her. "Thank you again."

"Goodnight, Bennet," Luke replied while noting how her face had somehow managed to become even prettier with the pale pink blush that had settled on her cheeks at the embarrassment over the old woman's words.

Letting out a sigh, Bennet turned towards her neighbor, "Okay, Mrs. Morateli, how about we get that ice cream inside before it melts."

Quickly glancing over her shoulder, Bennet was able to see Luke turn back towards her from further down the sidewalk and give a quick wave before she was forced to return her attention to helping her neighbor up the stairs and into the building. She was sure the look of regret she thought she saw briefly cross his face was nothing more than her imagination, a reflection of what she herself was feeling.

Chapter Twenty-five

Bennet walked into the Northhom on Monday morning riding the high of a wonderful weekend. The surprisingly pleasant dinner with Luke at Stew's Garden Palace on Friday proved to be just the beginning of a jam-packed two days. First she spent a long Saturday at the museum working with the art preparation team overseeing the beginnings of the installation for the Winthrop exhibition. A lot had been accomplished and she felt she had given herself a good head start on all the work she would have to accomplish in this last week before the opening. But it was the rest of the weekend that was making her feel really good, as it was full of congratulations and celebration as she shared with her family and friends the good news about her new role as a children's book illustrator.

Stella had of course insisted on taking her out for celebratory drinks on Saturday evening where they were joined by Terrance who made her smile with the enthusiastic way that he insisted on taking a large share of the credit for Bennet's success since, as he announced several times over dirty martinis, he was the one who had connected her to the author in the first place. Her family was equally thrilled for her when she announced her news at dinner at her mother's on Sunday evening. Both Jane and David said they could not wait until Charlotte was old enough to read her auntie's book and even Adelaide seemed genuinely happy for her, going so far as to lead a toast in her honor. It should not have mattered as much as it did, but Bennet found herself treasuring her mother's enthusiasm.

Despite how busy she was however, Bennet could not help herself from periodically returning to thoughts of Luke. She was just glad she had not shared any details of her evening with her friends as she knew they would have wanted to analyze every moment and review every last detail of who said what and how they said it, trying to make more out of it. Bennet had managed to convince herself that it was simply a nice evening between two people who had found a way to finally work together; a notable accomplishment considering on more than one occasion she had caught herself wondering what might have happened if her nosy neighbor had not arrived when she did.

The happiness Bennet felt walking into the museum lasted about as long as it took her to step into her office, take off her coat, and turn on her computer. Sadly, it had only taken mere minutes for her world to come crashing down around her, leaving her to feel as if the past two days and all the good moments they contained had been nothing but a figment of her imagination. With only one week left before the exhibition opening, Bennet now found herself smack in the middle of a mini-crisis; a reminder for her that as soon as she became happy, there was always something looming to cause her to be jolted back to the reality of her stressful life as curator at the Northhom.

While the catalogue for the exhibition would not be arriving until the end of the show, Bennet had done what she thought was a good job writing the text for the small booklet that was to be made available for visitors beginning on the night of the opening. It contained images of some of the most impressive works, along with a complete list of the paintings and sculptures that comprised the Winthrop gift. Most importantly, it was to include a brief but detailed description of the story of how the amassing of Vivian Winthrop's and her late husband's collection came to be, and an account of the events leading up to her decision to give the works to the museum.

Bennet had written the first draft of the text and reviewed it with Stella as well as the entire Publications Department. She had then given the copy to Katherine for her review who had insisted that she be the one to send the text to Vivian for her final approval before the booklet went to the printers.

When Katherine had returned the copy to her two weeks ago, complete with a number of editorial notes in bold red text, Bennet had assumed all was well. And so, as was procedure, she had incorporated the changes and passed the copy on to the Publications Department who oversaw its printing with an external press.

The booklets had arrived over the weekend, all twenty thousand in the original print run, and one had been waiting for Bennet on her desk when she arrived this morning. The publication had turned out better than she had hoped and Bennet was glad she had insisted they go with the more expensive high gloss paper stock because, as she had thought it would, it had made the colors of the paintings seem more vivid. As she flipped through the pages she was privy to an array of stunning images of amazing works that showed the full range of early to late modern masterpieces and she was just about to read the text about Vivian Winthrop when her phone rang.

Bennet did not even have time to say hello when the voice on the other line began to speak.

"Bennet? It's Harry."

There was something strained about Brent Stromwell's assistant's voice that instantly put Bennet on alert.

"Hi, Harry. How are you doing this…"

"Listen Bennet, Brent needs to see you in his office right now."

"Is there anything I should bring?"

"He asks that you bring all notes you have on the exhibition publication."

"I'm leaving my office now," Bennet replied.

"Thanks," Brent's assistant began, "and Bennet, I'd hurry if I were you."

As Bennet hung up the phone and gathered her file along with her copy of the fresh-off-the-press booklet, a horrible feeling of anxiety washed over her. There was no way this was going to be a friendly conversation or a congratulatory "way to go" on her work. She knew something was definitely wrong.

Reaching the director's office in record time, as Bennet entered the room she noticed Brent seated at his desk. While his demeanor seemed cold, it was Katherine's expression that most worried her. Standing next to Brent, she was glaring at Bennet like a hawk eyeing her prey.

While she could have guessed that Katherine would have been in the room to witness whatever humiliation was about to come her way, Bennet was surprised to find the head of publications, Lettie Waters, sitting on one of the two chairs opposite Brent's desk.

"Take a seat," Brent barked.

As Bennet did as instructed Brent continued, "We need you to take us through the steps you followed in regards to the creation of the copy for the Winthrop Collection exhibition booklet."

Confused and now fully on her guard, Bennet relayed step by step the stages of the creation process.

"Finally, after the Publications and Public Relations Departments had reviewed the copy," Bennet began as she neared the end of her recap, "I passed it on to Katherine, who instructed me that she would forward it to Vivian Winthrop for review and final approval.

"A day later, after receiving Katherine's edited copy, I sent it to Publications per established procedure, who then took on the oversight of the printing."

"That's correct," Lettie added, sounding as uncomfortable as Bennet felt. "We used our regular printing company and everything went well. The print run was delivered over the weekend."

"Well Bennet, even given what you have just said, I am having a hard time deciding if you are simply incompetent or deliberately trying to sabotage this exhibition," Brent began, failing to conceal his rage.

"I don't understand. I'm sorry, but someone needs to tell me what the problem is because I've been looking over the brochure this morning and I think it looks great," Bennet replied, totally unaware of what the issue was that had made Brent so furious.

"The problem is that after I had a copy of the booklet messengered over to Mrs. Winthrop yesterday, as a courtesy, she called me this morning quite incensed that she had not been given the opportunity to review the copy. She could not imagine how a museum of our caliber could be so grossly ignorant as to not allow her to give her approval before printing information about her in a publication for her own exhibition."

Unable to hide his anger, Brent added, "I will not even begin to explain to you how bad it looks for the museum and for me personally to have to hear something like that from one of our most generous patrons."

Bennet was shocked by Brent's words and her mind was racing trying to figure out why Vivian Winthrop would say such a thing.

Unsure how best to respond, when she finally managed to speak she knew her reply sounded weak.

"I really am sorry but I don't understand how this has happened. I sent the copy to all the appropriate departments internally. And then Katherine, you personally insisted that you wanted to be the one to review the copy with Vivian directly."

Katherine, who had remained uncharacteristically silent throughout Brent's tirade, now began to speak but not without first locking eyes with Bennet for the briefest of moments. "I do not know why you are saying this Bennet, but I never said any such a thing. I assure you I have more important things on my plate than to concern myself with doing your job. There would be absolutely no reason for me to want to review the exhibition copy with Vivian."

Bennet was beyond angry as the reality of her situation became clear. Having listened to what her boss had said, she now knew without a doubt that she had been set up by Katherine who must have been hoping this very thing would happen.

Still, all Bennet could do was stare in disbelief as Katherine continued to speak.

"If you have made a mistake Bennet, I would hope you would have the decency and professionalism to own it. Mistakes happen, albeit not usually this important of one, but the worst thing you could do here is to blame someone else."

"Katherine, you know very well that I…"

"We have no time for this," Brent said, angrily cutting Bennet off.

In that moment Bennet knew she was stuck. Katherine had planned this as a way to sabotage her and there was nothing she was going to say that would make Brent believe otherwise. He too had been expecting her to fail with this exhibition and this was his moment as much as Katherine's, even if he was not aware of what Katherine had done to achieve it.

"I am only going to say this once," Brent continued. "You have until tomorrow morning to rectify this situation with Vivian Winthrop. If you have to go crawling to her on your hands and knees and beg her to okay this exhibition copy then you do it. We are not spending the money nor do we have the time to reprint these booklets."

"I will handle it," Bennet said.

"Yes, you damn well will."

When no one moved, Brent shouted, "Well then go! What are you still doing here?"

Bennet had no idea how she managed it, but she somehow propelled herself up and out of her chair and began moving towards the doorway. As she did so, she saw a look of sympathy flash across Lettie's face which was almost more than she could bear.

Only after exiting the administrative corridor did Bennet finally allow herself to breathe again. She was so angry she did not trust what she would do, but she refused to cry or show any expression of her anger in front of the museum visitors.

While she had begun to walk back toward her office, at the last second she turned and went instead in the direction of the staff exit.

Once outside, despite being in the fresh air, she felt like she was having trouble breathing.

This must be what a panic attack feels like, Bennet thought as she tried to force herself to take in a deep breath and then slowly exhale.

After a few minutes of steadying her nerves and concentrating on her breathing, Bennet had succeeded in calming herself down enough that she was able to walk over to the museum's small outdoor garden where she took a seat on one of the wrought iron benches set amongst the perfectly landscaped greenery.

Steadier now, Bennet found herself admitting that even she could never have imagined Katherine capable of this level of despicable behavior. She had deliberately and calculatingly lied about her plans to review the copy with Vivian Winthrop. There was nothing Bennet could have done differently since there was no reason to suppose that when Katherine returned the copy to her, complete with numerous red edit notes, that she had not shown it to Vivian.

As this horrible reality set in, Bennet's shock over the booklet turned to anger. She knew that the only thing to do now was to try and fix the situation, because she was not going to let Katherine ruin her. She would succeed in this even if it meant she would have to throw herself on the mercy of Vivian Winthrop; something that infuriated her almost as much as Katherine's actions.

"I thought I might find you here."

Bennet looked up to see Stella standing in front of her. It was clear from the expression on her face that she knew what had just taken place. By this time Bennet feared her mistake would have already become gossip for the entire museum staff.

"So you know?" Bennet asked.

Stella nodded. "Lettie told me when she came back to our office. She was really worried about you."

"There was nothing she could do," Bennet said as a wave of humiliation washed over her.

Lettie had been as much in the dark about this problem as she was. Bennet had simply turned over the edited copy to Publications and told Lettie everything was set to be sent to the printers when Katherine had returned the booklet proof to her because that was what she honestly believed at the time. Maybe if she had told her that Katherine had insisted she be the one to review the copy with Vivian then Lettie might have been able to tell Brent that she had been aware of Katherine's involvement with the brochure. It probably would not have mattered though since it would still have been Bennet's word against Katherine's and Brent was never going to believe her.

"Are you okay?" Stella asked as she took a seat on the bench next to Bennet.

"I swear to you Stella that Katherine told me she was going to show the copy to Vivian Winthrop. Either she dropped the ball and wants me to take the fall or, what I think is more likely, is that she is actually setting me up to fail."

"I think she is capable of either or both," Stella replied. "What are you going to do?"

"I don't really have much of a choice, do I? I'm going to do the only thing I can do; I'm going to fix it. I haven't worked this hard on the exhibition to let it be ruined now."

"You know you could talk to Luke," Stella suggested. "He might be able to smooth things over with his aunt."

"No," Bennet answered firmly.

Thinking of the nice evening they had shared only nights before, there was no way Bennet was going to go crawling to him for help now. She refused to let him see what a giant mistake she had made and could only imagine what he would think of her if he did find out.

"Absolutely not. I'm going to confront Vivian Winthrop directly and just fall on my sword." Shaking her head in anger, Bennet added, "There's no way I'm going to let that bitch Katherine get away with this. She is not going to win this one because I'm going to fix it."

"All right then," Stella said as she stood up and reached out for Bennet's arm to help her up. "You better get back to your office and pull yourself together. Something tells me this will not be a pleasant task."

Chapter Twenty-six

Thirty minutes later, having been informed by the cold yet ever efficient Nora Mason of Vivian Winthrop's schedule, Bennet found herself walking into the Dartmore. A five-star restaurant located in the lobby of one of the city's most elegant hotels, the Dartmore boasted a patron list of Manhattan's most elite residents including dignitaries, celebrities, politicians, and old money millionaires. On her best day Bennet would have felt out of place but today, as she entered the restaurant it seemed as if everyone not only recognized that she did not belong but somehow knew about the disaster that was the reason for her presence. Even Nora Mason had known what a mess she was in as Bennet recalled how her voice dripped with condescension as she had readily provided information on how her employer could be reached, which Bennet took to mean the museum's great benefactress was not only anticipating her call but was also most likely expecting some major groveling on her part.

Letting the maître d' know whom she was here to meet, Bennet was quickly escorted through the restaurant to the back of the large room where Vivian Winthrop was seated. Even from a distance, she saw how unapproachable she looked, pristinely sitting at her table with her back ramrod straight and not a hair out of place. The mere sight of her caused an image of the Titanic sailing into a giant iceberg to flash through Bennet's mind; a visual metaphor in which Bennet knew she was the doomed ship.

While this was never going to be a pleasant task, just as Bennet was about to reach the table it turned into a potential nightmare when she realized that the man sitting opposite Vivian at her table was Luke. In that moment whatever slim chance she had of preventing him from finding out about this horrible mishap vanished.

Despite Bennet desperately wanting to give in to her sudden urge to simply turn and run out of the restaurant, she also knew she would lose her job if she did. Accepting there was no other viable option, Bennet did the only thing she could and, using all her nerve, tried to appear as professional as possible as she came to stand before their table.

"Ah, Ms. Reynolds, I was just asking my nephew to forgive this thoughtless interruption of our lunch," Vivian Winthrop said coldly by way of an introduction. "I assured him this unpleasant disruption would be brief as you would only be staying a few minutes."

Something I'm sure you enjoyed, Bennet thought as she cursed her luck that Luke would be here. Just once she would have liked to catch a break.

Luke cringed at his aunt's words. Since their dinner Friday evening, he had spent more time than he probably should thinking about Bennet Reynolds and when he might see her again; this however was certainly not the way it had played out in his mind and he was as uncomfortable with the unfolding situation as Bennet appeared to be. If he had known earlier what had happened with the museum he would never have agreed to join his aunt for lunch, but now that he was here, he vowed to himself that he would do his best to help Bennet in any way he could.

"Thank you for taking the time to meet with me, Mrs. Winthrop," Bennet began. "I promise I will do my best to make this quick."

"Do sit down," Vivian snapped. "I refuse to have you stand there making a scene. In addition to everything else you have done wrong, I will not allow your poor social graces to make me the subject of gossip among the rest of the guests attempting to enjoy their lunch."

"Sorry, I… I mean, yes, of course," Bennet mumbled as she fought back the overwhelming urge to tell this miserable woman where she could stick it.

Seeing that Luke had started to rise from his chair as she was about to take her seat, Bennet was quick to motion that he should not bother. She feared any gesture on his part to be accommodating to her might only serve to further annoy his aunt.

"Luke, nice to see you again," Bennet added as she hurriedly sat down at one of the table's two empty chairs.

"Yes, yes," Vivian began, making it clear she had no interest in any attempt at pleasantries on Bennet's part. "I have just detailed for my nephew the issue with the exhibition booklet. Needless to say, I am very displeased. In fact I think it imperative that I tell you how upset I am that you would print something without my approval when it relates directly to me. I would never have imagined the Northhom Museum capable of such sloppy and wholly unprofessional behavior."

Why does Luke have to be here? Bennet thought as she wondered what horrible things he must be thinking about her now.

"Mrs. Winthrop, I assure you that the fault is completely ours," Bennet began, knowing she had no choice but to do what she had come here to do; grovel to this condescending woman who she knew would take great pleasure in watching her do so.

"I was made to understand that you had been shown the copy or I would never have allowed the publication to go to print otherwise."

As Vivian Winthrop made no move to say anything and rather just glared across the table at her, Bennet was forced to continue.

"It's just now, if changes have to be made, I am not sure we can get everything done before the opening. It would be such a shame if…"

"Well if the Northhom has made a mistake," Vivian began, interrupting Bennet, "it will be their job to see that it is fixed and to pay whatever it costs to rectify the situation. I fail to see how any of this is my problem."

"No. Of course it is absolutely not your problem, but the publication would so enhance the exhibition that it would be unfortunate if you were not recognized in print in this way.

"And, if I might add, while I am sure my opinion does not matter," Bennet began, taking away the chance for Vivian to say exactly that, "I do think the exhibition brochure looks beautiful."

As Vivian remained silent, Bennet began to fear that she would be unable to satisfactorily resolve this situation on her own. As much as she dreaded it, she was starting to believe she would be forced to go back to Brent and Katherine and tell them that the museum would have to pay for the rush reprint of the brochures.

Up until now Luke had remained silent, but he took this moment to interject himself into the conversation.

"I feel compelled to say something, Aunt Vivian. If you had told me about this matter earlier, I could have clarified everything and spared Ms. Reynolds the trip down here on what I am sure is the start of a very busy week for her with last minute exhibition preparations before the opening.

"I reviewed the copy word for word before it went to print and thought it provided a glowing account of your and uncle's collection."

As shock registered on Vivian's face, Luke continued to explain. "I thought it fell within the list of tasks you wanted me to oversee for you when you asked me to help out with your exhibition. If I thought for even a minute that you would have wanted to trouble yourself with this mundane task I would have insisted you review it as well. I just assumed, however, that you would be far too busy."

Vivian Winthrop shifted her gaze away from Bennet and now stared at her nephew as she tried to decide the veracity of his words.

"You really should have discussed it with me, Luke," Vivian replied.

Knowing he was winning the argument, Luke softened his approach slightly. "Yes, but you did insist I be involved in the exhibition so you did not have to be. Wouldn't the review of a simple brochure copy fall under my job responsibilities then?"

"Yes, yes, I guess it would." Vivian knew she could not make much more of this without contradicting Luke in front of what she considered to be mere museum staff. Social protocol in her world would never allow for that.

Glaring at Bennet once more, she added, "If that is all then I do not see why we cannot just use those booklets. Now, if you will excuse us, your interruption has significantly cut into the time we had allotted for our lunch."

"Unless you would like to join us?" Luke asked, the words flying out of his mouth before he even had time to consider how awkward that might be for Bennet. As much as he had found himself desiring to spend more time with her, a meal shared with his aunt was not the way to do it.

Bennet had sat speechless as Luke had lied to help her out of this situation with his aunt. She was grateful, but also more than a little shocked that he had done so. While she felt an overwhelming urge to explain everything to him then and there so he did not think her completely incompetent, she also knew now was not the appropriate moment.

"No, thank you, but I've already taken up too much of your time," Bennet replied.

Then, almost hesitantly, she added, "However, with everything that has happened I am afraid I will just need you, Mrs. Winthrop, to sign off on the booklet proof so we can have it for our records. I will messenger a copy of the proof over to you as soon as I get back to my office if that isn't too much of an inconvenience."

"Send it to Luke," Vivian replied with an air of disdain. "He can sign for me since he seems to have taken such an interest in this publication. He will be sure to get it back to you tomorrow."

Vivian Winthrop's words made it clear that while societal norms may have dictated she drop this matter, she was less than pleased by the entire event. Luke may have provided a good explanation regarding this situation, but she was still clearly upset. In some ways, Bennet knew she had a right to her feelings. It was inexcusable that the copy had not been sent to her for review. The fact that none of this was her fault however, could never be explained and Bennet knew that this incident had further diminished her in this woman's eyes. While she really did not care what Vivian Winthrop thought of her, she found it mattering a great deal in this moment that Luke thought she was so bad at her job as to have let this oversight occur.

Bennet knew when she was being excused and, wanting nothing more than to leave the restaurant, she quickly stood up from the table.

"That will be fine. I look forward to seeing you both at the exhibition opening on Saturday."

Just as she was turning to leave, Bennet stopped for one brief moment, looked back to Luke and mouthed the words "thank you" before hurrying out of the restaurant.

Chapter Twenty-seven

Having returned to her office as quickly as she could after her escapade at the Dartmore, Bennet now found herself sitting at her computer composing an email; eager to inform her bosses that the exhibition brochure matter had been resolved. What she did not share with them was the fact that this resolution was due to Luke's stepping in and covering for her with his aunt. It made her stomach ache to think that Luke, without knowing what had really happened, thought she was unable to effectively do her job.

Still, despite the disastrous morning, Bennet knew things could have been much worse. Vivian Winthrop had been more or less appeased and Katherine had not succeeded in her plans to sabotage her, a fact that Bennet took comfort in as she hit send on her message.

Once it had migrated to the sent folder with a single whooshing sound, Bennet reread the email. Despite being furious at all that had happened she allowed herself a smile as she imagined a look of defeat settling on Katherine's face as she read it:

> *To: Brent Stromwell*
> *Cc: Katherine Hartis, Lettie Waters*
> *From: Bennet Reynolds*
> *Date: October, 22, 01:32:48 EST*
> *Subject: Exhibition Booklet*

Good afternoon, Brent,

I have spoken to Vivian Winthrop and she is now fine with the copy as we have printed it. All has been smoothed over, and she has given the okay to distribute the booklets as they are.

She has asked her nephew to sign the proof copy for our records. He will messenger that over to me by tomorrow morning at which time I will personally bring it to your office.

Regards,

Bennet

Brent's reply had been swift:

To: Bennet Reynolds
Cc: Katherine Hartis, Lettie Waters
From: Brent Stromwell
Date: October, 22, 01:41:07 EST
Re: Subject: Exhibition Booklet
Bennet,

Thank you for your quick attention to this matter. As all is fine now, I feel no need to look any further into the mishandling of this assignment on your part and what you claim to be your miscommunication with Katherine. In the future YOU are to handle all copy approvals ON YOUR OWN unless directly instructed by me to do otherwise. I am sure I do not need to say again how this entire situation would not have occurred if you had simply done your job in the first place.

Katherine has been included on this email and will know that it is YOUR responsibility moving forward should you try again to pass this task onto someone else instead of handling it on your own.

Brent

Having read the email three times, Bennet had to face the reality that there would be no further investigation into the incident. She would have to endure the blame for what had happened, even though it was not at all her fault. It would never come to light that it had been Katherine who had asked to correspond with Vivian Winthrop directly or had tried to derail the publication.

Still, all had been handled and nothing else mattered at this point. She knew Vivian would not bring the matter up again as Luke had made it seem that she was incorrect in demanding to have seen the copy in the first place. Despite the anger Bennet felt over the condescending email Brent had sent to her, she was just glad Katherine had tried to do her worst and failed. She may look blameless in Brent's eyes, but Bennet knew the truth.

While Bennet had made it through the rest of the day without any further interactions with Katherine and Brent, she was still relieved when five o'clock came and she could leave her office. The subway ride home had provided her little opportunity to clear her head however as thoughts of her morning exchange with Vivian and Luke were fresh in her mind. Whether it was wise or not, she had come to realize it mattered what Luke thought of her; based on what he had witnessed this morning, she was sure he thought that she was wholly incompetent at her job, or else how could she have let such a screw up take place.

While she would have likely spent the next few days agonizing over how she was going to explain to him it was not her fault without also revealing the duplicitousness of Katherine's actions and perhaps give him reason to doubt the professionalism of the Northhom Museum's administration, it seemed fate was not going to provide her with that opportunity. Just minutes before she was leaving her office for the day, Luke had called to once more offer his assistance. Believing she would want the brochure copy proof that his aunt had signed as soon as possible, he had asked if she would like him to drop it off for her at the museum. When she informed him she would be leaving soon for the evening and he could just get it back to her tomorrow he had, to her surprise, offered to drop the paperwork off at her apartment later after finishing up a meeting he had to attend that was taking place nearby.

Bennet had said yes without thinking anything of it, but was now worrying over whether it was appropriate for her to have done so. Surely Luke was just being nice by offering to drop it off, she reasoned, and her place was as he had said on his way back Uptown anyways. But now it meant she would have Luke at her apartment again and as she walked the three blocks from the subway station to her home she found herself not only trying to figure how she would explain this morning's debacle with the brochure but also what to do when he arrived. Should she invite him in or offer him a drink? Would he be expecting her to or would that be unprofessional? All these questions were running through her mind.

Don't be stupid and overthink everything, Bennet chided herself.

He probably saw what a disaster you were today and just wants to make sure you don't mess up anything else before the exhibition opens.

Rounding the corner onto her block, as her apartment building came into view, Bennet was surprised by the sight of her sister standing on the front steps with an expression on her face that made it clear that something was terribly wrong.

"Jane, what is it?" she asked as she rushed over to where her sister was anxiously waiting.

"Oh, Bennet, it's such a disaster. I don't know what we are going to do."

Bennet pulled her sister into a comforting hug.

"Come inside. We will figure it all out."

With no idea what could possibly be so wrong as to have her normally calm and in control sister look so distraught, Bennet tried her best to sound reassuring as she quickly moved Jane into the building's entranceway and up the three flights of stairs to her apartment.

"Here, sit down," Bennet instructed as she guided her sister towards the sofa. "Give me a minute and I'll be right back."

Walking into the kitchen, Bennet took off her coat and put it and her bag on a stool then quickly retrieved two glasses from the cupboard and filled them with wine from the half-full bottle in her refrigerator. Bringing them back with her into the living room, she handed a glass to Jane before sitting down next to her.

"Okay," she began, taking her hand. "Tell me what has happened."

At the sweet gesture of affection from her sister, Jane lost her usual veneer of control and burst into tears. It took her a few minutes to pull herself together enough to begin speaking again and when she did, her voice was heavy with a mixture of sadness and anxiety.

"You know how I have hinted at things not being fine between me and David. I can only imagine what you have been thinking, but it has all been about work. Things have been bad for a while."

"But I thought he was doing well at the firm," Bennet replied. It unsettled her to see Jane so out of control and emotional. It was usually Jane comforting her and now the sisterly roles had seemingly become reversed.

Taking a sip of wine, Jane struggled to continue. "Well that is of course all we would let you see. I have done my best to put off your questions assuring you everything was fine because that is what David wanted. And I guess I hoped everything would just work out if I didn't acknowledge anything but now I see how wrong I've been to try and ignore this whole situation."

"It's going to be okay, Jane. Just tell me what's happened."

Jane let out a heavy sigh before starting to explain. "There has been some rearranging of staff throughout the organization. David's position was fine and he should have just kept his head down and left things alone. I told him to, but there was a new vice president position that has become vacant and David was desperate to get it.

"What really angers me is that he stood a good chance of receiving the promotion just on the work he already does for the firm, but he thought if he could broker some big new deal that would really impress upper management by bringing in revenue and clients then he would be sure to get the job.

"The deal David came up with involved risks he would not usually take and he kept it quiet from the other members of the firm's management team, thinking once it was secure they would be both surprised and thrilled with what he had done. It was a stupid thing to do and if he had said anything to me I would have told him that myself; but of course he didn't say a word."

Bennet could not help but notice the anger mixed in with the fear in her sister's voice as she described her husband's actions.

"He has been really stressed with work the past couple of months and the last few days have been much worse. He stays at the office each night longer than he ever did before. He hasn't even made it home to put Charlotte to bed in a week. I knew he was trying for the new position so I just thought he wanted the bosses to see him putting in extra hours. But now I know it's because of this mess he has gotten himself into with this deal. I thought we shared everything with each other but I guess I was wrong."

Bennet was having a hard time reconciling what Jane was saying with the steady, conservative brother-in-law she had always known David to be.

"I don't understand. If he doesn't usually make those kinds of deals, how did he even pull one together so quickly?" Bennet asked.

"He went outside the firm. It was Jeremy Burlow who brought the idea to him."

At the sound of his name Bennet felt instantly sick. Her own limited experience with the man had shown her that he was a cad and certainly not someone to be trusted.

She had also not forgotten how Jeremy had said the issue between him and Luke was about business. She had been so quick to blame Luke back then; but now, even though she still did not know any of the details of their interaction, she knew Luke well enough to believe that if he did not have a high opinion of Jeremy's business dealings then it was for a good reason. Now as she was listening to her sister, she was beginning to fear Jeremy was worse than even she had first imagined him to be.

"What do you mean? Are you saying Jeremy searched David out? Did he actually approach David with a deal?" Bennet asked, doing her best to try and keep the anxiety she was feeling from manifesting itself in her voice.

"Yes; they had met a while back at some function and he supposedly reached out to him and reconnected a few months ago with this opportunity," Jane replied. "I don't know all the details and David has completely shut me out, but from what I could learn the deal seems to have been a setup. Jeremy got David to invest his share from a select group of his clients' money but then backed out, taking a portion of the jointly invested money and leaving it all to fall on David.

"Jeremy knew David would not be able to say anything without landing himself in serious trouble at work since he did not have full authorization from his firm to make the investment deal in the first place. David hasn't done anything technically illegal, but it goes against firm policy to make such deals without senior approval.

"Of course, people have done this kind of thing before at the firm and when it works it often leads to advancements and that is what David was counting on. But Bennet, when it fails, well let's just say it has had disastrous consequences. David is going to have to find a way to put back in the money on his own to cover the loss or it is going to be really bad. He could lose his job; maybe more. At the very least his reputation will be ruined."

"My God, what are you going to do?" Bennet asked, more to herself than Jane.

Then trying to speak with an optimism she knew she did not possess, she added, "But if the deal is solid and Jeremy just took off with the money than maybe if David can get a new investor to cover what has been taken initially; he could complete the deal before anyone is the wiser and before any real money is lost."

"I guess," Jane replied, "but I can't imagine who David could find to invest with him at this point. He certainly can't go around asking people he knows to take such a hit and invest with him without drawing unwanted attention that might make matters worse."

Jane shook her head as if she had already determined the unlikeliness of this task.

"Sure in the end a new investor could profit but he would have to sacrifice a large portion of his own money upfront, and really who would take such an initial risk? David looks completely untrustworthy now.

"For the last few days, since he discovered that Jeremy had backed out and took some of the money he's been trying to figure a way out of this on his own but he can't so this morning he finally lost it. He broke down and told me everything and I just sat there speechless and shocked with no idea what to do."

"But I just saw you Sunday night at Mom's for dinner. Yeah, David seemed a little quiet but he certainly wasn't behaving how you would think he would be if something so horrible had just happened," Bennet replied as she struggled to comprehend all that her sister was saying.

Jane let out a heavy sigh. "Well if nothing else, I guess I've learned he is good at hiding things. I think some part of him believed if he pretended it wasn't happening then maybe it would all go away. Pretty stupid right?"

Silent tears streamed down Jane's face as Bennet reached for a tissue from the box on her coffee table and handed it to her sister.

"I just feel so lost and I don't know how to help him," Jane continued. "You know the worst thing is that he has always been so worried about how things look and making sure he gives us the best. But Bennet, you have to believe me, I really don't care at all about any of it. That has always been Mom's thing. I fell in love with David for who he is, not what he does. I would live in a shack with him if he asked."

"I know that; of course I do." Bennet put her arm around her sister's shoulders, pulling her into a loving embrace. "You just have to find a way to make David understand it too."

While her thoughts were all over the place as she struggled to understand the magnitude of David's situation and what she could possibly say or do that might help, Bennet also knew her sister needed her to say something.

"Listen, I don't know what to do yet," Bennet began, "but we just have to believe that somehow we will figure out a way to…"

The sudden buzz of the intercom interrupted their conversation.

"Oh no; that's probably Luke."

In all the concern over her sister, Bennet had actually managed to forget about his stopping by.

Jane pulled herself from their embrace. "Luke who? Not Luke Dawlton? You mean the nephew is at your door?"

Bennet nodded. "He was meant to be dropping off a document from his aunt. I was on my way out of the museum when he called and so he offered to drop it off here."

Not long ago the idea of Luke coming to her apartment had filled Bennet with anticipation and had been all she could think about, but now her concern for her sister overshadowed all else.

"Let me just go downstairs and get the papers from him and I will be right back."

"No, don't," Jane said forcefully. "I'm a mess and I have to go anyways. I left Charlotte with the sitter. I have to get going or I will be late. Besides, I can't talk about this anymore tonight anyways."

"Jane, I just think…"

"It's okay. Really, I'll be fine."

Trying desperately to reinject some confidence and control in her voice, Jane added, "Buzz him in. I'm going to leave now, but we will talk again soon; I promise."

Giving her a quick hug, Jane finished her wine in one gulp, stood up, grabbed her coat from the sofa and, before Bennet had time to even try and stop her, had rushed to open the door and stepped out in the hallway.

Having followed her sister to the doorway of her apartment, Bennet watched as Jane turned back for a second to look at her.

As the tears had begun to once more spill from her eyes Jane added, "Please, don't tell a word of this to anyone, not even Mom okay? I can't take her knowing anything. David will be furious if he knows I told you."

"I promise. We will figure this out somehow; I know it. I'll call you tomorrow."

"Sure," Jane said with an air of hopelessness, as she began to rush down the stairs.

The sadness in her sister's voice caused an ache in Bennet's heart.

Then as the intercom buzzed again, she reluctantly pressed the button.

"Hello, Luke. Come on up. Third floor. It's the apartment on the left."

Seconds later Luke Dawlton was at Bennet's door. What only an hour ago had caused her to be overwhelmed with a sense of nervous excitement had in the last twenty minutes evaporated with her sister's news. In this moment she could think of nothing but Jane.

"Good evening," Luke said with a smile.

Despite everything Bennet could not help but notice the light blue cashmere scarf, the same color as his eyes, that Luke was wearing tied loosely around his neck that rested perfectly against a long charcoal gray trench coat. The man definitely knew how to dress; she would give him that.

"I hope I'm not interrupting any plans."

"No, it's no problem. Please, come in," Bennet said, stepping aside from the door and motioning for Luke to follow her inside.

Overwhelmed by all that Jane had just shared and having never figured out how to properly explain what had happened this morning to him, as Luke walked into her apartment, Bennet found herself begin to blurt out a rehashing of the brochure debacle; launching into the topic with such force that it surprised even herself.

"I owe you an explanation about what happened this morning. I assure you I was told your aunt approved the copy or I would never have sent it to the printers. It helps no one to get into the details regarding what went wrong on my end, but I just don't want you to think that I didn't know what I was doing."

Not waiting for a reply, Bennet continued, "Still, I so appreciate you stepping in and helping me with your aunt. You can't even begin to imagine how much it saved me. The truth is, I'm mortified about the whole situation."

"There is absolutely no need to feel that way," Luke replied. "I know enough of your work ethic by now, Bennet, to be certain that if there was a mistake then it was not of your making.

"I assure you, I have firsthand experience with dealing with my aunt and know how she will often go out of her way to be purposefully difficult. I would not have put it past her if she had forgotten she had given her approval and now was holding you accountable anyways.

"Besides, even if the mistake was on the Northhom's end, you did not deserve her misplaced wrath, no matter the reason for the mix-up. I was glad to have helped diffuse the situation and, that said, I just thought you would appreciate having the signed proof as soon as possible."

Pausing for a moment, as if unsure whether to continue, Luke seemed almost hesitant when he next spoke. "Although if I'm being completely honest, I should tell you that I had a second motivation for wanting to personally deliver the document to you tonight. I was hoping now that I am here, you might show me the illustrations you are working on for the children's book. I would really like to see them."

Bennet was surprised by his request, but it pleased her as well.

"Well, I'm not sure you will find them that interesting, but if you really want to see them I'd be happy to show them to you. They're only preliminary sketches though and I still have work to do on them.

"Would you like a drink while I go get the sketches?" Bennet asked as she motioned for Luke to follow her into the kitchen.

"That would be nice; thank you."

On the drive to Bennet's apartment, Luke had surprised himself by how much he was looking forward to seeing her again. Yet now that he was here, there was something about the tone of Bennet's voice as she had been explaining this morning that made him think something more was wrong than the exhibition brochure copy mishap.

Luke paused as he began to walk past a picture of Jane and Charlotte hanging in the hallway. "I know this may sound crazy, but I think I just saw this woman hurrying down the stairs as I was heading up to your apartment."

"Yes, that's my sister Jane. She was in a rush to go pick up her daughter from the..." Bennet found herself unable to finish her sentence as she burst into tears.

"My God, Bennet, what's wrong?"

Confused by what was happening, Luke quickly switched into crisis control mode.

"Here, sit down," he said as he guided her to one of her kitchen stools. Turning on the faucet he took a glass from the drain board, filled it with water, and placed it front of her on the counter.

"Thank you."

Mortified at her outburst, Bennet grabbed a napkin and began dabbing at her eyes.

Luke, who was now seated across from her, gave her what he hoped was a reassuring smile.

"I realize we don't know each other that well, but it might help if you talk about whatever is bothering you."

"I'm sorry," Bennet began. "You have to believe me; I usually don't cry in front of people like this. It's just that you showed up at the worst possible time. I just heard some disturbing news and I don't know what to do about it."

Starting to stand up from the table, Bennet added, "But I am sure you have more important things to do than to listen to..."

"Please, Bennet, talk to me." Luke said cutting her off. "You can trust me."

Luke was looking at her with such concern and she was feeling so overwhelmed by what Jane had just told her that much to her surprise, Bennet sat back down on the kitchen stool and found herself beginning to explain everything.

"I don't want to betray my sister's confidence; but at this point I guess it is only a matter of time before it all comes out anyways. It seems my brother-in-law David has made an investment deal that is about to fall apart."

"Those happen all the time. Deals come and go, but firms always bounce back," Luke replied as he tried his best to sound reassuring.

Bennet shook her head.

"If that was all there was to it, then yes, I'm sure you would be right. But the thing is, he made the deal without the approvals he should have obtained. He wanted to impress the senior management and land the open vice president position at his firm. But now his investment partner has dropped out, taking a large portion of the funds David put in from his side with him.

"He can't go public with it and expose what his partner has done without losing everything. He will be left to take all the responsibility and will probably end up losing his job; not to mention how horribly his reputation will be ruined."

Bennet shook her head at the thought of what she knew she was about to say next.

"But that is not the worst of it I'm afraid."

Looking up at Luke's face which was so full of sympathy and concern, Bennet dreaded having to say anything more.

"I've just learned that David's partner in this deal was Jeremy Burlow."

No longer able to look Luke in the eye, Bennet rambled on, her voice becoming more agitated with each word. "When I first met him at the gala he mentioned that he and David were working on a project, but he said it so casually I didn't really pay it any attention. Honestly, I had forgotten all about the conversation. Then later, when I learned firsthand what a jerk he was, I had just wanted to block him out of my mind all together."

Bennet was embarrassed all over again thinking about what Jeremy had done to her and having to bring it up in front of Luke of all people.

"If I would have remembered that he knew David and I had said something about him to my sister, maybe I would have been able to make them see what type of guy he was before it was too late. Maybe it would never have gone this far. As it stands now, I am afraid they are going to lose everything and I feel like it is partly my fault. I might have prevented some of this if I had told them what I knew about Jeremy."

Luke had gone silent as Bennet had been talking. When she finished and he finally spoke again, it was more forcefully than he had intended. "Listen to me. None of this is your fault. Your brother-in-law should have been more careful who he invested with, yes, but what happened is not only his fault." Reaching out and grabbing Bennet's hand, Luke added, "I'm sure everything will work out."

Then, realizing what he had done, Luke quickly pulled his hand back, got up from his chair, and began to move away from the table.

"I am sure you have things to discuss with your sister and I must get going actually. There is somewhere I have to be and I don't want to be late," Luke said, his words firm and final.

Taken aback by his abrupt need to leave, Bennet did the only thing she could and began to follow him to her door.

"I didn't mean to keep you. Thanks for bringing me the signed proof copy and again, I'm sorry for my outburst."

"There is no need to apologize," Luke said as he hurried out the doorway.

"Luke, wait," Bennet said calling out to him just as he was about to start down the stairs.

As he turned back to face her, Bennet felt a crushing weight settle on her.

"I know it is only a matter of time before this becomes public, but I would appreciate it if you could keep this to yourself until then."

"You can be assured that I will say nothing. Good night, Bennet," Luke said before turning away from her once more to begin his descent down the stairs.

A few seconds later, Bennet heard the outer door of her building slam shut. Stepping back inside her apartment, she went into her living room and collapsed in a heap on the sofa.

Daisy, sensing her mood, jumped into her lap and curled into a ball. As she began to absently stroke the cat's soft fur, Bennet wondered what had possessed her to confide in Luke. She had transformed in front of him into what she hated most: a weepy female. But what was worse was the fact that she had betrayed Jane's trust by telling him. It would be horrible if the news became public any sooner than it inevitably would because of something she had done. Still, whatever she might have thought about Luke in the past few months, she felt certain he would keep her secret.

Bennet fought back a rush of sadness as she remembered the transformation that had taken place in Luke's demeanor at the mention of Jeremy's name. Before that, he had seemed so keen to help her; he had been kind and comforting. But then, when he found out who David's partner had been in the investment deal, his whole manner had changed. Once she had shared that part of the drama, it was as if he could not get out of her apartment and away from her fast enough.

Bennet's opinion of Luke had altered so much since their first horrible interactions. She now knew he was nothing like the jerk she initially thought him to be. Instead, she had discovered that he was a good man who cared about a lot of the same things she did. It sickened her to think about how every time Luke thought of her from this point forward she would be linked to Jeremy Burlow; the horrible man that, for some reason she was still not clear on, he so utterly detested. How she wished she had never met Jeremy. It was humiliating enough that Luke knew she had gone out with him, but even though that was over now, she had brought it all up again by sharing this story with him.

What must Luke think of me? The thought was like torture to Bennet.

Taking a sip of the wine from the glass she had poured for herself when her sister arrived, Bennet grabbed the blanket from the top of her sofa, wrapped it around herself, and laid down. Pulling Daisy into her chest for comfort, she closed her eyes in an attempt to block out all that had just happened. Yet despite her best efforts to shut out the world, Bennet could not help but recognize what she knew to be the truth. In the last thirty minutes, she had lost any hope of real friendship or possibly, just maybe, even more with Luke Dawlton.

Well I will just have to finish this exhibition and then I can forget all about him. I will never see him again after that.

Besides, I can't think about Luke anymore. I have to worry about Jane and David now and what I can possibly do to try and help them.

Still trying her best not to, Bennet's last thought before drifting off to sleep was how sad it was that Luke was out there somewhere thinking ill of her.

Chapter Twenty-eight

After a restless night, Bennet arrived at work the next morning equally frustrated over her inability to figure out a way to help her sister and her failure in trying to banish the memory of her most recent interaction with Luke from her mind. She was grateful for the distraction of the exhibition opening in less than a week and the pile of work associated with it to keep her busy. And so, the next four days passed quickly for Bennet as she worked around the clock with her art prep team to finish the installation of all the Winthrop paintings.

Only days ago she had begun to imagine that Luke would have been a part of this last step in the exhibition preparation process, as all their hard work had led up to this moment. But she had not spoken to him since he had left her apartment Monday evening. The only interaction they had shared was a single email Bennet had sent him on Wednesday morning regarding a question about one of his aunt's paintings. He had responded with the information she needed and let her know that he had a lot of work over the next few days and so he would be unavailable to return to the museum until the night of the opening.

While the email was both cordial and professional, it was also these very things that let Bennet know, without having to hear him say it, that any chance at friendship between them was gone. Other than at tomorrow's exhibition opening, she doubted she would ever see Luke Dawlton again.

"You ready for tomorrow?" Stella asked as she walked into Bennet's office.

Turning to face her friend, Bennet smiled at the way in which Stella had flopped down in the chair next to her desk and dramatically let her tote bag and jacket drop to the floor.

"Just a few last-minute nerves. You know how I get right before an exhibition opens. I'll be happy when the first night is over and then things can get back to a regular routine."

"And Luke?" Stella asked gently. "Any word from him?"

While she had not filled her friend in on all the details, and certainly nothing of Jane and David's troubles specifically, she had provided Stella with the gist of what had happened on Monday night at her apartment, sharing with her how she had fallen to pieces in front of him and made a fool out of herself.

"Nothing other than an email letting me know he would be attending the opening," Bennet replied.

"Right. Enough of this," Bennet added as she powered down her computer, stood up, and began preparing to leave. "It's not like I had any reason to expect anything more."

Stella gave Bennet a look which, while sympathetic, also conveyed to her friend how little she believed what she had just said.

"It's fine, Stella, really. Let's get out of here. I just want to go home and try to relax a little before tomorrow."

"All right," Stella replied as they began to make their way towards Bennet's office doorway. "But after the opening tomorrow night we are definitely going out for drinks."

"Deal."

Forty-five minutes later, armed with takeout, Bennet had unlocked her door and was just about to let herself into her apartment when she heard Mrs. Morateli's door open.

"Is that you, Bennet?"

Oh please, not now.

Bennet turned to face her neighbor while keeping her body wedged in the doorway, doing her best to ensure a quick getaway.

"Hello, Mrs. Morateli."

Despite herself Bennet was unable to hide a smile at the old lady's appearance. Dressed in one of her trademark housecoats, this one green with big purple and pink flowers, the vibrant outfit matched her larger-than-life personality. Every time she saw her in one of these garments Bennet was struck by how much the artists of the Surrealist movement would have liked her nosy but well-intentioned neighbor, as she often looked like she could have walked right out of one of their paintings.

"Did you have a good day?" Mrs. Morateli asked.

"Yes, but it was a busy one. I'm looking forward to a quiet night in."

"So no date then?"

"No, Mrs. Morateli," Bennet said as she let out a sigh.

"You know it is Friday evening. That is a good date night. I thought maybe you would be going out with that nice man that you were with last week. What was his name again?"

"His name was Luke."

"Yes that's right. You're not going out with him tonight?"

What's so hard to understand about it? No, I'm not going out with Luke Dawlton because he probably hates me and my family all because of that horrible waste of a man Jeremy Burlow.

"No. Not tonight, Mrs. Morateli," Bennet replied, trying her best not to sound frustrated.

Not ever again I'm sure. In fact I'll probably be joining you in one of those housecoats soon.

"Well he was certainly a handsome one, wasn't he?"

Bennet sighed again. "Yes, yes he was."

"He looked like one of the old movie stars. Men knew how to be men back then," Mrs. Morateli said wistfully. "They dressed nice and opened doors for women. That's the problem for you young girls nowadays. There are no more gentlemen in the world today. And that accent. Where was he from?"

Not waiting for Bennet to answer, her neighbor continued, "Well I was hoping maybe you could come over tomorrow for tea. My nephew Louie will be there."

Here we go.

"And since he will be visiting me, I thought perhaps the two of you should meet. He is a nice man. Divorced twice; can you imagine that?"

"No, Mrs. Morateli, I can't imagine. But I'm sorry, I won't be able to come over. I have my big opening at the museum tomorrow night, remember?"

"Oh, that is just too bad. Well they were both horrible women."

"Who were?" Bennet asked.

"His ex-wives. But with a nice girl like you, I think he could maybe get it right this time. Besides you have been single for so long that I figure you can't afford to be too picky about looks. It's not his fault he has that one lazy eye."

Good God. Can this get any worse?

Suddenly Bennet's phone rang.

Saved by the bell.

"Sorry, Mrs. Morateli, but that's my phone ringing. I have to go."

Bennet quickly walked the rest of the way into her apartment and closed the door behind her while her neighbor was still talking.

I wonder if she even knows I'm not there anymore? Bennet mused as she hurried to grab her phone from off its base on her hall table.

"Hello."

"Ms. Reynolds?"

"Yes." Hardly anyone she knew ever called her landline and so while the voice was somewhat familiar, Bennet had no idea who might be calling.

"This is Ian Bristle. We met at Vivian Winthrop's cocktail reception a few weeks ago."

"Yes, of course. How are you?"

"I'm just fine, thank you. I hope I'm not bothering you."

"No, not at all. How can I help you?" Bennet asked. She wished she had something more profound to say but she could not imagine why this important man would be calling her or how he had even got her phone number for that matter.

"I was wondering if we could speak about an opportunity that I think might be of some interest to you and I am hoping you might be able to help me out."

"I'm sorry, Ian, but I'm not sure what help I could be," Bennet began as she tried her best to hide her confusion.

"Well you mentioned when we were speaking at the reception how you liked the work of my foundation and it relates to that. However, this really is something that would be easier to discuss in person. Could we perhaps meet for coffee?"

Bennet tried to remember the exact details of their conversation. There was no denying that she was intrigued.

"Bennet, are you still there?"

She had been so lost in her thoughts that Bennet had missed his last few words.

"Sorry, Ian, but could you repeat that please?"

"I wondered if you would be able to meet for coffee. I have some time tomorrow. I know it is the weekend and short notice, but I was hoping you might have a few minutes."

"I have my opening in the evening, but I'm free in the morning," Bennet replied.

After finalizing the details for the meeting, Bennet ended the call. She spent the rest of what she had hoped would be a restful evening thinking about what on earth Ian Bristle would want to discuss with her and what she could possibly have to say that would be helpful to one of the city's greatest philanthropists.

Chapter Twenty-nine

Saturday morning, nine hours before her exhibition opening, Bennet was seated across from Ian Bristle at a coffee shop in Midtown having what could best be described as a surreal, almost out-of-body experience. While she was excited at what had just taken place, she was also a little afraid this was all a dream from which she was surely about to awaken.

After exchanging pleasantries, Ian had launched straight into the reason he had reached out to her and explained that while his foundation was well established he was always looking for new ways to expand its philanthropic outreach. One of the areas which he was interested in pursuing more in-depth was within the field of the visual arts. To that end he would soon be launching a new initiative within his foundation focused on arts outreach for children living in the five boroughs of New York City.

He had described the details of his new initiative to Bennet and then, to her utter shock, he had asked her to run it. She would have a staff she would oversee and she would be working closely with Ian as they developed new pilot programs to implement for the initiative, the first of which would be an afterschool arts program for at-risk children.

While the salary was generous and significantly more than she was making at the museum, it was the idea of engaging children with art and being able to develop new programs that had Bennet the most excited. Without putting herself through her usual inner monologue of debate as to the pros and cons of such a major life decision, Bennet had said yes with zero hesitation; that's how sure she was that she wanted the job.

"I am extremely pleased you will be accepting this position," Ian said as their conversation was wrapping up. "I know in the coming days we can start going into all the specifics of everything involved with this position and regarding the new initiative itself, but do you have any further questions for me today?"

"I know this sounds crazy," Bennet began, "and honestly I could not be more thrilled about this new position, but I have to ask if you're really sure that you want me. I mean there must be hundreds of people in this city alone with far more significant experience than me."

As she nervously waited for Ian's answer, Bennet feared he might realize he had made a huge mistake and want to take the offer back.

Ian laughed. "I assure you that you do not get to be where I am by making any decision lightly, especially one as important as key staffing appointments.

"I was impressed with our discussion at Vivian Winthrop's reception. You have a clear passion and evident enthusiasm for the need to engage children with art. That is what the head of this initiative needs most. The rest can be learned as you go along."

As he continued to speak, Bennet found she still had to struggle to believe it was all really happening.

"You would have had no way to know that I was in the final stages of defining this new initiative when we spoke at the reception, but I already knew you would be perfect for it if I could court you away from the Northhom Museum.

"I of course did my homework after our conversation that evening, including a review of your stellar work at the museum. I also received a glowing personal recommendation from Luke Dawlton, although I did not tell him specifically why I was asking about you. His approval is worth its weight in gold as far as I am concerned.

"However, there is more behind my offer than all of that. Vivian Winthrop's reception was not the first time I've had the opportunity to see you in action."

"See me in action?" Bennet asked. "I'm sure I would have remembered meeting you before."

"Please, allow me to explain," Ian began as a smile broke out across his face at the memory of what he was about to tell her.

"Do you remember, it would have to be a little more than two months ago now, when you spoke with a young girl about a painting? She was on a tour with her second-grade class at the Northhom and she had just seen something in the work that no one else did. Her classmates were teasing her about it and so she asked you if you saw it also."

Bennet immediately recalled the group tour as it was also the day of her meeting with Luke when he was waiting for her at the front desk.

"I do remember. She wasn't afraid to see something in the abstract colors. I think she saw a flower."

"Yes, she did. Good memory. Well, that was my daughter Emily. I was standing off to the side as one of the parent chaperons with her class and was able to witness firsthand your interaction with her.

"I was impressed at how you described that the power of a painting is that each person has the right to see in it exactly what he or she wants to see. You not only validated what she had seen, but also encouraged her to have the freedom to see the painting her own way.

"When I find someone that impresses me I make note of it, and I have been keeping my eye on you ever since. I have to admit that my coming up to you at Vivian Winthrop's reception was not simply a happy coincidence. I knew you would be there and wanted to speak with you."

"Wow," Bennet replied, a sentiment completely inadequate to describe all she was feeling but in the moment it was all she could think of to say. "Well then, I guess all that is left for me to ask is, when would you like me to start?" Bennet added, unable to keep from smiling.

An eager Ian Bristle continued the meeting long enough to finalize next steps which included setting up a more formal and lengthy session for them to review all that would be involved in her new position. They also agreed that Bennet would need sufficient time to wrap up her work at the museum and would then take a few extra weeks as a break before starting the new position to allow her time to finish working on her illustrations. Ian had been genuinely excited when earlier in their conversation she had mentioned that she would be working on the drawings for a soon-to-be published book. That she was also about to become a children's book illustrator was something Ian saw as an added benefit for his new director of the Bristle Foundation's Children's Art Initiative.

Chapter Thirty

Having said goodbye to Ian, Bennet knew she should head back home to get ready for tonight, but instead she decided to take some time for herself and just walk for a bit. Never had a day felt so full of promise and she was overwhelmed with excitement about this new opportunity. A job in which she would effect real change and help children become interested in art was something she had always hoped for, but even in her wildest imaginings she could never have pictured herself with a job as prestigious and potentially impactful. There was really no end to what she could accomplish with the weight and resources of a foundation like Ian's supporting her work.

As she reflected on their conversation this morning Bennet found it more than a little difficult to believe that her interaction with Ian's daughter had left such an impression as to make him start to take notice of her work and to consider her for this position. What had surprised her almost as much was what Ian had said about how Luke had spoken highly of her which had helped lead to her selection for this new position. While it had pleased her to know what he had said, she could not help the nagging feeling that this was before their conversation in her apartment less than a week ago. She shuddered to think what Luke would have said about her character now. He probably could not even be bothered to mention her name anymore thanks to Jeremy. Once more she was overcome with regret at how things had, she feared, irrevocably changed between them.

As thrilled as Bennet was about her new job, she also knew she would never be able to fully enjoy the events of the morning since thus far she had failed to figure out a way to help David and Jane. It seemed unfair that she could be so happy while Jane's world was in the process of being turned upside down.

On any other day, her sister would have been the first person she would have told about this new job, but it did not feel right to do that now with her so unhappy. Still, she was only a few blocks from Jane's apartment so, while she would not tell her about the job, Bennet decided to stop in before she headed home, knowing that just seeing her sister and her sweet little niece for a few minutes would do her good.

A frequent visitor, as she reached Jane's apartment building, one of those impressively intimidating high-rise structures that populate a good stretch of Fifty-seventh Street, the doorman recognized Bennet and waved her through with a simple nod and a smile. She then spent the brief elevator ride to the eighth floor reminding herself not to let her expression betray to David that she knew anything about his troubles.

It turned out however that Bennet's preparations had been for nothing since her knock on her sister's apartment door was swiftly answered by what could only be described as an exuberant David.

"Bennet, what are you doing here?" David asked with a smile. "Don't you have an opening to be getting ready for?"

"I do, but I had a meeting a few blocks away this morning so I thought I would stop by for a minute and say hello first."

Bennet could not figure out how David could be in such a happy mood given all his troubles.

"Well then, come on in my lovely sister-in-law," David said cheerfully. "I guess you could say we are having a bit of a good morning."

Bennet followed David down the long hallway and into the kitchen where Jane was seated at the table. Her mother was also there, entertaining Charlotte on her lap by leafing through the pages of a pop-up book.

"Bennet, what are you doing here?" Adelaide asked.

"Just stopping by for a few minutes," Bennet replied, unable to hide the confusion from her voice

"Did you hear the good news about David?"

"No. What news is that?"

"David just made an impressive deal for his company and they rewarded him with a big promotion. I knew my son-in-law was brilliant and everyone else just needed to see it. Isn't that wonderful?" The smile on Adelaide's face as she spoke made it clear she knew nothing of his previous troubles.

Bennet sent a questioning glance in Jane's direction before flashing her brother-in-law a smile. "It certainly is. How wonderful, David. Congratulations."

"Yes, well for a while there I wasn't sure I was going to be offered the position," David began, obviously unaware that Bennet knew the entire story, "but it all worked out better than I could have hoped."

"That's really great," Bennet replied, meaning every word.

Bennet had no idea how things had turned around, but she was happy it had all somehow worked out.

"It is," Jane said returning Bennet's gaze with a look that seemed to imply there was more to this than David's simple explanation. "Do you have time to stay for lunch?"

"No. I should probably get going. I will see you all tonight though, right?"

"Definitely. We are going to take Charlotte to the park after lunch and then David's mother is coming over to babysit for the evening."

Jane went over to her mother, took Charlotte from her lap, and handed her to Bennet.

"Charlotte, say hello to your Auntie Bennet."

As she passed her daughter over, Jane whispered to Bennet, "Everything is good. We will talk later. I promise."

Bennet nodded and then, once her niece was safely in her arms, spun her around and around as she giggled with the pure joy and free abandon reserved solely for toddlers. Only when Bennet began to get dizzy did she stop spinning and gave Charlotte a kiss on the cheek before reluctantly depositing her back on Adelaide's lap.

As everyone was in such good moods and all seemed right once more with her sister, Bennet decided to tell them about her job offer. Everyone was happy for her, including her mother, who had instantly begun planning how she could brag to her friends about her daughter's role at the Bristle Foundation. Bennet knew by the time her mother was done explaining it she would be running the entire organization, not just one program; but still if it made her mother happy it was worth it. Simply relieved she had not somehow managed to disappoint her again, Bennet figured her mother could say anything she wanted.

Jane was so excited for Bennet that she hurried to the fridge to pull out a bottle of champagne she said they had been saving for just the right occasion. Claiming they now had a double reason for a family celebration, Jane filled four flutes and passed them around, then gave a tear-filled toast to both Bennet and David's new jobs.

While not wanting to leave what had turned into one of the happiest family gatherings she had experienced in a long time, Bennet knew she should be heading home if she wanted enough time to get ready for the evening; and so after another twenty minutes of chatting, she reluctantly pulled herself away from the table and made her excuses to go.

Bennet was outside the building and had just begun to try and hail a cab when Jane came running from the elevator.

"Bennet, wait!" Jane called out as she hurried to join her on the sidewalk. "I just want to say thank you for being there for me through all this."

"Is it really going to be okay?" Bennet asked.

Jane nodded. "It is. David got a last-minute new partner to invest. I can hardly believe it, but the deal is secure."

"I'm so glad. But I thought you said it would be near impossible to get a new investor to take such a risk after what had happened." Glancing down at her watch and realizing the time, Bennet knew she had to leave or she would run the risk of being late for tonight. Not waiting for her sister to answer, Bennet gave her a quick hug as she added, "Jane, I wish we could talk about all the details now, but I have to go get ready. Besides, you have a date for the park if I'm not mistaken. Just promise me you will tell me everything later."

Jane debated with herself for a few moments before muttering, "The hell with it."

Bennet was already at the edge of the sidewalk and had begun the process of again attempting to hail a cab when Jane came up to her once more.

"There is something I need to tell you. I'm not supposed to. In fact, I promised I wouldn't, but I don't care. You need to know."

"Okay. Now you're making me nervous," Bennet replied.

"It was Luke Dawlton," Jane blurted out.

"What was Luke?" Bennet asked as she felt her body freeze at the mere mention of his name.

"He is the last-minute investor. Luke is the one who gave David the funds to save the deal."

At Jane's words Bennet felt like the air had been knocked right out of her.

"I don't understand," she said, struggling to get the words out. "How… I mean why would he…"

"David told me everything this morning," Jane began to explain. "A few days ago he received a phone call from Luke. He had never met him before and only knew him by reputation but, when Luke said he wanted to meet, even though David could not understand why he of course said yes. He said Luke Dawlton is the kind of guy you don't keep waiting.

"When they got together the next day at Luke's office, he told David that he had learned about what Jeremy Burlow had done and that he wanted to help him out by becoming his new partner in the deal.

"You can imagine how David was hesitant to believe any of this was real or why someone like Luke would want to help him just out of the blue like that. He tried to explain as much but Luke refused to take no for an answer. He insisted that he wanted to be part of this deal and would replace all the money Jeremy had taken plus bring in additional clients of his own. With Luke's firm involved, the deal will more than just survive; it is sure to turn a good profit.

"And of course once David's bosses learned of the deal they were absolutely thrilled about the new clients and new revenue. But for them the icing on the cake was when they heard that not only had David managed to involve their firm with Dawlton Capital but that Luke Dawlton himself would be partnering on the deal. They were so pleased that they gave David the promotion right then and there.

"It goes without saying that David was thrilled that it all worked out. Honestly he couldn't believe it. But he was really shocked about the whole thing too. He could not understand why someone like Luke would want to help him or how he even could have found out about the investment deal."

Bennet could not believe what her sister was saying. While she had been standing frozen in place as Jane had shared the story of what had happened, at her sister's last words she knew she finally needed to speak.

"Well, that part is my fault," Bennet began. "Remember when you were leaving my apartment on Monday and Luke was on his way up to drop off a document?"

As Jane nodded, Bennet continued explaining. "I was so upset at what you had just told me that I actually broke down and started crying in front of him. I was mortified but he was so nice that I ended up telling him about what was happening to David. I didn't mean to, honest I didn't, but it just came spilling out.

"At first he was so supportive, but then when he heard that the person David had been in business with was Jeremy Burlow he went cold. After that it was like he could not get out of my apartment fast enough. I haven't seen him since. The only communication we've had was a brief email exchange about the exhibition. Honestly, I thought he was mad and I was convinced that he wouldn't want to speak to me again. I don't have any of the details but I know he can't stand Jeremy and that this animosity goes way back.

"I'm sorry Jane, but what you're saying just doesn't make any sense. I mean why would he help like this? To become partners with David and invest not only his share but cover what David lost to Jeremy of all people; I don't understand it."

"Well now I'm starting to," Jane said, as the corners of her mouth began to turn up into a smile. "Luke's only condition for David was that outside of their respective firms, he must remain a silent investor. He made David promise that you specifically would not learn of it. I just assumed it was because of your connection to the Northhom Museum and his aunt's gift that he didn't want to blur professional lines. But that was before everything you just told me.

"I'm just so glad now that I found out. I don't think David would ever have revealed who the investor was, but this morning I saw Luke Dawlton's name appear on the Caller ID on David's cell phone. I couldn't imagine why he would be calling and so I would not stop pestering David until he caved. I made him tell me everything.

"David explained how when he met with Luke he told him that he knew something about Jeremy Burlow's unscrupulous character in relation to a business transaction that had taken place several years ago. He said he should have exposed what Jeremy had tried to do back then, but was worried about how it might impact his own reputation if he did. And it was because he had never made Jeremy's bad actions known in the financial community that Luke felt responsible for Jeremy still being able to do business in this city and for what had happened to David. Luke said that he felt it was his duty to help him out now.

"David made me promise not to tell you but I don't care. I think you have a right to know."

As Jane had been relaying these facts, Bennet was struggling to process everything.

"But why would he do that? I don't understand."

"Don't you?" Jane asked. "Because I think I do now. I believe Luke helping David out has as much to do with you as it does about an attempt to right a wrong involving Jeremy from years ago."

Jane fixed Bennet with a kind but intense stare. "You are about to start a fantastic new job. And even before that happens, tonight is about the work you have done with the Winthrop exhibition which is amazing and shows how great you are. That exhibition is all you."

"Luke helped," Bennet added.

"That's right, he did. And why do you think that is? Why do you think he kept doing more than he had to with the project? You shouldn't doubt for a minute that someone like Luke Dawlton might be capable of doing this because of what he thinks of you; because I believe that is exactly why he acted the way he did."

As Bennet began to shake her head in disagreement, unable as she was to believe what was being said, Jane reached out and pulled her into a hug.

"Just promise me you won't close the door on something wonderful because you don't think you are worth it. You are worth it, Bennet. Believe me, you are."

"I love you, Jane," Bennet said, tears welling in her eyes.

Bennet might not have been sure of much else and certainly not why Luke had done what Jane had just explained but she knew she was happy that everything had worked out for her sister who she loved more than anything.

"I love you too," Jane replied. "Now go and get ready for tonight. We will see you later at your opening."

As Jane stood watching Bennet rush down the street to grab a cab, she could not help but smile thinking about her sister and what her future might hold.

CHAPTER THIRTY-ONE

Slowly pulling up the zipper that had been expertly hidden on the side of her dress, Bennet stared at her reflection in the closet door's full-length mirror. The woman looking back at her made her smile even though she found she almost did not recognize herself.

Maybe it was the events of the morning with their promise of a new chapter in her career about to begin that gave her a glow. Or maybe it was the way the vintage designer dark purple-colored dress with its billowing elbow-length sleeves fit her so perfectly. Tonight she had paired it with simple black heels, a long silver beaded necklace, and silver hoop earrings which created just the right mix of bohemian chic and art world glamour for the curator of an exhibition opening at a prominent New York City museum. Whatever it was, she knew she felt different and because of it she looked different too. She was still herself, but now she was a little something more; confidence, contentment, the promise of something new about to begin, or maybe all of it together had made her feel more herself than she had ever felt before.

The only thing left to do before leaving for the Northhom was to transfer her essentials into her black clutch which Bennet was in the process of doing when the buzzer on her intercom cut through her apartment, interrupting the jazz recording that she had softly playing on her record player.

"Yes?" she asked, after rushing to the hallway and pushing the intercom's button.

Bennet had no idea who could be at her apartment. Her family was meeting her later at the reception and she could not think of anyone else who would be coming to see her at this moment.

"Ellings Priority Delivery Service. I have a package for a Ms. Bennet Reynolds."

"Can you leave it in the lobby?"

"No. Sorry, but I need a direct signature and I need to see proper identification."

Bennet let out a sigh. "Okay then. I'm on the third floor in the apartment on the left. I'll buzz you in. Just come on up," she instructed.

In a few seconds the courier was at her door holding a medium-sized box.

After showing him her driver's license and signing for the delivery, Bennet shut the door and walked back into her apartment, feeling the weight of the package as she tried to figure out what might be inside.

Bennet knew she should get going if she wanted to accomplish all she had planned to do at the Northhom before the opening got underway. As she did not have much time she briefly considered waiting to open the package until later tonight; but without a return address listed on the package and no idea what it could be or from whom, she was far too curious to wait.

Placing the box on her kitchen counter, she used a knife to pry open the lid of the wooden box. Inside was a small, square package wrapped in brown paper, approximately one-foot by one-foot in size which she carefully unwrapped to reveal a framed drawing.

Bennet let out a gasp as she looked down at a sketch of a bird by Sébastian Reno similar to the one she had so loved as a child. Her training told her instantly that this was not a copy but an original artist drawing.

Gently she lifted up the picture to look at it more closely and as she did, she saw a white envelope lying on the paper wrapping. She had never had such a valuable work in her home and so she gently placed it back down on her counter, unable to stop herself from running her fingers lightly over the glass to trace the simple shape of the bird.

Then, with trembling fingers, she opened the envelope, pulled out a white note card, and began reading.

> *Dear Bennet,*
>
> *When you first told me of your love for Reno's bird sketches and how they were a fond memory from your childhood that helped to inspire your future love of art, I was taken aback by the coincidence. This is the other sketch that I requested from my aunt's collection. It, along with his figure sketch I already showed you, brought me such joy when I looked at it as a child hanging on the wall in my uncle's study.*
>
> *Now I would like you to have it as a small token of my appreciation for all your efforts on this exhibition. Perhaps when you look on it you will remember our time spent working together.*
> *Good luck this evening,*
> *Luke*

Chapter Thirty-two

An emotionally overwhelmed Bennet spent the cab ride to the museum trying to process everything that had just happened. She had thought this morning's new job offer was the biggest surprise she could have experienced for one day but the last hour had shown her just how wrong she had been. First, she had to wrap her head around the idea that there was a Sébastian Reno drawing waiting for her in her apartment. What were the odds that Vivian Winthrop would have owned one of his bird sketches and, even more unbelievably, that it had been one of Luke's favorite things as a child. Bennet and Luke's shared love of those sketches and the important impact they seemed to have had on both their lives had somehow tied them together and as she thought about it she could not help but smile as she mentally reread the note that he had written her.

Still, Luke's generous gift paled in comparison to what he had done for her family. Even now as she remembered the conversation she had with Jane outside her apartment building, Bennet struggled to make sense of it all. She had believed Luke was upset with her family's involvement with Jeremy Burlow and yet it seemed he had been the one to come up with the plan to save David's deal and his career. Jane had said she thought he had done it for her and while at first Bennet found the idea completely ridiculous, after receiving the drawing and his note, she wasn't sure of anything anymore. Bennet could not help but wonder what her sister might think of Luke's gift as she herself struggled to understand the meaning behind his actions and the magnitude of his gesture.

Twenty minutes later as the cab pulled up to the Northhom, Bennet looked at the grand stone building that had dominated so much of her life for the past several years. There was something almost magical about seeing the museum at night, all lit up in preparation for the evening's festivities. Today two large sapphire blue banners had been installed on either side of the front entrance announcing the opening of the Winthrop Collection exhibition, which lent the occasion a sense a grandeur.

Making her way around the building to the staff entrance, as Bennet walked into the museum she found herself overcome with a sense of relief mixed with a little sadness as it hit her for the first time since accepting the position with the Bristle Foundation that this would be the last exhibition she would curate for the Northhom. While initially the Winthrop exhibition had caused her nothing but problems and things had been so difficult in the early days of the planning, she now somehow found it fitting that her final show would be one of such importance to the future of the museum.

With more than an hour to go before the opening, the museum was relatively quiet but for the bustling of a few staff members and the maintenance crew completing the setup for the reception. Despite the empty feeling, she knew that Brent would be in his office as she had received an email from him forty minutes earlier asking her to come by his office as soon as she arrived so she could provide him with a final overview of tonight's proceedings.

A pre-exhibition rundown with the director was standard procedure before an opening, but unbeknownst to Brent and Katherine, whom she was sure would also be present at the meeting, Bennet knew this night was going to be far from normal as she was planning to reveal to them her future plans. Just the thought of telling them her news had put her nerves on edge as she imagined how everything would go down.

Quickly depositing her belongings in her office, Bennet wasted no time walking through the galleries to the administrative corridor. Still, upon hearing the beep of her staff pass as she used it to unlock the door, she found she had to take a deep breath and steady her nerves before stepping inside.

Here we go, she thought as in seconds she had walked the short distance down the hallway to the director's office.

"Ah, Bennet, come in," Brent said upon seeing her appear in the doorway.

Walking into his office, Bennet took a seat on one of two open chairs across from his desk. Katherine, she noted, was in her usual position, standing beside him and leaning on the credenza and Bennet thought how fitting it was the two people who had made her life so unnecessarily difficult at the museum should hear her news together.

Well, the next few minutes might go a little differently than you planned Katherine Hartis, Bennet thought, her body surging with nervous energy.

"I just came from a brief walk through the exhibition," Brent began. "I must say I was more than a little surprised how good it looks. You actually did a decent job."

Ah, how nice; yet another of your insults masked as a compliment. You can't even simply acknowledge the good job I did and leave it at that.

Bennet smiled. "Well thank you Brent. I'm so glad you're pleased."

You small-minded, little man.

"Yes, you can really see Luke Dawlton's hand in the exhibition. It is a good thing he was there to help you out, Bennet," Katherine added. She knew the exhibition looked impressive and it was clearly killing her.

Wanting more than anything to be done with this conversation and out of this office, Bennet took a breath, steeled her nerves, and began to speak. "Well before anything else, I wanted to give you a quick rundown of the schedule of events for tonight. The guests will begin arriving at 6:30 pm. An hour later, the plan is to have all the attendees gather in the main gallery where the opening remarks will take place. I've had the maintenance crew bring over the podium and set it up in the far west corner. Drinks and food will be set out in the café after 8 pm, and the exhibition stays open until 9:30 pm. As far as the remarks, I thought I would briefly…"

"That's where I will have to stop you," Katherine interrupted. "We feel strongly that with this being such an important exhibition for the Northhom that it should be me that gives the introductory remarks, and then Brent and Vivian will speak."

After years of dealing with all the vile things Katherine had done to her, somehow the words she had just uttered had still managed to surprise Bennet. It had always been the curator's job to give the introductory remarks at the opening but in Katherine's twisted, jealousy-filled mind it made sense that since this was such a high profile event that she would not allow Bennet to be the subject of any of the spotlight.

"It's just as curator everyone will be expecting me to speak," Bennet continued, struggling to maintain her composure.

"Well, we feel that this is a bit more important than you can handle," Brent said as Katherine nodded in agreement.

Thank you. Thank you for making this so easy, Bennet thought as she prepared herself for the bombshell she would soon be dropping on them.

"Well it's your call to make of course. You obviously know best."

"Yes, we do," Katherine snapped. Thinking she had achieved her victory, Katherine could not help but smile as she added, "If that is all then I think we should all go get ready to…"

"Actually, there is one last thing I need to fill you in on if you would allow me just a few more minutes of your time."

As neither objected nor made an effort to reply, Bennet continued. "I was struggling a bit with how to tell you this when I first walked in but suddenly I find that's no longer the case. In fact, I should really thank you both as what you have said to me just now has made what I'm about to say so much easier."

While Brent and Katherine seemed surprised at her unusual display of boldness, they could never have guessed what was coming next.

Pulling out a sealed letter from the folder she had been carrying, Bennet slid it across the desk to Brent. Then, looking directly at him, she began speaking the words she had practiced several times in her mirror before arriving at the museum.

"This is my letter of resignation. You will find I am giving a month's notice which, while more than required by my employment contract, I feel is appropriate to ensure I can satisfactorily wrap up all my outstanding projects at the Northhom before leaving."

If she had taken off all her clothes and told them she was flying off to Paris to join a troop of mimes, Bennet could not have shocked them more. It showed on their faces as they just sat there staring at her.

After what seemed like minutes but was in reality no more than thirty seconds, it was Brent who finally broke the silence.

"I don't understand. You're leaving the Northhom?"

"I am not sure what's confusing about it, but yes, I am resigning," Bennet replied. "I've taken another job and so I'm leaving to pursue that."

Bennet watched the transformation of the look on his face from an expression of struggling to comprehend to one of pure anger, as if someone had just snapped their fingers and made it happen.

"How can you leave? What will it look like?" Brent asked.

And there it is, Bennet thought. *They don't care one bit about me or the work I've done for this museum. All they care about is how it will look for them that the curator of this new exhibition is leaving.*

Bennet did her best to remain calm. "With all due respect, I really don't feel that it's any of my concern anymore. Still, I'm confident you will do just fine without me."

Then turning her attention fully to Katherine, Bennet added, "You don't even want me to speak tonight at the exhibition that I organized. No other curator in this city would be expected to put up with an insult like that. I am not appreciated here and I certainly think the Northhom will manage with a new person in my position. He or she can do your bidding from now on because I've had more than enough."

"Where are you going?" Katherine asked, unable to keep her voice steady. "It certainly cannot be to anywhere better than the Northhom Museum."

Bennet struggled to keep herself from smiling. She knew how much her next words would annoy Katherine.

"Well as the announcement will be released officially next week, I've received permission to tell you this evening that I have accepted a job with the Bristle Foundation as director of its new Children's Art Initiative. I will be developing and spearheading exciting new programs, and my team and I will be helping to implement them throughout the city.

"Oh, and I guess I can share this with you as well since I'm so excited about it; I've also been hired to do the illustrations for a new children's book. So you see, I'll actually be quite busy."

"You have always been ungrateful," Katherine began, spitting out the words. "I should have known you…"

"Katherine, I'm going to have to stop you there," Bennet interrupted. She was impressed by the command and calm in her voice and proud of herself for thus far not letting the conversation get away from her.

"From the moment I was appointed to this job you both made it clear that I was not your first or even second choice for the position. And yet despite a complete and utter lack of encouragement, and in your case Katherine the many instances of you actually trying to sabotage my work, I have put forth well-reviewed and attended exhibitions that have enhanced the visibility and reputation of the Northhom Museum.

"Despite everything, I have enjoyed the work I have been able to achieve as curator here; even though all was done with little to no support from you. That said, it is time for me to move on to this next exciting opportunity.

"I would however respectfully ask that you not share this news with the staff until next week when we are all back at the museum. I'm sure you will both agree that this night should be about Vivian Winthrop and her impressive gift."

Katherine's silence let Bennet know that she had delivered the final blow and managed to win the undeclared war that they had been engaged in since she first took on this position. She had done so by achieving the ultimate upper hand: leaving the Northhom for a far more impressive position.

Brent eventually recovered enough to stand and extend Bennet his hand.

"Well we wish you luck in this new opportunity," he said, albeit without any sincerity.

Katherine remained silent, making it clear that there would be no attempt to even try and be civil on her part.

"Thank you, Brent," Bennet replied as she stood to shake the director's hand. "Now if you will both excuse me; I do have a few last-minute preparations to attend to before the opening begins."

As she walked out of Brent's office, down the long corridor, and back out into the gallery, Bennet had to stop herself from shaking with the rush of nerves and excitement over what she had just done. She knew as long as she lived she would never forget the look on both of their faces as she delivered her news. If someone could actually die of jealousy she knew Katherine would have, right there in Brent's office.

Strangely enough however, while it was certainly a victory, Bennet found that when all was said and done she cared less about it than she thought she would. She felt good at the realization that she had just too many exciting things waiting for her to spend one more minute thinking about Katherine Hartis or Brent Stromwell. They no longer held any power over her.

Rather than returning to her office straightaway, Bennet chose instead to go upstairs and take a quick walk through the galleries in which the Winthrop gift of artworks and sculptures were installed. This was her favorite part of opening night, the final minutes before anyone was in the space when she could travel from room to room just taking in the complete physical manifestation of her curatorial vision. After months of work, the exhibition was now real and there for her to view.

Much to her surprise, Bennet felt a few tears start to form. Maybe it was just relief that the exhibition had managed to come together despite everything that had happened; or maybe it was the impact of Luke's gift and what he had done for her family that had moved her so much; or maybe it was the reality hitting her that despite all the new opportunities awaiting her what she had just done symbolized the start of her last days at the Northhom Museum. Most likely it was a combination of all these things that had brought her to this moment of standing in the empty gallery being moved to tears.

Glancing down at her phone Bennet knew these empty spaces would not remain that way for much longer and that soon the exhibition, her exhibition, would belong to everyone. In fifteen minutes the guests would be allowed into the galleries and among the crowd of visitors would be her family and Luke, just the thought of whom filled her with a rush of warmth and anticipation. Bennet had no idea what she would say when she saw him or how she could thank him or begin to express everything she was feeling.

Chapter Thirty-three

Back in her office, Bennet had just finished touching up her makeup and was about to head up to the exhibition when she stopped, closed her eyes, and allowed herself a moment to reflect on everything that had taken place over the course of the last few months.

It was almost unbelievable how much her life had changed in such a short period of time. Who would have thought Vivian Winthrop would have become the catalyst for her entire future happiness? Without the Winthrop gift and the chain reaction of events it had set off in her life she might never have found the courage to move on from the museum. Maybe she would never have met Ian Bristle. She certainly would never have met Luke. Most importantly, she might never have become the hero of her own story; but in this moment, she realized she had become just that.

"I thought I might find you here."

A smile spread across Bennet's face as she opened her eyes and turned to see Luke standing in the doorway.

Now face to face with her, Luke found himself struggling for words. "You look incredible."

While the compliment thrilled her, it was the sight of him that was threatening to take Bennet's breath away. She had never seen someone so handsome as he was just now. Impeccably dressed, she was drawn not only to his piercing blue eyes—that she was in that moment sure she would never tire of looking at—but also to how a wave of his chestnut brown hair had fallen across the left side of his forehead, which she had to fight back the urge to reach out and smooth away.

"So do you," Bennet replied. Suddenly nervous as to how to say what she knew she wanted to tell him, she rushed to add, "I need to say thank you."

"When you first spoke of that drawing and how much it meant to you, I knew you had to have it," Luke replied.

"No, I mean, yes, thank you for the drawing. It really is too much. I shouldn't even think of accepting it, but I love it so much that I don't know if I'm strong enough to refuse it."

Luke smiled. "I'm afraid I would not let you return it even if you tried."

Bennet stared up at him, overcome with emotion. "Well, I'm glad for that. But I also have to most sincerely thank you for what you did for my family; for my sister and for David."

"So you know," Luke said, looking suddenly uncomfortable.

"Please don't blame Jane. David did make her promise not to say anything, but she could not help herself.

"I thought when you left my apartment so abruptly that night after I mentioned Jeremy Burlow that you could no longer stand to be around me. I knew you didn't like him, and now that he was associating himself with my family I thought you were angry with me once more. I could never have imagined you would be the instrument of saving my family from that man."

"I think it is me that owes you and your family the apology," Luke began. "If I had been more upfront about Jeremy this would never have happened. So, you see, in many ways this was all my fault."

While Bennet wanted to tell him that nothing was his fault, the urgency in Luke's voice let her know that he needed to speak and so she said nothing as he continued.

"I feel I should explain about him, and I should have done so much sooner. Shortly after I returned from England and began the process of establishing my firm in the city, I learned that Jeremy was managing some of my aunt's investments and was about to cheat her out of a significant amount of money. I immediately severed his connection to her and took over control of all her accounts.

"While she suffered no losses, she was utterly embarrassed. In fact, her fears over her mistake being made public was what he was counting on to enable him to get away with the scheme. God only knows how many people he has swindled that way.

"While it was my responsibility to have made Burlow's actions known, I did not want anyone to know that my family and by extension myself could have been connected to such a poor investment. I know it seems vain of me and it is no excuse, but I felt at the time it might have hurt my chances of building up my office in the city. I was more worried about my reputation than making things right.

"If I had come clean and made it known what a shady character he was, he would never have been able to dupe people such as your brother-in-law. I assure you I have rectified the matter now. I made it clear to Jeremy Burlow that if he ever tries to make a deal in this city again, I will go public with everything. I know we will not be seeing him anymore."

"You saved David's job. You became his co-investor and revived the deal," Bennet replied, the words tumbling out of her mouth as she struggled to express everything she needed to say. "He even got the promotion he had been angling for which caused all of this mess in the first place."

Luke smiled. "Yes, but before you pin a medal on me, you should know that your brother-in-law is very good at what he does. He may have fallen victim to a scam, but the investment deal they put together before Burlow stole the money was a solid one and will stand to make me a good deal of profit for my clients and my firm. I will end up ahead in the long run, and I think I will enjoy working with David."

Taking a few steps forward, Luke lessened the space between them. "Besides, if I'm honest, my motivations were less than one hundred percent altruistic. I wanted to make things up to you. I admit I was jealous when I saw you with Jeremy that night at the gallery opening and then I handled it so poorly. I don't know why, but I never seem to act my best around you."

Bennet stood frozen in place as he continued.

"There was a large part of me that just wanted to look good in your eyes; to change what I fear is your bad opinion of me."

Finally finding her voice, Bennet thought it sounded strange when she heard herself reply, "My opinion of you? I do not think my opinion of you could be any greater.

"Yes, I admit I did not always feel this way, and we did get off to a rocky start; what with your petty thievery," Bennet added with a smile. "But what you did for my sister and her family and for me; I don't think you realize the magnitude of all you have done.

"It was because of what you said to me that night at your aunt's reception that played a large part in motivating me to make those drawings, and now I am going to illustrate a book. And I'm sure your recommendation of me to Ian Bristle contributed to his offering me a job heading a new initiative for his foundation this morning; an offer that allowed me for the first time since I started at this museum to wipe the smug looks off of Katherine Hartis and Brent Stromwell's faces when minutes ago I handed in my resignation."

Now it was Luke's turn to look surprised. "That's fantastic. When Ian called me asking about my experience working with you, I told him I honestly could not think of a better person to work with. But you should know that my opinion did not matter. You impressed Ian Bristle all on your own. Believe me, I know what impeccably high standards he has."

Bennet smiled. "So many good things have happened in my life recently and, in one way or another, you have been a part of each of them. And to think I thought you were such a jerk when I first met you."

As Luke laughed, she added, "I can still picture the arrogant look on your face when you bit into that croissant."

"And I can still remember the look on yours, when you saw me in Brent's office and realized you would have to work with me," Luke replied. "You know, you are quite adorable when you get flustered."

It was now Bennet's turn to laugh. "Then I must look good a lot of the time; especially around you it seems."

Luke stepped forward once more and was now standing so close to her that only a sliver of space remained between them.

"I hope you know how much I care for you Bennet. I find myself unable to think of anything else. I think… no, I know, I have fallen in love with you."

Bennet was filled with such joy at his words she was sure she had never felt anything like it before. "I love you, too."

Reaching out, Luke placed his hand on the side of Bennet's face. His touch, equal parts firm and gentle, was enough to send a bolt of electricity coursing through her body. Then lightly tipping her chin up towards his, Luke bent down and brought his lips to hers. In that moment it was as if time stood still as what started out as a soft exploration of his mouth on hers grew deeper and more passionate; each of them desperate to convey all the feelings and words they had yet to express to each other.

While she wished she could stay that way forever, Bennet eventually and with reluctance forced herself to pull away. As she did, she worried she might never regain control over her words. Yet, as she looked up at him, she derived pleasure in the realization that Luke looked as equally hungry for more as she felt.

"We have to go," Bennet said, her voice heavy with regret.

"Well I guess it wouldn't look good if we were late for this opening," Luke admitted. Although everything about the expression on his face told Bennet that was exactly what he wanted.

"Maybe when this is over you could come back to my place and help me hang the drawing?" Bennet asked, the subtext in her voice absolutely clear.

"I can think of nothing on earth I would rather do." Flashing one of his charming smiles, Luke held out his arm for Bennet to link through his. "Shall we go to your exhibition, Ms. Reynolds?"

"You mean our exhibition, Mr. Dawlton; and yes, we shall. Why don't you lead, since I know you know the way," Bennet suggested, unable to stop herself from smiling.

Luke laughed at the memory of how annoyed she had been when he had showed up at her office unannounced that first time.

Overcome with a feeling of pure happiness, together with the man she loved, Bennet headed out of her office and up the basement stairs to make the long trek to the exhibition galleries.

This time she was in no rush at all.

Jessica DiPalma is an art historian and writer. She is also the author of the novels *The Jump*, *The Jump: A Medieval Adventure*, and *The Jump: A Vaudeville Adventure*. They are the first three books in her art jumping adventure series. She lives in New York.